SLEIGHT OF MIND

RISE OF MAGIC
BOOK 2

STEFON MEARS

Also by Stefon Mears

The Rise of Magic Series
Magician's Choice
Sleight of Mind
Lunar Alchemy
Three Fae Monte
The Sphinx Principle
Double Backed Magic
Mercury Fold (forthcoming)

Cavan Oltblood Series
Half a Wizard
The Ice Dagger
Spells of Undeath

Power City Tales
Not Quite Bulletproof
No Money in Heroism

Standalones
The Hireling
The Captain's Cat
Save Whiskers!
The Ogre of Threepeaks
Between the Cracks
Sects and the City
Prince of a Thousand Worlds
Devil's Night
Portal-Land, Oregon
Stealing from Pirates
Fade to Gold
With a Broken Sword
Twice Against the Dragon
The House on Cedar Street
Sudden Death
On the Edge of Faerie

Short Story Collections
Spell Slingers
Twisted Timelines
Longhairs and Short Tales: A Collection of Cat Stories
Dangerous Space
Confronting Legends (Spells & Swords Vol. 1)
The Patreon Collection, Vol. 1-8 (Vol. 9, coming soon)

Nonfiction
The 30-Day Novel and Beyond!

Spells for Hire Series
Devil's Shoestring
Zombie Powder
Spirit Trap
Dragon's Blood

The Telepath Trilogy
Surviving Telepathy
Immoral Telepathy
Targeting Telepathy

Edge of Humanity Series
Caught Between Monsters
Hunting Monsters

Jumpstart Duchy Series
Into the Torn Kingdoms
The Dragon's Gold
The Gift Castle
The Deadly Feast
The King's Test
Triumph in the Torn Kingdoms

Published by Thousand Faces Publishing, Portland, Oregon

http://1kfaces.com

Starfield image © Ashestosky | Dreamstime.com (File ID: 11418999)

Venus illustration © Olga Kurbatova | Dreamstime.com (File ID: 145496119)

ISBN: 978-1-948490-10-8

SLEIGHT OF MIND

*The year is 2026
Six decades after the Rise of Magic*

1

Donal Cuthbert sprinted through the near-empty private section of Kennedy Spaceport on Earth's moon, Luna, cursing his footwear. Loafers were all wrong for this. No support. No grip.

He should have been wearing sneakers. His girlfriend's fault. Li Hua had Donal dressing better and looking sharper, but he never thought to buy shoes enchanted for combat the way she did. Even her high heels.

But then, Donal rarely had to run for his life.

Unfortunately, once might be enough.

No help around him. Just wide blue-gray spaces that echoed his pounding steps. They would echo his pursuers in short order.

In the public part of the port he would have found security guards, other passengers, maybe a small crowd to lose himself in. But here he saw no one. Not even a janitor. Only hangar openings that seemed to go on for days, and arrows pointing the way to the one he sought: Bay Forty-Nine.

The place even smelled deserted. Nothing in the air but a vague herbal smell leftover from alchemical ship maintenance.

Donal sucked air and clutched his messenger bag — distressed leather, of course, which suited his state of mind. He could feel the bag rubbing his hip and shoulder raw as his legs stretched for more speed and his feet protested with blisters.

How much further was the damned ship?

Suddenly running beside him appeared his familiar, Fionn, a spectral deerhound of emerald green, a meter tall at the shoulder and eyes that blazed with courage. It spoke in an accent somewhere between Scottish and Irish.

"I have alerted the ship, but the captain dismisses this as a local problem."

Donal wanted to swear, wanted to beg Lugh or the Dagda for help, but could not spare the breath. His heart pounded faster than his feet. Sweat blurred his vision alongside matted strands of black hair. His legs burned with effort.

"What ... about..."

"We should seek shelter in a hangar and try to lose them."

"No time," Donal managed. "Spoil ... aim."

Fionn understood. The *cú sidhe* fell back and would weave in the path to distract any attempts to use slingers, alchemical projectiles that could carry deadly effects. Difficult to make, expensive to commission, and illegal outside of military applications, slingers required spells strong enough to make them obvious to even the most casual customs inspections or weapons checks.

Just Donal's luck that he fled from a local family powerful enough to carry slingers anywhere they wanted this side of a helioship.

Cramp building in his stomach, legs beginning to falter from the sustained speed, Donal pressed on. Two more hangars to pass...

A spell ball the size of Donal's fist flew past his head. Smashed on a hangar wall. The spell took, cracking lines even in the thick, shaped rock. Donal pushed his legs harder, trying not to think of what that spell would have done to him, wishing he could have pulled off a moving protective circle.

Every part of Donal's body screamed in protest at his exertion. He had to have run flat out for at least a kilometer by now, but still he could hear his pursuers. They had the air to shout curses, damn them, even while Fionn mocked them in Gaelic that would have made Donal's mother blush. Probably his father too.

Not his big brother Bran, of course, but Bran would have been in good enough shape to lose them. Or he would have taken them all on and won. But that was Bran.

At least no travelers crowded around Donal this time, to risk becoming 'collateral damage.' Not like on Mars.

Donal put his head down and threw the last of his energy into a final sprint.

JOHN JACOBS PACED THE BREADTH OF HIS STARCHASER SPACELINES office. He should have been at the docks. He had a ship to inspect, a route plan to confirm one more time, and no doubt another dozen forms to fill out. Someone in the San Francisco bureaucracy must have decided that forms meant fees, which meant more money.

And now Zoltan, his business partner, was late.

Jacobs paused at the sound of wood under his boots as he stepped off the throw rug in front of his huge purpleheart desk. He spent so many of his days listening to the sound of ship ceramics underfoot that oak flooring sounded wrong in his ears. Artificial. How could he consider retiring when only ships felt like home?

Jacobs returned to pacing, five steps fore, three steps starboard, five steps aft, three steps port, and on. He paced as though in his office aboard the *Horizon Cusp*, the ship he had commanded for the last decade, and not in his spacious Earth office, with its conference table, hide-a-bed sofa, and comfortable visitors chairs, most of which went unused even when Jacobs was on Earth. Clients met with Zoltan. But Zoltan insisted that Jacobs, as co-owner, had to have a big office in the home branch of Starchaser Spacelines. Something clients would find impressive.

Jacobs paused to shake his head. Appearances shouldn't impress. People should learn to judge actions, histories. But with his eighty-sixth birthday approaching, Jacobs felt like little more than history himself, one of the dwindling few who remembered life from before the rise of magic.

A knock at the door. Finally.

"Come," said Jacobs, and Zoltan entered.

Jacobs felt his eyes narrow, his jaw clench at the sight of his partner: jowls shaking just a touch, fingers playing with the buttons of his silk shirt, and pants wrinkled, which at oh-nine-hundred meant that Zoltan had been awake for hours already, had likely not slept well. Even his graying curls had not been tamed to their normal positions.

Jacobs' nostrils flared a calming breath. Zoltan had earned the right to deliver bad news his own way.

"Rough night?"

"Rough couple of days. Mind if I sit?"

Jacobs held back the urge to say 'out with it.' Zoltan was not a member of his crew. Instead Jacobs nodded, and returned to his own ridiculously large padded leather chair.

"John, you know business has been down since the *Beamrunner's* accident."

"It's been rebuilding, and the business-class shuttle runs we've added have made the difference. Worried about your bottom line?"

"Always." For just a moment Zoltan smiled and looked like himself. But then the smile faded. "And you should be worried about your retirement."

"After this next voyage. I promise."

"You said that two years ago."

"This is different. The Venus run." Just the thought of it sent a thrill through Jacobs' system, made him rub his hands together like an eager boy. "A final hurrah for me, and peerless advertising for Starchaser Spacelines. We can sell when the value of the business is high, and—"

"I've already sold."

Jacobs's head snapped back, feet down flat on the floor and hands flat on the desk.

"What?"

"I've already sold." Zoltan took a deep breath. "John, even you have to admit this flight is risky—"

"You're abandoning ship?"

"—and if this goes wrong the press will murder us. We'll never recover."

"I captained the first commercial flight to Mars. I think I can handle—"

"And how long ago was that?"

"Don't you dare—"

Zoltan leapt to his feet, leaned across the broad, dark desk. "Sell! Retire! Take that cat of yours and get that place in Mazatlan you've talked about."

Zoltan must have seen the battle stations in Jacobs' eyes, because he softened his tone. "You've had a hell of a career. Accomplished things that will get your name in the history texts. You've done enough. Live to enjoy it."

"Not enough. Not yet."

"I knew it." Zoltan shook his head and deflated back onto his overstuffed chair. "I had to try. Have it your way, John." He sighed again and looked up. "One last drink with your old partner?"

"At oh-nine-fifteen?"

"You never give a fraction, do you?" Zoltan stood, dusted his shirt and pants with his hands. "Your new partner will be here in an hour or so. If you can forgive me, stay in touch. I've left my contact information with Cindy."

Zoltan started toward the door. "Good luck with the Venus run."

"Zoltan." Jacobs waited until Zoltan looked back at him. "It's been good working with you."

Zoltan smiled and left. Jacobs wondered whether he should have had that drink after all. He had a feeling he might need it.

DONAL WAS LOSING GROUND. HE KNEW IT. HE HAD TO BE.

His pace flagged, despite how he pushed. His legs weighed tons. His lungs burned. Even his arms and back were sore.

Another slinger-shot flew past. Fried a section of spaceport flooring to Donal's right. Too close.

Any second they would be on top of him.

Finally Donal reached Bay Forty-Nine, and he saw the twenty-meter-long owl shape of the helioship *Archimedes*, tawny wing up and passenger portal open. He could see the young steward standing at attention just inside the portal, memoboard against his side and with the clear intention to not interfere.

Donal's legs gave out and he tumbled forward into the landing bay, barely able to keep his head from slamming against the stone flooring, even though every other part of him seemed to bang into it.

Pain jolted through him. Squeezed tears from his eyes and a sob from his throat as he stretched with one hand toward the ship, determined to reach safety.

"Easy, Journeyman," said a strong, certain voice behind him. "You're safe now."

Another person might have only looked up to see a tall, handsome man with flowing brown hair and tailored clothes. A man who looked slender more by habit than by exercise, despite the rapier at his side.

Donal saw these things too, but what he saw first was power: immense personal power, more than Donal could ever have mustered, even more than most of Donal's professors back at U.C. Santa Cruz, when Donal was still studying for his Bachelor's in Thaumaturgy. And Donal recognized this man. This Hierophant. Had met him once at a conference years before.

And by the power Donal felt now, he would guess that Nicholas Mason had achieved much even since attaining his Doctorate in Thaumaturgy.

Donal knew he should have felt elated at reaching certain safety, but instead he felt humiliated. Exhausted, sweaty, crying and pursued by would-be murderers was not how Donal wanted to renew his acquaintance with what amounted to a childhood hero.

Mason stepped into the hangar doorway and waited. Fionn arrived and came to his master's side. "I made them waste only the one shot, I fear. No doubt they have others..."

"I doubt ... that matters now..."

"True." The fae deerhound regarded the Hierophant. "If such a one stands with us, we are safe."

Donal managed to sit up as the pursuers arrived, considerably less out-of-breath than Donal thought they should have been. Ten men, dressed in security jumpers, eight of them carrying Pacifiers, batons enchanted to disable even without a direct hit. On their chests they bore the crest of the Romanov family.

"I declare this man under my protection," said Hierophant Mason, one hand relaxed on the hilt of his rapier. "Come against him at your peril."

"We represent Natalia Romanova," said the leader with a slight Romanian accent, "who sends her regards, Hierophant." The leader bowed, and his men followed suit.

Mason acknowledged them with a nod of his head.

The leader continued, "Donal Cuthbert is participating in a moral crime against the Romanov family, which grants us power to pursue him under Lunar Code Section four eight—"

"I may not have maintained my champion's license in many years," said Mason, his voice still so casual he might have been discussing sports scores of teams he did not care about, "but I am acquainted with all sections that pertain to the Lunar Code Duello."

Mason raised his voice the barest bit. "Donal Cuthbert, can you swear to me that you have committed no legal or moral crimes against the Romanov family?"

"I can swear ... that I have not knowingly ... committed any crimes at all ... since I entered Lunar space ... and that I have behaved ... at all times ..." Donal drew a deep breath to finish, "...in accordance with my duties as an IIX courier and a certified Journeyman."

"Good enough for me," said Mason. He folded his arms. "Please return my regards to Natalia Romanova, and inform her that I still intend to accept her invitation to hospitality on my next visit. However, my statement of protection stands."

The security men gazed uncertainly at each other, then those gazes all settled on their leader. He drew a deep breath and said, "We have slingers—"

"I was consulted in the invention of slingers. Before your men could pull their triggers, I could have your toys dump their spells on the lot of you."

Mason raised one hand, leaving the other on the hilt of his rapier. "Shall we consider this matter ended? Or do you require a demonstration?"

The security guards hesitated. Even their leader seemed at a loss for how to respond.

"The weak points in the bindings are really quite simple to exploit. I could make a lesson of it for young Cuthbert here. You still intend to pursue Enochian research, do you not, Donal?"

Donal could not decide if he felt more flattered to be remembered or embarrassed at his arrival. Either way, he managed a shaky nod, and Hierophant Mason continued.

"Their binding spells are largely Earth of Earth. Air-aspected Air of Fire works best against them. Snaps them like so."

The Hierophant focused a tiny erg of the power Donal saw about him and made a show of moving to snap his fingers...

Before he could, the leader bowed again and said, "If contacted, will you confirm that we found Donal Cuthbert, but that you refused to allow us to complete our duty?"

"Of course," said Hierophant Mason. "So long as you do not embellish my actions."

The security guards left, and the tall magician gave Donal a hand up.

"Thank you, Hierophant," said Donal.

"When I was your age," said Mason with a wistful smile, "magicians didn't stand on ceremony. Not among ourselves. Once you proved yourself competent to be called a Journeyman, you got to speak to other magicians as equals, no matter their skill or experience."

He shook his head. "But times change, and I'm too young to lament the past."

If Mason were a day over thirty-five, Donal could never have guessed it from looking at him. Of course, Donal knew that some magicians experimented with age magics...

"Enough of that," said Mason. "You might avoid Luna for a time. The Romanovs are a powerful family, and they know how to nurse a grudge."

"But I didn't even go near them."

"Your delivery had to do with the Dockers Guild?"

Donal opened his mouth, but checked his initial reply and said instead, "I'm not supposed to answer—"

"Questions about a package. Of course. Just consider it an educated guess. On to other topics then. How is your brother Bran? I understand he successfully challenged for the rank of Magister without first completing his MaT training." He began to lead Donal toward the helioship. "First American I've heard of who accomplished that. You must be very proud."

Donal sighed. Of course that was why a Hierophant like Mason remembered him. Everyone remembered Bran. Donal was always an afterthought.

"Of course, Hierophant. We all are."

Donal recalled Fionn into the inappropriate silver faun pendant that served as his familiar's material base, and boarded the ship with Mason, telling the Hierophant about his brother's successful mission to explore Ganymede and a few of his other various successes.

If only Donal could think of a few of his own accomplishments to mention.

Starchaser Spacelines: *the ships that launched a thousand forms*, mused Jacobs. It seemed to him sometimes that he spent every stop in port at his office desk, filling out forms for one local authority or another. Mars was still the worst, but San Francisco was starting to give them a run for their money.

At exactly ten hundred hours, the comm pad on Jacobs' desk glowed red. He slapped it, and the round face of Cindy, the receptionist, appeared above the pad. Jacobs still felt uncomfortable calling her by her first name, but she seemed to find it more cordial.

She saved him the trouble by speaking first. "A Ms. Tai Shi Li Hua here to see you, Sir. Says she's expected."

Expected? Then his new partner had to be...

But no. Even Zoltan would not have sold to...

"Send her in," Jacobs said, steadying his breathing and forcing his fists to unclench.

Tai Shi Li Hua entered the room with the feral grace of a predator, which was one of the reasons Jacobs respected her. She wore a spotless chestnut brown skirt suit with matching heels that even Jacobs had to admit complemented the red Martian overtones of her Chinese heritage. She stopped two paces inside the room, and her patient posture told Jacobs that she meant the distance as a gesture of respect, to give him the opportunity to invite her in or dismiss her.

Under the circumstances, that showed more presence of mind than he would have expected from someone under thirty. But most magicians developed their presence of mind faster than regular people.

"Captain Jacobs," said Tai Shi. "Thank you for seeing me."

"So Mancuso bought out Zoltan."

"Technically, 4M bought Zoltan's share of Starchaser Spacelines to reflect the growing concern of space travel to our business interests. But the effect is the same, yes."

Jacobs gestured for her to sit. He definitely should have had that drink. "Coffee?"

"No, thank you," said Tai Shi as she sat, her posture relaxed, but balanced. Ready. As though even here she expected an attack.

"I thought you handled 4M security for Mars. How did you end up playing messenger?"

"I'm not. The recent expansion of our business interests has prompted Mr. Mancuso to create the position of Director of Security for Inter-Business Relations. I've been promoted."

"Sounds like a very specific position."

"With broad reach. Anyone we do business with has to accept my oversight of their security."

"To prevent the infiltration of your security teams, such as happened on the Mars run?"

That damned Mars run. Smugglers, murderers, conspiracy theorists and a threat to destroy the ship.

"Exactly."

Firm confidence in her voice suggested that she had figured out exactly what had gone wrong on that voyage and that she knew how to prevent anything like it from happening again on her watch.

Her watch?

"Wait," said Jacobs with a scowl. "Does this mean I'm expected to let you oversee security for *my* ships?"

"*Our* ships now, Captain Jacobs. 4M owns half-interest, and has equal say in—"

"I run my ships my way. My chief handles my security."

"Nevertheless I need to run a personnel check."

"I'll sell."

"No one will buy. Mr. Mancuso will see to that."

"I'll quit."

"Captain Jacobs," said Tai Shi with wearing patience in her voice. "If you try to quit, Mr. Mancuso will sink the business, write off the loss, and not lose a moment's sleep over leaving you ruined."

Jacobs stared at her impassive face and felt anger pump through his veins. *Belay that, Old Man. She's the messenger, not the target.* He made her wait while he wrangled his temper under control, never letting any of it get past his eyes.

Tai Shi simply sat, without so much as a fidget.

"Fine man you work for."

"I like my job. Doesn't mean I always like my employer."

"He's going to ruin me anyway, isn't he?"

"No. He wants you to stay through the Venus run. Then if you still want out, he will buy out your shares at two hundred percent value."

"So that's why Zoltan sold."

"Normally," said Tai Shi reaching into her inner jacket pocket, "I would send this to you from my zephyrpad, but I recall that you prefer actual paper."

She pulled out a trifolded piece of paper and slid it across the desk to Jacobs.

Jacobs picked it up and read it twice. Sure enough, Mancuso seemed to be offering to purchase Jacobs' share of Starchaser Spacelines for two hundred percent of peak market value over the two week period following the successful completion of the Venus run. That would give the public time to absorb the news and for everyone to think of Starchaser Spacelines first when they thought of traveling off-planet.

The offer even included a retirement bonus large enough to buy Jacobs a house anywhere he wanted, and guaranteed health and care insurance for life for himself, and included a provision for a spouse should he marry.

As though Jacobs would ever meet someone who could replace Rhonda. He never had. Not in the fifty-eight years and seven months since her death.

Jacobs looked up at Tai Shi, who smiled as though honestly pleased.

Jacobs needed a moment to remember why she was smiling.

"It's a good offer," said Tai Shi, "and all you have to do is what you were going to do anyway. Captain the first commercial voyage to Venus."

"What's the catch?"

"Well," said Tai Shi, and Jacobs felt his jaw set. Just that one word told him he would not like what followed, but she had more to say. "The circumstances of that voyage will not be what you expect."

She passed Jacobs another piece of paper. This one a passenger list and cargo manifest.

"Ridiculous," said Jacobs, his eyes still on the paper. "There are twenty names on this list, double the maximum passenger load for a little ship like the *Lark's Song*. And three times as much cargo as we're allowing."

He slid the paper back to her across the desk. "Besides, a proper full load of passages has already been sold."

"About that…" Tai Shi drew a deep breath. "Those passengers were false fronts, 4M employees buying the spaces to hold them while Mr. Mancuso prepared to purchase—"

"Did Zoltan know?"

"I was not involved in this aspect of the transaction."

"So this is why Mancuso didn't come himself."

"You did punch a representative of Transterran Properties on the Mars run."

"That idiot was stabbing someone he had no business stabbing."

Tai Shi tried to say something, but snorted out a laugh.

"Excuse me. It's just that I agree. Mr. Mancuso, however, is a man of a different sort of action."

"Fine."

"I beg your pardon?"

"The passenger count and cargo tonnage are both too much for the *Lark's Song*, and since the *Last Night* and the *Star Wave* are committed to other flights, we'll have to use the *Horizon Cusp*. That means a more experienced crew, but greater risk and greater expense. 4M is picking up all costs above and beyond those budgeted for the voyage as I've planned it, agreed?"

"Agreed." Tai Shi tried to continue, but Jacobs spoke over her.

"Furthermore," he said and waited until he had her attention. "My ship, my security, my way. Goldberg handles *all* security for *this* flight. No 'private guards' this time, 'personal bodyguards,' or anything of the like. You get executives and support staff only."

"Agreed, with the proviso that I will be among the executives and oversee—"

"Anything Goldberg allows you to. You'll meet with him before takeoff, and I'll tell him what's coming. If he agrees to your oversight, you get it. Otherwise, the best you get to do is assist him. Yes." Jacobs let command infuse his deep voice, and even the walls rang out with compliance. "Your boss has pulled his tricks to get a Venus flight with me in command. Well, heaven help him, he has it. And that means I run things my way. No oversight. No interference. This is a dangerous voyage, and I'll be damned before I'll risk my crew on the meddling of landlubbers.

"Is that clear?"

"Yes, I believe so," said Tai Shi, eyebrows up and face impressed. She handed him a business card. "Have Security Chief Goldberg contact me at his convenience."

After she left, Jacobs gathered the forms he would need for the docks, at least those he had finished, leaving behind the ones now rendered inaccurate by changes to the passenger list, cargo manifest, and most of all the helioship.

The *Horizon Cusp* was too much ship for this voyage. Added risk. But, Jacobs admitted with a sigh, at least Benny Sugg would be happier. The old tomcat hated change as much as Jacobs did.

TWELVE HOURS AFTER HIS CONFRONTATION IN DOCKING BAY FORTY-Nine, Donal disembarked the *Archimedes* with the other efficiency-rate passengers, probably a good half-hour after Mason would have departed from his luxury-class personal cabin.

That thought made Donal smile. Someday he too would fly in luxury-class personal cabins at someone else's expense. In five months he would move into his graduate student accommodations on the CalThaum campus in San Luis Obispo, ready to begin his own doctoral studies. No more courier work with its promise of exotic travel and its reality of cramped quarters and occasional threats to life and limb.

At least it paid well, especially when threats to life and limb got involved. And in a few years, Donal would make Hierophant himself and get to choose his field of research. People might remember him as more than Bran Cuthbert's little brother.

Donal stepped out of the hangar and into the Spaceport of San Francisco proper: huge, organized, and teeming with life. The third largest spaceport in the United North American States — after Toronto and Durango — tens of thousands came through every day. And with the chaos of noise and movement pressing on him, Donal felt as though every single one of those travelers surrounded him right now.

Too much.

After three days among the sparser population of Kennedy, Donal was not ready for the press of San Francisco's spaceport. Luna's population counted in the millions now, but they never seemed as crowded as the cities of home. There they moved in knots and groups. Here they moved in packs and throngs.

The smell was better here in San Francisco though. Solid enchanting work kept a fresh spring scent in the air.

Still, Donal retreated back into the hangar for relief, where the only other people were low-grade alchemists in their stained jumpsuits, here to see about the *Archimedes* fuel needs.

Donal calmed himself with a breathing technique. Regular practice had enabled him to shift his levels of awareness — key to his magical perceptions and work — but at moments like this he found their familiarity comforting.

He called forth Fionn, who emitted as a green beam of light from Donal's pendant before coalescing into shape. The emerald spirit deerhound determined the lay of the land in a sniff of the air, a shifting of its eyes and a quick angling of its ears.

"Are we hunted?"

"No," said Donal. "The Hierophant took care of that."

Fionn sat and regarded the immense foot traffic, then looked back at its master with emerald ears still pointing to check for threats.

"Exactly. I need you to keep an eye on me while we head for the IIX office. I need to catch myself if I tighten up."

"You still consider field work." Fionn snorted with a twitch of its head. "Research is safer and more to your taste."

"People keep trying to kill me. I need the skills of field work, even if I don't use them to earn money."

"Your continued association with Tai Shi Li Hua endangers you."

"Because she loves field work?"

"That, and her employer." Fionn thumped its tail. "You should sever your connection with her. Sooner is better."

"Look," said Donal with a sigh, "just keep an eye on me, all right?"

And with that, they moved into the crowd, working their way through clusters of humanity — some accompanied by familiar spirits or illusory guides — and down the broad halls.

Subtle magics worked into the carpeting and walls freshened the air and drew out the smells of travel: fast food, sweat, competing perfumes and colognes, and periodic improper hygiene.

Donal passed alcoves where hallucinatory scenes advertised travel destinations and local products, barely sparing them a second glance. Of course, it helped that local noise regulations kept their volumes low enough not to interfere with casual conversation. At least, not any more than the thousand competing casual conversations did.

He did pause at an interactive map, seeing that the port had improved their map system again. When Donal had left for Kennedy, the maps had been two meters wide and could tilt, zoom and search when travelers used the proper series of gestures and key phrases.

But now Donal saw people surrounding a nearby map and pulling down personal copies, each still fully interactive, that looked as though they would maintain their integrity for some time.

The siren song of new spellwork called to Donal, and he stepped out of the traffic zone to shift his consciousness and dig into the spells, intending to study the decay rate of the duplicated images. He hoped to find some new approach to direct enchantment duration, a weakness in his own work.

The feel of Fionn's teeth lightly denting Donal's wrist brought him back into his own head before he had gotten his answer. Donal gave Fionn an irritated look.

"Research magicians can pause to study new spells," said the familiar. "Field magicians must keep their attention on their surroundings."

Donal sighed. Fionn was right, as usual. Had someone been following Donal, they could have taken him down with even a commercial-grade Pacifier while he was busy focusing on the map. On the other hand...

"I have a familiar to track threats while I study."

Fionn sat and regarded its master, head at a slight angle and ears perked in silent statement.

"...and if I thought the area might be hostile I would have sent you off to scout." Donal checked his messenger bag, an empty reflex as he had no package to deliver. "You want me to say it? I'll say it. You're right."

The *cú sidhe* sat. Waiting.

"You think I missed something else?" Donal scanned the crowd, saw no threats among the throngs. "If you aren't going to tell me, we should get moving."

Fionn looked once over its shoulder, and Donal would have sworn that his familiar managed to assess their entire surroundings in that single movement. Fionn then stood and fell into step alongside Donal as he began to walk.

Three steps later, realization made Donal slap himself in the forehead. Fionn must have been waiting for Donal to start walking.

Fionn snorted, possibly to cover a chuckle.

Some five minutes later, the two entered the main office of IIX, Intraplanetary and Interplanetary Express. The businesslike storefront had no counter, only generous floorspace surrounding private cubicles, and roving salespeople in suits eager to help anyone who needed enough security on a package to have it delivered by a magician.

Three elegant illusions demonstrated the service to passersby: one, silent, that scrolled through images and text showing every city, nation and planet IIX delivered to; the second, a three-dimensional montage of famous and important people receiving IIX deliveries by hand (simulated from real events, so the couriers would look more handsome or beautiful than any Donal knew of on staff); and the third and most impressive, a scene of IIX partner Hierophant Jane MacDougall thaumaturgically sealing a package against tampering.

Donal knew that the scene was also simulated, to avoid giving even a hint about the spells used to protect IIX packages, but he still enjoyed looking at it. Hierophant MacDougall was a handsome, statuesque woman who looked decades younger than her rumored sixty-three years.

And he found the "spell" itself entertaining: dramatic gestures and Gaelic chanting (actually a list of ingredients needed to make haggis), vivid jewel-tone colors moving in patterns that looked nothing like actual spell structures, and a subtle press against the skin of those watching, as though the spell created pressures that pushed out even through the dramatization.

Donal occasionally wondered which shadow play director had designed that display, but he never got around to asking. And he had no intention of losing himself in yet another spell while still in what amounted to a public place.

Donal nodded to the salespeople he knew as he passed through on his way to the back door leading to the employee area. He slipped on his courier signet ring and knocked twice with the ring, letting the ward chime a verifying acknowledgment before he opened the door and stepped through.

Donal had studied that ward once, a complex enchantment also performed by Hierophant MacDougall. After a solid half-hour of deep contemplation, he had learned that it tracked who passed, verified the ring and the wearer, sealed out detection spells and probes, barred unauthorized personnel and familiars, and also contained an intricate self-defense system.

And Donal knew he had only scratched the surface.

He stepped through the employee lounge, with its Spartan couches and chairs, on which two other couriers attempted to nap while their familiars — a crow and a snake — exchanged ideas in that language that all familiars seemed to know. To Donal they sounded as though they spoke some variant of Arabic, but he knew they were not using any human language.

In one corner sat the sort of kitchenette one might see in an moderate hotel room: drawers, cabinets and counters of cheap-but-decent wood, plus one heating plate and one chilling plate. Two sodas sat on the chilling plate, frost coating their glass bottles and suggesting that the sleepers had forgotten them.

Donal continued through the room and down the hall, passing the rest rooms, to the manager's and accountant's offices at the back. He turned right and paused in the doorway of Aafiya, the accountant. Donal had always thought accountants were supposed to be middle-aged, overweight men with bald spots, but Aafiya kept trim and dressed sharp, his small beard and black hair as tidy as his gray pinstriped suit. And if Aafiya was any older than Donal, Donal could not have guessed it.

Donal waited in the doorway for acknowledgment while Aafiya finished manipulating numbers in the chimeric display floating above his desk. Finally the accountant looked up and smiled.

"Donal, back from the moon in one piece I see. No combat pay this time?"

"Actually..." said Donal as he entered and sat in the square guest chair, Fionn settling on the floor beside him.

"Oh, come on. Not again."

"Check it." Donal tossed his enchanted silver IIX seal onto the desk. "That's both my off-planet flights and the Sydney mishap. I'm starting to think there's a target on my back."

"I don't believe it." Aafiya shook his head as he swept the seal through his chimerical display and it acknowledged the chase, the shot from the slinger, and Donal's vitals throughout. "I'm starting to think you've found some way to rig this thing."

Fionn emitted a low growl, and the *cú sidhe's* fur began to rise.

"Come on, Aafiya," said Donal, waving one hand to placate his familiar. "I'm just a Journeyman. How am I going to rig it?"

"You have two more years of magical training than most of our couriers, and you specialize in conjuration and deception. Maybe you figured something out. Hate to say it, but it looks like I'll have to ground you until I can get your signet checked."

"I had a feeling you were going to give me a hard time about this." Donal reached into his messenger bag and pulled out his zephyrpad. He transferred a document to the accountant, and saw it show up in the chimerical display. "Hierophant Nicholas Mason witnessed, and was good enough to sign a testimonial."

Donal smiled at Fionn while Aafiya looked the document over. "Like my mom always taught us: 'get it in writing.'"

Aafiya broke into a broad smile. "That's why I like you, Donal. You make my job easy. I'll need a few minutes to verify this, but I should be able to approve your combat pay within the half-hour."

A knock came from the door frame behind them. The two men looked up to see IIX Regional Manager Tracy Washington, who dressed as neatly as her accountant, with skin the color of wet, fertile soil and just enough height and weight to lend intimidation to her already impressive title.

"Cuthbert. My office. Now."

2

Donal knew that tone, like a hanging judge ready to pronounce sentence. He recalled Fionn back into its silver faun pendant as he stood to follow Ms. Washington.

"Good luck, Donal," whispered Aafiya. Donal forced his lips into a small smile in response, and spent the short walk across the hall from the accountant's office to the IIX San Francisco Manager's office wondering what he had done wrong. He always got his packages where they needed to go as fast as he could manage it (within the budget guidelines set by IIX).

Two steps outside her office, Donal raised his head and set his shoulders in defiance. He could think of nothing he had done to merit that tone, and in a few short months he could ditch courier work forever. In fact, with the combat pay from this last delivery supplementing his expectations, he could squeeze his money and survive until the grants kicked in...

Except that his girlfriend was accustomed to a certain standard of living that did not allow for much penny-pinching. Plus, Mom and Dad would rip him a new one for unnecessarily draining his savings.

Crap. Donal did need this job for a while yet. He set his jaw and took his seat.

Ms. Washington's office always impressed Donal with its simple elegance. Instead of paintings, each wall had a single lit sconce featuring a neoclassical statue sculpted by Edmonia Lewis. Her dark ash wood desk had a single drawer, and she had arranged her chimerical work display to take only half of the desk's width, allowing her to comfortably meet a guest's eye even while her display was active. Next to her small comm pad she had a single coffee cup (empty), resting on a coaster that showed the image of a museum, but Donal could never get a good enough look to know which one.

Most of the IIX offices smelled like coffee. Hers just smelled like wood.

Ms. Washington sat and gave Donal a sour look, lips pulled slightly to one side and eyebrows coming down toward her nose.

Donal knew better than to start this conversation. He settled into his chair, which looked like simple ash to match the desk, but soothed Donal's muscles gently with earth magic: a creature comfort to relax guests. But Donal could not quite relax. He found himself shifting despite the comfort as her silence stretched.

Finally, she said, "More combat pay, I hear."

"That wasn't my fault. The Romanovs—"

"Three times in six months, Donal. That's more than most couriers see in ten years."

"Well, the Mars run—"

"Yes. The Mars run." Ms. Washington glanced into her empty cup, then sat back. "Do you know why I like hiring Initiates instead of Journeymen?"

"You can pay them less?"

"An Initiate on the Mars run could have hidden in his cabin while the other passengers tried to kill each other. An Initiate would not have accidentally brought a zuglodon down on the ship. An Initiate—"

"Are you firing me for being a Journeyman?" Donal leaned forward, shifting his consciousness just a little to pull free of the earth magic on the chair. "We went over all this—"

"Don't interrupt." Ms. Washington tapped her comm pad hard

with her middle finger. She spoke before her secretary's face appeared in the air above the pad. "More coffee for me. Water with lemon for Cuthbert."

Donal blinked. He had asked for that the only time he had ever had a drink in her office. A year ago. And Donal never saw her take notes.

Ms. Washington kept them silent until her secretary brought in the drinks, including another coaster for Donal, this one depicting the image of a waterfall, labeled 'Saut-d'Eau, Haiti.' Once the secretary left, Ms. Washington sipped her coffee, set down the cup, then turned her attention back to Donal.

"What do you know about Rowan MacPherson?"

The name sounded familiar, but Donal might not have placed it if he had not already shifted some of his consciousness. As it was, he slipped through details and connections in his head until he remembered the red-haired beauty ... and what he later heard about her.

"I met her once, on Mars. Doesn't she have something to do with Red Sun?" The connection fired in Donal's head — Red Sun had been behind the murder and attempted murder on that fateful Mars run. Not that their connection had been proven. Bin Zuka took the fall, and bin Zuka was dead.

"Have you ever worked with her?"

Ms. Washington scrutinized Donal with an intensity that would have done his old professors credit. She might have missed her calling by not studying magic.

"No. I didn't even let her buy me coffee." Donal started to pick up his glass of water, but hesitated, his hand still on his armrest. "The Red Sun people on the flight mentioned her too, when they tried to enlist me to help them kill Mr. Mancuso."

"That's what bothers me." She pulled in a deep breath and blew it out with her bottom lip forward, jetting the air up as it went. "You turned them down flat, but they still want you. MacPherson herself came in yesterday. Wants a package delivered to Venus. Asked for you, specifically, to deliver it."

"We don't deliver to Venus."

"Don't keep up with the news when you're on a delivery?" Ms. Washington smirked. "I like that. Shows focus. Anyway, first commercial flight takes place next week, and the company doing it is an IIX partner. We can get a package on that ship."

"So what's the problem?"

"This sounds like trouble, and you're in the middle of it. Again."

"So send someone else."

"MacPherson made it clear: you or no one."

"So—"

"We'd be a poor delivery company if we started turning down jobs because of politics. We can be the first courier service with a route to Venus. Besides, I'm charging her over the top for the delivery. But Donal," — Ms. Washington leaned in, and for just a moment Donal felt convinced that this woman could break him in half — "no bullshit on this flight. Keep your head down and make your delivery. Don't go looking for trouble."

"I don't have to look," said Donal. "Trouble finds me anyway."

No one smoked in Smoky Jerry's, at least, not in the main room. Common gossip claimed that the name came from the entryway, where a haze of shifting varicolored smoke gave privacy to the customers while freely admitting all who sought entrance, so long as they were old enough. The first time Jacobs came in, the proprietor had explained that the spell was cheap to maintain and saved him the cost of a bouncer.

Jacobs had visited the bar six times over the course of a year and half before he had learned of the 'smoking room' in the back, where patrons could indulge in spell-treated tobaccos of varying purpose and legality.

That information might have persuaded Jacobs to take his custom elsewhere, but Smoky Jerry's had a homey feel that Jacobs liked. Rich dark woods, comfortably warm temperatures, and some sort of air freshener that kept the suggestion of frying steak in the air.

Besides, Smoky Jerry's sat conveniently near the spaceport, always kept Brigid's Own Irish Whiskey in stock (always at least fifteen years old, though Jacobs preferred at least twenty), and didn't clutter up the room with shadow plays, sports or music, apart from the occasional acoustic guitarist.

Jacobs liked acoustic guitar. It reminded him of the local blues bars of his native Georgia. How long had it been since he'd been back to Atlanta?

"Evening, John," said newly promoted Captain Kristoff Tunold, clapping Jacobs on the shoulder as he gestured to Jerry for some of that bourbon swill he favored. Tunold, despite his halyard-thin physique, dropped onto his barstool heavily enough that Jacobs thought he saw it wince in pain.

Tunold leaned one elbow on the bar. "You wanted to see me?"

"About time. I'd already started reminiscing. Settled in yet?"

"I've got the office squared away, and I'm moving into your old cabin tomorrow. Speaking of, you better pick up Benny Sugg. I swear the big tom thinks I've mutinied and done away with you. He's knocked three paperweights off shelves like he's trying to bomb me."

"Did you move his office cat bed? Last time I did that he started yanking bookmarks out of whatever I was reading." Jacobs smiled, then sighed. "Well, I won't be picking him up just yet."

Tunold jutted out his prow of a chin, but held his tongue.

Not bad. Just six months ago Tunold would have already yelled a complaint. Jacobs decided he had been right that Tunold was ready for the big chair. Which made what he had to say that much harder.

"I'm going to have to take the *Horizon Cusp* to Venus."

"Too much ship for that run, you said." Tunold's words came out an almost ursine growl.

"Stand down, Mister."

Tunold slammed both fists on the bar, then startled to see his drink between those fists. Jerry gave Jacobs a wink and continued down the bar. Tunold looked at Jacobs, then picked up his drink and tossed it down his gullet.

Jacobs shook his head. Tunold knew his old captain's view of drinking, so that had to have been spite. Perhaps Tunold wasn't as ready for command as Jacobs had thought...

Then Jacobs gave a lopsided smile. He had no right to criticize any man for temper. But Tunold narrowed his eyes at Jacobs' smile, so Jacobs had to cover.

"You're probably better off not tasting that swill anyway." He savored the air above his own whiskey before drawing a sip onto his tongue: smooth and rich, with just a hint of honey. "Now the good stuff—"

"Why?"

"That should have been your first—"

"No lectures today, John. You've been dangling a chair of my own for over a year now. I've more than proved myself. I deserve to know why you're yanking it away."

"First of all, I'm not, and this is not a punishment." Jacobs gestured to Jerry for a second bourbon while he gave Tunold a chance to let that sink in. "You want a command now? Take the *Lark's Song* and run the Luna-Mars-Earth charters until I bring the *Horizon Cusp* back. But I'd prefer you didn't."

Jacobs eased another sip of whiskey onto his tongue. "This Venus run is going to make that first Mars charter look like a stop in Toronto. And I'm not getting any younger. I need my best ex oh by my side, one more time."

"I've been waiting a long time for the big chair."

"You have."

Tunold took a small sip of his bourbon that impressed Jacobs with its restraint, even if Tunold had to hide the sour taste of his swill behind a quick grimace.

"Wait." Tunold turned to look Jacobs square in the eye. "What are you holding back from me?"

"Mancuso bought out Zoltan."

Tunold tossed down the rest of his drink and gestured for another. Jacobs did the same.

"Jesus, John, you're taking on water and you haven't even left the dock."

"I know. Double the passengers, triple the cargo, plus *oversight*." Jacobs spat out that last word, and rinsed the taste of it from his tongue with a sip from his fresh glass.

"Quit. I've got a friend at SF State, could get you on the History lecture circuit. Not much, but it'll keep a roof over your head."

Jacobs might have considered quitting when confronted by threats, but in the face of facts, he knew he could not.

"Let that son of a bitch Mancuso chase me out of my life's work? I'd kill him first."

"Tai Shi'd cut you down before you got close enough."

"True," said Jacobs, though inwardly he wondered. Tai Shi had youthful vigor and magic on her side, but Jacobs kept his conditioning as well as any man might in his mid-eighties, and he had more experience than she could begin to guess.

But then, maybe these days 'experience' just meant that he was old. Too old for this line of thought.

Both men took a morose swig of their drinks.

"The *Lark's Song's* a nice ship," said Tunold. "Small, but the charters—"

"Kris..."

"All right, here's the deal." Tunold spun on his stool, grabbed Jacobs' shoulders with his huge hands, leaned in until Jacobs could smell the rank bourbon on his breath, and said, "No heroics. No looking good for the customers. If Mancuso is deciding who goes" — he paused long enough for a confirming nod from Jacobs — "and he's your partner, then commercial passengers or not, this is an in-house gig. You play the old school captain. You make all the big calls and keep us on mission. I'll handle the crew, passengers, and any on-ship problems."

"I'm not too old to—"

"Never said you were, John," said Tunold in a softer voice. "But even forty years ago you would have needed help with this one. I would, if it were me."

Jacobs nodded. Once.

"All right, Kris."

The two men shook, then drained their drinks in a toast to flying the first commercial voyage to the morning star itself.

"Since you're handling on-ship matters," said Jacobs, "I should warn you that Tai Shi and Goldberg may be fighting over seniority..."

Tunold grinned like a bear with a salmon.

"Bring 'em on."

Donal recalled Fionn as he waited outside the spaceport for a public runner to bring him to within walking distance of his apartment. A light breeze carried to Donal the steady clacking and ticking of hooves and claws as well as the accompanying scents. Runner traffic had thinned over the last year in San Francisco as horses came back into fashion, but Donal could still see many of the furry or scaly vehicles moving up and down the streets on two to ten legs each, their passengers riding comfortably inside, as though they had been actual giant animals hollowed out for human use — albeit far more comfortable that that phrase implied.

Fionn emitted from the silver faun pendant as a beam of emerald light, and coalesced into its deerhound shape. "Field protocols?"

"Not now. Red Sun is back."

"I see three strong escape routes from this spot. Mask our movement and follow—"

"Not here." Donal waited until the fae hound sat and twitched its ears, ready to listen. "Rowan MacPherson wants to send me to Venus for a delivery. She asked for me specifically."

Fionn snorted with a shake of its head, the fur of its shoulders ruffling slightly.

"Yeah, I know. I should quit. I don't need the risk." Donal snapped his fingers. "And hey, Magister Machado left me that standing offer to intern with him for a flight or two. Pay wouldn't be as much, but it should be safer, plus—"

"You should take the delivery, Master."

The familiar's words stunned Donal into slack-jawed silence.

Fionn waited for Donal to settle himself, then continued, "If Red Sun wants you on that ship, your benefactor will be there."

"You still think Mr. Mancuso might be this 'shadow dictator' that bin Zuka warned about?"

Imenand bin Zuka: magician, businessman, murderer. He believed his murders would prevent a shadow government from forming, but he died suddenly after killing only one of his two targets. Could Mr. Mancuso have had him murdered?

"Can you afford to have doubt?"

"Taint the foundation and you taint the results," muttered Donal, reciting an axiom of magic. The very axiom he had quoted to Mr. bin Zuka in an attempt to dissuade the man from murder.

Louder Donal said, "And the result will be my future doctorate, maybe doctorates." Donal sighed. "Plus any findings from my research ... any contributions I make to the future of magic...." Donal let that sink in. "Mr. Mancuso said that 4M would always be there with funding for whatever I do. That means they'd expect to be the first to see my results, to find ways to benefit."

Fionn merely sat, tail twitching as though conducting the orchestra of Donal's thoughts, or perhaps keeping time with the beat.

"Mr. Mancuso *will* be on that flight. He has to be. Maybe this is my chance to find out once and for all what kind of man Donatello Mancuso really is."

"And if he is as bad as the image Imenand bin Zuka described?"

"Then I have to find a way to stop him. Even if it costs me my funding."

"Or your life?"

"Or my life."

Donal half-expected his familiar to try to dissuade him at that point. Fionn had always shown a clear priority of keeping Donal alive and safe. That the *cú sidhe* said nothing now meant that it agreed with the risk.

Donal wondered whether that should make him feel better, or worse.

3

Ship's Mage Machado held a leisurely pace along the golden ceramic corridors of the *Horizon Cusp*, as much to irritate his companion as to conserve his energy. Jitters, as he called Ship's Engineer Jang in the privacy of his own thoughts, would likely have jogged all the way from their new research lab to the bubble, even though she would have saved less than a minute.

But then, she lacked the authoritative weight of Machado's features and stature. Jang's nervous energy kept her short body positively tiny, like a squirrel that thinks it has five minutes to live. Further, she wore her engineering overalls everywhere, clothing more appropriate for an alchemist than a magician, and not at all like Machado's own tailored shirt and slacks. She smelled like an alchemist too, like someone had blended a dozen random flavors of herbal tea, then left the mixture on to boil too long.

All of these things added to the chance of her being mistaken for an exuberant child instead of the competent professional she was.

"We should check the formulae again," said Machado, "before we bother Goldberg with this."

"You're just mad that you didn't think of it first."

"If it had been a good idea, I *would* have thought of it first."

Jang spun on her heels, eyes narrowed and fingers twitching as though clutching air. Then she seemed to remember that, for all her experience and space certifications, she was only an Initiate, while Machado was a Magister.

Machado stretched his lips in a lazy smile, eyes half-lidded, certain that he had read her right. But a true magician knows when to show magnanimity.

"All right, there is some merit to your notion of tying into the central systems an emergency switch that could hit an entire room with a pacify effect—"

"Ha!"

"But it needs more development before it's worth talking about. Right now you haven't allowed for a failsafe, its implementation is too broad, and its trigger too vulnerable to outside magic. And this doesn't begin to address concerns about how the layers of spells would interact with other systems—"

"No point in going forward if Goldberg wouldn't want it," said Jang with a shrug, pushing her pace a little, probably to try to force Machado to keep up. He held his stroll, and she fell back into pace after a few steps. "If he nixes it—"

"Goldberg will love it. Tunold will probably approve it. But until our new captain makes it through probation, you'll need Jacobs' consent, and he'll never go for it."

She seemed to think about that while Machado absently checked the broadcast spells on a Starchaser Spacelines logo as they walked. The spells were solid, and would carry announcements well. Good bit of enchanting on Machado's part, if he said so himself.

"He might," said Jang, bringing him back to the conversation at hand. "He hates big fights."

"Too much risk. And you know I won't sign off on it until it's seen a hell of a lot more development."

"Jeez, Mash, can't you acknowledge someone else having a good idea?"

"I don't know that it's good yet. It still needs..."

Machado gave Jang a sideways look, saw her cheek twitch: she was hiding something.

"Are you bucking for your Bachelor's?"

"I..." Jang scuffled three steps and spat. "Wouldn't mind the pay raise, even if it means I have to pull my head out of the engines for a bit."

Even if it means that you'll have to develop some art to go with your technique, thought Machado. He didn't believe she would ever make Journeyman. He'd never seen enough creativity in her spell work. But despite their personal problems, he couldn't bring himself to discourage her. Who was he to judge how far her talents could take her?

"Just make sure you don't mess with my spells. I'd hate to see you make Journeyman only to have to kill you myself."

Jang snorted through a lopsided grin and clapped Machado on his back as they reached the water tube. She pulled the lever to call the bubble. "Help me with my homework and there'll be *caxaça* in it for you."

"I'll think about it." Much as Machado enjoyed his cane rum, he didn't need the headache of tutoring Jang. "Heard anything about the new ex oh?"

The bubble arrived, a large pocket of air containing a steel cage that could hold close to a dozen passengers, and carried by undines in the tube. As they boarded, Jang said, "Security Deck," to the water elementals, and to Machado she said, "I hear it's going to be Daher. She's only commanded little boats like the *Daedalus Dream.* Needs big ship experience if she wants to move up."

"Better learn to watch your mouth," said Machado as the bubble came to a gentle halt, the cage opened, and they stepped out into the corridor. "I hear she doesn't take backtalk well."

Machado continued to hold Jang back to a stroll along the pale blues of the Security Deck. The two had not gotten halfway to Goldberg's office when they heard him bellow:

"Over my dead body!"

Machado and Jang looked at each other, then ran the rest of the distance to the open doorway. Jang easily outdistanced Machado, but had the sense to wait for him in the hall.

Through the open doorway they saw Chief Goldberg, looking grizzled and angry. He leaned over his old, stained desk, and spoke in a low tone to a woman in a charcoal gray skirt suit who held a relaxed, ready posture. Even from behind, Machado recognized Tai Shi Li Hua as much by the pleasant contours of her form and the black sheen of her long, straight hair as by the magical signature he could see in her personal power.

Two members of Goldberg's watch tried to pretend they didn't exist, sitting in chairs against one wall, next to the chief's distasteful physical filing cabinets.

Machado sent a mental call to his familiar, *Saravá*, and readied a few spells to protect his fellow crew members, if needed. Machado knew that as pleasant as she could be to look at, Tai Shi could take down the chief before the watchmen could bolt from their chairs. She might not even need magic to do it.

"Chief," said Tai Shi in an even tone that made Machado relax just a little, "I have a great deal of respect for you and your work. Your record sparkles. But Starchaser Spacelines is now a part of the 4M family of companies, and all 4M security is subject to my review and approval."

Machado and Jang looked at each other. Starchaser Spacelines was part of 4M? Since when?

"4M only owns half the business," said Goldberg, words spitting out of his mouth as though he wished they were punches. "That makes us affiliated, not owned."

"That's not how affiliation works, but I take your meaning. Nevertheless—"

"The last time you had security oversight of people boarding this ship, some of them turned out to be involved in a conspiracy—"

"The entire purpose of my promotion was to prevent a recurrence of such an incident by—"

"Didn't ask. The answer is no. I handle security on this ship."

"And this ship falls under my scrutiny."

"Scrutinize *this!*" said Goldberg, with an accompanying gesture that made Machado smirk and Jang giggle.

"Chief, if you don't cooperate, I can have you fired."

"*Bong!*" Goldberg drew the word out in an imitation of the wrong-answer gong used in a popular shadow play contest. "Check my contract. Only Jacobs can fire me."

"Unless you present a clear and present danger, at which point any superior in the organization can fire you." She tossed a business card on the desk. "Care to read that title again?"

Machado felt *Saravá* approach and sent a mental command to his *onça* familiar to ensure that Tai Shi's spirit dragon familiar had not gone wandering.

Goldberg slammed his fist on the desk. "How do I 'present a clear and present danger?'"

"'Any 4M company or related company refusing to cooperate with the Director of Security for Inter-Business Relations shall be considered to present a clear and present danger to 4M executives.'"

Tai Shi placed her hands on the desk and matched the chief's lean.

"I would fire you. You would sue. The courts would sort out whether or not half-interest in the company gave me the necessary authority." She pushed in closer until they were eye-to-eye. "Maybe you get a payday out of it, but you miss being an officer on the first commercial flight to Venus.

"Which is more important to you?"

"She's good," whispered Jang. Machado said nothing.

Neither did Goldberg, at first. He tried to hold her with his glare, but Machado could tell that Goldberg had a long way to go before he could match the glare of a master like Jacobs. And against a magician? Machado could have told Goldberg not to waste the effort.

Finally, the chief said, "Fine. I'll let you review any new hires I need for this voyage, and you can veto any you don't like *if*, and I do mean if, you can show me cause. Maybe you have resources I don't." He shook his head, but wasn't done speaking. "Also, I'll let you inspect the ship and any cargo before takeoff, provided you are accompanied by a security officer of my choosing and either the ship's mage or the ship's assistant mage."

Tai Shi drew a breath as though to speak, but Goldberg charged ahead with one more detail.

"Anyone currently part of the crew is to be considered secure, and not subject to your inspection or approval."

"Exception: anyone hired since the Mars charter is to be considered a new hire and therefore subject to my review and veto."

"No."

"Need I remind you that those Pacifiers were smuggled aboard this ship by your own purser, then a recent hire?"

Goldberg hesitated, and Tai Shi added in a softer voice, "Give me this and we have an agreement."

Goldberg extended his hand. Tai Shi shook it.

"Exception," said Machado from the doorway, turning all five other sets of eyes to face him. "Assistant Ship's Mage Aaron Cromartie could be construed as a new hire after that Mars run because it was at that time that he joined the crew permanently. However, he had been hired and vetted for security work for that voyage, and I will vouch for him."

Machado folded his arms over his massive chest. "More than that, I will take it as a personal insult worthy of a duel if my word in this matter is deemed insufficient."

"There's no need for that, Magister Machado," said Tai Shi, while over her shoulder Machado saw Goldberg grin. "Initiate Cromartie comported himself well on that voyage, and I will accept your guarantee of his character."

Tai Shi looked back and forth from ship's mage to engineer to security chief, then said, "And it seems that some ship business presses, so I will take up no more of your time. Chief Goldberg, when shall we meet about the newer hires?"

"Give me two days."

"Done."

And with that she left. Machado had to check his urge to watch her walk away, lamenting that she had declined his dinner invitation after that Mars charter.

"She's going to be trouble," said Jang.

"She'll get worse?" said Goldberg. "Oy!"

He shook it off, dismissed his waiting watch personnel with a sarcastic remark, and turned back to the two visiting magicians.

"So what can I do for you two?"

Jang glanced at Machado, but he let her take the lead. She said, "I have this idea about ship security..."

***

THE ORB: SAN FRANCISCO'S PREMIERE RESTAURANT CATERING exclusively to the magically adept. Donal gazed longingly at its elegant, black-and-silver décor as the public runner carried him down Market Street. Donal had tried for a reservation before he had left for Luna, imagining that a week would have been enough lead time for his welcome-home date with Li Hua.

His estimation fell more than six months short. But then tables at The Orb were always in demand. Even visiting magicians from other planets added San Francisco to their itineraries for the chance to eat at The Orb.

Donal wondered if the restaurant prioritized reservations by a magician's credentials...

Fionn would probably have advised Donal to save The Orb as a treat for getting his doctorate. Donal had to guess, because his spirit deerhound remained housed while aboard the runner, per San Francisco public transit regulations. In Donal's opinion, that regulation mattered less on runners than on the cable cars, where too many extant spirits might interfere with the elementals that kept the old relics running. But he didn't make the rules.

At least the runner was comfortable. Cloth bench seats inside what looked like a headless, six-meter-long, twelve-legged grizzly bear, seating about twenty plus the woman at the reins. Only ten other passengers today, unlike the packed, standing-room-only trip home from the spaceport Donal had yesterday.

No rushed and hostile travelers around him this time, only business types at the end of their work day. Two carried dueling swords, but probably just for show. A movement had sprung up among the United North American States to abolish dueling codes as anachronisms from the chaotic early days following the rise of magic. But no other nations had gotten rid of theirs yet, so Donal expected those codes to stay on the books, even if they weren't needed as often as they once were.

Besides, swords were an excuse for ornamentation for either gender, though it was a more popular affectation among men.

Bran, of course, kept in practice with his dueling sword. As though, if challenged, he would pick anything other than spells as his weapon. Donal hadn't touched a sword since his failed attempt to join the dueling club in high school.

Finally the runner arrived at the stop nearest the restaurant where Donal *had* gotten reservations: The Jade Monkey. Donal hopped out of his seat, dusted off the light summer jacket he wore over his ocean blue, short-sleeved shirt and dark gray pants, and stepped off the runner and onto the sidewalk.

Another passenger got off behind him, one of the sword-carriers. Probably nothing, but still Donal called Fionn out of its pendant and muttered, "rear guard," in Gaelic. Fionn retained invisibility to normal vision and kept an eye on the possible follower.

The Jade Monkey waited a block and a half away, but if this man followed, he would know where Donal was headed and see him with Li Hua. That last part should not have been a problem ... unless Li Hua was the reason for following.

Donal thought about that as he let his eyes drift along Octavia Boulevard. Not so busy as Market had been. Donal could see two or three other knots of pedestrians, a half-dozen horses, and one two-legged runner. No movements that suggested that sword boy had a partner — assuming he *was* following Donal.

"He has turned into a florist shop, master," said Fionn, rejoining

Donal as he walked down the pocked sidewalk. "The woman behind the counter had a dozen roses ready for him."

"So, likely innocent then," said Donal with a chuckle.

"Likely," said Fionn in a more serious voice, "but not certain. Shall I continue to watch him?"

"No. He wouldn't be after me, anyway. I'm not on a delivery."

"But you will be, and the matter may contested. Consider also that the Romanovs might have connections here."

"Hierophant Mason assured me that the 'moral crime' defense wouldn't extend past Luna-controlled space."

"That does not preclude assassination."

"There's a happy thought." Donal glanced over his shoulder by reflex, but saw only a young boy dashing toward an apartment building. "Let's be honest here. If the guy were headed this way with violence on his mind, he would probably be after Li Hua."

"And you are close to Tai Shi Li Hua. I will return to my watch."

"No," said Donal, stopping at the door of the restaurant, a design that blended African and Middle-Eastern designs. "Time for you to return to your pendant. We're here."

***

Jacobs tossed his pen down on his desk in disgust. These chimerical workspaces used in land-bound offices simply did not replicate the way a ship's phantasmal interface worked. Too vague. Too ... inflexible. Zoltan had promised him that the ones they purchased were as close as he could get, but they just were not good enough for plotting courses.

Zoltan.

Jacobs deflated in a sigh that dropped him back in his chair. Zoltan had abandoned ship, leaving only Jacobs at the helm. And they were being boarded.

Jacobs rubbed that spot between his eyes that always seemed to irritate him these days. He wanted to hate his old partner. Wanted to curse his name and his fate before every great sea, sky and space god Jacobs knew. And a few he had invented.

But he couldn't do it.

Jacobs could not bring himself to hate Zoltan for doing what came naturally: making the best possible deal in a bad situation. That happy talent had helped them turn Starchaser Spacelines from a tiny shuttle service into a veritable fleet of passenger ships, a leader in commercial travel.

At least, it had been a leader until the *Beamrunner's* accident last year. But even then, Zoltan's business savvy and Jacobs' facility with ships had gotten them through the public relations nightmare. They had come through that disaster as they had come through every other for almost two decades.

And now Zoltan was gone, and Jacobs had to fend for himself with the business side of Starchaser Spacelines, including man-who-would-be-king Donatello Mancuso, President and CEO of 4M, and de facto leader of Transterran Properties and four other corporations, if Jacobs understood correctly. Hard to keep the facts straight after the rhetoric of bin Zuka and Red Sun, who seemed convinced that Mancuso would not be satisfied until he held the planetary governments themselves in his thrall and ruled all human territories from his shadow throne.

That was what Zoltan had left Jacobs to deal with on his own: an arrogant megalomaniac who might have imperial delusions. Jacobs' new partner.

Perhaps Jacobs could allow himself to hate Zoltan just a little bit then. Just enough to provide a dangerous look in Jacobs' eye and a cutting tone in his voice the next time they spoke. Yes. Jacobs could allow himself that much, at least for now.

Lord God Almighty did Jacobs need to get back to space, back where life made sense. How could he ever consider retiring to an Earth-bound house, even one in beautiful Mazatlan?

Jacobs picked up his discarded pen and noted: '*Daedalus Dream* as a retirement bonus?' Then he turned once more to his charts. Even with the latest data from San Francisco Port Authority — at least, the version of that data released for public use — the three dimensional view of space between Earth and Mars lacked the gradation and measurements as fine and precise as Jacobs knew the data contained. The margins were too wide, introducing an extra element of risk to the travel.

No good. This land-bound tool may have sufficed for the general fleet planning the business required, possibly even for quick evaluations of known safe routes. But for a first flight along a brand new route? Dangerous.

Jacobs snorted when he realized he could feel a bitter downturn at the edges of his mouth. Not that long ago he had charted all voyages by hand, with paper. Now, finally, magic had given him a tool he truly believed was better than anything technology could have provided, and he had let it spoil him.

Still. Six hours Jacobs had spent trying to double-check the route he was planning for his voyage to Venus. Six hours trying to accomplish what he could have done in two aboard the *Horizon Cusp*, or even aboard the *Lark's Song*.

But the *Lark's Song* was due to ship out in two days, off to Kennedy on Luna before heading out to New Leningrad on Mars. Jacobs had wanted to give Tunold as much time as possible to adjust to giving up the captain's office on the *Horizon Cusp*, but Daher would need to prepare the *Lark's Song* for her first voyage as a captain.

No help for it. Jacobs would have to finish aboard the *Horizon Cusp*.

A light knock at the door preceded Cindy into the room. She came in carrying a piece of paper held between her thumb and index finger by one corner, as though she might damage it. Her sheer discomfort with something Jacobs considered so essential made him contemplate ordering that the office begin to track all records on paper.

He dismissed the notion just as quick, deciding that the entire office staff would revolt or quit.

"The latest delivery schedule from IIX, Mr. Jacobs."

"Thank you." He glanced over it until he reached an entry that made him call the receptionist back in. "What's this about a delivery on the Venus flight?"

"That's right, sir. Mr. Zoltan arranged it. One of his last acts before he left." She crinkled her eyebrows suspiciously. "Actually, he said you would ask about it. He said, 'If John asks, tell him I used the unusual circumstances clause to charge ten times the standard fee.'"

Jacobs grimaced, and Cindy took that as her excuse to leave. *Smart girl.* The increased fee was a good touch, but something about this sat wrong in Jacobs' stomach. Could IIX have scraped up a delivery so fast after the formal press release a week ago?

Perhaps. Zoltan could have done it. Still, no man sailed as long as Jacobs had without learning which instincts to trust. And this time his instincts said that the courier would be trouble.

Just another detail to drop in Tunold's lap tomorrow. Jacobs would have to move back into the *Horizon Cusp* come morning anyway. He could not risk any imprecision in his course for this voyage. He needed a ship's phantasmal display, and the best would be the ship flying the route in question.

And, Jacobs had to admit, he needed the comfort of a ship around him amid all this turmoil.

Jacobs stared at the Venus entry on the IIX itinerary. He could not shake the feeling that a storm was brewing.

Donal was met at the door of the Jade Monkey restaurant by savory smells, the clinking of dishware, the buzzing hum of background conversation, and Mr. Mohatar, with his wrinkled brown skin and his bright white teeth.

"Donal! Weeks we haven't seen you! Off playing in the stars again?"

"Delivering packages, you mean." Donal shook the proprietor's hand with honest enthusiasm, unconsciously trying to match the man's infectious smile. "Boring work, but it keeps the hyenas from my doorstep."

"And may they never call your name at night," said Mr. Mohatar with a quick warding gesture. More casually, he rubbed his hands together. "Alone or with company tonight?"

"My *girlfriend* is already here I see." Donal pointed past a half-dozen full tables among the red-and-brown décor and Moroccan artwork to Li Hua, sitting under a mural of Mr. Mohatar's native Marrakesh, looking over the menu.

"Girlfriend? So this is why you have brought no dates lately! But wait, you're just bringing her here now?" Mr. Mohatar's eyebrows climbed high enough to convey just a little hurt alongside his amazement. "You are ashamed of our cooking."

"Never! It's just that she travels more than I do. Actual dates take planning."

"Fine. But I can't let you meet her looking like that." Mr. Mohatar gave Donal's outfit a critical once-over, dusting here and straightening there. "Better. Now come, let's not keep your lovely lady waiting."

Mr. Mohatar swept Donal along, managing to give each diner a smile or a kind word in passing, until they reached Li Hua's table, where he said, "My dear Ms. Tai Shi, if I may present your escort for the evening, the very fortunate Mr. Donal Cuthbert."

He gestured Donal to his seat with such a flourish that Donal almost applauded. Donal took his seat and turned to comment, but Mr. Mohatar had already moved on to another table, smoothing over a question about an entrée.

Li Hua gave Donal a smile that looked wry around the lips, but sincerity gleamed from her soft brown eyes with their hint of caramel.

"So you've dined here before?"

"You could say that."

Donal pointed to the open wine bottle with a questioning look, since both their glasses were empty, but Li Hua gave a slight shake of her head to indicate that the wine's tannins needed a few more minutes yet.

He continued, "I discovered this place my first week in the city, and Mr. Mohatar has always made it feel like home."

"Did I hear you tell him that courier work is boring?"

"I don't want to make him worry."

Li Hua's smile gave up its attempt to stay wry. "How do you do it, Donal? Everywhere you go, people like you."

"Trouble at work?"

"Everyone wants safety, but they all resent oversight."

"I don't think it's the oversight, so much, as your boss. Mr. Mancuso can be a bit ... much at times." Donal made a show of enjoying the sight of the reddish-brown dress that bared Li Hua's shoulders and hugged her contours. "Whereas I can't imagine anyone complaining about the sight of you."

"I've never given you orders. Well, except when people were trying to kill us." Her tone sounded droll, but her eyes showed that his words had mollified her. She glanced over the menu. "What do you recommend?"

"Try the *tajine*, with beef. It'll go great with red wine."

"Not just red. Look at the bottle again."

LI Hua's smile had returned to hover around her lips and eyes in that way that made Donal want to lean across the table and kiss her. But if he did, he would never hear the end of it from Mr. Mohatar, who might begin planning their wedding.

"A syrah. A Morgan '75." Donal's jaw dropped slightly as he considered how much the bottle had likely cost. But he knew why she had chosen it. "The same year as the first bottle we shared."

"On Mars. The restaurant made me homesick." She pointed to a couple of still-image depictions. "The colors, the open-air markets..."

"I never saw enough of Mars to miss."

"I'll have to give you a guided tour sometime."

"If the locals can go long enough without trying to kill us."

"I'm a Mars local and I've never tried to kill you."

Donal met her eyes, his cheeks fighting back a smile at her inadvertent reference to a personal joke they shared from their first night together. Li Hua caught the reference only a moment later, and the smile she gave Donal then made him want to skip dinner.

Whatever might have been said next was lost to the waiter's arrival. Donal and Li Hua both ordered the beef *tajine*, with artichoke hearts and peas, served with a Moroccan bread made from an old Mohatar family recipe. Donal had prepared a comment about how she might try to kill him later that night, but the moment had gone.

"I'm just tired of people assuming I have some deeper agenda," said Li Hua.

"Are you sure it's not the reduced risk of your position? When was the last time you had to fight off a threat?"

Li Hua blinked, then poured them each a glass of wine. Donal swirled his and inhaled the subtle scent with its touch of blackcurrant. A touch richer and fuller than the bottle they had shared on Mars.

The first taste delighted him. The bottle was worth every cent.

Li Hua had yet to sample hers. "You think I'm looking for fights?"

"No," said Donal, drawing the word out and raising his free hand to indicate that he didn't want one either. "I just think you deal with people in nerve-wracking situations, and you can feel the edge without the release."

"Maybe." She paused long enough to sample her own wine, then savor it for a deep, eyes-closed breath that came in smooth but went out rushed rather than relaxed. "Probably doesn't help that I generally meet these people around the time that Mr. Mancuso has proven his business acumen."

"You mean after he's gotten his acumen all over them."

"He *is* paying for your graduate school," Li Hua said with one eyebrow arched.

"And I appreciate it. But it's still true that 4M has been downright predatory in its business practices lately."

"'Predatory' has a specific business meaning."

"You know what I mean."

The waiter arrived with their bread, but the basket sat untouched between them as Li Hua continued. "You aren't back on that Red Sun garbage."

"No, but 4M has been on the move. Plus, you have to admit that Mr. Mancuso has been making as many waves in the society and political sections of the news as he has in the business section."

"Doesn't mean he's trying to set up a shadow government."

"Look." Donal set down his wine and spread his fingers on the table before him, a universal not-casting gesture that promised peaceful intentions from a magician. "I'm just saying that a company he deals with might view him as power hungry. So when his Director of Security for Inter-Business Relations comes calling, people might expect that your work is part of his effort to seize control."

Li Hua reached over and tapped the backs of Donal's hands, indicating that the gesture was not necessary, like clinking a host's glass instead of having one's wine checked for poison.

But instead of speaking, she reached for her wine, so Donal added, "I hope we're not going to waste tonight fighting. I'm going back to space in a couple of days."

"Me too," she admitted after her sip. "Wait. You just got back. I thought IIX guaranteed its couriers a week at home between off-planet deliveries."

"Two weeks when the combat clause comes into play."

"Again?" Li Hua's smile was back, and Donal felt muscles in his back and ribs relax at the sight.

"Seems one of the local rich families on Luna objected to my delivery."

"You see more action than I do these days."

"That could change..." Donal tried to make his tone flirty. Not one of his great skills, but enough to keep the smile on Li Hua's face, and maybe add a hint of promise behind her eyes.

"So why are they shorting your home time?"

"Special request for me to deliver a package to Venus."

"Venus?"

In the space of a single word, Li Hua's entire aspect changed: her tone urgent, her posture erect, her eyes scanning the room, one hand near her table knife and the other stroking a bracelet that Donal knew held ready enchantments.

"Who is sending you to Venus?"

Donal felt his stomach jump at her reaction, and it jangled a nervous thread through his words.

"It's just a delivery. And you know I can't identify the interested parties."

"This isn't a game, Donal." She huffed out an angry breath at Donal's narrow-eyed refusal to answer. "Who else knows?"

"I haven't told anyone, so just the client and IIX." Donal tried to shrug, but his shoulders had tightened and the back of his neck felt exposed to the door behind him. The gesture came out a twitch. "And anyone the client has told. The receiver, I imagine."

"When did you get the assignment?"

All flirtation had fled from Li Hua. Donal saw in her only the focused, dangerous woman who had killed the people trying to murder them on Mars. Donal found himself answering her question, only the mental discipline of his calling allowing him to control how much information he gave her.

"Yesterday. Just after I reported in when I got back from Kennedy."

"Where have you been since?"

"Just home. Now here."

Their food arrived. Mr. Mohatar smiled as he helped the waiter set down the plates, but he must have read their intensity because he left without comment, only sparing Donal a worried glance.

"Were you followed?"

"Maybe." Donal forced himself to pick up his fork to try a piece of the beef, but had to finish his thought before tasting what smelled so wonderful. "Some business type with a dueling sword got off the runner when I did, but he turned into a flower shop. Fionn said the woman behind the counter had a dozen roses ready for him."

Li Hua called Pinyin-Lung, her familiar, out of its home in her brooch. She gave the smoky, serpentine dragon rapid orders in Chinese, then turned back to Donal as it whisked away.

"I'm impressed that you had Fionn follow him. We'll make a field magician out of you yet." She reached out and stroked Donal's cheek, and the blend of adrenaline and desire flared confusion through Donal's system. She continued, "It may be nothing, but Pinyin-Lung will find out."

"So what do we do?"

"For now? We eat." Li Hua's smile was back, but this time it carried an undertone of excitement. "I don't know about you, but I'm starved."

4

"If you won't try the *sfenj*, at least let me bring you some *baklava*."

Donal knew the smile on Mr. Mohatar's face. Mr. Mohatar must have assessed the tension in the air during dinner. He also probably noticed the lack of angry words or postures, or the touching and looks that would have indicated sexual tension.

Donal's guess: Mr. Mohatar thought the evening was on the ropes and was trying valiantly to save it for Donal through the power of his excellent pastries.

And dinner *had* been tense. There had been moments of pleasure through the wine and *tajine*, but then Pinyin-Lung had returned. Donal could not pick up the information the familiar had passed to its mistress, and Li Hua had put off his questioning looks with a small shake of her head.

Not the time to talk about it, perhaps, but something was wrong. Something she had spotted that Donal had missed.

And now, dinner was finished, and Mr. Mohatar had to settle for his payment, and for assurances that Donal would return for breakfast or lunch before he next left port.

When Donal and Li Hua were at last alone again, Li Hua turned to Donal, excitement flashing in her eyes. "They're still out there."

"*They*?"

"You missed his backup?" She shrugged. "I wondered why you hadn't mentioned him. Anyway, there are only two, and neither is a magician, so it might just be a warning."

"Suppose there's a third..."

"There isn't."

"How can you be sure?"

Li Hua tilted her head forward and answered with one raised eyebrow.

"Because this is what you do," Donal said, and was rewarded with a graceful incline of her neck. He continued, "So they'll just want to talk?"

"I didn't say that." Li Hua stretched her fingers and rolled her wrists. "I just don't think they're here to kill me."

"You're sure they're after you?"

"Donal," she said, managing not to sound condescending. "You are an excellent magician, and you're starting to pick up some field skills. You beat bin Zuka in a serious duel, and you don't even need to control your breathing to shift consciousness anymore. But face it," — and here she paused to cover his hand with hers — "anyone coming after you would be a fool to let you reach me."

"You think this is corporate espionage."

"Most likely." She shrugged, and even through the tension Donal found the movement fetching in her off-the-shoulder dress. "If they think they'll distract me while they're doing something else, then they're foolish enough not to realize I've had Pinyin-Lung put my people on alert while we ate."

She finished the last of her wine.

"No, words or a fight, this will be a message."

"Then let's go see." Donal recalled Fionn and briefed him in Gaelic, Li Hua nodding along and adding details about positioning.

"Better to split up," said Fionn. "We should go out the back and let Tai Shi Li Hua deal with the threat."

"You want Donal to circle around and flank them?"

The emerald deerhound tilted its head with its ears at an angle that Donal read instantly as disagreement. He had no doubt that Fionn wanted Donal out of the way of a threat that did not concern him directly.

Except that, as far as Donal was concerned, a threat to Li Hua was a threat to him personally.

"They know I'm here," said Donal. "And they know I'm with Li Hua. If I don't come out with her, they'll suspect a trap."

"Or that you have seen the wisdom to evade unneeded trouble," added Fionn, twisting the words so that they only made sense to Donal, a special form of communication all familiars shared with their masters.

"Flanking might not be a bad option," said Li Hua in English. "If you can come around the side fast enough and quiet enough."

"No," said Donal. "Better for us both to come out and meet them head on. Two magicians. No waiting."

Li Hua smiled.

"You do know how to show a girl a good time."

***

KRISTOFF TUNOLD CAME LAST TO THE MESS HALL ON THE *HORIZON CUSP*, almost late to a meeting he had called. His officers chatted among themselves as they waited for him at the center table, just one of over a dozen round tables surrounded by simple wooden chairs.

Tunold had hoped to redecorate the mess hall of his new command: new tables, padded chairs, and actual art alongside the giant Starchaser Spacelines logo and mandatory still displays of duty rosters, maps, and ship regulations. Maybe get rid of that fish smell that always seemed to linger.

But the *Horizon Cusp* was not his ship. Not yet. Any more than these were really his officers.

Tunold stood behind his chair for a moment, looking over the assemblage, his jaw proudly forward and his posture almost the protractor-straight of Mr. Kelly, the yeoman. Not that anyone could match Kelly's posture or his precise gestures.

One by one the officers looked up from their conversations and personal notes: Goldberg, the security chief with his unkempt hair and his uniform worn just off enough to remind everyone that he had never been a Navy man; Jang, the chief engineer whose talent and enthusiasm more than made up for her almost childlike size; Dr. Ramirez, ship's physician, with his owl-like eyes always staring as though he sees some problem you have, but he's waiting for you to mention it first; Machado, ship's mage, whose arrogance would have merited censure or dismissal, if the man weren't every bit as good as he said; and Fredrickson, the potion-stained ship's alchemist who tapped her fingers to irregular beats when thinking, but who could, in a tight spot, stretch reagents and ingredients far enough to impress even Machado.

A terrific first crew. But not his crew yet.

"Sorry I'm late," said Tunold, taking his seat.

"You still had three minutes thirty-six seconds," said Fredrickson, "if we consider you present as of the moment you reached your chair. Three minutes forty, if we count your entering the room."

"I've called you all here because there's been a change of plans." Tunold noticed Machado and Jang exchange a look that, for once, appeared to lack animosity. Goldberg, for his part, leaned forward in his chair. Tunold continued, "*We* will be making the Venus run instead of the *Lark's Song*. Captain Jacobs will command, and I will serve as his executive officer. When you return to your stations, you will find the details waiting in your phantasmal displays. Questions?"

"How do I get Tai Shi off my back?" said Goldberg. "I don't need her breathing down my neck the whole way to Venus."

"The captain has assured me that once we're at space, the crew will not be subject to outside supervision."

"So I have to put up with her in the meantime?"

"No way around it, Chief. Do your best. Other questions?"

"I would like it noted for the record," said Dr. Ramirez in his slow, thoughtful voice, "that I object in advance to the captain undertaking any investigative actions or participating in any fights, skirmishes, or 'dust ups.'"

"Noted."

"Not that it will do any good," grumbled the doctor. "He'll do exactly as he damn well pleases and we all know it."

"Not this time, Doc." Tunold almost smiled at the speed with which his comment drew all eyes back to him. "The condition I placed on serving as his ex oh was that he plays the old school captain and leaves the affairs of the crew and passengers to me. Which reminds me..."

Tunold swung his chin to take in the assembly in what he hoped was a commanding fashion.

"Any problems on this voyage, anything you think might need to go to the captain, it comes to me first. Understood?"

"No," said Machado, who had the gall to look relaxed and casual at defying a direct order from his executive officer.

"What did you say, Mister?"

"That's *Magister*, which is my point." The hefty magician leaned forward, casually resting his round elbows on the table. "The ship's mage reports directly to the captain. I've never served in the armed forces, but I'm pretty sure you can't order me to violate the chain of command."

"Doc, you want to back me up about the captain's health?"

Before Ramirez could speak, Machado cut in again. "If he's healthy enough to command, he's healthy enough to hear what I have to say from my own lips." He raised a thick black eyebrow. "You want to incite a mutiny, Ex Oh, do it on your own time."

"*Mutiny?*" Tunold leapt to his feet, chair thrown back to slam into the next table. "How dare you—"

"How dare you?" said Machado, still as calm as though Tunold weren't about to twist him into an entirely new shape and put him on display in the Museum of Modern Art.

"Doing your job as ex oh is one thing. Trying to steal duties and decisions from the captain is another."

Goldberg and Fredrickson nodded their absolute agreement, and Ramirez and Jang reluctantly joined them a moment later.

Tunold started to sit, realized his chair was missing, and snatched one from the table behind him. "All right," he said slowly. "Bring me everything you can without violating regs. Better?"

"Much," said Machado.

"You would have been hell on a Navy ship," said Tunold. "Can you at least try to give me an unofficial heads-up when it comes to trouble? This trip isn't going to be a stop in Toronto."

Machado nodded as though the issue had never been in question. *Damn his arrogant hide*, thought Tunold. "Any further questions?"

Jang started to speak, but Tunold cut her off. "No experiments this trip. No tricks, no tests. By the book, as much as anything about this voyage can be by the book."

"Not that," she said, with a distant look the like of which Tunold had never seen cross her face before. "I just need to know. What's the deal with 4M? Do they own us now?"

"No," said Tunold. "It's more complicated than that. They bought out Zoltan's share, so they own half exactly. Makes some of the decisions difficult, but it won't have any impact once we hit space. At space the captain is in charge, unquestioned."

"Think it'll be that easy?" asked Goldberg in a tone that suggested he knew the answer.

Tunold suspected he knew the answer too. And he didn't like it.

Donal knew better than to try to be the first one to leave the Jade Monkey. The street was quiet, though Donal could just hear the ticking of runner claws from the traffic down on Market Street.

The sword carrier waited no more than two meters in front of the door of the Jade Monkey: short black hair slicked down, tanned, Eastern European features patient, stylish dark blue suit still crisp, dueling rapier casual at his side, and bouquet of a dozen roses cradled in his left arm.

"If those are for me," said Li Hua, "I should warn you that I have a boyfriend."

"So I see," said the sword carrier, his voice a touch too high to be smooth. "But I assure you that my interest is purely professional."

"Is that why you have backup?" asked Donal, letting his focus cover his surroundings to ensure that no enchantments were waiting for them to let their guard down.

"Not backup," he said. "An Unbiased Witness."

Donal heard the capital letters in the man's voice, but didn't know what they meant. But Li Hua must have, because she said, "4M doesn't have any current disputes up before the Fair Arbiters Guild."

"No, but people inconvenient to 4M have had a habit of disappearing lately. You guys are good, but even you won't cross the Fair Arbiters Guild, not here in San Francisco."

"We don't make people disappear either."

Li Hua's voice sounded tired, but Donal wondered if her eyes had narrowed a shade too much. Fionn might have agreed, for the *cú sidhe* focused on Li Hua instead of on the sword carrier, where Donal had expected.

"If you've got something to say, say it," said Li Hua. "But if you imply anything more about my company, I'll give you an excuse to break in that unused sword of yours." She smiled, full of danger. "In front of an Unbiased Witness."

Her words made Donal glance at the man's sword, and realize that it looked new, its scabbard so pristine it might have hung in a store window that morning. The sword carrier smiled like a boy caught playing out of bounds.

"The sword's for show, as I'm sure you can tell. All the executives at my firm carry them. Challenge me and I'll demand a champion."

"Don't insult me or my boyfriend and we can get on with our night in peace."

"First, these are for you." He held out the roses, but when Li Hua made no move to take them, he shrugged and set them on the sidewalk. "There's a card, but under the circumstances, I'd better just tell you the message."

The sword carrier raised his eyebrows, and at Li Hua's nod he continued.

"Please accept these flowers as a gesture of respect to your talents and abilities. We ask that you leave 4M, either for another company or to go into private practice. Failing that, we ask that you cancel your passage on a certain upcoming trip to Venus. In either case, you will be compensated for making the right choice."

"Vague and useless," said Li Hua. "Not even an amount or a signatory."

"The signatory is 'The Consortium,' As for the amount..." The sword carrier smiled with the winning confidence of a salesman. "That's the other reason I brought an Unbiased Witness."

If the man expected a reaction from Li Hua, he didn't get it. Donal flicked his eyes up and down Octavia Boulevard: a young couple enjoying riding double on a horse, and an old man leaving an apartment building, huddled into his coat against the cool spring evening.

The sword carrier gestured to the roses on the ground. "If you don't want those, I could—"

"Leave them," said Li Hua.

"Right," said the sword carrier, hands up and backing away across the street before he continued on his way.

"They look like nice roses," said Donal. Li Hua kicked them into the street. She turned to say something — something flirty by the tilt of her head — but a dark-skinned young man, clean-cut enough to be working his way through college, got out of a parked runner and approached them.

The man held up his right hand, fingers splayed so they could see the seal of the ring he bore on his middle finger. Donal reached for his tuning fork, but Li Hua stroked her earring. The ring flared green in response.

"You have been identified to me as Tai Shi Li Hua," said the Unbiased Witness, "and I have substantiated your identity to my professional satisfaction. I bear a message for you, the veracity of which has been confirmed and verified by the Fair Arbiters Guild. Do you wish to receive this message in private, or here in front of your acknowledged companion Donal Cuthbert?"

Donal wondered if his identity had also been substantiated, and what that process involved. Under the circumstances, though, he declined to ask.

"Here is fine," said Li Hua, "if the message is brief."

"The message is as follows: 'Tai Shi Li Hua, we of the Consortium have placed in escrow with the Fair Arbiters Guild the sum of fifty million dollars. You may claim half of that sum if you appear at their downtown San Francisco office in person at any time during the upcoming Starchaser Spacelines flight to Venus. You may claim the entire amount if, at that time, you present evidence or testify to the satisfaction of the Fair Arbiters Guild that you have terminated your employment with 4M and the 4M family of companies. If you choose the latter option, the names and companies of the members of the Consortium will be made available to you, and if you contact any of them you will be offered a director level position with salary and benefits commensurate with those offered by 4M.' This ends the message."

"That was brief?" said Donal. Li Hua nodded and the Unbiased Witness said, "Very."

"Message received and understood," and Li Hua. The Unbiased Witness nodded acknowledgment, then his posture relaxed and he jerked a thumb at the Jade Monkey and smiled broadly. "This place any good? I'm starved."

Donal's jaw dropped, and he managed a rapid nod as his eyes found Fionn and saw confirmation in the gaze of his familiar. When the Unbiased Witness entered the restaurant, Donal turned to Li Hua and said, "*Geas* magic? Seriously?"

"That's how they guarantee their results." She took his arm. "Come on."

Donal hesitated, tried to relax into a stroll with Li Hua while their familiars circled, watching for threats, but he could not quite manage it.

"So he has no idea what he said, but he was compelled to say it to you."

"His ring wouldn't even respond to a check right now. He's off the clock."

"Rough job requirements." Silence fell between them as they approached Li Hua's runner, a sleek, feline design with four furry legs but only two seats. "Speaking of jobs…"

"Later," said Li Hua, turning to face Donal and placing two fingers on his lips. Excitement burned in her eyes, her smile. "We both got amped up for a fight, but there was no fight. Do you really want to waste our adrenaline?"

Donal had not built up adrenaline, so much as nervousness. But he saw no reason to point that out.

Donal kissed Li Hua hard, his arms tight around her, and as she matched his passion he wondered how far back her runner's seats reclined.

Not much later, in a secluded spot, he learned that they reclined all the way…

5

By oh-seven-hundred the next morning, Jacobs stepped into the office that was once more his, aboard the *Horizon Cusp*. The bookshelves behind the huge desk sat bare, waiting for his many volumes to return to their accustomed spots from their crates down in the hold. The walls looked empty without his art, especially his gallery of the scores of ships he had served on, from old seagoing Naval vessels through the advent of magically borne aircraft, to the first space runabouts, all the way through helioships, the current leading edge of space travel.

Three things remained as they had been the last time Jacobs stood in this doorway: the air smelled slightly of the sea (from the cleaning staff's cleansers, a special concoction for Jacobs); his old, comfortable couch still sat under the huge porthole (that right now showed only a view of the San Francisco Spaceport where the ship sat at dock); and on that couch sprawled his slightly grizzled white tomcat, Benny Sugg.

As he so often did, Benny pulled Jacobs out of his reverie with a meow of complaint, as though the cat were horribly mistreated and had not seen so much as a kind hand in years, and he demanded to know where Jacobs had been anyway, and how dare he be gone for so long?

Jacobs chuckled. "I'm afraid you'll have to join me at the desk, Benny. I have too much to do right now to nap with you." Jacobs strode over to his desk and called up his phantasmal display before he so much as sat or tossed down the small bundle under his arm, a collection of reports and forms, along with the memopad he used for exactly one purpose: to transfer charts. He set it about that process now, while Benny Sugg, affronted, rolled over and went back to sleep with a huffing churr that suggested that he expected better treatment when he awoke.

Kelly had offered to handle the chart transfer, knowing as the rest of the crew did the discomfort Jacobs still took with the myriad replacements for the tools of his youth. But Jacobs declined. So far as he was concerned, space travel was the single greatest accomplishment of magic, and if Jacobs would use it then he felt he owed it to magic, somehow, to give it the respect of doing his work for himself.

Jacobs would no sooner allow Kelly to transfer his charts than he would allow Mr. Burke, the helmsman, to plot his courses for him. Tunold might have a point about Jacobs letting his ex oh handle more of the on-ship demands for this flight — as a Naval ex oh would — but so long as Jacobs sat in the big chair he would not relegate his responsibilities.

The transfer now complete, Jacobs called up a three dimensional image of Venus and the space around it within a decan, a clearer, more detailed view than he had gotten in his Starchaser Spacelines office.

Jacobs frowned at the sight. The planet should never have been colonized, but humans were ever impatient for expansion. A zuglodon hunting ground passed within half a decan of the planet. And if Jacobs read the correspondences right, that region of space lay closest to Earth this time of year.

Of course. What fun is a tricky flight without a zuglodon or two trying to batter down our wards and feast on our elements?

A red zone between Venus and Mercury had been expanded since the last charts Jacobs had seen, a warning update from the Navy. The details were classified, damn them, which meant they had their own exploration going that direction and designated a no-fly zone. That meant patrols and trouble, trouble the likes of which even Jacobs dared not skirt.

The whole zone might as well have been labeled 'Here There Be Dragons.'

No. Some idiot would take that seriously.

Could they be charting a course to Mercury already? No. Too much money going into Ganymede right now. That meant that the red zone represented a hazard, something the military didn't want to admit to. At least not yet. Fine then. Their problem, and they could keep it. Still...

Jacobs stretched the red zone in his display. A military no-fly zone meant military patrols. Military patrols meant support in case of trouble, or at least rescue in case of emergency.

Jacobs took note on his paper notepad to chart their course as close to the no-fly zone as he could get away with. If Mancusco had anything unsavory planned, Jacobs could turn him right over to the Navy. And though much had changed in the Navy since Jacobs served on the old steel ships, one thing had certainly not: the Navy took a dim view of people causing trouble at high space.

Three precisely even raps on the frame of Jacobs' open door announced the arrival of the yeoman, Kelly, who leaned at a crisp thirty degree angle through the doorway when Jacobs looked up.

"Mr. Tunold to see you, Captain. And welcome back, if I may say so, Sir."

"You may, Mr. Kelly, and thank you. Send him in."

Tunold galumphed in, as though his body were run by a bear's spirit that never acknowledged the human form's limitations. Not for the first time Jacobs thought that if Tunold had been born a thousand years earlier, his people would have put a sword in his hand, a bear skin on his back, and launched him at the enemy with the other berserkers.

But then, Jacobs own ancestors might have given him similar treatment (albeit in a very different region).

Jacobs indicated a chair with one hand while he adjusted his display with the other, preparing to make a point to his executive officer. But Tunold spoke as he heaved himself into his chair.

"Officers are on board with the mission. Goldberg is having troubles with Tai Shi."

"He can handle her. Look at this."

Tunold listed to one side for a better look, then narrowed his eyes.

"Jesus. Think the Navy wants enough space to themselves?"

"What do you think? Hazard or a project?"

"What difference does it make?"

"We swing too near a hazard and they'll be worried about us. Too near a *project*, and..."

"And they'll greet us as spies." Tunold shifted his massive jaw from side to side. "Who the hell would spy on the Navy?"

"Mars," said Jacobs with a shrug. "Corporations, probably. Hell, maybe the colonists. I can't imagine they flew all the way to Venus intending to live right under the Navy's thumb."

"Might be worried about a quick move for independence, like Mars tried."

"Tries," corrected Jacobs. "They're not done yet. But who they're worried about isn't our problem."

"You're right," said Tunold with a sigh that shook his whole torso. "Want me to check with a few contacts, see what I can dig up?"

"Make sure they know why we want to know."

"You mean you're going to share our flight path this time?" Tunold's eyes widened in wonder. "I figured that with Mancuso and his cronies aboard..."

"Can't be an official first commercial run without a verified route, confirmed by the ship's own nav system."

"All the crap dropping on your shoulders right now and you're still worried about getting this trip recognized as the first commercial flight to Venus?"

"Hell yes." Jacobs slapped his desk with one hand, and for just a moment the familiar position of arguing with Tunold across this desk almost made him smile despite the point he had to make.

"Think I'm doing this for my health? Starchaser Spacelines needs this to happen *and* succeed."

If Tunold felt any need to fight the lopsided grin that pushed its way onto his face, Jacobs couldn't tell.

"Going out on top, eh, Skipper?"

"Damn straight."

<hr>

Donal intended to sleep late.

Staying with Li Hua for the night meant waking up in the accommodations 4M provided her whenever she was in town: a corner suite on the top floor of the Hamilton, the most luxurious hotel to perch high in the San Francisco hills.

Unfortunately, Li Hua must have set a mental alarm, because she was up and moving before the morning fog had burnt off. Donal did get to enjoy a few lazy minutes of expensive silk sheets and subtle, relaxing spells that had been expertly woven through the mattress, but the sound of her chatting through a comm pad (with the display disabled) and the site of her moving about in nothing but an untied hapi coat finally drew him to wakefulness.

Donal slipped out of bed and into a hotel robe, almost as comfortable as the bed had been, and for similar reasons. The first time Donal had slept here, he had lain awake marveling at the scores of spells permeating the suite, but by now he had grown almost accustomed to them: relaxed enough to savor the delights without needing to gawk.

Not entirely unlike how he often felt about Li Hua, though he could not deny that Fionn was right. Donal's life was more dangerous with Li Hua in it. But what he could not make Fionn understand was that Donal's life was more *fun* with her in it.

He considered that as he stood beside the bed and watched her pose just outside her closet, one long finger tapping on her chin as she considered her clothes.

"You know," she said, "if you're going to insist on wearing a robe when you could be naked, you should at least bring something sexy."

She turned to look at him, the gape in her hapi coat making her point for her. "I see too little of you as it is."

"Take some vacation time. Let's travel a bit for fun before I start school."

"Too much going on right now. You know that."

"When isn't there too much going on?"

"Skip the Venus contract, Donal." Li Hua's lips formed a tight line. "Too big a coincidence that someone wants you on this flight."

"People tried to kill me on the moon, too." Donal shrugged. "I survived."

"You were rescued by a Hierophant."

"I wasn't ready for trouble. I will be this time."

Li Hua smiled. Not the bitter smile of someone accepting a fact she could not change, but a secret, deeper smile, that only barely showed around her lips but came across in full in her eyes, her posture. Donal almost thought she was going to throw off her hapi coat and make herself late for work, but she spoke.

"You love it now, don't you? That thrill I told you about, when your life is on the line and you need every resource you have to survive. That's the real reason you're taking this Venus job. You love it as much as I do."

"I need the money. And…"

Donal drew a deep breath. Li Hua waited, with seeming infinite patience, and the nature of Donal's thoughts kept even the sight of her from distracting him. He could not tell her his suspicions about Mr. Mancuso.

But he would not lie to her, either.

"I have responsibilities. I owe it to myself and my magic to see this through."

Li Hua winked, one raised eyebrow telling Donal that she knew he was not telling her the whole story. "Of course. Responsibilities. Well, I can't argue with that."

She turned and pulled a sapphire blue blouse and Navy blue skirt out of the closet and hung them on the door, her eyes checking for minute flaws. Donal almost turned to see about a shower, but she said, without looking, "You know, Donal. The only way to get what you really want out of life is to accept yourself for who you are."

She glanced back over her shoulder. "Once you do that. You can have anything."

Donal had to admit that she lived what she preached. Li Hua might have complaints about her job or her boss from time to time, but she lived in luxury, traveled more and further than over ninety-nine percent of the human race. And she loved her work.

Donal stepped into the plum blossom smell of the bathroom and hung his robe on the shaped silver hook that would slowly heat anything it held to a comfortable warmth and maintain that tempera-ture, however long the robe might wait there. He looked past the pale purple marble sink to the matching separate tub and shower, the latter with its multi-spray design.

This was how Li Hua lived every day. Far from the simple apart-ment Donal kept, and further still from the tiny house Donal grew up in, attached to his parents' woodworking business. Wealth, chal-lenges, satisfying work: she had a right to talk about how to get what one wanted in life.

But she never talked about meaning. Donal wanted more than thrills and perks. He wanted to make a real contribution to humanity. He worried about the long view.

Donal stepped into the shower stall, quickly bringing the water to the perfect temperature. He closed his eyes and soaked, accepting the truth he could not explain to Li Hua. She lived for the moment. But for Donal, each moment existed to set up the next. She had instants. He had transitions.

But, Donal wondered as he began to soap himself down, was that the truth, or only what Donal wanted to be true?

Donal had to admit that he had felt thrills when he had outwitted

Red Sun conspirators, thrown together an illusion that deceived even a zuglodon, and outfought bin Zuka in the *Comórtas Draíocht*, the duel of magic. Could Li Hua have been right? Did Donal seek the thrill of learning the truth about Mr. Mancuso and taking action, or did he merely want to make certain humanity's future was not shaped by a tyrant ruling from the shadows?

What did Donal really want from his life?

A soft hand stroked his shoulder, and Donal turned to see Li Hua, sans hapi coat, smiling as she stepped into the shower with him. Through the touch she slipped a thread of her personal power into his, sharing, not influencing, but still drawing Donal's attention on every level.

"Maybe I can't fit in a vacation just yet," she said, "but I have right now."

And in that moment, even Donal could not worry about what might follow.

JACOBS SAT IN THE BACK OF THE RUNNER CAB AND TRIED NOT TO THINK about the side-to-side sway of its lizard-like gait. Never seasick a moment in his life, never carsick or airsick, but something about the movement of runners discomfited Jacobs' stomach. He could not think of them as vehicles, however many times he might have ridden in one by now, however similar aspects of their interiors might have been to cars.

Cars had paint, not skin or scales or fur. Cars had wheels, not legs. Cars had "new car smell," a scent distinctly their own. To Jacobs, all runners smelled vaguely like dead animal. And cars never felt like speeding drunken camels.

But cars were gone, and Jacobs had never learned to ride a horse. So for his trip out of the city and down to Millbrae, a runner cab had to suffice.

At least the day had been productive. All of Jacobs' officers were ready for tomorrow's takeoff. Even Goldberg, who had spent the better part of the day in his office with Tai Shi, seemed confident about their readiness. Of course, when Jacobs had left the ship, the two remained deep in conference about security, but Goldberg knew better than to lie to his captain about progress.

And Tunold had promised to check on them.

Tunold's military contacts turned up nothing useful, so Jacobs charted a course to skirt that red zone as close as he dared. Of course, between Earth and Venus there were other hazards, but staring at the charts had not made them go away. In the end, the route had been plotted, quadruple checked by Jacobs himself then again by Tunold, Burke, and finally officially by San Francisco Port Authority.

Port Authority had complained about several of Jacobs' choices, of course, but damn them anyway. They only needed to log the *Horizon Cusp's* route, not approve it.

Only one thing remained before Jacobs hit space once more. And he had in mind to check it off his list before he returned to the ship for dinner with his crew.

The neighborhood was wild with growth, like much of the Bay Area. Old concrete broken up and returned to dirt in many neighborhoods, with the remains of the concrete going to alchemical plants for some damned purpose that no one had shared with Jacobs.

But no raw dirt in this neighborhood. Oh, no. Here the sidewalks and streets gleamed like jewels with just enough roughness underfoot for an easy grip.

The runner mercifully came to a halt. Jacobs' stomach came to its halt a moment later.

"Dispatch said you wanted to be picked up, too?" said the driver, a girl with a hard look that spoke of rough rides in much worse neighborhoods. But she had survived. Jacobs respected that.

"Just wait. I won't be long."

"All right, but the dial keeps spinning."

"I'd expect nothing less."

Jacobs got out and walked up the polished cobblestone walkway to the two story house that probably could have served as a hangar for the *Daedalus Dream* and at least two runabouts. And these days the house was probably paid for.

Jacobs raised his hand to give his normal, resonant knock, but his eyes flicked across the gloves he wore. He belayed his movement. Instead he reached for the bell pull and rang it once.

Jacobs forced his breaths to come slow and deep as he waited, even when he heard approaching footsteps. He flexed his hands to make sure their blood flowed nice and even.

The front door opened and Jacobs saw the trimmed black curls and beard, the pale face and broad jaw and narrow chin. Jacobs' right cross drove that jawbone back and up, up enough to pull expensive loafers off the shag carpet.

Zoltan landed flat out on his back, dazed and moaning. Jacobs stood in the doorway and waited, fists clenching and relaxing. He knew his old partner would get up soon enough. Zoltan might not have been a fighter, but Jacobs had held back his punch.

At least, a little.

"Owww," said Zoltan, finally, rubbing his jaw and shifting on his back as though trying to find a more comfortable spot on the carpet.

Jacobs stared at his former partner, possibly former friend, and waited. He didn't want to wait. He had many things he wanted to say. Or yell. But Zoltan had been his partner for a long time, long enough to earn a chance to speak.

"Jesus, Mary and Joseph, John." Zoltan managed a sitting position, one hand still rubbing his jaw and the other investigating spots on his back. "My back may come out of this worse than my face."

Jacobs felt his teeth grind, his fists clench a little tighter. But still he held his silence.

Zoltan looked up, a bit bleary. He got his first real look at Jacobs, and Jacobs had no doubts about the image of restrained fury he presented. Zoltan dropped his hands, then raised them in surrender.

"I had that coming, I know." Zoltan stood, a slow, painful-looking process that ended with him stooped forward. "I hope I can get an alchemist over here tonight." He raised his hands again, still stooping.

"I'm sorry, John. I had to take the deal. If I didn't, he would have buried us both. This way he gets his Venus flight and we both get to retire."

"You had this planned, and you dumped it on me."

"Given your reaction—"

"You should have told me." The words came out a low, almost feral growl, a tone that had silenced mess halls and bars in the past. "You were my partner."

"I should have told you." Zoltan dropped his hands. "The deal said I couldn't. But I should have found a way. Something coded in your ship. Something." Zoltan tried to smile, but winced and rubbed his chin. "I'm sorry. If you want to hit me again, I probably deserve that too, but I hope you don't."

Zoltan met Jacobs' eyes now, and Jacobs saw pain that went beyond anything Zoltan had suffered from that right cross.

"You were always the brave one, John. I had the business savvy, but you had the guts. I let him scare me."

Jacobs felt his fists unclench. "You did what you had to. I get that." Jacobs let out a breath that almost sagged him against the doorframe. Only a small act of will kept him upright.

"But if we're going to stay friends, you can't betray me like that. Not ever again."

"Never again, John. I swear. And if there's anything I can do to help you with Mancuso, maybe on a consulting basis, just let me know."

"Unpaid consulting."

"John…" Zoltan furrowed his bushy eyebrows. "All right, I guess I've made enough money off this to cover you."

Jacobs allowed himself a small smile now. Zoltan extended one hand and Jacobs shook it.

"You can shake my hand with the hand you used to flatten me," said Zoltan. "Insult to injury. Could you at least pretend you hurt your knuckles on my jaw?"

"Modern boxer's gloves," said Jacobs showing off the soft leather with spread fingers. "A gift from my ship's doctor. Apparently he thinks that his captain acting like a street brawler is insufficient reason to disrupt the flow of his duties."

Zoltan snorted, then winced. "Have a drink with a backstabbing bastard?"

"I wish I could, but I have to get back. The Mancuso storm hits tomorrow.

"Besides," Jacobs added with an evil grin, "I got what I came for."

<hr>

THE LUNCH CROWD AT THE JADE MONKEY WAS SPARSE ON THE DAY Donal would leave for Venus, only a half dozen suits scarfing down meals before they rushed back to work. So Mr. Mohatar made excuses to stand beside Donal at his table-for-two, with Fionn in the other seat, fully visible.

"She is beautiful, Donal. Shame on you for not bringing her here sooner."

"She is dangerous," said Fionn.

"All women are," said Mr. Mohatar.

"Says the man married longer than I've been alive," said Donal.

"That's right." Mr. Mohatar nodded his head emphatically. "My Amina destroyed my miserable single life utterly, demolished it beyond recognition or repair and trapped me in this existence of blissful happiness." Mr. Mohatar smiled so wide Donal's plate might have fit in his mouth. "Some dangers a man must conquer to be truly alive."

Fionn shook its head with a snort of disagreement.

"You will not sneeze on my food," said Mr. Mohatar with a wag of his finger at the *cú sidhe*.

"He's not sneezing," said Donal. "He hoped you would side with him."

"Against happiness? Never! Donal, I think you've bound a demon."

Donal laughed at Fionn's exasperated expression — finding such eye and jaw movements hilarious on an emerald green deerhound —

but before he could speak, the door chime sounded and Mr. Mohatar had to see to a new customer somewhere behind Donal.

Fionn spat out a few words that perhaps only familiars could understand before finally switching to Gaelic to mumble, "The one approaching you now would be better for you than Tai Shi Li Hua."

Donal wondered for a moment if Fionn spoke metaphorically, but Mr. Mohatar returned to Donal's table leading a woman about Donal's age whose smooth skin and fiery red hair called to Donal's mind the tale of Deirdre of the Sorrows. Even her casual blouse and slacks could not help emphasizing her figure, however thoroughly they covered it.

"Donal," said Mr. Mohatar, his eyes unreadable but his eyebrows threatening to crawl over his scalp and scamper down his back, "may I present Ms.—"

"Rowan MacPherson," said Donal, his stomach sinking despite his excellent, half-eaten lunch.

"We've met," said Ms. MacPherson, as though pleased about their acquaintance, and Donal grudgingly had to admit that even her voice was so beautiful that she could probably sing old Irish songs in a lyric soprano that would bring tears to his mother's eyes. Ms. MacPherson continued, "May I join you?"

Donal hesitated long enough to make Mr. Mohatar's eyebrows fly back down to crinkle over the bridge of his nose, but Donal said, "Certainly. Fionn, do you mind?"

Fionn slipped down through the chair to stride around the table and sit beside Donal in a position that gave the fae deerhound a clear view of the entire restaurant. Donal saw Ms. MacPherson spot that detail, but as she sat she made no comment about his familiar immediately slipping into a bodyguard position.

Mr. Mohatar set a menu, silverware, and a glass of water before her, then stepped aside, probably to give them a moment alone before concerning himself with her order.

"What do you recommend?" she asked, as though this were a business lunch date.

"I've had everything on the menu. It's all good. What can I do for you, Ms. MacPherson? Or should I say, what does Red Sun want with me?"

"Let me order first."

She called back Mr. Mohatar, complimented him on his restaurant and ordered something off the menu that sounded as though it came from the right region. Mr. Mohatar looked impressed.

Ms. MacPherson turned back to Donal. Her smile was bright. Charming. Everything it should have been, and might even have included sincerity, if Donal were to relax enough to leave that possibility open.

As it was, he had shifted his consciousness the moment he saw her and had already triple-checked her for magic: nothing. She had no training. She carried no enchantments. Even the delicate timepiece on her wrist had to have been entirely mechanical.

"Donal... May I call you Donal?" She waited for his nod before continuing, "Thank you. And please call me Rowan.

"Have you ever asked people to do something, knowing it might get them killed? Whether they succeeded or not?"

Donal shook his head.

"It takes a certain kind of person to volunteer for a potentially suicidal assignment. The person must have commitment beyond commitment, a dedicated belief that what you have asked of her is not only right, but necessary. Vital. The kind of person who can accept that even death in failure has not wasted her life because the cause was just and the attempt worthwhile."

"I'm not going to die for you."

Donal managed another forkful of lamb casserole, and found that at least her presence had not ruined his delightful meal.

"I don't mean you. I want you to understand that the people who kidnapped you aboard your flight home from Mars were not taking sanctioned action. You were to be asked for help, offered reward for your efforts. Not threatened into compliance."

"'No one is neutral in this fight.' Your words, in the New Leningrad spaceport."

"And I meant them, even though you declined to give me time to explain myself. But even armies at war acknowledge the difference between enemy civilians and enemy combatants."

Ms. MacPherson held that thought as her food arrived, and Donal marveled at the speed with which Mrs. Mohatar had managed the meal. Once Ms. MacPherson had tasted her first bite of something that looked to Donal like a type of lamb stew, and shot an approving smile to Mr. Mohatar who stood near the entrance to the kitchen, she continued.

"They treated you as an enemy combatant instead of an enemy civilian. I apologize for that."

"Thank you." Donal ignored something quiet that Fionn mumbled to him. "But I suppose I declared myself an enemy combatant the moment I challenged Mr. bin Zuka to the *Comórtas Dríocht*."

"Did you? Or did you try to prevent what you saw as murder?"

"It would have been murder. A murder you ordered. A second murder you ordered."

"The situation was not that simple, Donal."

"Mr. Mancuso would have been killed like Mr. al Rashid: deliberately, by someone who is not a government. That's pretty much the definition of murder."

"Murder is a legal issue, and this was interplanetary space. The death might not have qualified."

"*What do you want*, Ms. MacPherson?"

"Please, Donal. Call me Rowan." That smile again, but only for a moment. "My sources inform me that Donatello Mancuso feels safe around you. He is likely to allow your presence where he would not allow another's."

Donal tried to say something at this point, but she spoke over him. "I am not asking you to take action. I am asking you to do what your nature as a magician might make you do anyway. Pay attention. Do not deny facts you observe or reasonable conclusions they lead to." She started as though to reach for Donal's hand, but instead set her hand down on the table. "And should your own conscience cause you to take action, I want to guarantee you that Red Sun will be there to help you. We will take you in, support you. Whatever you need."

"I suppose you'd pay for grad school too."

"I could arrange that." She smiled again, and Donal thought he saw something more unexpected than charm: sincerity.

"I'll think about it," said Donal.

"That's all I ask," she said. "And now I'll leave you in peace."

She gestured to Mr. Mohatar to pack her food to go, and paid for both her meal and Donal's. She set her business card on the table, and left.

Once the front door closed behind her, Mr. Mohatar returned to Donal's table and said, "That is a woman who gets what she wants."

"Everyone faces disappointment sometime."

Mr. Mohatar laughed. "If you will not even consider her ... offer, then you must be in love with your Li Hua." He pointed to the door, though Ms. MacPherson was long gone by now. "That woman could tempt the devil into virtue."

Donal must have tried to stutter a denial, because Mr. Mohatar clapped Donal on the shoulder and said, "Well, *whatever* she wanted, she paid enough to cover dessert for you and still leave a generous tip. The *sfenj*?"

"Of course," said Donal, finally smiling.

As Mr. Mohatar went to see about the fried pastry with honey, Fionn returned to the empty chair and regarded Donal, patiently.

"Something you wish to observe?" asked Donal.

"You draw the wrong kind of women."

Donal sighed. But before he left, he took the business card. When he did, Fionn declined to comment.

DONAL LINGERED OVER DESSERT AS THE REMAINS OF THE LUNCH CROWD cleared out, which gave Mr. Mohatar the opportunity to speculate several times about what Rowan MacPherson had wanted from Donal, though Donal left him guessing. More important, Donal hoped to have taken enough time that any Red Sun escort accompanying Ms. MacPherson would be well gone before he set foot on the street again.

He and Fionn went through their field work routines on the way back to Donal's apartment in the Sunset District near Stern Grove, but if they were followed, they did not know it.

Donal had heard that the Sunset District had suffered greatly during the rise of magic. Densely populated at the time, when technology failed the locals initially fell to battling over remaining resources. Even spreading into Golden Gate Park and Sigmund Stern Grove helped little because too few had the skills to survive without technology.

Their troubles continued until Aoife Durnin herself, one of Lloyd Bird's greatest acolytes, began the restoration of San Francisco by bringing peace to the Sunset District. Donal sometimes wished he had seen her work. On evening walks, he occasionally spotted small traces of Durnin's spells, yet lingering after all this time.

Not many still living remembered blood in the streets of the Sunset District. But cities have memories of their own, and San Francisco would need more time to wash clean the stains caused by the fall of technology. So Donal's apartment with its view of two parks cost no more than half of what it probably should have. Not that Donal objected.

Donal had a corner apartment on the third floor of an old house, designed after the Tudor fashion. The house creaked and groaned like an old man when anyone crossed its floors, and the entryway and stairs smelled like age and must.

He smiled at a couple of neighbors as he passed them on the stairs, though he did not know their names: long term tenants who did not waste time introducing themselves to the newer residents until they had stayed longer than a year or two.

Donal pulled his tuning fork from his sleeve as he approached his door, ready to check his wards, but Fionn drew his attention with a small growl.

Donal turned and saw the sword-carrying businessman from the night before. He wore a different suit, but probably the same sword.

Donal twirled the tuning fork in his fingers significantly, reminding the interloper that Donal was a Journeyman. He took further advantage of the momentary pause to shift his consciousness and examine the stranger: enchantment on the belt buckle, Earth-based and Journeyman-cast. Something that aided endurance, but without more time to study it, Donal could not tell if it would help the man with dueling or drinking or even with paying attention during long meetings.

Safer to assume the worst.

"Here to offer me a job too?" asked Donal, but not as though he meant it.

"Offer a local job to a man about to start school down south? Sounds like a low-percentage gambit."

Donal expected a smile after a comment like that, but the man held a straight face.

"Where's your Unbiased Witness?" asked Donal.

That got a smile out of the man, but a cold smile. A mere raising of the corners of the mouth.

Fionn said, in tones only Donal could understand, "He has come alone. I sense no allies nearby."

"It's like this, Cuthbert," said the man. "Twice I've found you with no effort. I know where you eat, and when. I know where you're going to be before you do. I know you're a Journeyman and I have a pretty good idea about your limits."

"If you know I'm a Journeyman you should know that threatening magicians does not encourage a long and healthy life."

"I haven't threatened anyone. Right now I'm just apprising you of a few facts. Like it's a fact that I'll survive anything you could do, at least long enough to take you down if I have to. And it's a fact that I've killed Journeymen with a lot more field experience than you have."

He spread his hands, but Donal noted that the man still managed to keep one hand near the hilt of his sword.

"Just facts. Like the fact that this sword is not just for show. And the fact that not everyone thinks Red Sun is handling 4M right. And the fact that a lot of people want Mancuso dead." He wagged his finger as though giving Donal avuncular advice. "You should think about that one. You'll soon be in a position to manage that death, in uncontrolled space or even on Venus, where they have no laws."

He dropped his hands to his sword belt and something cold crept through his eyes. Donal became uncomfortably aware of how quiet the house was. No help nearby.

"And it's a fact that if Mancuso makes it back to Earth alive, some people are going to blame you. They might ask me to come see you again when I'm not in such a chatty mood."

Then Donal understood, and he snickered, a sound that continued long enough to make the man with the sword grit his teeth. He opened his mouth to say something, but Donal spoke first, relief and humor in his voice over the pounding of his own heart.

"Big bad killer threatens me because he's scared of my girlfriend."

"I don't think you—"

"Oh, no, I get it. You think you're a badass, but you can't get to Mr. Mancuso because Li Hua's too much for you. In fact, she's so good you want to hire her. But me, well, I'll be in the area so you want *me* to take a shot at *your* target. And I'm not a badass, so you figure I'll be scared enough of you to try, which means I'll either succeed or create a diversion for your people's real attempt. I'm betting you expect the latter."

The man with the sword tried to speak again, but Donal wasn't done.

"Now, of course, you have a problem, because I know. And I have no reason not to tell Li Hua. This pretty much ruins your plans, but you still can't afford to try to kill me, because your failure means that your people will have to rely on whatever Red Sun has in mind. And Red Sun needs me on the flight."

Donal made a show of yawning. "Now why don't you run along home? I've got a big trip in a couple of hours, and I'd like to catch a nap before then."

The man had one hand on the pommel of his sword now, his

knuckles slowly turning white. Then he puffed out a breath and released his grip.

"All right, Cuthbert," said the man, moving toward the stairs. "I'll leave. But realize this: your girlfriend may be dangerous, but you aren't. You I could kill on my way to lunch and not spoil my suit. So think twice before you cross us."

"Whatever. Try not to spoil your suit on the way out."

Donal nodded to Fionn, who followed the man out of the building. In the meantime, Donal struck his tuning fork and waved it over the wards. The tones of his wards resonated harmony, each tone coming from his personal magical signature: no one had tried to breach the wards, even to scry.

Donal slipped inside into his living room and let the wards re-knit behind him.

Donal leaned against the door, eyes closed, a trickle of sweat running down his forehead. After too long a delay, Donal felt Fionn shift into the room through an outside wall. Donal opened his eyes, but the *cú sidhe* looked relaxed.

"He boarded a private runner with a waiting driver."

"No partners waiting for us? No one watching the apartment?"

"No one."

Donal relaxed and slumped onto his old, vaguely bovine lime green couch. It didn't match anything else in the room, but it had stayed with him all through college. That couch, even the spot that sagged, felt safer and more like home than even Donal's own bed.

"I know," said Donal. "I shouldn't have taunted him. But—"

"That one will find cause to return and bring trouble with him." Fionn sent a ruffle of fur rippling down its back. "Better to have killed him now and had done with it."

Donal blinked at that, rapidly. He needed to finish packing and get to the spaceport. He knew this. But at that moment, all he could do was sit on his couch and stare at the emerald deerhound.

Fionn had always advised Donal to take the safest route, avoiding trouble whenever possible.

Never before had Fionn recommended killing.

6

Tunold stood high on the walkway overlooking the 'gangplank,' the crew's unofficial nickname for the *Horizon Cusp's* passenger loading deck. *Another little tradition started by our captain.* Tunold might have wondered what traditions he would leave behind him when he retired, eventually, but he had too much work to focus on just then. Ms. García, the new purser, approached with her passenger checklist. García had been working double-time to get up to speed at her new post, had probably heard the extent of the security check done on her by Goldberg and Tai Shi.

Tunold suspected she understood. She had to have heard about the smuggling incident involving the previous purser. If she felt offended in any way, Tunold could not see it in her dark eyes or practical manner. Tunold had only worked with her for two weeks, but so far the woman had proven herself to be one-point-seven meters of solid efficiency.

"All aboard, Sir," she said, passing a passenger checklist from her memopad to his with a flick of her finger.

"What's your read?" asked Tunold as he looked over the list of names, checking them against the pre-flight list he had been provided.

"Sir?"

Tunold looked up, and noted that she looked less puzzled than patient. "Your read. What do you think of them? Who are the likely troublemakers? Wiseasses? What have you?"

"No opinion, Sir. They're on time and their cargo meets all set requirements. Everything matches the customs check sheet down to the milligram. Anything else I leave to Chief Goldberg."

"Safe answer," said Tunold. "But keep in mind, you're going to see a side of passengers that they won't show the chief. Advanced warning can save both us and them a lot of headaches."

"Aye, Sir." She ran her eyes over the assembled executives and others, getting organized below them in the gold-and-sand colored seating area just shy of the hippogriff shuttle in its fake nest of a dock. She shrugged helplessly.

"They're mostly arrogant, privileged, used to the best. Some are out of sorts from travel. Wouldn't say any of them are looking for a fight though."

"That's a start. Next time pay attention to the little details. Talk to Chief Goldberg about how." Tunold checked his watch. "Dismissed."

The moment the purser left, that spooky ghost of a panther that Machado called his familiar phased up through the deck in front of Tunold.

"Executive Officer Kristoff Tunold," said the panther, in a Brazilian accent that almost matched the ship's mage. "My master wishes me to inform you that all thaumaturgic content brought aboard by the passengers is legal, safe, and permitted according to the specifications of the flight manifest."

"That doesn't mean there are no weapons."

"It means that there are no items legally classified as weapons, or whose purpose is primarily offensive."

Tunold grimaced. He hated when Machado reported through his familiar. It gave precise replies, but never expanded the information it provided. Tunold wanted to press further, but knew the spirit would add nothing. Machado must have felt confident in his assessment.

"Very well. Dismissed."

The panther vanished in a swirl of smoke. Only one left to hear from...

Tunold could hear the rapid-fire click of Goldberg's boots coming up the ceramic stairs. Then Goldberg came into view, as crisp and official as the chief ever got: wrinkled, but shirt tucked and all buttons buttoned.

"How's it look, Chief?"

"Clean enough to make me nervous."

"Come again?"

"Well half of those 'assistants' have combat experience or I'm a cleaning lady from San Jose." Goldberg smiled like a wolf watching another predator take down a deer. "But they aren't my problem. Pros I can deal with. It's the executives. Get a bunch of proud, accomplished people together and half of them treat us working folks like their servants' servants. And we got that attitude here. I can see it in their eyes. Especially the moon money woman..."

"Romanova," said Tunold, checking the list.

"That's the one. Gave me a two minute speech about the history of her court sword and its importance to her family, as though if she didn't I might use it to clean the grout in my shower."

Goldberg shook his head in disbelief. "But after all that she handed it over *without question.* No argument. Just like the others." He held up his checklist for emphasis. "All their weapons are safely tucked away, where only the captain and I have access to them, and not one of these fancy folk makes a peep? It's creepy."

"Who the hell said they can bring weapons at all?"

"We allow dueling weapons on all flights, and this one—"

"This is hardly a normal flight, and the last time we carried Mancuso—"

"We can't ask them to go to Venus unarmed unless we want to guarantee their safety when they arrive. We're already denying them bodyguards in transit."

"So let them have weapons waiting for them." Tunold could feel his jaw jutting forward as though of its own accord.

"Believe me, Tai Shi and I went round and round about that." Goldberg slapped his memopad with the back of his hand. "But damn it, she was right about this one. We can't leave them drifting if something happens to their arrangements on the other side."

"Wait." Tunold took a step back.

"That's right," Goldberg said through clenched teeth. "They get weapons, and they get a guarantee that if their welcoming committee isn't friendly, they get to stay aboard the ship under *our* protection until *we* get them someplace safe."

"Does the captain know about this?"

"The captain okayed it." Goldberg must have seen the fire flare in Tunold's eyes, because his voice got firm. "Come on, Ex Oh. This is no guaranteed safe port we're taking these people to. We're accountable for their safety. Why did you think I requisitioned the extra people and weapons?"

"Thought you were expecting another Mars run."

"I wish." Goldberg cracked his neck. "Fighting conspirators on our own ship is nothing compared to fighting a prepared enemy on land. Worse, our enemies would know the territory and we don't."

"This is insane." Tunold could hear the growl reaching his voice. He didn't fight it.

"I had to guess about what we might need." Goldberg did not sound any happier than Tunold felt. "What the hell kind of way is that to go into a fight?"

"Fuck this."

Tunold turned and sprinted to the nearest comm pad, on the wall near the bubble, and slapped it hard enough to sting his calloused hand. With his other hand, he yanked the lever to call the bubble.

"Bridge, this is Executive Officer Tunold. Hold lift off, on my authority. Repeat, hold lift off. I'm coming to the bridge."

Tunold slapped the pad again to cut the connection before even receiving acknowledgment. He knew the ship's communications officer, Ms. Jefferson, would relay the order, and he did not want to be patched through to the captain.

Tunold tapped his closed fist against the ward that sealed the water tube as he waited for the bubble.

No, this was a talk Tunold wanted to have in person.

Show time.

Jacobs perched in his command seat, high above the ring of duty posts that formed the bridge, looking outward through the transparent dome at the port hangar as it opened above him. Right on time. As always.

Below him his crew buzzed with activity as they went through last minute checks and prepared for liftoff.

He spun back to face the illusory replica of the *Horizon Cusp*, a tiny gryphon floating above his station. By placing his finger on the location of the engineering section he saw a display form above the gryphon with the latest numbers on the Deception Drive: current, all systems go.

Jacobs knew he had no reason to check the security report. He knew that Goldberg was amid his final check right now, and Jacobs would see nothing but the status as of about five minutes ago.

And yet it was a speculation he could not resist confirming.

No updates. A brief blue glow between the wings on the gryphon's back, in the position of the bridge, signaled that all passengers and cargo had been accounted for.

Jacobs spun his chair back to his bridge crew. "Helm, report."

"Moderate traffic," said Mr. Burke, "but they've given us a clear lane, Captain."

"And the pilot?"

"Ready for duty, Sir."

Burke had to know that his captain would keep a weather eye on him, and his performance during lift off would determine whether or not he got to land the ship on Venus. The boy had taken ships in and out of port without the modern mandated thaumaturgic guidance, but nothing the size or power of the *Horizon Cusp*.

Jacobs moved on to the next report before any hesitation could be noticed. "Scanners, report."

"All systems go, Captain."

"Damage Control, report."

"Five by five across the board, Captain."

"Then as soon as we get the final word from the port, we're ready for space."

At the communications station, Jefferson slipped her fingers through the pale blue, glowing web strands of the ship's communications network, receiving a communiqué. Certain this would be the go signal from port, Jacobs spun his chair to face Mr. Burke and drew breath to give the order.

"Captain," said Jefferson, "Mr. Tunold is ordering that we hold the launch."

"On what grounds?"

"He's cut the line, sir. He said he's on his way to the bridge."

"Prepare for launch as normal," said Jacobs, before his bridge crew could register confusion. "I want air under me the second I give the order, and space around me on schedule."

Jacobs turned to face the low, curved door that led down to the next deck by a sloping passage. Any moment now his ex oh would thunder onto the bridge.

Jacobs drummed his fingers on his console, but that was not enough activity. He came down the spiral stairs from his station to pace the circular walkway surrounding the duty stations, just inside the transparent bulkhead, waiting.

Tunold did not keep him waiting long. No more than a minute after Ms. Jefferson relayed his words, the door opened and Jacobs saw the light sheen of perspiration that told him that Tunold had double-timed it the whole way.

"I trust you have a good reason for this," said Jacobs, in a dangerous tone.

"Captain, what the hell is this about us allowing passengers weapons?"

"Stow that attitude, Mister."

Tunold slammed the side of one fist against the bulkhead, and Jacobs noted the eyes of the entire bridge crew on their executive officer. Tunold raised his hands wide, like the spread paws of an angry bear standing upright, then gushed out a breath, half-tipping forward.

He straightened himself out and said, his huge jaw scarcely moving, "Captain, as executive officer, why was I not informed that our passenger complement would be armed?"

"They're not armed," said Jacobs, his own words level and cool. "But we are allowing them to transport the weapons they might need on a potentially hostile planet with little government and less law."

"Captain, these people brought us trouble last time—"

"*One* of them brought us trouble, not the others. And I've already arranged their security with Goldberg. Keep current on your reports, Ex Oh."

"This will concern the ship in transit. I should have been informed."

"If it affects the ship in transit, then our passengers have managed to breach the best security we have just to get to those weapons." Jacobs did not try to resist the smirk he felt quirk his lips. "If that happens, I promise you'll be informed."

"Captain," said Jefferson, and Jacobs understood the slight tremor in her voice, "port has given us the go sign."

"Take her up, Mr. Burke," Jacobs said without looking away from his executive officer. "And you return to your duties, Ex Oh. I have a ship to run."

Jacobs turned away from Tunold to give his ex oh the chance to let his frustrations out without the risk of offending his captain, and hustled back up the stairs to his station. Jacobs refused to let himself hover over Burke at this key moment, but failing to oversee liftoff was an impossibility.

Burke guided them up flawlessly, and minutes later the *Horizon Cusp* was at space once more, roughly three days from whatever passed for a port on Venus.

A lot could go wrong in three days.

Donal knew that once he started graduate school, he would miss one thing about these special deliveries: they always came with the best accommodations. On his last regular delivery — to the moon and back — he had been cramped into the sort of restricted passage he could have afforded for himself. But for a custom job like this?

First of all, it smelled fresh. Like clean clothes. Not like the efficiency cabins, which always smelled a little like the past occupants, no matter how good a job the cleaning crews did.

And talk about spacious!

Donal spun in a circle in the middle of the main room of his suite, his arms spread wide. Something he could not have done on many flights. And this was just the sitting room, with its huge, plush couch and matching recliners — each bigger than Donal's first college bed — that rotated for a view of either the room or of space outside through room's three-meter-wide porthole. Not that there was much to see right now, except the port.

Across from the couch was an interactive entertainment display that looked more expensive than any Donal had ever been close to. This room even had its own bathroom, over near the door, next to the coat closet.

Subtle privacy spells woven into the walls, ceiling and floor kept the suite quiet in both directions. A marching band could have gone past the front door and Donal would not have heard it. And Donal could have screamed his head off without disturbing the neighbors on either side of him.

The other bathroom was in the bedroom behind him, next to the walk-in closet. *Walk-in closet.* Even Donal's apartment didn't have a walk-in closet. And that bathroom had a tub wide enough and long enough that Donal could stretch out any direction he wanted. And a misting shower that let the user move the main jets anywhere in a three-hundred-sixty-degree sphere.

The bedroom's huge, real-wood chest of drawers hardly seemed worth mentioning, or even the second porthole (the same size as the first), compared to the emperor-sized bed.

Donal didn't know if that was the official designation for the over four square meters of comfort that allowed for variable firmness, heat, and soothe, but it seemed to him to be fancy enough for an emperor. *It has a soothe control.* Not just elemental spells unwinding the sleeper's tension, but a grid panel that controlled the intensity and location of the relaxation magic.

Donal could not resist glancing at the spells when he first discovered the bed, but quickly realized puzzling through them would take weeks. And he only had the suite for three days, until the helioship reached Venus. Three short days to savor this luxury before he delivered his package and had to sleep in whatever passed for a hotel in a colony that had not yet opened itself to tourist traffic.

At least he would have the flight home to look forward to.

Donal heard a canine rumble, as of a throat being cleared, and he had the feeling that his familiar had been trying to get his attention for several minutes now.

"Come on, Fionn, you have to admit that this place is amazing."

"You have not spoken to me since we dismissed your would-be assassin. But we have much to discuss."

"You said I should kill him."

"I said that you would have been better off had you killed him." The emerald deerhound sat, its head tilting at an angle that Donal had come to think of as Fionn's professorial expression. "Your reticence to take life pleases me. I hope you do not lose it. But I never wish to see you underestimate a threat. And that man represents a threat that has not yet expired."

"You think he'll really try to kill me if I don't murder for him?"

"I think that whatever comes of this voyage, you should not relax until the matter of your would-be assassin has been ... resolved with certainty."

"I'll tell Li Hua."

Fionn flicked its ears, a slight ruffle weaving through its fur.

"While I do not approve of your association with her, I admit that in this case she is well qualified to tend to this for you."

"What else is bothering you?"

Fionn sat, impassive.

"Something's been bothering you since Ms. MacPherson joined us for lunch."

"You are surrounded by promises, but no one discusses their price."

Leave it to the fae to think of the price of favors.

Donal sank down into the couch, felt it cradle him from beneath and had to resist the urge to lay his head back and revel in the comfort. He drew a breath to bring his mind back to the subject at hand.

"I think she made her price rather plain. If I kill Mancuso, she'll take care of me."

"Rowan MacPherson never spoke directly of killing, and as she was direct in other matters, this may mean that she foresees several options for you. But that is the effect, not the price."

Donal thought for a moment. "The price is the removal of Mancuso from 4M, and the ripple effects that causes."

"If Donatello Mancuso is all that some say, then removing him from power may be the best option. But removing him would create a vacuum. And the question of what would fill that vacuum remains unanswered. And it must be considered."

"Can't I just enjoy my new room for a little bit?"

"Very well. Take this night for enjoyment, but pay attention. I will remind you of this conversation."

As Donal felt the ship lift off, he had the feeling that Fionn's reminder would come sooner than he wanted.

WITHIN THE WORKSHOP THAT DOUBLED AS HIS OFFICE, MACHADO SAT within the largest and most intricate of three magic circles inscribed in the floor. The room also had his small alchemy lab behind him, his extensive library to his right, and his desk to his left. Before him, on the deck outside his circle, his censer trailed the scent of goldenrod and dried holly into the air.

But Machado could perceive none of those things at the moment.

Machado's mind floated within the thaumaturgic patterns of the ship, the center of a network of spells that knit together Fredrickson's alchemy, the hull's carterite and ceramics, the elementals bound into key systems, the relatively few spells Jang had cast, and the vast number of enchantments he had woven himself.

Over the ten years Machado had served aboard the *Horizon Cusp*, he had found cause to remove and re-cast every single spell of its construction and maintenance.

Captain Jacobs might refer to the *Horizon Cusp* as his ship, but in a very practical way it belonged to Machado.

At the moment he waited, studying the lines and flows of power all about him. Soon the ship would lift off, and every system would experience stress beyond anything easily replicated for testing purposes. Machado expected to catch any current or potential trouble spots before the ship hit space.

Some magicians favored viewing interwoven spells as a web, but Machado preferred the image of tapestry. More artistic, and it helped him color-code and pattern-code systems and subsystems for ease of reference.

The projection of Machado's attention chuckled in a way that would have shaken his belly, had the laugh reached his seated physical form. If non-magicians ever learned how personal and idiosyncratic were the spells that supported their daily lives, they might try to resurrect technology.

Machado wondered for a moment whether they could.

While Machado kept an eye on the whole thaumaturgic tapestry, his familiar *Saravá* prowled the spells nearest the Deception Drive, the ship's engine. Jang might have been the most competent Initiate Machado had ever known, but he would not trust space travel entirely to the perceptions of an Initiate. His spirit *onça* would warn him of any problems requiring his immediate attention.

Then Machado felt it; flares swirled along the superstructure, keying the wings and legs of the great gryphon that was the *Horizon Cusp* as the helioship took to the air.

Once airborne, the sylphs that supported the ship within the Earth's sky pulsed information from the atmosphere to the crew about location, speed, and everything nearby.

Machado's attention drifted like a ghost past the bindings that held the air elementals in place and kept them about their assigned tasks: tight and harmonious. 'Ship shape' as Jacobs would say. Machado followed the links and ensured that the vibrations of the bindings harmonized with those that kept yet more sylphs supplying and refreshing the air within the confines of the ship.

The *Horizon Cusp's* Deception Drive needed only one lacuna, a single space elemental to transport them through the solar system (and, Machado admitted, another smaller lacuna to keep them appraised of the space around them). But the ship required more than a dozen air elementals to ferry it within a planet's sky.

Machado sent a mental note to *Saravá* to remind him later: Machado wanted to calculate the ratios of elementals needed for ship travel and determine where the optimal balance lay.

Machado tapped into the feed of information coming from the sensors' sylphs. Almost out of the hangar, perhaps ten minutes more before the lacunas could feel enough space around them to take over.

More systems checks, all responding within the parameters Machado considered safe. *Which*, he noted with irritation, *were narrower than those Jitters would have set, if I'd let her.*

Thoughts of the Chief Engineer brought a response from Machado's familiar: "Everything functions as you predicted, Master."

Machado swept once more through the main systems, double-checking his work, but by the time he felt the Deception Drive take over he had not found anything to concern him.

His official work finished, Machado prepared to withdraw from the tapestry and return his attention to his body, perhaps to celebrate his good work with a snack.

But so long as he was here...

Machado ran his thoughts along the designs of his most recent addition to the ship's thaumaturgic array — emergency wards that could partition the life support systems in case of a breach.

He had finished the third of ten latent magic circles inscribed in key places when a tremor in the tapestry drew his attention. He turned his focus to investigate, but it was gone.

Somewhere near the bridge, thought Machado.

If the *Horizon Cusp's* spells formed a tapestry, then the bridge was the key visual element that tied everything together. Machado dropped his other investigations and sifted through every spell connected to the bridge controls, beginning with life support.

Just as he dug into the control elements he felt the tremor again. Not coming from the bridge. Not coming from his spells...

Machado spread his mental self wide, encompassing the bridge and the two decks below it; every spell, latent and active, spread itself before his scrutiny.

There. A throb, almost like a pulse point in a wrist. The tremor comes from the resonance of ... the ship's safe?

Machado yanked his mind back into his body so fast his bulk careened from its lotus position like a drunkard. Back in control of his physical form, Machado slapped his hands against the deck for support and launched himself to his feet like a Buddha beginning a 100-meter dash.

He reached his desk and slapped his comm pad, speaking before Ms. Jefferson's head finished appearing above it.

"Bridge! This is Machado. We have a problem."

7

At his station on the bridge, Jacobs finished calming his ship's mage, and cut the connection. He looked up through the transparent ceramics of the domed hull and sighed at the stars.

Barely into space and already a problem.

As he descended the stairs from his station, he said, "A fine take-off, Mr. Burke. Mr. Grabowski, keep a weather eye on the scanners once we're past rush hour. Anyone tries to ride our wake to Venus, I want to know. Ms. Jefferson, find Chief Goldberg and send him to my office. Mr. Tunold, keep an eye on things for a few minutes, won't you?"

Jacobs heard the expected chorus of 'Aye, Captain,' with one exception. Tunold said, "Problem, sir?"

"Remains to be seen, Ex Oh." Jacobs stopped just shy of the low, curved door, turned back to his executive officer's frown, and said with a smile, "Don't worry, Kris. I won't hog all the fun."

Tunold said something in reply, but Jacobs was already closing the door behind him.

Jacobs held his pace to a leisurely stroll down the sloping passage to Crew Deck One. His office was not far, and he saw no point in hurrying down just to stand around waiting for Goldberg.

But when he reached his office door, Goldberg stood waiting, along with Machado, and the tall, dark assistant ship's mage, Cromartie. Machado's mouth pulled wide and his brow pulled down: irritation, likely at whatever's in the safe. Storm warning in Goldberg's eyes, his jaw positioned to crack his neck at any moment.

Someone's already on the Chief's bad side.

Cromartie had that distant look mages get when they're thinking about magic but should be thinking about the world around them.

"Captain—" started Goldberg.

"This comes first, Chief," said Jacobs. "Gentlemen, if you'll follow me."

He opened his door and led them through his office, through his personal quarters, and into the short, narrow hall behind them that ended in the ship's safe: two meters wide by two meters tall, fashioned from a carterite-steel alloy and sealed up with spells so tight that the hull probably felt inadequate by comparison. In the center sat a false combination dial in the shape of a twenty centimeter wide ship's wheel.

Jacobs turned to the three cramped men. "Chief, let the record show that we will be opening the ship's safe at the request of our ship's mage, who has detected a possible threat inside."

"Acknowledged," said Goldberg, enough curiosity in his voice to outweigh the impatience in his eyes.

"Mr. Machado, if you will recount the reason we are here."

"Sir, can't we just—"

"Regulations are clear. Unless the threat is imminent, we will follow procedure."

"Fine." Machado spat the word out as he might a jalapeño pepper found in his chocolate ice cream. He rushed through a summary of what he had detected.

"Without a formal passenger request, the chief of security and I must agree that the need is sufficient to open the safe. I agree. Chief?"

"I confirm."

Jacobs placed his hand on the wheel and said, "I, Captain John

Jacobs, acting in the interest of ship's safety and with the confirmation of the chief of security, hereby require the safe to open."

The door swung open. Inside the safe were several boxes of passengers' valuables (most often cash and jewelry), a few enchanted items that had to be safely stowed in transit, about a dozen dueling swords, and a sealed leather pouch, barely large enough to contain a memopad.

"The pouch," said Machado.

"Safe to touch?" asked Jacobs.

Cromartie narrowed his eyes, perhaps uncertain, but Machado gave a definite nod.

Jacobs reached for the pouch, but Goldberg cleared his throat, so softly it was almost too quiet to hear.

Jacobs closed his reaching fingers. He felt an urge to reprimand Goldberg for daring to correct his captain, but Jacobs had to admit that the sound had been the most diplomatic utterance Goldberg had ever made in his presence.

Jacobs drew his back straight and waved his hand in an after-you gesture. Goldberg pinched the edge of the pouch between his index finger and thumb, slid it to the edge of the safe, and lifted it high enough to give them all a good look.

"Pulsing at steady intervals," said Machado, finger moving to ensure his assistant spotted the pulse.

"Courier's seal," said Goldberg.

"Of course," said Jacobs. He held out his hand and Goldberg, with only a slight hesitation, handed over the pouch. Jacobs reached out his other hand and slammed the safe's door shut hard enough to make Machado and Cromartie wince.

"Chief, would you have someone fetch our courier?"

THE LAST TIME DONAL HAD FLOWN ON THIS SHIP, HE HAD FELT quarantined, isolated in a cabin at least six decks away from any of the other passengers. Admittedly, tensions had been high and it had been done for his own safety. Not that it had helped...

But still, it felt good to have a cabin — a luxury suite cabin no less — down on Promenade One alongside the rest of the passengers. And if Donal's cabin sat a little apart from the others, well, that was just enough to provide breathing space.

And with any luck, thought Donal, *having a cabin so close to Li Hua's will come in handy...*

Not that he expected her to have much social time on the cruise, since she was working. Donal had yet to even see her since they boarded.

Donal forewent the bubble and took an access ladder down to the Main Deck, entering through the hatch door. The main passenger deck spread out around him like a sanitized version of a Greek village. Shops and boutiques, bars and restaurants, game rooms and exercise areas spread out in rows of standalone buildings cut from marble, fitted without mortar, and polished to a shine. The air carried a hint of dust and sea smells, but those were illusions, like the ceiling, which appeared to be a vivid blue daytime sky, complete with fluffy clouds and a sun that moved through the sky on schedule, and would later set to let the moon and stars provide evening mood lighting.

The attention to detail made Donal smile. The sound of voices broadened his smile a little more. If other passengers were already exploring this deck, perhaps the voyage would feel casual despite the small passenger count.

Nevertheless, Donal recalled Fionn from its silver faun pendant.

The fae deerhound assessed the situation and said, "Hoping for an early massage?"

"You read my mind."

"Shall I scout ahead and get your name on the list? There may be competition."

"Donal!" came the commanding crack from a voice Donal recognized. He turned to see the speaker, Donatello Mancuso, business magnate, possible would-be dictator, and Donal's personal college sponsor.

Fionn immediately faded from visible to everyone to visible only to the sight of magicians.

Donal smiled, hoping it didn't look forced. Mr. Mancuso — *Donatello, he wants me to call him Donatello* — stood with his pair of secretaries, Ms. Stevenson and Mr. Davis, who both looked so blonde and crisp that they could have modeled for a young married couple. His and hers midnight blue suits.

Donal didn't know the four others standing with Mr. — *Donatello* — but they had the look of money: old enough to be out of college but young enough to not go gray, with tailored clothes expensive enough to pay the cost of Donal's suite for a full year's cruise.

But apparently looking over the crowd required a moment longer than Donatello wanted, because the whip-like man with the pencil mustache and black hair raised his hands in a clear gesture that said, 'I am not accustomed to waiting.'

Despite himself, Donal trotted down the row between buildings to reach the conversation. He could feel Fionn withholding comment as he slapped his smile back in place, extended his hand, and said, "Good to see you, Donatello."

"Glad to see Tai Shi's been improving your wardrobe," said his patron, while gripping and pumping his hand as though trying to throttle money out of a deadbeat, "but what the hell are you doing here?"

Between Donatello's rapid-fire delivery and the amused looks on the faces of the three men and one woman Donal did not know, Donal had not yet managed an answer before Ms. Stevens leaned in and whispered in her boss' ear.

"A delivery?" barked Do— *Mr. Mancuso. He may want me to call him Donatello, but there's no way he'll be anyone but Mr. Mancuso to me.* "Why are you delivering packages? Why aren't you in school? Stevens, has there been any breakdown on our end?"

"None, sir."

Mr. Davis cleared his throat politely, and Mr. Mancuso said, "Right. Pleasantries. Donal Cuthbert, meet Natalia Romanova of The Romanov Group, Ricardo Montenegro of United Manufacturing, and

Saito Akio, of Saito Industries. Donal here saved my life, and is apparently continuing to work as a courier despite the fact that I'm paying for him to become a Hierophant."

"A magician," said Mr. Saito, with a slight bow that kept his eyes on Donal. "Excuse me." And Mr. Saito stepped away as though he expected Donal to start casting spells. Mr. Montenegro uttered something polite and pleasant before making his own quick getaway, but Ms. Romanova said nothing. She only narrowed her eyes at Donal, then turned and sauntered away.

Wait. Romanova?

A flick of Donal's eyes told him that Fionn had made the connection as well, and his *cú sidhe* circled around to stand guard between Donal and a potential enemy.

"Petty idiots," said Mr. Mancuso with a disgusted glance after his departing companions. "As though any magician who would save my life would threaten their secrets. You aren't here to steal secrets, are you Donal?"

"No, sir. I—"

"Then would you care to tell me why you appear to be refusing my gift?"

Something dangerous moved through Mr. Mancuso's eyes. Not as though Donal were in any immediate danger, but as though Mr. Mancuso was not a man to look kindly on those who rejected his largess.

"I'm not." Donal held up his hands in near surrender. "I can't move onto campus until the end of August, and I've got to eat and pay the rent in the meantime. Plus Li Hua isn't the cheapest date I've ever known."

That last got a chuckle out of Mr. Mancuso.

"I bet she isn't. But I've told you, boy, we've got you covered. You like to earn your own way, and I respect that. But you should have come to us if you needed money. Stevens, I left enough in the Cuthbert Budget to handle incidentals?"

Stevens gave a single, tight nod.

"Thought so. Never cut corners to save a dime, Donal. Always ends up costing you a dollar later."

"I wasn't—"

"And don't play poor when you've got a rich uncle. Now you give up this courier business and let 4M take care of you until you've got at least one doctorate and can start earning some real money."

As so often seemed to happen to Donal while talking with Mr. Mancuso, he felt at least three sentences behind.

"All right ... Donatello ... I'll make this my last delivery."

"Yes, I suppose you have to finish it. Wouldn't do to leave a job half-done..." Mr. Mancuso tapped his fingers together as though looking for a loophole.

Donal half expected him to somehow find one, but they were interrupted by a white-uniformed member of the ship's watch. Donal noted that the bruiser of a woman had a Pacifier strapped to her hip, like a white billy club declaring to all who saw it that the watch was ready if trouble called.

"Donal Cuthbert," she said. "I'm going to have to ask you to come with me."

"Later," said Mr. Mancuso. "We're talking."

"I'm afraid I have to insist, Sir. Ship's business, by order of the captain."

"It's all right," said Donal, relieved to have an exit from the conversation, even if it meant he was in some kind of trouble. Mr. Mancuso always put him in mind of his grandmother's stories of the *daoine sidhe*, and Donal felt that Mr. Mancuso would have been more than at home among the unseelie. "Probably just a question about the security requirements for my package. Nothing to worry about."

Donal hurried after the watchwoman, Fionn following as though Donal needed a rear guard. Of course, if the Romanovs were still angry about the package Donal delivered on Luna, he might need more than a rear guard.

Donal entered the captain's office and felt his breath catch. The captain, seated at his desk, had the scowl of a commander ready to order men to their deaths. Standing to the right of the desk was the chief of security — Mr. Goldberg, if Donal recalled correctly — and to the left stood Magister Machado, with Initiate Cromartie hovering behind the heavy magician. None of them looked happy.

The Magister's eyes tracked Fionn's entrance, but he said nothing.

The captain, the chief of security, and the ship's mage. All waiting for Donal. He could imagine no way this meeting could go well, especially with that look on the captain's face.

Sitting on the desk in front of the captain was Donal's courier pouch. Still sealed, at least.

Captain Jacobs gestured and the watchwoman who had escorted Donal stepped out into the hall, locking the office door behind her.

The door shut with a click that rang out all too final in Donal's ears.

<hr>

Poor kid looks like he's been brought to trial, thought Jacobs. *Pale, ready to start shaking or sweating any second.*

"Have a seat, Mr. Cuthbert." Jacobs knew better than to force a smile that would have come off as a snarl. He waited until the boy settled on the edge of his chair, eyes sliding between Machado, Goldberg, and Jacobs himself.

Jacobs pointed to the pouch on his desk to give Cuthbert something to focus on. "We need to know what you're carrying."

"I'm afraid I don't know, Sir. Couriers are never told what we're transporting."

"Protects the package against mind magic used on the courier," said Cromartie in his deep, smooth voice. "I did a stint delivering off-world a couple of years back."

Jacobs saw Goldberg nod absent confirmation of Cromartie's statement, though whether he was confirming the assertion or the facts of the Initiate's personal history, Jacobs could not be certain. He decided it didn't matter.

"And I suppose you can't tell us where it's from or who's going to receive it?"

"No, Sir. Sorry, Sir." The kid at least had the grace to look apologetic. "May I ask why it matters?"

"Did you notice the way it pulses?" asked Machado, with what sounded to Jacobs like more curiosity than suspicion in his voice.

DONAL FELT PUZZLEMENT SPREAD ACROSS HIS FACE, BUT RATHER THAN ask he slipped his mind through to a deeper phase of consciousness and looked at the package. First he noticed the tight, protective weave of spells that sealed the contents against damage or tampering: everything remained intact. Next Donal spotted the wispy remains of the concealment spells he used to divert attention from the courier pouch when he was carrying it.

Donal felt embarrassed about Magister Machado having seen those remains, and Donal was sure he had. Letting the spells decay instead of properly removing them might not cause problems, but Donal could not deny that the practice looked sloppy. Careless. Like having an invited guest see old, gelled cereal in a bowl on the coffee table.

Apart from that detail, everything looked...

And then Donal saw it. A momentary flare of magic, distracting with its brightness.

"It's never done that before. Not around me," said Donal. "No way I would have missed it, much less my familiar."

"He speaks unvarnished truth," said Fionn, formal words in Gaelic, the official language of human magic as established during its rise.

"I didn't think so," said Magister Machado, in English, with a heavy sigh. "And, Captain, I can confirm that it's not Cuthbert's signature."

"All right then," said the captain. "Open up that package, Cuthbert. Let's take a look at what we're carrying."

"No, Sir."

Donal felt a bead of sweat form on his forehead and roll down his nose. He was struck by the sudden image of trading his wonderful luxury suite for a cell in the brig.

"I can't do that."

———

Jacobs felt his intimidating stare spread across his face, starting with the lowered brow, then the slowly set jaw, and finishing with the eyes.

In his early days as a captain, Jacobs imagined that his eyes warned their prey that Jacobs would beat them to death and enjoy it.

Jacobs knew better now.

It didn't matter what Jacobs thought as he fixed his intimidating stare. He had enough presence and experience that his victim would imagine far worse tortures than any he could concoct, though he knew he could come up with some horrors.

As if to prove his point, the courier squirmed in his seat as though in physical pain.

Jacobs let that last for seconds that must have felt eternal to the boy, before saying, "What. Did. You. Say?"

Jacobs expected a delayed response, but Cuthbert replied immediately. "I wish I could help you, Sir. I really do. But I can't open that package."

"He can," said Cromartie. "All couriers carry a signet ring that allows them to open a package with authority the magical seal will acknowledge."

"That's only in case of emergency," said Cuthbert, regaining his composure and sitting tall and proud, as though defying a death squad. "Once open, a package is considered undeliverable."

"If it's a threat to my ship," said Jacobs, "I'd say that counts as an emergency."

"It doesn't," Cuthbert insisted. "Emergency is defined by IIX as an immediate threat to life and limb." Jacobs drew breath to make the obvious retort, but Cuthbert cut in to say, "Mine don't count."

Jacobs continued as though the boy had not spoken.

"My ship's mage has detected unknown magic with an unknown purpose, originating from that package. As captain of the *Horizon Cusp*, I declare this an emergency, and will confirm to your company that I required you to open the package to prove that it does not contain explosives or other weaponry that might harm this ship and its crew.

"Open the package. Now."

***

DONAL WIPED THE SWEAT FROM HIS FOREHEAD WITH THE BACK OF HIS hand, and found himself wishing fleetingly that he were back in his uncomfortable conversation with Mr. Mancuso.

"No, Sir." Donal shook his head, slowly, as though the movement might ward off his sense of impending doom. "That's not enough reason to open the package. IIX magicians test all packages before they are handed off to couriers. IIX guarantees that all packages they ship are safe to carry, safe to transport, and safe to deliver. IIX does not deliver weapons in any form, not active, nor inert, nor in alchemical or thaumatugic component form."

"That guarantee is no good to us if we're dead," said Jacobs.

"I believe your IIX contract stipulates that Starchaser Spacelines will not impede or interfere with an IIX courier or delivery in any way. If I open that package of my own free will, I not only won't get paid for this trip, I'll have to reimburse IIX for my travel costs, which I cannot afford. If you force me to open that package, you'll be in violation of your contract."

Donal drew a deep breath, stood, and met the captain's eye.

"As an IIX representative, I formally request that you return that package to the ship's safe. And if there's nothing else, I'll take my leave."

Donal didn't know if he expected the captain to explode, or just promise death with his eyes, but Donal definitely did not expect what the captain actually did: he smiled. Not a broad, happy smile, but a small, slightly lopsided, chagrined smile.

"You're dismissed, Mr. Cuthbert," he said. "Thank you for your assistance."

"You're letting—" began the chief, but the captain cut him off with a glare.

"Thank you, Sir," said Donal, who turned and got himself and Fionn out of that room as fast as he could manage without actually running or quite slamming the door behind him.

Once Donal reached the bubble, he yanked the call lever and half-collapsed forward against the water tube's ward.

"Holy crap, Fionn. I thought we were going to the brig for sure."

"The captain is a fair man," said the *cú sidhe*. "He will not hold you accountable for the danger you have brought aboard his ship."

"So you think the package is trouble?"

"I never thought otherwise."

Donal rolled sideways to lean his shoulder against the tube and stare at his familiar.

"Then why did you agree I should take this delivery?"

"To get you close to Donatello Mancuso. You need to assess for yourself, once and for all, whether or not the man is a threat that you must deal with."

The emerald deerhound tilted its head in a canine shrug.

"Why else?"

Jacobs stared at his closed office door for a moment, and he could feel tension build in his officers. If he let the silence stretch too long, one of them would break it. Probably Goldberg.

"He's grown up some since the Mars run," said Jacobs, wondering how he would have handled Carl, had his son lived long enough to defy him the way Cuthbert just did. "I may have to stop treating him like a boy."

"Why did you let him go?" asked Goldberg, frustration seeping through his tone. "We need to see what's in that package."

"Take a breath or take a walk, Chief," said Jacobs. "And no, we don't. We now know it's not a weapon. Ergo, it's a tracker, isn't it, Mr. Machado?"

"That's my best guess. Whoever commissioned the delivery wants to keep tabs on us."

Jacobs slapped the comm pad on his desk, waited for Jefferson's ghostly head to appear. "Link me through to Scanners, please."

A moment later, Ms. Jefferson's face melted into Mr. Grabowski's, a process that Jacobs still found disturbing.

"What's the latest, Mr. Grabowski?"

"We're past the local traffic now, with no signs of anyone pointing our way. Looks like clear space, Sir."

"If that changes, I want to know the moment you do. Captain out." Jacobs whipped one hand through the illusion of Grabowski's head to cut the channel. He turned back to Machado and pointed at the pouch. "Can that thing pull nav data from us?"

"No. The seal is Hierophant cast, so trying to scry through it would be difficult at best, and I mean difficult *for me*. From what I've been able to determine by the pulses, there's no way the spells inside are good enough or complex enough to reach past that seal, break into our systems, pull the data, then store or transmit it."

Machado twisted his thick lips to one side. "Well, maybe that last part. Transmitting is all this thing seems to do. But it won't get anything from us to send along."

"So the point must be tracking. But our route's in the official logs. Why would…"

Realization hit Jacobs like a jab to the jaw. "A rendezvous. Someone plans to intercept us."

Jacobs took off his captain's hat and ran his hand across the tight black curls shorn close to his scalp. "Chief, we're going to be glad you brought on extra security. Mr. Machado, I need you to quarantine this thing. Lock it down so the signal can't get out."

"I should be able to trap the pulses," said Machado, "but that may not be enough."

Mash looked as though he had more to say, but his fingers moved the way they did when he ran silent formulae in his head.

Jacobs grew tired of waiting. "Why not?"

"If I were going to do this, I would keep some of the original materials used in making whatever's in that pouch. Then a basic link could home in on it."

"Why the pulses then?"

"The difference between speaking and shouting." Mash still had that faraway look on his face, but it resolved all at once in an expression of disgust accompanied by some of Machado's finest Portuguese swear words. "Pointless. We might as well throw it back in the safe."

"I want that thing locked down."

"Won't help." Machado shook his head hard enough to make his cheeks continue quivering when he started to talk. "I've seen the pulse enough times now that I can tell the pulse is an effect, not a purpose."

Cromartie's head snapped to attention, like the statement meant more to the Initiate than it did to Jacobs.

"Meaning..." Jacobs said, letting the word trail off.

"The pouch doesn't contain a spell. It contains half of a spell. The other half will be on the ship intending to rendezvous with us. The pulse is just the natural response of the spell trying to connect with itself. It's that attempt at connection that will let the other ship find us, no matter what we do to that pouch."

Machado nodded to Cromartie. "They probably tried to suppress the pulse, but couldn't find a workable method in time."

"What if they—" began Cromartie, but Jacobs cut him off.

"Fine. To hell with IIX and to hell with loopholes. We may not be able to open that package, but we can toss it into space."

"Captain," said Goldberg grimacing like he had an ulcer inside an ulcer and he'd just eaten a jar of horseradish. "Much as I might like to be the one casting that thing into space, I have to remind you of something. And you won't want to hear it."

Goldberg's grimace grew, squeezing his eyes shut and grinding his teeth. Jacobs wondered what could...

Then he knew, and that knowledge made Jacobs slam his fist down on his desk hard enough to send splinters of pain into his elbow and shoulder.

"Even that would violate our IIX contract," grumbled Jacobs, loud enough for all to hear. "Our *lucrative* IIX contract."

"Yes, sir," said Goldberg, his voice still strained but his face less pained at not having to reveal this uncomfortable truth, even if he was the one giving it voice. "Something you shouldn't do without consulting your partner."

Jacobs felt an urge to throw that partner out into space along with the courier pouch. But then someone would inherit the man's shares of the company, and Jacobs had the sneaking suspicion that if Mancuso died by foul play, those shares would go to one of Jacobs' enemies.

And Jacobs had lived long enough to have made his share of enemies.

8

DONAL YAWNED AND STRETCHED, STILL FACE DOWN ON THE SQUISHY massage table, even though the Swedish angel (this one was actually Filipina, Donal believed, though the massage style made them all Swedish angels in his mind) had left to give him privacy while he dressed. Soft guitar music seeped out of the carpeting, inviting Donal to nap. And seemingly from everywhere, the barely-there scent of sage.

They let me nap last time. Maybe... nah. This time other passengers might need the room.

Donal sat up in the tan-and-brown room with its cactus decorations and high desert paintings, his muscles and mind loose and easy despite his earlier stress. 'A calm mind makes a good magician,' Professor N'Kembe had said so often. If that were true, then Donal in that moment felt like the greatest magician ever born, possibly even greater than Lloyd Bird himself.

Donal chuckled, and called Fionn out of the pendant that was all Donal wore apart from the towel around his waist.

"I smell sage," said Fionn.

"The Albuquerque Room," said Donal, "not actual incense."

"Good. I did not wish to correct what you had already lit, but the purity of this concoction would prove insufficient for spell work."

"I know," said Donal, hopping to his feet and fighting another yawn. "No character without a blend. Even a pinch of verbena would help." He raised an eyebrow at his familiar. "I'm not *that* bad at alchemy."

Fionn snorted, and assessed its master as he walked toward the pile of clothes on his chair.

"Your body and mind have calmed, but uncertainty obscures your aspect. If you plan a significant working, I suggest a full ritual bath."

"A bath? Can I help?" said Li Hua from the interior doorway. Donal looked over to see the Chinese-Martian beauty clad only in a towel herself, though hers covered the whole of her torso. "Wait, if this is a ritual bath, I probably shouldn't."

She leaned against the door frame, posing in a way that had to be deliberate. "Wouldn't want to distract you from your designated purpose."

"Of course you wouldn't," said Donal, one eyebrow raised. "But suddenly I find myself thinking of whole avenues of magic you and I haven't ... experimented with."

Fionn snorted with a shake of its head that snapped its ears to and fro, making both Donal and Li Hua laugh.

"I don't actually need a ritual bath," said Donal. "Fionn and I were talking about relaxation and alchemical incense."

A voice called Li Hua's name. She said, "Looks like I'm up. I'll have some time after dinner. Meet me on the Observation Deck?"

"Of course," said Donal with a grin that made Fionn roll its eyes.

Li Hua moved off toward her room, and the door swung shut behind her. After she was gone, Donal asked, "Did Pinyin-Lung check on us?"

"No."

"Then how did she know I was here?"

"Your name is on the temporary placard in the interior hall," said the *cú sidhe*, as though the answer were the most obvious in the world.

"You were in the faun until I called you, and you haven't left the room."

"During the first massage you had aboard this ship, I studied the layout and procedures." The emerald deerhound tilted its head. "Shall I confirm this for you now, Master?"

"No, you're probably right." Donal dropped his towel and started dressing at high speed. "But if Li Hua is here, maybe I can arrange a private conversation with Mr. Mancuso."

"If you determine that he poses a problem, you will not be able to avoid Tai Shi Li Hua's intercession on his behalf."

"True," but that doesn't mean she" — Donal struggled with a shoe while standing on one leg, finally leaned against the wall to manage — "needs advance warning."

Donal could not have explained to a layman how he said what he said next. In his mind and in his mouth, he formed words in Gaelic, but in his intention he formed words that only Fionn could hear. He understood the magic of it. Familiar-specific speech was a technique that expressed thought through the essential bindings that first brought Fionn through to this world, the spells referred to as 'creating' a familiar. Strictly speaking, vocalized words should not have been necessary at all, and Donal knew that Magisters and Hierophants could hold lengthy conversations with their familiars, even over distances, without uttering a sound.

Donal had not reached that point yet.

But for his next words, he needed complete privacy, and merely directing his intention along those lines twisted the sounds that emerged from his mouth, such that only his own familiar could interpret them. But what he said was, "I will head for the restaurant areas. Scout ahead and search out Mr. Mancuso for me."

By the time Donal had offered his profuse thanks and left The Relaxation Station, Fionn had shifted through a wall and vanished.

But finding Mr. Mancuso would be the easy part. What could Donal say to him?

Donal stopped five steps into the row of entertainment businesses, between a bar (open, but empty) and a dance club (closed until dark). Mr. Mancuso was the last person Donal should talk to. Literally. Donal needed to start with others and work his way to the center. Donal needed to find some of those other businesspeople first.

MACHADO FOLLOWED IN CAPTAIN JACOBS' WAKE, DOWN THROUGH THE corridors of the crew sections of the ship, down the crew-only bubble to the security deck and across to the only passenger bubble that intersected both crew and passenger sections, in this one location.

Machado felt a wave of respect for the pace his captain set. On his own, Machado would have meandered, or perhaps strolled. Jacobs maintained a determined march that left Machado sweating by the time they reached the first bubble and panting slightly by the time they reached the second. Jacobs himself hardly seemed to have noticed any effort.

Impressive, for a man more than twice Machado's age.

During that second bubble ride, Jacobs' eyes slid over, obviously noting the puffing for breath, the forehead wiped on Machado's sleeve. Little ever embarrassed Machado, but in this case he felt his cheeks grow warm.

"Perhaps I should ask Tunold for some workout tips," said Machado, with an attempt at a smile.

Jacobs said nothing, which meant that whatever the captain thought, he considered it more politic to keep to himself than to insult one of his officers.

"Why do you need me for this anyway, Sir? Usually the last thing you want when talking to Mancuso is a witness."

That got a wolfish smile out of the captain. The man's shoulders lost a bit of their hunch.

"Sorry to keep you from your duties, Mash. I may need someone to explain the technical side of the magic to make sure he understands the strength of the wind crossing our sails. I'd let your second do it, but Mancuso's the type to respect credentials more than information."

The bubble opened before Machado could offer his own view of Mancuso, that of a Faust. *Mancuso's the sort to gather and verify all the best possible information, then make the decision that most furthers his own goals.*

The corridors were wide on this deck, easily three meters across and high, with rich golden carpeting and even the occasional painting: mostly Greek and Roman themed.

Ten paces off the bubble Jacobs stopped outside the door of one of the premiere luxury suites. The captain raised his right fist, checked his movement, took a deep breath, then knocked politely.

Machado snorted before he could stop himself, drawing an evil eye from the captain intense enough that Machado almost raised a ward by reflex.

Scarcely a moment passed before the door opened, revealing a tall blonde man in a suit and haircut to match, the sort of man that tries to use conditioning and expensive tailoring to make up for a lack of personal strength. "Captain Jacobs, a pleasure to see you again. What shall I tell Mr. Mancuso brings you here?"

"Just let him in, Davis," called the sharp voice of Mancuso. "Jacobs doesn't wait any better than I do."

Davis took a step to the side, and Jacobs strode into the room, leaving Machado to follow, an assumption that Machado would tolerate only from his captain.

Machado had never been inside one of the top luxury suites of the *Horizon Cusp*, and what he saw now nearly made him whistle in admiration. He made a mental note to improve the accommodations he required on the rare occasions that he allowed himself to be flown off-world for consulting purposes.

The plush sea-green carpeting emitted a gentle wave of relaxation that soothed the feet with every step. The coat room to his right had spells woven into it that could clean any article of clothing left in it overnight, similar to the ones Machado had cast on his own dresser and closet. Next to the closet was a bathroom with secondary purification spells on the faucets, filtering their water beyond what the main system did. An unnecessary extravagance in Machado's opinion, probably done to impress those who would notice.

The main room itself had three indigo couches surrounding a coffee table that looked to have been carved from a conch shell. Over by the porthole — a porthole that took up most of the external bulkhead — sat another couch the color of golden sand, flanked by two matching recliners the size of loveseats and a quartet of end tables that looked to have been pressed out of yellow sand. Spells of comfort wove through all the seating, and the tables had sections designated for maintaining warm or cool temperatures for drinks and food.

Right now each of those tables had an assortment of finger food — all Earth-based — mostly fruits, vegetables, cheeses and candies.

In the recliners by the porthole, reading, sat a woman who could have matched Davis for blondness and suited-ness, save that Machado's quick read of her spoke better of her strength and confidence. Something in her bearing.

Mancuso and a guest sat on the triangle of couches, where they had clearly been having a relaxed chat. Mancuso's suit lacked its jacket, and his expensive-looking black shoes were propped on the coffee table. Across the table from him, dressed in a more casual sweater and slacks, sat an Arabic man with a red tint to his features that spoke of more time on Mars than in the lands of his ancestors. Younger than Machado would have expected from someone having a casual conversation with Mancuso, probably only a couple of years older than Cuthbert.

Mancuso gestured to his two standing visitors with a tumbler of brown liquid that Machado suspected of being Scotch old enough to remember technology.

"Captain Jacobs. Making a personal visit to my humble abode without so much as a link of warning. And with the ship's mage in tow no less. Pity Tai Shi's not here. She might have learned something."

Still not pausing for breath, Mancuso directed his next words, but not his eyes, to the man seated opposite him.

"Farbod, may I present Captain John Jacobs, my partner in Starchaser Spacelines, and our ship's mage, Ronaldo Machado. Gentlemen, may I present Farbod Kianoush, CEO of Sandstorm Transit. What can I do for you, Captain?"

Machado noted that Mancuso pronounced every name with exact precision. Machado's own name had sounded so natural coming off the man's lips that it would have matched the accents of Machado's native São Paolo.

Jacobs nodded at Kianoush, changing Machado's mind about extending a hand for shaking. Machado almost did it anyway, but decided his captain needed to take lead here.

"Good to meet you, Mr. Kianoush," said Jacobs. "I do not mean to be rude, but I must ask you to excuse us. I have pressing ship business I must discuss with my partner here."

Machado saw Mancuso's eyes widen the barest fraction. The blonde woman rose from her seat and began to approach, her book abandoned on an end table behind her.

Before another word was spoken, Machado saw an emerald green deerhound phase in through the wall. *Cuthbert's familiar?* Without sparing a hint of focus, Machado called forth *Saravá* and sent the ghostly *onça* to intercept, allowing a fragment of his own attention to ride along.

When Mancuso did speak, he said, "We'll have to pick this up later, Farbod. The timing may be inopportune, but if Jacobs says it's pressing business, it is."

Kianoush nodded, made his goodbyes, and left. As he did, Machado slid more of his attention over to the familiars, but the deerhound had already left. In the swift mind speech Machado shared with *Saravá*, they quickly exchanged:

What was that about?

The Journeyman needed the tycoon found, Master.

Purpose?

Innocent, by my judgment.

Machado let the situation stand at that for the moment and returned his attention to the conversation in front of him. Kianoush had left and Jacobs was saying, "Someone's using the courier package to track us. I want to dump it, but that would violate our IIX contract."

Mancuso steepled his fingers. Machado stared at that, wondered at the sort of man who used such an obvious gesture as a conversational gambit.

"Machado," said Mancuso, "I assume you're here to tell me that the tracking magic in the package can't be disabled?"

"Hard to judge for certain without opening the package, but I don't think so. If I had designed the spell, I would—"

"Do something impressive, no doubt. Your credentials aren't in doubt here, Machado, but that doesn't mean I expect to follow all of your explanations. Send Tai Shi a copy though. She should hear about anything that affects security. For right now we'll accept as given that you two believe our options are: either accept being tracked or break Starchaser Spacelines' most valuable asset."

"Our ships and crews are our most valuable assets," said Jacobs.

"Ships and crews do us no good if no one buys passage," said Mancuso. "When all is said and done, this voyage is going to look to the press like either a vibrant business expanding into a new market or a desperate company praying a publicity stunt will keep it in the black. Dump that package and which do you think we look like?"

"PR doesn't do us any good if we don't survive."

"I saw the increased security bill that 4M has to pick up for this little trip. You can't fool me, Jacobs. You were expecting trouble."

"The last time you were aboard my ship, someone was willing to kill us all to get to you."

"So you're ready for a fight. And you seem to know fights and space travel. But tell me something, what will double the price of your share be worth if Starchaser Spacelines loses its *exclusive* IIX contract?"

Machado didn't fight the rise of his eyebrows at that question. Was the captain thinking of selling? Jacobs' hesitation answered the unspoken question.

"Not much," Jacobs finally said. "But you'd be the one buying." Jacobs smiled then, the sort of feral smile Machado remembered from barroom brawls in the occasional spaceport during the early days of his tenure with the captain. "I'm an old man. I've been expecting to die at space for decades. But you, you have big plans. Are you willing to risk those plans for one business deal?"

Machado checked the urge to smack himself in the forehead. How Jacobs could not have known the answer to that question, Machado could not have guessed.

Mancuso smiled, a smile less violent, perhaps, than Jacobs', but no less predatory.

"Captain," he said, "you have no idea what I have risked for a business deal."

"Then I guess we keep the package," said Jacobs.

"I suppose we do. But that does not mean we must be foolish about it. Machado, consider Tai Shi available to help do whatever can be done with that package to minimize our risks. And I should think Cuthbert could help as well."

"The courier works for IIX," said Jacobs. "Better to leave him out of this."

"As you like," said Mancuso, with an air of dismissal. "Stevens, check the IIX contract for a ship endangerment loophole."

"Yes, Sir," said the blonde woman, who produced a memopad out of a pocket in her suit jacket.

"Then we're done here," said Jacobs. "Machado," he added, by way of an order to follow, and the captain marched out of the suite. Machado followed, *Saravá* on his heels.

Out in the corridor, Jacobs shook his head and said, "What do you think the chances are that someone will kill him on Venus?"

"I think it's a tribute to Tai Shi that he's alive at all."

Jacobs chuckled and started off, probably for the bridge. Machado almost followed as far as his workshop, but remembered the deerhound intrusion, and turned his steps toward the Main Deck.

DONAL DUCKED BEHIND A CRENELATED ALABASTER COLUMN ON THE steps leading to the *Horizon Cusp's* space museum on the Main Deck. Between Donal and the Observation Wall, a twenty-meter-long section of bulkhead that had been rendered transparent, stood three passengers Donal had not met, all men not much older that Donal. Their clothes were expensive casual, each outfit probably costing more than Donal had spent on his single formal suit. Or even his formal robe.

But were these men executives Donal had not yet met, or assistants? They spoke in relaxed tones, laughing about a topic Donal could not overhear from his vantage point, and pointing out details in space to each other. Currently the ship passed near a tremendous golden cloud, and Donal wondered fleetingly what magical significance it might have.

One deep breath of cool air and back on topic. Donal had delivered enough packages and dealt with enough bureaucracy to know that executives and assistants required different approaches, and that neither would necessarily be more likely to offer up information to a curious stranger.

And Donal could not count on them knowing who he was. *Or maybe I should hope they know nothing about me. For every good impression they might have gotten from Mr. Mancuso, they're just as likely to have gotten a bad impression from the Romanova woman.*

And a good opinion from Mr. Mancuso might make them distrust me anyway.

If my suspicions about him have any validity...

Donal leaned back against the column. This was foolish. He was not ready to approach strangers about Mr. Mancuso. He faced too many unknowns. Every one of his professors had warned Donal, "A good magician acts when he is ready."

Of course, the unspoken corollary was that every magician occasionally falls short of the ideal.

But not Donal. Not this time.

Donal rubbed his forehead. So much to think about. Venus was still more than four days away, and the chances were good that everyone would gather at Ambrosia — the ritziest restaurant on the *Horizon Cusp* — for dinner tonight. Donal would have opportunities then to study how others reacted to Mr. Mancuso. Perhaps then he could at least figure out who would be worth talking to.

Maybe I'm not cut out for field work. Not thirty minutes into my first investigation and I already want to go back to my research.

Donal puffed out a breath and entered the museum, hoping his bearing and attempted eager expression would convince any observers that the museum had been his goal all along, even though he could tell after a single step inside that the contents had not changed since his last flight. Programmed illusions covered the history: early thaumaturgic fliers that restored man's ability to take to the air after the old airplanes failed; the disastrous attempt to take a flier outside the limits of Earth's sky; the pioneering effort to reconfigure an old submachine — *no, submarine* — to successfully carry a small crew to the moon, and the lunar 'rail' system that ran for three years before Hierophant Carnes broke the secret of space flight.

Donal was turning his attention to the interactive ship development display when Fionn drifted down through the ceiling.

"I found Donatello Mancuso in his quarters, meeting with Captain John Jacobs and Ronaldo Machado."

"About the package?"

"I believe so, but I did not risk tarrying. *Saravá* advised me to leave with haste so that none could accuse you of spying." The deerhound's emerald ears flattened for a moment, then popped back up. "The course of action they would take regarding the package seemed to be under dispute."

"Wait, they're not going to try to open the package, are they?"

"I could not determine their decision without remaining. Would you prefer that I had done so?"

"No, better to avoid accusations of spying. The captain seems the sort to take that badly." Donal turned from the display and started back out of the museum and toward the nearest bubble, Fionn by his side. "I don't like the idea that they want to go behind my back about the package though. I can't let them damage it."

Donal reached for the bubble's lever, but before he could pull it the cage arrived, carrying Magister Machado, who had a troubled crinkle around his eyes.

"Just the Journeyman I was looking for," said the Magister.

"I didn't do it," Donal said, hands coming up, drawing curious expressions from both his familiar and the heavy magician.

"Didn't do what?" asked Machado, slow emphasis on that last word.

"I haven't cast any spells since I boarded. Well, apart from a couple of false trails for the package, but those were standard procedure, strictly by the book and within my rights as a professional courier. I haven't cast anything that might threaten or work beyond the boundaries of your spells."

Machado's eyes narrowed. His lips flattened and curled in, almost disappearing as his chin pressed forward. He raised a single, pointing finger with the inevitable slowness of doom...

...then started laughing.

Deep, raucous amusement shook the mage's whole body, infecting Donal until he too chuckled.

"Why are we laughing?"

"Because..." Machado leaned his hands on his knees and caught his breath. "You don't have a year's experience since getting your Journeyman's license, but you're already so used to trouble that you can rip off a formal denial without even having done anything wrong." He reached out and clapped Donal on the shoulder, with more strength than Donal had expected.

"Come on." Machado steered Donal toward the cage. "I'll show you my workshop while you and I discuss a few matters. And on the way I'll tell you about the time I got kicked out a hotel bar in Los Angeles for setting up a spell that stripped the clothes off of everyone who had a drink in the bar. That was quite a party."

Donal held up a forestalling hand. "First, I need to know. Is the captain going to force the package open?"

"Are you kidding?" Machado smiled again. "They'd throw it into space first. Now come on."

Donal followed, but he couldn't decide if he trusted the Magister's answer.

Jacobs stormed onto the bridge. The moment the door closed behind him he noticed the silence of his bridge crew. Not just silence. Stillness.

Could be nothing. Could be sensitivity to the Old Man's anger at his 'partner's' bullshit. Then again...

"Mr. Tunold, how is my ship?"

"Steady as she goes, Sir," said Tunold from his station, facing Jacobs who still stood just inside the bridge door. "All reports show five by five."

"Current as of..."

"Five minutes ago. How's His Highness?"

"Same as ever," said Jacobs, and he shared a look with his executive officer, the same look shared by many captains and executive officers throughout naval history: V.I.P actually stood for Very Invasive Pain.

"Let me handle him. Free up your time for something more important."

"I could handle a dozen Mancusos if I had to," said Jacobs, ascending the stairs to the captain's station. "In fact, a dozen would leave me a few extras in case of ... accidents."

Jacobs settled into his chair, and tried not to think about how good it felt to get off of his feet, to let his back relax against the padding. *Stay sharp, old man.*

"Mr. Grabowski, any bogies in my sky?"

"Clear space, Sir. Nearly as far as I can see."

"Nearly isn't clear, Mister. Which is it?"

"Clear enough," said Tunold.

Suddenly that padding held no comfort for Jacobs' shoulders.

"Mr. Tunold, check on Chief Goldberg. Last time I saw him he looked harried, and I'm betting Tai Shi's the cause."

"Aye, Sir. Ms. Jefferson—"

"Face to face, Ex Oh."

Tunold looked up, irritation all over his face. Jacobs gave him only steel in return, daring his executive officer to challenge the order. Tunold hunched and relaxed his shoulders twice, then finally said, "Yes, Captain. Right away, Captain."

Jacobs gave his miniature gryphon display a quick check while he waited for Tunold to leave the bridge. No systems flashed red, always a good sign.

The moment the door closed behind Tunold, Jacobs said, "Give me details, Mr. Grabowski. What is not clear about my sky?"

"It's probably nothing, Sir."

"Mr. Grabowski, I am going to assume that you chose those words out of respect for your executive officer and as an attempt to avoid saying anything that might countermand the expressed opinion of a superior officer.

"However.

"I did not ask Mr. Tunold to evaluate the data. I asked you for a report from our scanners. And if you ever again tell me something 'is probably nothing,' I will give you a safe suit and send you out into the black to investigate it personally. Do I make myself clear?"

"Aye, Sir."

"That goes for all of you," said Jacobs taking in the whole of his bridge crew. "When I ask you for a report, I expect a complete report, as accurate as you can make it, and not omitting a detail that is 'probably nothing.' 'Probably nothing' sinks ships, ladies and gentlemen. 'Probably nothing,' gets us killed."

Jacobs let that sink in while he sat back in his chair.

"Now, Mr. Grabowski. What is this 'probably nothing' of yours?"

"For the last hour or so—"

"Mr. Grabowski, this is not a casual jaunt to the moon. We are following a route that has only been flown by military vessels, explorers, and colonists. Approximations are insufficient on this flight. I thought I made that clear in our pre-flight briefing."

Giving his beleaguered scanners officer a moment to collect himself, Jacobs turned to his pilot.

"Mr. Burke, did I make that point clear during our pre-flight briefing?"

"Aye, Sir," said Burke, face flaming red at having to throw a fellow officer under their wake. *Good man. That should never feel comfortable.*

"Ms. Jefferson?"

"Aye, Sir, but may I point out that this level of expectation is unusual for our voyages and may require time to adjust?"

"You may," said Jacobs, not hiding his smile. *That's it. Stand up for your fellows without challenging your superior. More politick than I would have been at your age.* "And I have not issued any formal reprimands. However, consider this the end of the grace period. Continue, Mr. Grabowski, and remember: precision."

"One moment, Sir." Grabowski called up his own log in his phantasmal display, but before he dug through he grabbed the handles of the scanner systems and got the distant look of a scannerman, his mind sweeping through the ship's surroundings.

As Grabowski released, Jacobs noted that he set a quick alert that would ping him if anything came within a set distance. Not as accurate as active work, but good enough to spare Grabowski attention for his log.

"It was one hour seven minutes ago that I first logged an anomaly aft of us at one-seventy-eight by one-ninety-two, distance zero point zero three seven decans, approximately ten thousand three hundred klicks. The anomaly vanished before I could attempt a clearer scan at that distance. The anomaly appeared to me as a slight shimmer, like the sun above the sea near dusk."

"Color?"

"None that I could discern. I've spotted it twice since then, with no predictable interlude between sightings. The distance is consistent, but the location varies. Full details about times and locations are in my log, Sir, and have been sent to your station."

"Professional opinion. Any guesses what that anomaly might be?"

"Unknown, Sir. I've never seen space shimmer before. Any chance this is a good thing?"

"I've never heard of a mistral wind in space." *Let me be wrong. Let this be innocent.* "Mr. Burke, anything in the Navy reports about this section of correspondences and decans that might account for this 'shimmer?'"

"Negative, Sir. Clear space was predicted for the next twelve hours."

"Mr. Grabowski, when was the last sighting?"

"Sixteen minutes ago."

"So we're due."

"Aye, Sir, as due as we get. I have attempted to pre-program a deep scan response on detection, but I'm not sure the lacuna can respond that quickly."

"Good plan and good thinking, but I suspect you're right. We'll have to take another approach." *A fool's approach, Old Man. You can't be considering this.* "Mr. Burke, raise speed one-eighth. Let's see if that distance stays consistent."

"Aye, Sir."

With that, Jacobs turned his attention to the ship's reports, first of his bridge crew and then the remaining key systems. As he did, he tried to talk himself out of a risky plan.

DONAL LAUGHED ALONGSIDE MAGISTER MACHADO AS THEY ENTERED the Magister's workshop. Donal could not decide if going drinking with the man would be fun or lead to his first prison sentence. *He never seems to get arrested though. Another perk of an advanced degree?*

Fionn followed along, chatting with *Saravá* in that language all familiars seemed to speak, but no one else could understand.

"What do familiars talk about among themselves?"

"They're still spirits, Donal." The laughter had vanished from the Magister's manner fast enough to draw Donal up to full height, unimpressive though that may have been. Machado continued, "They are part of us, but partly still of the Outside. They'll never quite see things the way we do, and they keep secrets among themselves that they will never share with us. I have my suspicions, of course, but I keep those close to my chest, out of respect for *Saravá*."

Donal almost let that statement pass with a generic sound of acknowledgment, but... "So you don't know either."

Machado laughed. "If anyone does, they've never spoken or written about it. I'd've heard. And the familiars, of course, aren't talking. But try to cultivate an air of mystery, boy. You're a magician, for *Oxalá's* sake. We have a grand and glorious tradition of looking smarter than we really are, and you better uphold your end."

"Yes, Magister," said Donal through a chuckle.

"Right," said Machado. He snapped his fingers and the door to the workshop closed, giving Donal a moment to stare with no forced awe at the complex structures of thaumaturgy woven into three separate magic circles, some of which were tied to the small alchemy lab at the back. And he also marveled with no small amount of envy at the personal library along one wall that fairly reeked of magic.

"Speaking of familiars," said the Magister. "Don't let me catch yours poking around a passenger's cabin again." He held up a hand to forestall Donal's protest. "I know. Your plan was only to find someone. But businessmen guard their secrets as tightly as we do, and your *cú sidhe* nearly overheard something it shouldn't have.

"Now." The Magister turned to face Donal square. "I want you to swear by your power that you are only aboard this ship to deliver a package. And remember, I know that deception magic is one of your specialties."

"I..." Donal tried to find a loophole while Fionn watched. But the real problem was that, with the Dagda as his witness, Donal didn't want to find a loophole. He liked Magister Machado. "I can't."

"I thought so," said the Magister with a sagely nod. "Come on." He led Donal over to his desk and eased his bulk into the overlarge roller chair, leaving a seat for Donal that was a tiny squib in comparison. "Out with it. What scheme is cooking in that overreaching mind of yours?"

"I want to find out, once and for all, whether Mr. Mancuso is just a business man making business deals, or really—"

"Shadow tyrant, ruling all humanity?" Whatever Magister Machado had been expecting Donal to say, it must not have been that. His nostrils flared even wider than his eyes. "You got caught up in that?"

"Well, you've got to admit that the man makes sharks look like prey animals. And I was there when Mr. bin Zuka dropped dead."

"You saw a spell kill him?"

"No. There was a flare of power. Fionn identified it as death magic. Then everyone scrambled and the port security mages shut me out."

"And they were right to do so," Magister Machado said with slow emphasis. "Here you're suspecting murder, but security mages on the scene never officially reported murder. If they had, the whole crew would have buzzed about it."

"So you think suicide?"

"A crazed mind shapes magic poorly."

"He seemed coherent enough during our duel." Donal couldn't help the wounded pride showing through in his voice. "Nearly killed me."

"And you said he relied entirely on the magic of disharmony, which works strongest for an unquiet mind. Death spells are a bit trickier."

Donal remembered the ease with which Li Hua slew a runner full of assailants on Mars. She needed less time than Donal had needed to summon a dust devil. But Donal saw no need to tell Magister Machado about Mars.

"I've never studied death magic."

"Nor should you." Magister Machado shook a heavy finger in Donal's face. "The way you overstretch yourself, you'd end up your own target."

"I'm getting better about that."

"Don't tempt me to make you prove it." Magister Machado drew a breath so deep his whole body seemed to inflate. He puffed it out at the ceiling, and Donal would have sworn the mage was larger than before he had drawn that breath.

"On second thought. Prove it. Don't overreach while within my demesne. And don't harass the passengers or I'll cut off your magic until you're back on Earth."

"But Venus is—"

"So don't harass anyone."

"I don't intend to, but—"

"Journeyman, you are out of your depth." Magister Machado swore in Portuguese for a moment, then continued in English. "Damn it, you're a clever kid, but there's no margin for error on this flight. Think Mancuso's doing more than he should? Report it to the Commission for Space Safety when you get back to San Francisco. I know they aren't a governing body, but all the governments listen to them and they have resources you don't even dream of."

"But what if that's too late?"

Machado snapped his hand into a fist and Donal felt a jolt through his aura, like he'd been slapped everywhere at once and now every body hair stood up.

"Ever think the reason Red Sun didn't go to the C.S.S. was that they were lying? Don't be a fool, Donal. Enjoy the flight. Sleep with your beautiful girlfriend, who, by the way, would probably not like to hear you making accusations like that. So think long and hard before you speak them aloud again to anyone."

The Magister looked sideways at Donal, and some of the fire left his tone. "And keep your head down. Goldberg already told me he thinks the Romanov has it in for you."

"She might," said Donal, although his thoughts were on Li Hua. If he brought a complaint to the C.S.S. they might start a formal investigation, and Donal doubted his name could be kept out of it. "The Romanovs didn't like a package I delivered on the moon. They blamed the messenger."

"More reason for you to avoid mixing potions you don't need to drink."

"He's putting me through grad school. Is that something I can accept if he turns out to be more than a businessman?"

"Foundation concerns?"

Machado sounded honestly surprised, as though Donal had given the Magister an angle he hadn't considered by reminding him of one of the axioms of magic: taint the foundation and you taint the results. The Brazilian magician ran the back of his hand across his chins, then shook his head.

"Even if he is. The factors balance neutral because you saved his life. Accepting the repayment of a debt does not create debt."

Donal hoped that was true. He wanted it to be, but he couldn't shake the idea that Mr. Mancuso would consider this more than simple repayment. He would expect a return on his investment.

But how do I explain that to Magister Machado?

"Now go on," said the ship's mage, "and do something that won't make me come down on you. I don't enjoy it, and I have real work to get back to."

Donal lingered a moment longer, but at seeing an impatient eyebrow raise on the Magister's face, Donal gestured for Fionn, said his goodbyes, and headed toward the door. But before he could bring himself to open it he turned back to the Magister, who scribbled something in his zephyrpad with his finger.

"Magister?"

"What?" said Machado, with a note of warning clear in his voice.

"What was that spell you cast?" Donal held up an empty hand and closed it.

"You've never seen the Jenkins Flash? It's the entire basis for thaumaboxing." When Donal shook his head, Magister Machado continued. "I shouldn't be surprised. Can't have the undergrads getting caught up in fight games." He shook his head. "Don't get your hopes up. It's not good for much more than what I did with it, not without the spells setting up the thaumaboxing ring."

He must have seen the curiosity burning in Donal's eye, because the Magister pursed his lips in thought. "Tell you what. If we make it all the way to Venus without you causing any trouble, I'll teach you how it works."

"I'll do what I can," said Donal, and with that he left the workshop, slow steps carrying him down the echoing, narrow corridor the bubble. After he pulled the lever to call the bubble, he turned to his *cú sidhe*.

"What do you think, Fionn?"

"I am acquainted with similar techniques. They rely on skills outside your chosen areas of focus."

"No, I mean about the rest of it."

"Ronaldo Machado raises good points. Perhaps this burden can pass from you."

"I don't know. Mr. Mancuso always puts me in mind of the Fae. No offense, but my grandmother always said that debts to the Fae weren't like debts to other people: they always dug deeper, reached further, and lasted longer than any mortal human being had a right to expect."

If the fae deerhound took offense it gave no sign. "So what is our next course of action?"

"Let's go back to the room." Donal ran his hands over his face, then through his short, black hair. "I need time to think. Figure some things out."

9

"Captain," said Jefferson from the communications station, "Mr. Tunold reports that he is on his way back."

"Excellent. Have him meet me in my office." Jacobs continued giving orders as he descended the stairs from his station. "Helm, hold current speed for another half-hour. Let's see how our shimmer responds. Scanners, I expect as much attention on the rest of space as on likely locations for the shimmer's next appearance. Never assume it isn't a distraction. Comm, route any important links through my office. I'll be back soon."

Nerves set Jacobs' pace faster than usual down the sloping passageway to his office on Crew Deck One. He was not in the Navy anymore, had not been for decades. He had no right to order men into harm's way.

Jacobs knew the ethical choice. But Jacobs also knew the ethical choice and the best choice for survival did not always coincide.

Jacobs let himself into his office, and poured two tumblers of Brigid's Own Irish Whiskey. He set one on his desk in front of a visitor's chair, and swirled the other gently in his hand as he took his seat.

He would not sip. Not yet. But he took some comfort in having the drink ready.

No more than a minute passed before a frame-rattling knock announced the arrival of his executive officer. From another man that pounding might have been a sign of anger, but Tunold only knew one way to knock.

"Come in, Kris, before you knock it off its hinges."

Tunold entered and began speaking on his way to his chair. "You were right. Tai Shi's been riding Goldberg about how security needs to be handled when we land. As though we don't have days to hammer out the details. The chief was almost ready to try to throw her in the brig."

"I'd have liked to have seen that. She may be a caster, but I've seen him take down casters before. If only..."

"If only it wouldn't have been horrible for passenger morale." Tunold noticed his glass, then looked at it more directly, then slid his eyes back to take in his captain.

"You knew. That's why you sent me down in person instead of talking on the link."

"Partially," said Jacobs with an acknowledging incline of his head. He waited for Tunold to pick up his glass and take a drink — only downing half of it. *Improvement, at least. Better than slugging the whole glass.*

"However. Your 'probably nothing' looks to me like a ship that's somehow evading our scanners."

Jacobs sipped his honeyed whiskey, holding it on his tongue long enough for the sweet scent to add depth to the taste. In doing so, he gave Tunold time to digest Jacobs' meaning, which led to the unfortunate side effect of Tunold slamming down the rest of his whiskey.

Jacobs shook his head, a bare movement that was probably lost on the younger man.

"That's right," Jacobs continued. "It might be a ship, but from here we can't be certain. But we damn well need certainty, because if that *is* a ship, the chances that its intentions are honorable are about as good as the chances of Mancuso donating everything he has to charity and joining a monastery."

"We don't have a proper scout ship. You want to let Mash do his projection thing?"

"The last time a magician projected off of this ship he accidentally brought two zuglodons down on us. No, we need to send someone in the hippogriff shuttle to check it out and see if proximity gets us any more information." Jacobs looked at his whiskey, swirling in his tumbler. "Ethically I should not ask anyone to take this risk if I'm not ready to take it myself—"

"Not going to happen," Tunold said in a tone of absolute certainty that rankled Jacobs' contrary side. "Obviously a command level officer needs to lead this mission, so I'll go. I'll take—"

"But," said Jacobs, loudly enough to silence his angry bear of an executive officer. "Ethics also allow me to take volunteers for the job, and on this ship volunteers are rarely in short supply."

Jacobs turned his gaze on Tunold, matching the younger man's passion with some fury of his own.

"So you're volunteering? Well, *maybe* I'll let you go, and maybe I won't. I agree that command needs to be represented in this little venture, and I agree that my ex oh should go in my place. But does that mean you?"

Tunold's jaw jutted far enough forward that his narrowed eyes looked as much like a function of angle as of suspicion. "What do you mean?"

"I mean I need an ex oh who treats me like *the* Old Man, not *an* old man. Limiting the information my crew gives me? I won't have it. Not on my ship. So you need to decide right now if you're spacer enough to handle serving under my command."

"It's not that I don't trust you, John." Tunold looked away, an action so unlike him that surprise tried to pale Jacobs' skin. "Dr. Ramirez caught me before takeoff. He's worried about you. Zoltan jumping ship, Mancuso your new partner, now this flight.

"You're the oldest helioship captain still flying. He's worried about the stress and your heart."

"My heart's as strong as anyone on this ship, and stronger than most."

"He begged me to do as much for you as I could. Take all the pressure off you I could."

Jacobs grimaced and shook his head. "How long have you known me now, Kris?"

"Hell, I don't know," said Tunold with a wave of his hand. "A long time."

"Which do you think is better for me? Sitting back and letting someone else do my job, or digging in and getting my hands dirty?"

"He's the doctor, John. Retirement's no good if you don't live to see it."

"Enough!" Jacobs slammed his fist down on the oak desk. "Ramirez doesn't command this ship. I do. And you don't report to him, you report to me. So make the call. Are you my ex oh or do you quit?"

Tunold rubbed his eyes with those great paws of his.

He has to think about this?

Finally, Tunold said, "John, I'd hate to see you die if I could stop it, but my guess is you'd rather die commanding from the big chair than live watching with the passengers while your crew struggles."

"Too goddamn right."

Tunold breathed out a chuckle. "How are you going to survive retirement?"

"I'll deal with that after I survive this voyage."

"Fair enough," said Tunold in that growling tone that meant he only conceded a point for purposes of the current discussion. How many times had Jacobs heard that tone over the years? So many that hearing it now almost made him smile. But Tunold wasn't done talking. "So I'm in. And, Captain, I formally apologize for exceeding my authority."

"Accepted. Now I need you and Cromartie to take that shuttle and check out this bogey. Grabowski can feed you aggregate coordinates and likely locations."

"Cromartie?"

"I can't imagine him not volunteering, and the expedition could use a magician." Jacobs tossed down the rest of his whiskey. "Besides, would you want to risk taking Mash off this ship?"

"As if he'd volunteer to leave his comfy bunk," said Tunold with a laugh. Then the two men put their heads together and planned a scouting expedition.

———

BACK IN HIS SUITE, DONAL SAT CROSS-LEGGED ON THE CARPETING, DEEP within a circle of his own thoughts. Eyes closed, his body moved only to the rhythm of breaths so deep they fully expanded his lungs and diaphragm. Each single breath took perhaps a minute to complete from the moment the inhalation began to the moment the exhalation completed.

But Donal's mind spared no attention for these details. The body would attend to them without conscious intervention. Donal's mind had spent time it had not tracked divesting itself of speculations, conclusions, hopes, fears, concerns, impulses, and finally details, each thought joining the others to whirl about the circle in which Donal sat. Nothing escaped him, but nothing troubled him. Not just then.

Absent of thought, Donal hung in a suspended moment of perfect peace. Perfect ... until he felt the gentle touch of his familiar's mind.

"Master, Ricardo Montenegro knocks upon your door. I have informed him that you meditate, but he feels his need is sufficient to interrupt."

Returning took time, but how much time the effort required, Donal could never tell. He could tell only that his thoughts seeped back into his mind like rolling fog, then he became aware of the tingle of air on his scalp, the smell of dragon's blood incense in his nose, the sensation of his shirt on his shoulders and chest, the weight of his arms as they moved to stretch above his head, the plush comfort of the carpeting underneath him, and finally the prickling tingle of his sleeping legs.

"Just a moment," Donal called to the knock, a reflexive response that made him realize he could hear the world around him again. He rolled onto his back, then side to side to help straighten his legs, and finally used his hands to help get his feet under him.

He stood by bracing himself on the coffee table as his legs agreed to hold his weight. To Fionn, he said, "Is Mr. Montenegro carrying any enchantments?"

"One, on a tie tack, that would defend against mental intrusions or manipulations."

On his way to the door, Donal's gait had to have looked as awkward as it felt, his feet and thighs still protesting as though they properly belonged to another body. At last he managed to get the door open to see Ricardo Montenegro, a middle-aged gentleman whose coloring and bone structure told of heritage somewhere south of the United North American States. His black hair had grayed at the temples, but his tailored suit looked as crisp and new as though it had just been sewn.

"There you are, Cuthbert. I was starting to wonder if your familiar delivered my message."

"Deep meditation..." Donal almost explained about states of mind, but remembered Magister Machado's advice about an 'air of mystery.' *Not a complete fabrication,* thought Donal. *Just the proper spin doctoring.* "...involves direct communication with primal forces. Even a critical interruption wouldn't excuse a rude exit on my part."

Donal felt his right knee begin to shake with the need to move more blood. "What can I do for you, Mr. Montenegro?"

"May I come in? I have an important matter to discuss with you before dinner."

"Of course," said Donal, moving to one side and gesturing for the man to enter. "But I should make clear that I'm not allowed to take on side contracts while out on delivery."

"I don't need your magic," said Mr. Montenegro, who sat in one of the two recliners and made a show of surveying the room before bringing his eyes back to Donal.

Donal saw expectation there, but as he followed into the main room after closing the door, he could not guess what the man wanted.

That expectation hung in the air between the two men until Fionn muttered, in tones only Donal could hear, "He's waiting for you to offer him a drink."

"Oh!" said Donal. "I'm sorry. Can I get you anything?"

"No, thank you," said Mr. Montenegro, but Donal noted that the formality had relaxed the man a little. He sat back more casually, but continued speaking as Donal approached to sit in the other recliner. "I do not intend to take much of your time, but there is something I must know."

Again silence filled with expectation. But Donal didn't need Fionn's prompting this time. "What's that?"

"Why did you choose to save Mancuso's life?"

"Are you suggesting I should have let Mr. bin Zuka murder him?"

"I'm not suggesting anything. I'm asking. I know that Red Sun gave you the hard sell." He must have seen Donal's eyes widen, because he raised a forestalling hand. "I won't tell you how I know, but I will tell you that I am not allied with Red Sun.

"You could have left the matter to ship's security. You could have taken a deal from Red Sun. Instead of doing either, you risked your life fighting a duel to save Mancuso. I just want to know why."

"Why does it matter? Isn't all life worth saving?"

Mr. Montenegro raised one eyebrow. The movement required only the smallest fraction of a millimeter, and yet Donal felt that the man had just read, assessed and evaluated him.

"I suppose a certain amount of quid pro quo is in order. I have an opportunity to do business with the man, which means I have dug further into his life and history than you could probably imagine." Those dark brown eyes smiled now, but the smile never spread to the rest of his face. "Oh, I assure you, he has done the same to me. It is the life we have chosen.

"While my research indicates that Mancuso is a man to inspire many responses, noble sacrifice is not on the list. Which makes you an anomaly. You weren't on his payroll. You aren't in a line of work that demands or rewards unnecessary risks. Your goals, so far as I can tell, involve lab work and research."

Mr. Montenegro shook his head, a quick, irritated movement as though bothered by the buzz of a mosquito.

"You had no reason to care. But you risked your life to save his. Why?"

"Maybe I knew I'd be rewarded with money for grad school."

"If that were the reason, you wouldn't have continued courier work. You'd have gotten a living stipend to tide you over until school started. Pocket change to a man like Mancuso, and probably a write-off of some sort."

Am I the only one who didn't think of that? "Maybe it was just the right thing to do."

"Maybe. Is that the reason you're giving?"

"I'll tell you the truth, if it matters so much. But before I do, you have to answer a question for me. And I want the truth too."

"I'm not taking off my protection."

"Put it in writing and I'll verify the truth by magic, then destroy the entry."

"There is no need. My research tells me you are honorable enough, for a magician. So I'll tell you the truth if you'll swear it won't leave this room. In return, I'll keep whatever truth you tell me to myself. Are we agreed?"

They shook hands.

"Mr. Mancuso has been accumulating a lot of power," said Donal. "What do you think his ultimate goal is?"

"That is your secret question?" Mr. Montenegro laughed, a sudden but rolling sound that continued for a moment before drifting away. "Very well. Mr. Mancuso's ambition does not have limits. He wants it all, and when he gets it he'll look for ways to gain more. He's the sort of man who will bankroll exploration and colonization just to create new markets to conquer."

Donal thought about that, and Mr. Montenegro laughed again. "Do you need further elaboration?"

"No…"

"Then please be so kind as to answer my question: why did you save his life?"

"Because even if everything Mr. bin Zuka said about him was true, murder wasn't the answer. Magic teaches us that whatever Mr. bin Zuka might have hoped to accomplish, tainting the process would taint the results."

Mr. Montenegro rubbed at an old scar on the inside of his left wrist.

"So despite never having fought a duel before, you challenged bin Zuka to a duel to the death to save a man's life, over a point of philosophy?"

"It was the right thing to do."

Mr. Montenegro played with his tie tack for a moment, staring out the porthole at the passing space. Finally he said in a distant voice, "I will never understand magicians." He stood, an abrupt movement that had Donal halfway into a defensive gesture before he could stop himself. Mr. Montenegro said, "But I have taken enough of your time, and you have given me much to consider. Thank you very much. I will see you at dinner."

Mr. Montenegro let himself out and Donal turned a puzzled look on his *cú sidhe*. Fionn lay its head on its crossed paws. Donal decided that Fionn didn't know what to make of the man either.

10

Tunold settled into the pilot station of the Hippogriff shuttle.
The station felt too short for a man his height. His knees nearly
bumped on the bottom of the console. And the chair felt too narrow,
even though it had space enough for someone half-again the skinny
ex oh's breadth.

But then, maybe the problem was that this shuttle was entirely
insufficient to its assigned task, and Tunold knew it. Not enough
acceleration. Not precise enough scanners. No defenses built in, only
whatever Cromartie could bring to bear, and the man was only an
Initiate.

Doesn't mean this is a suicide run. Just have to be careful, Kris.

Tunold could hear Cromartie now, coming into the shuttle and
setting up over by the station that handled both scanners and communications. Tunold glanced back at him, and felt a moment of camaraderie. Cromartie had to have felt as crowded as Tunold: they were
both of a height, and Cromartie's shoulders were broader with muscle.

"I've got the extra supplies," said Cromartie, holding up a small
pouch that probably had eye of newt and toe of frog, or whatever the
hell else it was that alchemists put into their brews. "If we're out long

enough to stress the bindings, I should be able to smooth things over and keep us in good running shape."

"So you can handle the basic engineering for a ship this size?"

Tunold waited until Cromartie nodded before asking his next questions, even if that nod came with a furrowed brow.

"What about scanners? Ever handle scanners before?" Like the communications station, the controls of the shuttle seemed simple next to those of the *Horizon Cusp*, but Tunold knew they contained subtleties that they might need for this mission. "I can give you a quick rundown on the basics."

"I'm fully rated with runabouts, shuttles, and airborne craft." Cromartie's face split in a smile. "Some of us like to get out of the lab once in a while."

"Will your magic be any help if we run into trouble?"

"Depends on the trouble, but I *did* help fight off those zuglodons. I know what I'm doing, Ex Oh."

"All right, Mr. Cromartie. I'm not trying to ruffle feathers. I just needed to know you're ready for this."

"Ready as you are, Sir."

"Fair enough." Tunold ran through the pre-flight sequence, and transferred the planned route from his memopad into the navigation system. If all went according to plan they would sweep out in a broad arc that would carry them past the four likeliest locations for the shimmer, see whatever there was to see, and get back to the ship without running into any problems.

I should be so lucky.

All the pre-flight checks from both stations came up clean. Tunold ran through final details with the bridge, then spread the hippogriff's wings, lifted off from the nest, and soared out into the not-quite-black of space.

Immediately Tunold felt claustrophobic. From the bridge on the *Horizon Cusp* he could have seen every direction except straight down, but the bridge of the shuttle sat in the hippogriff's chest. A forward view only, maybe one hundred sixty degrees. He had a good angle to see relative down in front of the ship, but his view of relative up was impeded by the throat and head of the hippogriff.

Tunold's eyes kept flitting from the space ahead of him to his small phantasmal display of the sphere of space about the ship, fed to his station from the scanners.

Behind him, he could hear Cromartie give the final exit report. "*Horizon Cusp*, this is the mule. We are away and beginning sweep. Will report as needed."

Tunold waited until the *Horizon Cusp* signed off, then said, "Mule?"

"We're in a shuttle shaped like a hippogriff that flies out of a gryphon's nest. Figure that means mixed parentage, and probably an inability to breed." Cromartie waited until Tunold glanced back at him before finishing, "Besides, we needed a code name."

Tunold shook his head and went back to flying. He needed to spend more time flying the shuttle once the *Horizon Cusp* was his ship. Hopping up and down to the docks didn't draw attention to the slight starboard pull of the controls or the sluggish updating of the navigation elementals.

"You better check the shuttle over when we get back," he said. "I think the nav binding has a problem."

"I checked the bindings before we left. They're fine."

"It's almost a half-second too slow."

"That's not the binding, that's the compulsion. It must be... Wait, do you actually want the details?"

"No, I want the damn thing to work."

"Right." Cromartie got quiet, and when Tunold glanced over his shoulder, he could see the Initiate finish a quick probe through the scanners, then dig into the pouch for ... something small. Tunold turned his attention back to his flying, but could hear Cromartie mumbling something that didn't sound like English.

The Initiate hopped out of his seat and threw a handful of reddish gray powder onto the navigation display and barked out orders in some harsh, guttural language. Before Tunold could say anything, Cromartie was back in his seat, checking the scanners.

Tunold checked the nav and sure enough, its response was quick and clear.

"The helm pulls a little to starboard too," said Tunold.

"Deal with it, Ex Oh. I only brought so much, and we may have greater need later."

Tunold raised the speed to three-quarters. They were as ready as they were going to get.

———

Jacobs trudged up the stairs to his perch above the bridge, his legs bone weary from the long, stressful shift, but his back straight and his head high. A man might grow exhausted, but a captain had to stay strong for his crew. Much as he might have wished to settle down to dinner in the crew mess with his officers, he knew that was impossible.

Jacobs stood atop his perch, looking aft through the transparent section of the enchanted ceramic hull at the black of space and the swath of royal green in the distance. Somewhere out there two of his men risked their lives for his crew. Jacobs could do nothing less than stand ready to save them if needed.

And abandon them if the safety of the ship left him no choice. A small part of him knew that too, though most of him pretended otherwise.

"How is our prodigal?" he said.

"They've chosen the call sign 'mule,' Sir. They're about two minutes from the predicted trouble zone." Grabowski stopped talking as though he considered his report complete.

Jacobs shook his head. "Mr. Grabowski, when I told you to keep an eye on the shuttle, what else did I tell you?"

"Space clear within predicted parameters in all other directions," Grabowski said with the speed of the guilty. "And no recent sighting of the anomaly, Captain."

"Much better. Ms. Jefferson, please ask the mess to send my food here, then contact Duran and Ketterman, and begin dinner rotations."

Another concession to budgets, thought Jacobs. *Instead of three full rotations for each station, I'm stuck with a dozen floaters. If we ever get a flight longer than a week...*

"Captain."

Jacobs looked past his grousing to see Kelly and his perfect posture at the foot of his stairs. Even now the man's at-ease pose looked textbook perfect, down to the angles of his elbows. The hands behind his back probably didn't waver.

"Yes, Mr. Kelly?"

"Sir, you are expected in the main dining room of Ambrosia in two minutes."

"Much as I love dining with the passengers," Jacobs said, irony dripping through his words, "I have two men risking their lives for this ship. I'm right where I need to be."

"Shall I inform Ms. Stevens that you are delayed by a ship emergency?"

Jacobs knew that tone. He hated that tone. Kelly was not yet thirty years old, probably a third Jacobs' own age, so how did he manage to master guilty expectation in so few years?

Perhaps it was a yeoman's job requirement, the power to make strong, experienced captains feel the urge to squirm.

Worse, Jacobs knew Kelly had chosen the perfect words to make his meaning clear. The man's diction was as precise as his posture. 'Delayed by ship emergency,' the exact phrase in the Starchaser Spacelines charter that enumerated the only circumstance under which a ship captain was excused from dining with the paying passengers. The fact that the chief paying passenger on this cruise happened to now be a partner in the company did not remove Jacobs' obligation to the remaining passengers.

Jacobs could not remain on the bridge without formally announcing their situation as an emergency, which meant frightening the passengers, going to threat rotation, and a lot of other unnecessary bother for his crew.

And all because Mancuso had two assistants who did their jobs as well as Kelly did his.

"Fine," said Jacobs with a sigh. "I'll head down as soon as I've made a brief stop by my office."

Kelly brought his right hand around, holding up one of Jacobs' tumblers. "Brigid's Own, the twenty-one year old, two fingers, neat."

Jacobs smiled as he descended the stairs and took the glass from the waiting yeoman. "To your health, Mr. Kelly." Jacobs drank down the whiskey, not in a gulp but in a slow steady trickle. Not as good as savoring it would have been, but time pressed. He handed the glass with a nod of thanks.

To the rest of the crew he said. "Continue meal rotations as normal with one exception: Mr. Burke, you have the bridge until I return."

"Captain," said Ms. Jefferson, "on behalf of the others, I would like to formally request that we remain on watch until the mule returns. We mean no disrespect to the relief staff, but—"

"I understand." Jacobs casually scribbled in his notepad that the bridge crew had chosen Jefferson to speak for them. That sort of sign indicated leadership potential. Perhaps he would have her watch the bridge next time and find out how she handled it.

"You may delay meal rotations up to two hours. After that, you'll all have been on shift too long to be sharp." Jacobs started on his way, saying over his shoulder as he went, "Keep an eye on my ship."

He left the bridge to a chorus of "ayes," and went to face a fate worse than pirates: socializing with executives.

Donal stood outside Ambrosia, the *Horizon Cusp's* fanciest restaurant, with its three large dining rooms and Greek decorating scheme. Unable to decide how he should dress when he did not know if he would be dining alone, at a large table with a selection of V.I.P.'s, or perhaps even at a table-for-two with Li Hua, Donal had changed outfits three times before settling.

As he stood with Fionn under the pseudo-starlit sky of the Main Deck, the vague hints of sea air in his nostrils, Donal wore a midnight blue silk shirt with ivory buttons up the front and at the cuffs. His slacks were black, an alchemical blend that hung like wool and breathed like cotton. He wore his best black loafers, the only shoes he always kept polished, though maintaining their shine was a small piece of thaumaturgy. One of the benefits of his chosen art.

Fionn had circled three times, back in the room, before declaring Donal fit for any of the possible dinner combinations they foresaw. But Donal wondered if his familiar had not been entirely certain. The fae deerhound kept sniffing at the loafers, as though unhappy about the choice, or perhaps disagreeing about the socks. But the socks were black, if thin, and Donal could think of no reason they might prove a problem.

But before Donal entered the restaurant, he had one more thing to do, loathe as he felt to do it.

"Fionn, I think you better return to your base for now."

"While I agree that you are unlikely to suffer physical violence, I think it better if I remain. You may need assistance dissecting the verbal sparring later."

"True, but you saw how paranoid the executives got about having a magician around, and after Magister Machado's warning…"

"I disagree with this decision, but if you wish, Master, I shall return to the pendant."

Donal felt his stomach pucker at the formal words from Fionn. Fionn only reverted to such terms and phrases when it considered the situation important. But Donal felt he had to stick to his guns. "I'll call you back the second I expect trouble."

"Better to do so the second before you expect trouble." And then Fionn twisted its words so that only Donal could understand them, even though Donal could spot no observers. "Remember our field work practice, and maintain your guard. This may appear a simple meal, but you enter a den of vipers."

Donal was saved from having to reply by Fionn's conversion into a beam of emerald light that flowed into the small silver faun pendant around Donal's neck. Donal checked to make sure the pendant remained tucked into his shirt, steadied himself with a deep breath, and entered Ambrosia.

The door seemed to disappear as it closed behind Donal, and just like that he found himself standing atop Mount Olympus. A marvelous network of illusions provided a breathtaking scene. From the peak of Mount Olympus, Donal could see ships at sail on gentle seas, ancient Greek towns at ease by firelight far below, and even shepherds tending their flocks on distant hillsides. The air felt fresh as a warm summer evening, carrying the slightest hints of salt, and earth, and grass.

A tiny red speck among the faint stars above marked the position of the *Horizon Cusp*, relative to Earth.

A *maître d'* dressed in the robe and tunic of a simple shepherd — if a simple shepherd ever had his robe and tunic cleaned and pressed — approached Donal, thumped his crook, and said, "Donal Cuthbert, I believe?" No sooner did Donal nod than the *maître d'* said, "Mister Mancuso apologizes for not inviting you to join his table, but business concerns make that impossible this evening."

"That's fine. I'll sit wherever."

"Miss Stevens and Mister Davis request that you join their table, should you feel so inclined."

"They're not dining with Mr. Mancuso?"

The "obviously not" look the *maître d'* gave Donal made heat rise in his neck, but the man's continued silence made clear that he waited for an answer.

"Certainly, I'd be happy for the company."

The *maître d'* led Donal across the grassy apex of Mount Olympus, between tables and beautifully rendered statues of Greek gods. Donal half expected Apollo to strum his lyre, or Aphrodite to offer a flirtatious wink.

Only a few tables were actually in use. The captain's table in the center, of course, where Captain Jacobs sat at the head and other chairs were occupied by Mr. Mancuso, Mr. Montenegro, Ms. Romanova, Mr. Saito, and a Martian-Middle Eastern man Donal had not yet met. Given that the table could have sat twelve, Donal wondered why only half the seats were filled.

A ring of smaller tables surrounding the executives had two diners each, probably support personnel for the various executives. Donal wondered why they did not mix. Surely business matters among them were not so strained that the support staff could not even dine together.

At a table behind the captain sat Chief Goldberg and a half-dozen members of the ship's watch, apparently there to eat, though Donal had seen the crew mess on a previous voyage.

Magister Machado also sat at that table, the only magician in the room apart from Donal. The Magister gave Donal a smile and a nod, which Donal returned while feeling grateful that he had dismissed Fionn. He would hate to have the ship's mage misunderstand the presence of Donal's familiar during a simple meal.

Moving among the tables were the wait staff, clad and enchanted to resemble satyrs and nymphs, albeit dressed to convey elegant beauty rather than lasciviousness.

The *maître d'* dropped Donal off at his table and left, summoned by a nymph to tend to some small problem. Donal looked at his dinner companions, dressed in something apart from business suits for the first time in his experience. Mr. Davis wore a cashmere sweater over an olive green shirt and chocolate brown slacks, while Ms. Stevens wore a sky blue dress, conservative cut with a high neck and long sleeves, but flattering in how it hung.

"Thank you for inviting me," said Donal as he sat. He glanced about as subtly as he could, but he saw no sign of Li Hua.

"If you're looking for Li Hua," said Ms. Stevens, "she's dining with the other security executives."

"I knew they wouldn't follow the no-bodyguards rule," said Mr. Davis.

"Well to be fair," said Ms. Stevens, "Li Hua can pull double-duty. They'd have felt at a disadvantage if they didn't bring help of their own."

"I didn't see any other magicians," said Donal.

"Nothing like that," said Ms. Stevens. "They couldn't go that far. But each of the other companies suddenly happened to have a security executive with an ops track record."

"Ops?" said Donal, feeling almost as far behind this conversation as he might have if Mr. Mancuso had been leading it. Perhaps they picked up the ability by osmosis.

"Field operations," said Mr. Davis. "They all have combat experience."

Ms. Stevens leaned forward a little. "They're still a step behind. Rob and I both have combat experience. It just doesn't show up on our records."

Donal casually put both hands on the table in the universally accepted not-casting gesture, a reflexive show of peaceful intentions. "So you're expecting trouble?"

"Officially?" said Ms. Stevens. "No."

"Unofficially?" said Mr. Davis. "Always."

"Give me a wider read, damn it," said Tunold staring more at his three-dimensional display of the space around the shuttle than out the front viewport. They were ten minutes out from the *Horizon Cusp* and entering the hunting grounds proper. "I'm flying half-blind here."

"I'm getting you reads as fast as I can," said Cromartie, irritation all through his tone. "This lacuna's pulling double duty. The shuttle's not designed for this sort of thing, you know."

"Well we'll be flying it to Davy Jones if this shimmer gets a jump on us."

"Davy Jones? Really?"

Tunold spared a glare over his shoulder. At least Cromartie kept hard at his work as he groused. Still...

"Navy traditions didn't stop when we left the seas, Mister."

"Where's his locker these days, then? Does it orbit any given planet? Or does it fly a long cycle like a comet."

Tunold cursed under his breath. He knew there was no requirement for commercial spacers to have ever served in the Navy, but damn it, the ones that didn't had no sense of history.

"Just find me the damn shimmer before it drops on top of us."

"Aye aye, Sir. And if it's the Dutchman, we'll lay a couple of broadsides agin' her timbers before she knows we're here."

"There!" Tunold snapped the word out and Cromartie cut off his laughter mid-breath. But that was merely a side benefit. Tunold had seen it. Just for a moment, true, but for long enough for him to jab that spot in his display, sending the data immediately back to Cromartie at the scanners.

"Got it," said Cromartie. "Ten minutes at best speed."

"We'll take twelve then. I don't want it to know what we can do." Tunold spared a glance and was gratified to see Cromartie hard at work, analyzing the scant data as best he could. "Any idea what that was?"

"Not ... yet. I've got a rough idea of the size, maybe two-thirds the size of the *Horizon Cusp*..."

Cromartie trailed off and Tunold let him, angling for a smooth approach while letting the magician work his magic.

"I can't get anything else right now. As far as the lacuna is concerned, there was something odd about a section of space for an instant, and then it was fine again."

"No memory to search?"

"None that would help. They don't think in our terms."

"Then I guess we'll have to go find out firsthand. Better strap in. The ride might get bumpy."

Tunold pushed the speed toward eighty percent of capacity and wished he had a weapon trigger to ease the itch in his fingers.

No matter how smart someone may be on land, mused Jacobs, *in space one landlubber is just like another.*

It didn't matter that the five people at his table wore jewelry worth at least the cost of a small helioship or that their tailored finery looked equally expensive. As though their clothes might give them a negotiating edge.

They all asked the same questions when they sat at the captain's table. "How long have you been at space?" At least this crowd knew enough not to say "in" space, which would have suggested that they were floating free outside a ship. But still, if they had bothered to read their pre-flight brochures, they would have already known the answer to that question, as well as how long the *Horizon Cusp* had been in service, what sort of engine it used, and whether or not it was armed.

Jacobs never understood why anyone asked that last one. Surely everyone had to know that the Navy took a dim view of arming civilian ships.

But it was the dreaded pirate question that Jacobs had been hoping to evade tonight, especially since that shimmer behind them might just turn out to be a ship. But no sooner had the wine been poured and the appetizers served — seasoned calamari with Martian clams to go with the Greco di Tufo — than Kianoush had to ask, "How often are pirates a problem?"

Kianoush had asked not as a curiosity, but with the intent eyes of someone considering the question as part of some deeper calculation. This was unlike Mancuso, Romanova, Montenegro, and Saiko, who all seemed to consider such questions a part of the small talk portion of their dinner conversation. Perhaps even an attempt to include their host before they moved on to more weighty matters.

But Kianoush stood out in another way as well. He alone did not dress as though announcing his status to the world around him. He wore a simple reddish brown sweater with darker brown slacks, the sort of clothes that might have come from a department store, even if his looked hand sewn.

So Jacobs paused before giving his pat answer to the pirate question, sipping his Greco di Tufo and considering the man who asked. The pause made Mancuso's eyebrows rise, perhaps remembering the pat answer Jacobs had given when he asked a similar question.

Similar, but not quite the same. Mancuso had asked if Jacobs had ever faced pirates. Kianoush's question assumed that piracy was a problem.

"Pirates are a rare problem for a passenger liner at space. Even when a ship's route is known, the vagaries of flight can make interception difficult and time consuming. Further, the crews tend to be larger than cargo vessels carry, and people are more likely to fight to protect their personal possessions than for a company's products."

Zoltan would have wanted Jacobs to apologize for any inadvertent offense given at this point, since these people were quite likely the sort to employ cargo vessels with crews that did not fight hard for their wares. But Zoltan was gone, and Jacobs felt he had said nothing that merited an apology.

"No need to take Farbod's question so seriously," said Romanova in an offhand manner as she studied her wine. "He just wants to sound interested in your business."

"Easy to say for someone whose business is dock-bound," said Kianoush. "But those of us with ships must keep abreast of new developments. Sandstorm Transit has not ventured into passenger travel, and I wanted to know what I might deal with if I decide we should."

"Fewer pirates," said Jacobs, "but on the other hand a shipping container never complains about the facilities."

Everyone laughed, so Jacobs smiled and pretended he had been joking. Mancuso began to steer the conversation, then, to discussions of a family named Klemperer. Jacobs knew the Klemperers had provided major private funding for the colony on Venus, or at least the portion that had not been subsidized by Earth governments. But two minutes into the conversation he had figured out that Mancuso had had problems in the past with one Felix Klemperer.

But that was nothing compared to the problems at the table.

"Wait," said Donal. "What sort of trouble are you expecting?"

"Well, the Romanov Group and Sandstorm Transit have been

fighting for years over rates," said Ms. Stevens, gesturing for a waiter and ordering a vegetable platter and a Morgan '23 sauvignon blanc for the table. "But honestly, there was bad blood between them before that."

"Didn't old Rodion try to expand to the Mars docks a few years back?" asked Davis.

"Yes, and the Kianoush family was instrumental in blocking him, ostensibly in support of local work for local workers."

"But Mars has always tried to fight off-world businesses, hasn't it?" asked Donal, wishing he could take notes.

"They used to nod to it, but it became the rallying cry around the time the Romanovs attempted expansion. Gave us fits until we started hiring Mars locals for upper executive positions."

"We are a truly interplanetary company," said Mr. Davis with a smile that Donal decided had to have been companionable humor. It didn't look plastic enough for a marketing gimmick, plus Ms. Stevens gave him a droll eyebrow.

The waiter returned with the vegetable platter, which included the obvious things like carrots and olives, and more obscure Earth treats like sliced oca, bright green romanesco, and peeled nopales. But the selection also included Martian orange cucumbers (stiffer than their conventional cousins, and a touch spicy) and celery (much like its Earth cousin, but twice as juicy), and the only vegetable unique to Luna to date: dadan, which grew in crisp pale blue spines and tasted to Donal almost like a heavy mustard.

As the waiter identified everything on the plate, a second waiter poured the first glasses of wine and left the bottle in the middle of the table.

When the waiters left, Mr. Davis picked up as though there had been no pause. "But really," he said as he sniffed at a dadan spine, "that's nothing compared to the trouble between Saito and Montenegro."

"They're just competing for research facilities on Venus," said Ms. Stevens as she sipped her wine.

"Not at all." Mr. Davis turned to Donal. "If a boy jilted your kid sister, how would you feel about doing business with his big brother?"

"In my family? There'd have been a duel."

"There already was," said Ms. Stevens. "Two. Legally the matter is settled."

"And I'm sure that's the end of that," said Mr. Davis with a roll of his eyes. "But enough shop talk. What about you, Donal? How could you have gone after Li Hua and not given so much as a glance to Tina here?"

Donal almost spat out a sip of wine, and he felt his eyes grow wide.

"He's just teasing you," said Ms. Davis. "Believe me, I think we're all happy Li Hua is ... dating."

"Actually," said Mr. Davis to Ms. Stevens, "Li Hua's not the only one who could use a few *dates*. The pair of you are all business, I swear."

The two began a shorthand version of what was clearly a favorite argument between them. Donal could not follow the details, but by the time they seemed to remember he was there, he had deduced that, as Mr. Mancuso's social secretary, Mr. Davis had a never-ending string of opportunities to ... date while on the job. Ms. Stevens, on the other hand, appeared to have a relative dearth, though if Donal followed the thread correctly, she did date; she merely kept her private life private.

Right then, Donal wished his was.

Their discussion contained enough offhand comments about improvements to Li Hua's temperament now that she was getting *dates* — and they continued to emphasize that word, as though fearing Donal might miss what it substituted for — that he had trouble keeping himself from blushing.

"So why do the security executives have to eat in another room?"

Mr. Davis and Ms. Stevens looked at each other, each with one eyebrow raised, mirroring the other. Donal began to wonder if conversing with them was less about the conversation itself and more about some sort of game between the two of them.

"Officially," said Ms. Stevens, "they are discussing security plans for the various groupings once we arrive on Venus, and will be each night of the voyage."

"Unofficially," said Mr. Davis, "the top executives are getting all of the combat-ready folks out of the room to prevent the possibility of assassination—"

"Leaving you as the only wild card," chimed in Ms. Stevens.

"—because you've already saved Mr. Mancuso's life. Also, they're sizing each other up."

"In case they have to fight each other?" asked Donal

"Yes," said Mr. Davis. "Though partially it's just what they do. Get two marksmen in a room and they want to know who the best shot is. That kind of thing."

"In this case, though," said Donal, trying to break the rhythm of their back-and-forth, "Li Hua's got the clear edge. She's the only magician."

"And don't you think the other executives are pleased about that," said Ms. Stevens. "Everyone loves the idea of increased security, but when Mr. Mancuso created Li Hua's position—"

"It felt like a power grab," said Donal.

"Which is was," said Mr. Davis.

"Someone had to do it," said Ms. Stevens, "and 4M was in the best position to handle it."

"What if the four of them team up against Mr. Mancuso?" said Donal.

Ms. Stevens and Mr. Davis shared a laugh, but she was the one who said, "You've obviously never watched him work."

TUNOLD FELT AS THOUGH HE MIGHT STRAIN HIS EYES TRYING TO SCAN the minutia of his small phantasmal display. Extrapolating for estimated speed, the hippogriff shuttle had to have been practically on top of the shimmer, but neither he nor Cromartie could find any trace of it.

"Could any of your spells help?"

"Scrying's not my area," said Cromartie, his distant voice telling Tunold that his focus was still on the scanners. *Where it should be.*

"What if we—"

Before Tunold could finish his question, a fold in space shimmered into view dead ahead, close enough that it filled most of the forward viewport. It looked like a lightning strike the size of a mountain next to the field mouse that was their little shuttlecraft.

The opening was visible for barely a moment, but in that moment Tunold saw a ship, easily a hundred meters long and at least fifty wide, shaped like a great flying gargoyle.

"Got it!" shouted Tunold, tamping his voice down to continue, "I got a good look at our bogey in that split second."

"As did I, Sir," said Cromartie. "But the bad news is that I'm pretty sure it got a look at us too."

JACOBS MIGHT NOT LIKE THE MAN, BUT HE HAD TO ADMIRE THE SKILL with which Mancuso worked. Through the main course — reindeer steak with garlic mashed potatoes and summer squash for Jacobs — Mancuso had appeared to grow tipsy, but Jacobs noticed how he played the enmities of his dining companions against each other. An offhand word here, a minor reference there, all appearing to be innocent in context, but Jacobs could afford to watch with nothing personal on the line.

Mancuso kept them sniping at each other so they never managed to unite against him. In the process, he subtly manipulated the accomplished businesspeople into letting the conversation stay within the boundaries he established.

For a man who was famous for railing against politicians, Mancuso played politics with the astute hand of a master.

Fortunately for Jacobs, this also had the happy effect of drawing attention away from him, so he could enjoy his meal almost in peace. Much better than the near sideshow attraction that most dinners at the captain's table became. Jacobs even briefly considered the possibility of a second glass of wine — something he never indulged in around passengers, only around crew — but knew better than to take things that far. He was Mancuso's partner now, after all, which meant that if Jacobs showed weakness, the man would no doubt try to *handle* him as he did these others.

Jacobs was almost tempted to let him try.

Owning half of Starchaser Spacelines might make Jacobs a businessman in fact, but he was a spacer first and foremost, and he had no doubt that Mancuso was unprepared to deal with a mind the likes of his.

He had been considering joining the conversation when one of the waitresses leaned in to whisper in his ear, "Captain, they're asking for you on the bridge. They said to tell you, 'there's a problem with the mule.'"

The poor waitress clearly did not understand the significance of her words, and had to jerk back as Jacobs snapped to his feet.

"My apologies, but ship's business calls and I must answer." He saw questions forming on several sets of lips but Jacobs raised his hands and let command seep into his voice as he said, "I assure you that there is no immediate danger, and there will not be so long as I respond immediately. Enjoy your dinner."

Jacobs gave a significant look at Goldberg and saw the chief nod that he understood: Goldberg had to ride herd on the passengers for now.

Jacobs threw down his napkin and marched out of the restaurant before anyone could call him back.

DONAL HAD BEEN GLAD OF THE MAIN COURSE'S ARRIVAL. NOT ONLY DID it mean he got to enjoy his lobster — stir fried with ginger and scallions — but Mr. Davis and Ms. Stevens took enough pleasure in their food — both filets mignons, with spiced squash mash and edamame — that Donal's ears got a little rest.

He appreciated all the information, but he needed time to process so he could begin to figure out what it all meant, and how it could affect his chances of figuring out what Mr. Mancuso was really up to.

Donal also needed to talk to Fionn.

Besides, if Ms. Stevens and Mr. Davis had continued at that pace, the finer points might have begun to jumble in Donal's head. But this break meant that he could afford to shift a bit of his consciousness to aid his memory of the details for later comprehension during meditation.

Donal had actually been ready to comment on the food himself when the captain stood from his table and left abruptly, with scarcely a word to anyone.

"What do you—" began Mr. Davis, but Chief Goldberg stood and said, "I know the captain's exit is going to leave a lot of you with questions, and that some of you might feel tempted to direct those questions to myself and my staff.

"I'm going to ask you to resist that impulse. If the captain says it's a matter of ship security, it's a matter of ship security. And that means no one on the crew can talk about it until the captain gives us permission." Chief Goldberg rolled his shoulders. "Before that happens, he will make a statement that will answer most of the questions any of you are likely to ask. If you still have questions, please feel free to bring them to me then."

Chief Goldberg stopped and looked around the room, as though expecting an objection that didn't come.

"In the meantime, please enjoy your meals, and rest assured that if there were any immediate danger, the captain would have had us escort you safely to your cabins."

Chief Goldberg spared a glance at Magister Machado, then said, "Now I'm going to go carry this information to your security executives myself. While I'm out of the room, please consider our ship's mage the senior officer present, in case you need anything."

The chief turned and walked toward a second dining room. Donal half expected Magister Machado to make some sort of statement himself, but the ship's mage appeared more interested in his *feijoada*.

But that was a show for the businesspeople who, unlike Donal, could not have seen the Magister's ghost panther familiar take shape and phase through the walls in the direction of the bridge.

TUNOLD SWORE IN THE LANGUAGE OF HIS FOREFATHERS AND GAMBLED that no ship designer would give a gargoyle look to a craft designed for maneuverability.

He jerked the hippogriff shuttle up and to port, spinning with the wings and legs stretched in an effort to persuade the gargoyle's scanners that it was a much bigger mule than it really was.

Tunold spared a thought to hate the term mule, and swore that if the shuttlecraft got them safely back aboard the *Horizon Cusp* he would give it a much better name. *Lifeline*, perhaps.

Behind Tunold he could hear Cromartie chanting rapid-fire in that harsh language he'd used earlier when casting...

Wait, he sounds like he's right behind me.

Tunold spared a glance over his shoulder as he held the spin but eased his hard turn into a gentle arc that would eventually intersect the *Horizon Cusp*. In that glance he saw that Cromartie had abandoned the scanners and communications, and was sitting on the cramped cockpit floor, facing aft and gesturing and chanting like a madman.

Great. I'm flying solo because my co-pilot needs to defend the ship.

Tunold began transferring basic controls for that station to his own, doubling the number of details he needed to track. Tunold should have had a co-pilot separate from the magician he brought for defense. He should have had a faster shuttle, one rated for real flights, not just suborbital and emergency landings.

And damn it! I should not die aboard a shuttle called 'the mule.'

Tunold poured all the speed he could manage into their escape.

After a flat out sprint between bubbles and finally up the ramp, Jacobs arrived on the bridge, sweating and panting and trying not to think about Dr. Ramirez and his concerns about Jacobs' heart. Jacobs had no doubt that his heart was fine, however fast it might have been beating right then.

The moment Jacobs' crew saw him, they began giving reports.

Jefferson: "They reported contact, but have been out of touch for two minutes."

Grabowski: "They almost landed on top of the shimmer, but there's been no sign of it since they linked in."

Burke: "I've slowed to one-half to try to let the shuttle catch up."

Jacobs' head felt too light, his body a little faraway, redness pressing in on his vision. He grabbed the back of Jefferson's chair to steady himself and almost tipped her over in the process.

Still, he barked out at Burke, "On whose authority?"

"Mine, Sir," said Burke, trying to swallow the words even as he said them.

"Get us ... back to speed..." Jacobs could feel a creeping sensation up the back of his skull, but refused to let a head rush black him out. He went down to one knee, head forward and arms bracing him on the other knee. "Never ... drop speed ... under pursuit..."

Don't you dare pass out and leave children running your ship, Old Man. Deep breaths.

"Do not ... drop speed again ... on this voyage..." One more deep breath and Jacobs began to feel steadier. He pushed as much of that steadiness as he could into his voice. "Unless you have a direct order from myself or the ex oh."

Jacobs stood, holding his back straight as though he were Kelly.

"And if the ex oh orders it, you confirm it with me."

Jacobs ran his gaze around the stations and saw concerned faces everywhere he looked. So he pretended that sympathy was not directed at him. "I'm worried about them too, but the safety of the ship comes first."

Jacobs turned and started up the stairs to his station, leaning a little more heavily on the rail than he tried to let on. "Mr. Grabowski, I want updates on that chase. If our bogey is after them, you find me something I can give Machado for a target. Ms. Jefferson, get them back on the link. I want solid information, not—"

"I have them, Sir," said Ms. Jefferson. "Linking through to your station."

A moment later the furrowed brow and angry grimace of Tunold appeared above Jacobs' comm pad. "It's a ship, Captain. Shaped like a gargoyle, maybe two thirds the *Horizon Cusp's* size. It saw us too."

"What's it doing now?"

"Unknown." Tunold lost a moment fighting with controls, if Jacobs judged the grit of his teeth correctly. "Can't get a read and fly at the same time, Captain, and my scanners officer is busy casting spells."

"Then stick to flying and let him handle pursuit."

That earned Jacobs a tilt-headed no-shit look. "I'm complaining about my lack of manpower, Sir. Not asking how to fly a noncombat shuttle ... in combat conditions..."

Tunold trailed off. Jacobs tried to wait patiently as Tunold stared fixedly at something Jacobs could not see.

But patience just then was too much to ask.

"Something to share with the class, Ex Oh?"

"Yes, Captain. This ship handles like someone wrote the bindings in molasses. I feel an urge to report my speed in knots. I—"

"Anything beyond complaints, Mister?"

"I don't think it's moving to pursue." Tunold shook his head. "Can't be sure without a solid read though. I'll have to go back and—"

"Belay that!" Jacobs leaned forward, putting himself almost nose-to-nose with the three-dimensional representation of his executive officer's head. "Get back here and debrief."

"Captain, I—"

"Now." No yelling. Just one word with a simple undertone of command, but Jacobs knew that from him it sounded as though

daring to violate whatever order it carried would have dire consequences beyond the capacity of the poor recipient to imagine.

"Aye, Sir. Returning at best speed."

"That's more like it. Call home again at the first sign of trouble,
but otherwise, focus on getting here. And the moment you do I want
both you and Cromartie in my office, reporting."

***

DONAL WOUND UP ENJOYING HIS FIVE-LAYER DARK CHOCOLATE CAKE
alone. The captain had not been gone two minutes before dinner
broke up at the main table, the various executives gathering their
staffs and leaving separately amid an undertone of private
discussions.

Ms. Stevens and Mr. Davis had been gracious enough about their
own exit when Mr. Mancuso twirled his finger in the air to gather his
people. Still, the whole group of them left quickly and without much
fanfare.

Li Hua did spare Donal a smile as Mr. Mancuso hustled his group
out of the restaurant, and Donal remembered that she had asked to
meet him on the Observation Deck after dinner. He estimated she
would need a good half hour to get away, so he had time to linger
over Ambrosia's wonderful chocolate cake.

Chief Goldberg had his ship's watch file out in groups, between
the various factions, as though he expected a bunch of executives to
start a brawl.

Donal amused himself with that mental image, ridiculously
expensive ties used to turn faces purple. Hands without a hint of
callous bruising and tearing knuckles on finely shaven chins.

Magister Machado tipped an imaginary hat to Donal as he made
his own meandering way out of the restaurant, the last of the crew to
do so, leaving Donal alone with his dessert. One of the nymphs
offered to pack the slice of cake into a box so that Donal could take it
with him, but he declined. Donal believed that restaurant desserts
always tasted best in the restaurant that served them.

So Donal savored forkful after slow forkful, the smooth, thick chocolate further enhanced by rich, South American coffee. As he neared the final bite, he saw approaching the sinuous, smoky form of Pinyin Lung, Li Hua's spirit dragon familiar.

"Is she on the Observation Deck already?" asked Donal.

Pinyin Lung bowed the top half of its serpentine form and said, "Tai Shi Li Hua offers her sincerest regrets, but has asked me to inform you that she will be unable to meet you tonight. Pressing business matters will require her attention into the late hours. She does offer her promise to make this up to you."

"Then please tell her I look forward to that and hope that her night does not become arduous."

"I shall do so."

"Thank you, Pinyin Lung."

That got a second bow out of the spirit dragon before it departed. But the arrival and departure of Li Hua's familiar made Donal realize his own was no longer forbidden to his company. After all, it wasn't as though he had anyone else to spy on in the empty restaurant.

Donal called forth his *cú sidhe.* Fionn assessed the room with a glance, then sniffed the air, flicked its ears, then circled Donal's table once.

As Fionn did this, Donal said, "Li Hua had to cancel our date."

"That is probably for the best." Fionn looked over at where Magister Machado had been sitting, then back at Donal. "Did you learn anything of substance during your dinner?"

"Save that for the room," said Donal in words pitched only for Fionn. "Why do you keep looking over there?"

"A spell lingers. I believe you are under observation."

"Well, I can't very well argue with the ship's mage."

"You are a paying passenger. If he continues to do this, it could constitute harassment."

"Studying law on the side?"

"It is a simple matter of tactics. He is in a position of protective authority, but such actions could violate the trust of his position."

Fionn snorted with a shake of its head. "I will mention this to *Saravá* later."

"What do you familiars talk about among yourselves?"

Fionn said nothing in reply to that. The fae deerhound merely gave Donal the best attempt at an innocent canine stare that Donal had ever seen from his familiar.

Donal knew better than to believe it, but he knew that look meant he would get no answers to that question.

11

Jacobs sat at his desk in only the yellow light and kerosene smell of his archaic oil lamp, and waited. His depictions of all the crafts he had served on or commanded had been returned to their proper places on one wall, but he did not regard them. The bookshelves behind him were once more organized with his library of seamanship, airmanship, and spacemanship (a term he hated and used as little as possible), but he did not consider their contents while he waited. Not the more modern refillable volumes, nor the more plentiful older books that could only ever contain a single set of words.

Jacobs did not drum his fingers as he waited. He did not pour himself a glass of whiskey. He did not run down to the gangplank to meet his men when the shuttle landed.

He considered doing all of these things, but chose none of them.

He knew the pictures and still illusions well enough that he felt no need to look them over, any more than he needed to pore over books he could have gone through and corrected.

Drumming Jacobs' fingers would have reminded him of Fredrickson and her insistence on rhythmlessly tapping her fingers whenever she thought through a problem. And having had a glass of whiskey before dinner and a glass of wine with dinner, another glass of whiskey now might have distracted Jacobs from the questions he would need to ask as soon as his men arrived.

And Jacobs did not rush down to the gangplank, because that was the act of an inexperienced captain.

It would be the act of a younger man too.

What Jacobs tried most not to think about as he waited was the head rush. In those moments that he could not help himself but consider the topic, he tried to tell himself that he needed more cardio in his workout, though he included at least fifteen minutes of such work every day, and thirty minutes more days than not. He tried to tell himself that the heavy reindeer steak had drawn all the blood down to his stomach, and even the doubtful voice in Jacobs' head — which always spoke the tones of Dr. Ramirez — had to admit that it had probably been a factor.

No, the idea lurking in the background of all the thoughts Jacobs' mind danced around as it waited was this: even in his seventies a run from Ambrosia to the bridge — with two bubble rides along the way, for rest — would not have left Jacobs on the verge of passing out.

It was one thing for Jacobs to know it was time to retire. It was another to have the facts of it shoved down his throat.

Jacobs also did not think about the fact that he should bring the incident to Dr. Ramirez's attention.

Besides. He knew he did not have to. Either someone on the bridge crew would tell the doctor of the incident, or they would report it to Tunold, and *he* would run to the doctor with the information.

On some level Jacobs knew that such signs of worry from his people were a good thing, that it demonstrated loyalty to their captain. Perhaps even affection. This was certainly true of the bridge crew, and Kris was a good enough friend that Jacobs knew, *knew* deep down, that his worry was sincere.

But still Jacobs could not quite shake the feeling that Tunold was trying to steal his command.

Why had he tried to go to the officers behind Jacobs' back?

The door shook with a thunderous knock, and its timing gave Jacobs a wry smile. *Poke the bear and you'll wake him up.* Aloud he said, "Come."

Tunold entered followed by Cromartie, and Jacobs wondered if it were coincidence that both men were so tall, or if the human race had begun growing again. Tunold had the clamp-jawed, ruffled look he usually had after an irritating shift, but Cromartie's dark skin looked wan, and his steps less certain.

The two men took their seats as greetings were exchanged, but before Jacobs could bring them down to business, Tunold said, "Captain, may I ask why we are sitting here half in darkness?"

"It suits my mood." Jacobs leaned back in his chair. "So tell me about this gargoyle."

"It's a ship all right," said Tunold, rubbing that massive jaw of his. "Only saw it for a split-second when the lightning flashed, but clear enough. Big enough to threaten us if it can use those massive arms as a prow."

"Any chance it's reporters?" asked Cromartie, even his voice a little weak, unlike his usual deep, resonant tones.

"No," said Jacobs. "I checked before we left. No one has filed to follow our route, and there's no percentage in the press doing it without making a big announcement in the process."

"Think it's pirates, Captain?" said Tunold.

"Stupid pirates, maybe, if they think we'd be worth hitting, but stupid pirates aren't anything to worry about." Jacobs shook his head. "No. These people have bad intentions, no doubt about it, but they've got to be chasing us because of our passengers.

"That's not the right question anyway," said Jacobs, and he saw Tunold grip the arms of his chair at Jacobs' choice of words. *Well maybe he's sick of my lessons, damn it, but he still has a lot to learn.* "The question is, are they operating alone?"

"If they weren't they are now," said Cromartie. Jacobs looked a question at the young magician, and Cromartie continued, "My repertoire of illusions is pretty small beside Magister Machado, or even Journeyman Cuthbert, but I hit that section of space with everything I could think of: hazards, monsters, and lots of false signals."

"If we assume they have magicians on board—"

"Then how long it takes them to work through my spells tells us something about the level of competition."

"Good man," said Jacobs, the depth of his approval infusing his tone and making the assistant ship's mage smile with weary pride. "What did you two figure out about the shimmer?"

"I've got some theories," said Cromartie, "but I want to run them past Magister—"

"We think they're trying to conceal themselves," said Tunold, "but the spells are messing with their lacunas, so either they're glitching or they have to surface occasionally."

"But," said Cromartie with a sour stretch to his lips, "a brief glimpse like we had makes it tough to say for certain. Magister Machado will help me work it through."

"I look forward to the full report." Jacobs turned back to his ex oh. "What else can you tell me about that ship?"

"Recent model," said Tunold, "no more than five years old. Didn't look like it was straining, so I'd say it has more speed yet. Probably retrofitted with a Deception Drive, since we're known to have one. Worse, I'm betting that they went with the gray, gargoyle look because there's more carterite in their hull than ceramic."

Jacobs stared out his immense porthole at the passing stars as he considered that. A mostly carterite hull would respond better to the lacuna, making it faster and more maneuverable than the *Horizon Cusp*.

"They know what our resources are," said Jacobs. "And we have to assume they know which passengers we're carrying. And while I'm confident in your spells, Mr. Cromartie, they wouldn't come after us unless they think they have someone who can stand against Mash.

"No, we have to assume they'll cut through your deceptions pretty quickly. And we have to assume they have the other half of that spell in our safe."

Jacobs rubbed his hands, a slow, thoughtful motion. "The only real question is: are they on their own or do they have someone coming to meet them from the other side."

"Want to pick up speed?" said Tunold. "If the shimmers are a response to their lacuna's needs, they might have to drop their hiding spell entirely. We could force a confrontation before they're ready."

"I've got a better idea," said Jacobs. "Let's hail them."

ON THE WALK BACK TO HIS CABIN, DONAL CHATTED WITH FIONN ABOUT all the various ways he could think of to disrupt their flight. If Magister Machado intended to keep him under surveillance, Donal might as well give him something worth listening to, even if he never intended to complete any single action he mentioned. Especially not trying to contact a trakhaa, a creature only rumored to exist based on evidence that implied that something out there could hunt and kill zuglodons.

Donal even joked about trying to lock the *Horizon Cusp* into perpetual Venus orbit based on the thaumaturgic landing technique required by larger spaceports.

He could do it too. All he would need was...

Donal stopped two steps shy of his room, excitement lighting up his face.

"I've got it!" he said and snapped his fingers. "Fionn, go find Magister Machado. I've got to talk to the captain."

When Fionn appeared to hesitate, confused at its master's sudden shift of mental direction, Donal yelled, "Go!"

The fae deerhound phased downward through the deck, and Donal jogged back down the hall to the bubble and its nearby audio-only comm pad, activating the latter with a light pat.

"This is the bridge," said a woman's voice.

"This is Donal Cuthbert. I need to talk to the captain."

"The captain is in the middle of something very important, Mr. Cuthbert. Could I link you through to our chief of security?"

"No, it has to be the captain." Donal began thumping his fist against the bulkhead to control the urgency in his voice. "Tell him I know how to stop the package from pulsing."

Jacobs sat at his station and rubbed that spot between his eyes.

Today had been a very long day, and it was only their first day out. He hesitated to consider what tomorrow might bring. That way lay madness.

But sitting there surrounded by the half-painted canvas of space beyond the transparent bulkheads, Jacobs was half-tempted to go ahead and hail that gargoyle ship and be done with it. He hated cat-and-mouse games when he sailed the seas, liked them no better in the skies above Earth, and now, at space, he liked them even less.

Better to confront the problem head on and deal with it.

That thought made him smirk. How many problems had Jacobs literally face head-on, breaking noses with his forehead in barroom brawls?

Jacobs shook his head. No, this was a fight to avoid if he could, for the sake of his crew, his business, and yes even for the sake of his passengers. Although he felt sure that this pursuing craft was the direct fault of one of them. And if it wasn't then the reason for its presence likely came back to Mancuso. The man might not be the source of all ills, but he had proven himself a pain in Jacobs' backside many times over.

Still, Machado would know if Cuthbert's idea had merit. And if it did, then it needed to be done. Anything Jacobs could do to hinder the efforts of the pursuing craft.

And if it happened to force their pursuers into a confrontation before they lost track of the *Horizon Cusp,* so much the better. A rushed attack would lead to mistakes.

But, Lord, Jacobs was ready to go to sleep. The day had been so very long.

Jacobs put his hands on his knees and forced himself to a

standing position. He took a deep breath, and let one hand use the rail to steady him as he descended the steps.

Has this staircase always had so many steps?

Jacobs did not even look at the crew members manning the bridge stations. He did not have to. He could feel their eyes, feel them wondering about their captain's weakness, wondering if Old Man Jacobs could manage this last demanding flight.

He covered by issuing orders his whole way to the passage door. Nothing unusual, just his standard push for attentiveness to duty. When the bridge door closed behind him, Jacobs let himself slump against the bulkhead for just one moment, before making the slow walk down the sloping passage to his office.

He felt so very, very tired.

<hr>

DONAL'S SECURITY ESCORT TO THE CAPTAIN'S OFFICE WAS A GIRAFFE OF a man, so tall and thin that in places his joints looked too large for his body. But Donal remembered him from escort duty the last time a delivery had brought Donal aboard the *Horizon Cusp*, and the guard treated him like an old friend: asked after family and developments, shared his successes in correspondence school, and generally behaved so comfortably that he forgot to introduce himself.

Four times the man had escorted Donal someplace secure on the ship, and Donal still didn't know his name. Worse, the man seemed so at ease that Donal didn't have the heart to ask him this time either.

Still, Donal arrived at the captain's office, Fionn trailing behind as rear guard. Donal wondered if the *cú sidhe* expected the Romanova woman to step out of the shadows and try to assassinate him.

He decided against asking. The answer, Donal felt certain, would only make him more nervous.

And Donal felt nervous approaching the captain about this idea. It went beyond the scope of anything he had tried before. But he found the possibility of success so exciting that he had to check himself from skipping down the hall. *Magister Machado would never forgive me.*

The watchman stuck around while Donal knocked, but gave Donal a smile and a thumbs-up when the captain's voice called, "Come!" The watchman walked away, and Donal opened the door.

Inside the well-lit office, the captain sat at his desk, as Donal expected, but the only other person present was Magister Machado, who reclined on the well-loved couch under the porthole. Donal had half-expected the entire command staff to be waiting for him, or at least the chief and Initiate Cromartie, like the last time they had asked him about the package.

"Have a seat, Cuthbert," said the captain, "and tell me how you can cut off that damned signal flare of a package."

The captain held himself straight as ever, and his voice sounded strong and clear, but something in the man's eyes made Donal think the captain felt exhausted.

But Donal didn't have time to waste wondering about that. He hustled into a guest chair on the other side of the desk, and said, "I can't really *cut off* the signal, per se, but I think I've figured out a way to ... shunt it, so it's coming from somewhere else."

Magister Machado shifted on the couch, and despite a lack of any outside signs of increased attention, Donal had the feeling that the Magister's full attention was on him, a feeling he remembered from taking oral exams from his professors in Thaumaturgy courses at U.C. Santa Cruz. Old fear gripped Donal's stomach that he hadn't studied enough, hadn't prepared enough, had wasted too much time having fun, and now he was going to fail in front of...

But this wasn't an exam, and Donal managed to contain that fear with a deep breath.

"I have to travel so much that I keep a memory circle in my apartment—"

"You brilliant bastard!" cried Magister Machado lurching to his feet, practically vibrating with excitement. "Of course! I live on the ship, so I never need one, but—"

"Would someone tell me what a memory circle is?" said Captain

Jacobs, and the speed with which the ship's mage locked down his own eagerness assured Donal that he was not the only one who heard warning in the captain's tone.

Magister Machado gave a sweeping wave of his hand to let Donal explain.

"Magicians tend to have a lot of ideas. We're always researching something. Like right now I'm—"

"Getting off track," said Captain Jacobs.

"Right. So. A few years back," — *he doesn't want the history, give him the crux* — "someone came up with a kind of ... thought holder, for giving yourself little reminders that you either can't or don't want to write down, because of your circumstances."

Donal dug through his pockets and pulled out a small vial. "This is a sample of the paint I used to paint the circle, and that paint has never been used for any other purpose. So through the principle of contagion I can send ideas home to myself with a quick spell, and the circle traps them and holds them until I get back."

"The pulses aren't your thoughts," said the captain. "Won't that pose a problem?"

"Let me," said Magister Machado, coming over to sit in the other guest chair beside Donal. "In a word, yes. He'll have to take the rest of the paint in that vial and use it to cast a connecting circle around the package. He'll lose use of his memory circle until he can cast another, but it should shunt the pulses to the circle for the rest of the voyage."

"And if they're linked to the pulses," said Donal, "then their link will lead them to my apartment in San Francisco."

"They won't follow that far," said Captain Jacobs. "When the pulses disappear from their immediate proximity, they'll figure that we've found a way to neutralize it and abandon it as a tracking device. Could they still complete their spell and accomplish something else?"

"If they can complete the spell at a distance, I doubt this will stop it from happening," said the ship's mage. "But it will add a layer of difficulty, and I'm not convinced they can complete a spell that would cause us a major problem. They would have to have made a leap forward in that process, and getting a magician to make a discovery like that and keep it to himself, well, that's all but unprecedented."

"'All but' means it can happen," said the captain. "So we'll have to be ready anyway. When you do this thing, take the package to Promenade Ten, all the way aft. That should keep any potential fallout away from any passengers or important systems."

Captain Jacobs gave Donal a deeper and more searching look than any that Donal's professors had ever managed. The Morrigan herself would give a general such a look, before deciding whether to aid him in battle. The captain said, "Can you do this, Cuthbert?"

"No, Sir. Not by myself." Donal meant to only provide a simple statement, but the details came pouring out before he could stop them. "I've never managed the connection through deep space. I've tried three times and—"

"I'll assist, of course," said Magister Machado. "As an IIX courier, you have authority over the package. That'll help." The Magister began enumerating details on his fingers. "But you'll still need a full circle, incense, and for this I think—"

"Keep it between yourselves." Captain Jacobs pulled the package out of his desk drawer.

Donal looked from the package to the captain. That package was supposed to be in the ship's safe. Nothing from the ship's safe was supposed to be retrieved, except—

"That's right," said Captain Jacobs rubbing a spot between his eyes. "I took the liberty of having it ready. You're not enchanting the whole safe, so I interpreted your offer as a request. And yes, Chief Goldberg approved. Do you want to see the paperwork?"

Something about the way the captain said that made Donal think he had actual paperwork, instead of an entry in a memoboard. Still, Donal shook his head.

"Then take your package and make this happen. I am going to bed."

"Captain?" said the Brazilian magician. "He should have a full night's sleep before attempting this."

"No. Mash, if you need a reason, ask Saul. Cuthbert, you'll just have to take my word that the need for this may be pressing."

"Of course," said Donal, who would have liked that night's sleep before attempting so complex a working. "We'll get on it right away."

Magister Machado's lips turned down as though he wanted to argue, but he said, "Aye, Sir. We'll make this happen."

DONAL FOLLOWED MAGISTER MACHADO INTO A STATEROOM ON Promenade Ten that reminded Donal of the room he had had on his last flight aboard the *Horizon Cusp.* Passably large and comfortable, it had seemed spacious for helioship accommodations, except that now Donal had his suite to compare it to. This whole stateroom, including closet and bathroom, could have fit in the social area of Donal's suite, with space left over. And the bed Donal would enjoy in his suite later that night had to have cost more than all the furniture in this stateroom combined.

The air didn't move as well here either. It felt still, and smelled vaguely of mothballs. Donal wondered if the cabin's air freshening system conserved resources by shutting down when unoccupied.

I better make it as a Hierophant, thought Donal. *I'm getting used to all this posh living.*

"We'll have to move that table," said Magister Machado, indicating the small table and chairs under the meter-wide porthole. "The bed would be too much hassle."

The two of them wedged the table and chairs along the wall opposite the bed, chairs against the wall between the prefab desk and simple chest of drawers and the table cutting the walking space down to a thin tunnel between the table and the bed.

As they did this, their familiars, fae deerhound and spirit panther, went over the perimeter of the room, cleansing the space of any psychic odds and ends that might interfere with their working.

Donal started a piece of charcoal burning in the incense censer the ship's mage had loaned him. It was brass chased with silver, and had a loop that could hang on a matching tripod or be held if the ritual required that the incense be swung. In this case, it needed only to burn so Donal kept it on its hook.

Meanwhile, Magister Machado ground together the blend of chicory, eryngo, eyebright, horehound, and star anise that they would burn.

When the ship's mage declared the incense blended, he handed the mortar and pestle to Donal who gave mixture three clockwise twists, then both magicians touched the result with a hint of power.

Donal took a generous pinch, held it above the smoldering charcoal, and rubbed his fingers together to trickle the incense onto the charcoal, while saying three times softly, "Burn as here, connect as there."

Pungent smoke rose, and both magicians inhaled deeply. Donal caught a handful in each hand, and pushed the smoke at the two familiars, whose nostrils flared as the smoke reached them.

Donal lifted the censer off the tripod. Magister Machado held up a hand as though to intervene, but pulled the hand back down without saying a word. Donal walked once around the area they had cleared, smoke gently wafting in his wake. He replaced the censer.

Donal pulled from his pocket the vial of vermillion paint. With one hand he held it. With the other he took hold of the stopper, ritually sealed with wax.

On an out breath he broke the seal.

Donal knelt on the carpet, and, one middle finger stoppering the vial, he tilted back and forth, then used the paint left behind on his middle finger to begin painting the circle, adding power with each drop, focusing his thoughts on the circle he had cast this way in his apartment near Golden Gate Park.

The process was slow, but the circle had to be drawn this way and Donal had to draw it. But his attention wanted to drift. The hour was too late, the day too stressful for the precision demanded by such work. His mind wanted to review the coming steps of the ritual, but more than that his mind wanted to imagine the waiting comfort of his bed. He could feel an aching tingle in his skin where his body yearned to slip into those sheets...

Fionn's nose, in front of Donal, snapping Donal's focus back to the present. Fionn's mind, touching Donal's, not with words but a general sense of support, helping Donal stay where he had to be: in the moment.

Donal returned all his attention to the drops of paint, the touch of power, and the circle he drew on the thin carpet. His familiar moved along the circle, just ahead of him, helping Donal keep his resources where they belonged: on the spell which Donal would have exactly one chance to get right.

Centimeter by centimeter he constructed the circle, seeing little sign of his passage, but feeling the presence of his magic every step of the way.

When at last the circle connected, the sudden flare of power jarred Donal. He fell backwards into the waiting hands of Magister Machado.

"Always be ready for the connection," he said in soft tones that seemed to augment his Brazilian accent. "Don't let it catch you off-guard."

He helped Donal back to his feet, and Fionn looked up from assessing the work so far and gave a single nod of approval.

Donal drew a deep breath, but his mind was already deep in his magic. He could see his power flow deosil along the simple circle, ready for the second stage.

Magister Machado handed Donal his courier pouch. The Magister could not have entered the circle without breaking it, but Donal could. A magician's magic always knows the magician.

Donal reached across the barrier of power and felt it tingle, not in his skin, but in what some called his aura or his aetheric counterpart, that portion beyond Donal's skin that was still Donal. He set the pouch in the center of the circle, then withdrew to stand just outside the circle.

Despite the evenness of the flow of power, he could even see the starting point, the place the first drop had been applied. Not that this spot represented a flaw. It represented the beginning, from which all things must flow, including the cycling green power of his circle.

Donal stepped to the spot just outside that beginning point. He spread his arms, as though to encompass the whole of the circle. Donal gathered the feel of the circle within himself, the flavor of the power — his own signature, modified by the nature and alchemy in the paint and the blend of herbs and powers that formed the ritual incense.

When he felt that he had it, Donal chanted Gaelic words of connection and union, and drew his hands together to cup them in front of his face. In his hands he held a linking spell, and he breathed warm air onto it through his wide-open mouth, sealing the links.

Magister Machado stepped up to Donal and held up a small pot of viscous, iridescent brown fluid, an alchemical blend Machado had concocted himself to aid in forming connections between spells that must separate by very long distances. Donal merged the power of his linking spell into the Magister's unguent, and both magicians said five times, "Link one to one, one through one, one become one."

Donal staggered back a step, reflexively wiping sweat from his forehead that he had not realized was there. He sat on the bed as the Magister performed the next stage, anointing the circle with the oil at seven key spots, chanting musical words in Portuguese.

Donal wanted to watch the Magister work, study the dance of his power as he amplified Donal's spell so that the next stage would be possible. But Donal's mind reeled from his efforts. His thoughts ran to his waiting bed, and wondering what Li Hua was doing, and whether she had a similar bed of her own, and what her place on Mars was like, and what Donal's graduate student housing would be like. He only had his U.C. Santa Cruz dorm rooms and apartments to compare to, but he had heard that the doctoral students got accommodations comparable to the faculty. Donal started imagining a split level condo, maybe with a loft...

Fionn's nose, right in front of Donal's face again. Fionn's mind, gentle, but present, pulling Donal's thoughts right back to the present, right back to this stateroom where *Saravá* stood just behind Fionn, checking on Donal. Where the Magister had completed the second stage of the spell, and stood ready to join Donal for the third stage.

"I'm still here," said Donal.

"Believe me," said the ship's mage in a gentle voice. "If I could tie this spell off and let you continue it in the morning, I would. But if the captain says time is of the essence, then you better believe it is."

Donal didn't remember the captain using those words, but decided not to point that out. Right now, he needed to stand, didn't he? Yes. Stand. Standing was good. He was standing right now, maybe teetering a little, and wasn't teeter a funny word?

A sharp shock jolted through Donal's system, snapping him back to wakefulness as though he had been slapped ... everywhere at once...

Donal looked at Magister Machado, who held one closed fist high.

"You ready to cast now?"

"You didn't have to—"

"Yes, I did. Now are you ready to work, or do I need to do it again?"

Donal rubbed his face, trying for more alertness. "You've done more today than I have. How do you stay so ready?"

Magister Machado grinned with anticipatory malevolence. "Donal, if you think grad school in Thaumaturgy is just learning new spells, you're in for quite a wake-up call."

That statement gave Donal a thousand questions, but he knew that this was not the time to ask them. Further, that grin told him that the Magister had phrased his statement to test Donal's focus. So Donal rolled his shoulders and swept his arms out wide, bringing his hands together in front of him and gathering his focus as he did.

"All right, let's finish this."

Donal returned to the circle's beginning point and the ship's mage took up a counterpoint position on the other side. Fionn stood behind Donal, while *Saravá* stood behind Machado. Both magicians raised their arms, met each other's gaze to key their timing, and stretched their power together to form a circle outside the circle, blending both their power together. The Magister's power hit Donal like a kick to the head, but this time he was ready and channeled that kick into the flow, clockwise like the inscribed circle.

The two familiars began to pace a third circle, perfecting the arrangement: one interior circle that was mostly Donal's power and would connect to his memory circle in his San Francisco apartment back on Earth; one center working circle, more Machado than Donal for the practical reason that the Magister had so much more power to contribute, but it balanced the disparity of the first circle; a final circle equally Donal and Machado, balanced and maintained by their familiars to contain the working and ensure that all energies used went to the goal and did not dissipate, wasted.

Donal and Machado began to pace their circle in tandem, chanting spells of connection and binding together in Gaelic. After three repetitions, Donal could feel sweat matting his hair and dampening his armpits. After five repetitions, Donal felt heat rising under his collar. His focus was here, but his steps grew unsteady, his words not quite slurring, while the Magister continued as though he could do this all day and night. Donal's attention *almost* slipped to wonder if Machado ever had...

Seven times, and Donal's feet shuffled now, tried to trip him. His arms had grown heavy, and he had to work to pronounce every word of the chant right. Only his parents' insistence on speaking Gaelic around the house as Donal and Bran grew up kept the harsh syllables of Donal's chant from clashing together and losing their meaning.

Eight times, and Donal's arms had drifted down from parallel to the floor to a forty-five degree angle, and shook to stay even that high. His eyes blurred from sweat, and his shirt and pants felt glued to his body. His feet trudged, slowing his pace and forcing the Magister to slow to match him.

But Donal kept his thoughts on his spells, forming each word as clearly as he could manage.

As they finished the ninth cycle, Donal fell to his knees, his head spinning, but he knew he was not finished.

Nine times, in all, they had circled. Nine times they repeated their spells. Nine, and then the final seal had to come from Donal.

Fionn's cold nose on the back of Donal's neck, and Donal felt some semblance of sense return.

Not enough. Donal began to drift...

With a sharp crack, the Magister's open hand slapped Donal back to awareness. Awareness of stinging pain through his cheek and neck, but awareness all the same.

"Finish it, Journeyman! Finish it or this has all been for nothing."

There, before Donal, he could see the perfect construct of the spell, waiting for the final words that would key it, would connect this circle to his memory circle and transmit all thoughts and pulses of power that went through it across the blackness of space and to Donal's little apartment.

"Two circles ... one cause..." Donal forced his exhausted arms to raise, digging deep within himself for one more surge of power. "Remember for me. Carry for me. Hold for me. Mine to mine. So ... mote ... it ... be!"

With that last word, Donal snapped out everything he had left, and for a fleeting instant he could feel his memory circle with its waiting idea about Lunar magic and Air aspected Earth...

But then it was gone and Donal was on his knees in the stateroom, Fionn pacing him and examining him.

"Good work, Donal," said the Magister. "You can rest now. I'll make sure no one bothers you."

Donal awoke stiff and sore, unsure of where he was. But then he saw the circle and realized he had fallen asleep on his stomach, fully clothed, on top of the bed in the stateroom where he had been working with Magister Machado.

Donal tried rolling his neck, but felt it kink, seizing somewhere in his right shoulder blade. He managed to roll onto his side and saw Fionn, seated beside the bed, chin resting on crossed forepaws.

"How long have I been out?" Donal's voice came out a strained croak.

"Ninety-two minutes. Ronaldo Machado said that you would do better to rest first, then move to your own bed."

Donal's head ached, like he'd slept hard then tried to wake up and missed. He dug his fingers into his shoulders.

"Can you..." A stab of pain forced a wince out of Donal. "Can you get me back to my room?"

"I will guide and guard the way."

Donal devoutly hoped the fancy bed in his suite could take care of muscle spasms.

12

JACOBS ROSE TO AN EARLY ALARM, EXPECTING TROUBLE.

It came while he was shaving.

Jacobs stood half-dressed beside a sink full of hot water — a luxury beyond gold to an old Navy man — in a bathroom larger than his first berth had been. He shaved straight edge and soap, the way his father taught him. He had finished both cheeks, chin and lip, and was just moving on to his throat when he heard the audio alert from his nearest comm pad: his own voice said "link from the bridge."

Jacobs dropped his straight razor into the sink, grabbed a hand towel, and wiped his face down on his way to the nightstand beside his queen-sized bed. The captain's cabin did not compare to the fancy suites or even the top-of-the-line cabins on the *Horizon Cusp*, but it was more than roomy enough for Jacobs, even with the nightly encroachments by Benny Sugg, Pillow Thief.

Jacobs slapped the red, glowing comm pad and Tunold's face phased into being above it.

"Captain, the shimmer winked out a few minutes ago, but the gargoyle's now in full view and flying to gain on us. Must have abandoned that trick when they lost their link to the package. I've got us up to ahead three-quarters, but there's tight space ahead. Keep this quiet? Or—"

"Not this time. Wake Mash up, but alert Goldberg first. We need his people to contain the passengers before that ship can reach us. And prepare to sound general quarters the second I reach the bridge."

Tunold was mid-confirmation when Jacob waved his hand through the image to break the connection. He thrust his arms into his shirt and jacket. He slipped his socked feet into shoes, pulled his cap into place, and hustled out the door, buttoning his shirt and jacket on the way.

———

MACHADO AWOKE NAKED, DEEP WITHIN THE COMFORT OF HIS KING-SIZE bed. It was too much bed for his quarters, requiring him to make do with little sitting room and use his workshop for additional personal storage, but Machado knew where his priorities lay.

On a normal morning, he would have awoken to a pre-set internal alarm, allowing him fifteen minutes to revel in the comfort and enchantments of his mattress and sheets as he contemplated some thaumaturgic question or other, but his alarm was not due to awaken him for another hour.

That realization made Machado sit up, his arms behind him, propping him in place. He closed his eyes and felt one of his spells pull at his attention ... the scanners. Machado slipped his mind into the tapestry of spells that tied the *Horizon Cusp* together, then along connections and threads, following the tug of his own alert to the scanners.

His spells had detected a ship where none should be.

Machado had almost forgotten this particular bit of spellwork, because it could only trigger when a foreign ship approached at speed in an unpopulated area of space. It was an alert he had established after the last time the *Horizon Cusp* had faced pirates, some five years past.

Pirates?

Machado snapped his consciousness back into his body and called forth *Saravá*. "Find out if Cuthbert made it back to his room. If not, wake him up and send him there. Then go awaken Aaron and have him meet me in my workshop. Tell him to bring our breakfast."

Machado sighed. At least this time he would have a passable assistant in Cromartie.

"And make it a big breakfast. We may have a busy day ahead of us."

<hr>

JACOBS ARRIVED ON THE BRIDGE, STILL STRAIGHTENING HIS CUFFS. Tunold had the bridge crew hopping, but too keyed up for Jacobs' taste. Even a glance was enough to show Jacobs that every one of them held their controls too tightly, expecting a fight that Jacobs hoped to avoid.

Well, most of him wanted to avoid it.

He knew that running was the safest option for his crew and passengers. Certainly it was the responsible option.

But part of Jacobs, the old hellion who used to start fights in bars for the joy of fighting, the part of him that had tucked into his pocket those modern boxing gloves Dr. Ramirez had given him, that part of Jacobs wanted the fight to happen. Wanted one last fight before he retired, wanted to show Tunold, show Mancuso, show Ramirez, show all of them that John Jacobs at eighty-six was still more a man than any of them.

Jacobs tried to quell that belligerence on his way up the stairs to his station.

"Sound general quarters, Mr. Tunold. Confine all passengers to their cabins for the duration."

He drew a deep breath as the klaxon began to sound. "Scanners, how's it look out there?"

"The gargoyle's gaining, Sir. At current rate, they'll be right on top of us in five minutes."

"Helm, ahead full. Let's see how fast they really are."

"Sir," said Mr. Tunold. "Sending my analysis of approaching space to your station."

"Acknowledged, Ex Oh. Now go help Goldberg with the passengers and get things ready for the fight I'm going to try not to have."

"Aye, Sir," said Tunold, and the ex oh saluted with a look in his eye that did more to reassure Jacobs about how things stood between the two men than anything Tunold could have said.

Tunold was off to handle the people while Jacobs handled the ship. The old school way. Jacobs spared a moment to wonder if he had not allowed his ex oh enough room to take care of his own duties.

But then the general quarters klaxon sounded again, and the moment was gone. Jacobs had a ship to run. He took a quick glance at the systems reports through the illusory gryphon display, but everything appeared to be in order, at least as of five-to-ten minutes ago.

On to Tunold's report then. Tight space indeed. To stay on course, the *Horizon Cusp* would have to thread the needle between a violet gas cloud and a bank of asteroids. At normal speeds this would be nothing worth noticing, but at evasive speeds both represented increased risk and limited maneuvering that would be necessary to keep ahead of that gargoyle, a ship that, if the assessment of its carterite content was correct, was probably faster and more maneuverable than the *Horizon Cusp*.

Worse, the violet clouds were known to be feeding grounds of lacunas.

While lacunas were not normally a hazard to ships, they could get big, and the big ones could get interested in large things that occupied space and reeked, metaphorically, of other lacunas. A description that applied to all helioships.

No doubt, the gargoyle ship had Jacobs at a disadvantage. He needed to buy time to find a way to steal that advantage back.

Machado walked into his workshop to see Initiate Aaron Cromartie laying out a breakfast of pastries, scrambled eggs, linguiça, and orange juice on a cleared section of worktable.

Saravá looked up from where it lay curled on the floor next to the three inscribed circles and said aloud, in English, "Shall I fetch Donal Cuthbert as well? Or perhaps Tai Shi Li Hua?"

"No to both for right now," said Machado, nodding his thanks to Cromartie and picking up a link of linguiça. Its taste was sharp with just a hint of spice, and Machado noted to send his complements to the mess hall.

To his familiar he continued, "I may have you fetch Cuthbert if it looks like we'll need the help, but there's too much politics in involving Tai Shi."

"What's the plan?" said Cromartie, looking and sounding fresh and ready after a good night's sleep.

"First we eat. Next we'll prepare some basic deceptions to throw them off our trail. After that, we may have to play it by ear. I'll need permission from the captain before we could directly attack them."

"I've never heard a battle stations call before," said Cromartie with a shake of his head. "Damn near straightened my hair."

Machado chuckled. "Don't call it 'battle stations.' The captain hates that term. On this ship it's 'general quarters' or you'll find yourself on a most unpleasant duty."

Machado chuckled again, remembering the time the captain had ordered him to scrub all the toilets on the main deck for a similar offense. But that had been back when Machado was younger, and naïve in the ways of military men.

"Now," he said to Cromartie around a mouthful of bear claw, "what can you tell me about that ship's magic?"

"Didn't have time to get much." Cromartie, like Machado, wolfed down his food as he spoke. "I don't know how they pulled off invisibility, but I think the shimmer resulted from the fits it gave their lacunas—"

"Obviously, and that level of invisibility would require either an exceptionally talented Journeyman or a Magister, so don't worry about analyzing that. Stick to your gut. You felt them detect you, I believe." Machado waited for Cromartie to nod confirmation while sipping orange juice. "What else did you pick up? How fast did they respond? How aggressive?"

"I went straight into throwing illusions. I didn't have time for analysis."

"This is why you need a familiar."

"I know." Cromartie dropped his shoulders. "I can't make sense of the spells. Conjuration—"

"Later. How did they handle your illusions?"

"Can't be sure. I don't think they intended to pursue us, and that's what I tried to prevent."

"Well, we're coming into this blind, and they probably think they have a pretty good idea of what we can do."

Cromartie started to apologize, but Machado stopped him with a wide smile. "Are you kidding? This sounds like fun!"

Machado downed half a glass of orange juice in a single gulp.

"Let's get to work."

Donal awoke surrounded by bliss. The kink in his neck was gone. The stiffness in his back was gone. That weird headache from waking up wrong earlier? Gone. He felt only luxuriant comfort as he snuggled into his sheets, the question of how he could have awakened from such joyous respite barely able to form in the back of his mind, much less garner his attention.

Donal began to nestle back into his pillow, fully prepared to return to what must have been a glorious dream, but someone kept calling his name. In fact, this person had been doing so for several minutes now.

Donal decided that whatever this person wanted could not possibly be more important than letting his mind drift away from consciousness for just a little while longer. Not for too long. His personal alarm would wake him by ten, and it hadn't yet, and there was simply no way anything could have such urgency as to require Donal to jump out of his bed and deal with it.

On some level, Donal knew that was not true. But on most levels he succeeded in telling himself it was, and only moments after realizing someone had been calling his name, Donal began to slumber once more.

Then he felt what could only have been Fionn's teeth denting the skin of his hand.

Donal's eyes snapped open.

"What? Who? Fionn?"

His familiar released its grip on his hand. "I apologize, Master," said Fionn in its lilting tones, which sounded less than entirely apologetic to Donal's sleep-addled ears. "No one wishes more than I to see you sleep deeply and fully following your exertions of last night. But alas need may require it."

Donal forced himself to a sitting position, half considering that having access to so enchanted a bed might cause one to oversleep. He wanted to say at least a dozen different things, but none of them could quite find their way to his mouth.

"A short time ago," Fionn continued, "the ship called its crew to general quarters, which appears to be how they call action stations."

Donal didn't know either of those terms, and curiosity finally came together with the right nerves and he produced sound.

"Is that like battle stations?"

"Indeed. The arrival a short time ago of two guards confirms this. They asked for you, but were content to leave a message with me. Their message: a nearby ship presents a possible threat, and all passengers are confined to quarters until the all-clear announcement comes."

"But I'm a magician. They may need me to help out."

"In the brief interval between the visit from the guards and the moment I began calling your name, Tai Shi Li Hua sent Pinyin Lung to check on you. Through Pinyin Lung, Tai Shi Li Hua requests that you remain in your suite and refrain from anything that could be construed as heroics."

"Is that really how she said it?"

"I'm paraphrasing. Would you like her exact words?"

"No," said Donal trying to rub sleep out of his eyes and deciding that this would not be entirely possible until he got out of bed.

"Moments later," continued Fionn, sitting in his 'patient dog' pose, head tilted slightly to one side, "*Saravá* arrived carrying a message from Ronaldo Machado. Ronaldo Machado requests that you eat a good breakfast and prepare yourself in case you are needed."

"I can't exactly visit a restaurant right now, and if the ship's on alert, I can't imagine they have room service run—"

A knock came from the suite's social room. Without missing a beat, Fionn said, "Ronaldo Machado said that he had arranged for your breakfast."

TUNOLD REACHED GOLDBERG'S OFFICE AT A BRISK JOG. HE EXPECTED TO find the chief bent over his desk, discussing tactics with watch leaders and pointing out details on actual paper maps. Goldberg was the only officer aboard the *Horizon Cusp* who shared the captain's love of keeping and tracking paper records, and it meant that he kept archaic filing cabinets along one wall, cutting down on the space available for watch men and women who needed to wait in his office for one reason or another.

It also meant that Tunold found the chief with his desk covered in paper more often than not. But this time was different. The desk was clear, and the drawers of the filing cabinets all fully closed.

Also absent from the room was the chief himself, but Tunold knew Goldberg had to be around there somewhere because a dozen ship's watch filled the office, donning their safety skinsuits.

Safety skinsuits looked like body stockings the color of adobe, with hoods covering everything but their eyes, and goggles to protect those. Tunold had heard Jacobs describe the safety skinsuits as "ninja outfits, as interpreted by a ballet company," but Tunold thought they looked like skintight pocketless combat fatigues. Not much good for stealth, though, unless the wearer had to blend in among the reddish deserts of the North American southwest.

Invented to aid in riot suppression in the early days of the Rise of Magic, the skinsuits had defensive charms designed to reflect the force of anything stronger than a light pat. The modern version not only protected its wearer but also doubled her striking strength.

They were quite effective, but too expensive to maintain on an everyday basis. The *Horizon Cusp* kept a dozen available in case of emergency.

"I need the chief," said Tunold.

"Right here, Ex Oh," said one of the skinsuits, close enough that Tunold actually jumped and immediately hated himself for it. But sure enough, the speaker lifted his goggles and Tunold saw in Goldberg's eyes the smile he'd never let reach his face at such a moment.

"Never thought I'd see you willing to put one of those things on," said Tunold.

"We might get boarded, Ex Oh. I can't protect my ship if I'm unconscious on the deck."

Tunold nodded, then indicated the others with his chin. "How soon are you ready to move?"

"I already have my lieutenants taking teams to break the confinement news to the passengers and quell any general questions. They'll leave a skeleton crew behind to monitor and the rest will join us here."

Goldberg looked around the deck. "The Main Deck may be the most central, but it's from here that we can reach any part of the ship at speed."

"Need anything?"

Goldberg shook his head. "So far this is running like a drill. But when the party starts..."

He shrugged, then picked up a gleaming white billy club: a Pacifier. "Could definitely use you if you want to stick around."

Tunold grinned and accepted the Pacifier.

JACOBS CHECKED DETAILS ON HIS THREE-DIMENSIONAL MAP. THE CHOKE point between the violet cloud and the asteroids approached rapidly, and Jacobs could find no way of avoiding it that would not allow the gargoyle ship to catch them even faster.

"Mr. Burke, how's your sewing?"

"I can thread a needle, Captain."

"Then hold our speed as long as you can and bleed it only when you have to. We're going in."

Jacobs shook his head. They might as well slow to half for all the good their speed did them. The gargoyle still gained. It might not have achieved speeds much higher than those of the *Horizon Cusp*, but a little higher could be enough.

Jacobs poked a finger into the part of the gryphon display that represented the ship's mage's workshop. The workshop flashed green, signaling that Machado and his Initiate were ready to defend the ship.

Ordinarily, Jacobs hated to be the first to take action, because in most cases there existed the possibility of coincidence, that the other ship happened to find itself crossing Jacobs' path through an unfortunate confluence of circumstances.

But not this time. No other passenger ships had filed routes as of then minutes before the *Horizon Cusp's* launch. Jacobs had checked. And no captain would have been so foolish as to attempt this route without logging his flight path. A military ship would have obvious markings, or have hailed them by now, as would a news ship.

One twist of Jacobs' finger while touching the location of the ship's mage's workshop and he would open a communication link with the ship's mage. He drew a deep breath and prepared to give the order.

"Captain," said Jefferson. "The other ship is hailing us."

Jacobs withdrew his finger and cast a suspicious glance over his shoulder in the direction of the gargoyle ship, but said, "This should be interesting. Link it through to my station."

The man's head that formed above Jacobs' comm pad looked German: pale with almost colorless blue eyes, short, spiky blonde hair, and a wide jaw. But the Aryan-poster-boy connection that tried to form in Jacobs head — an admitted relic from his youth and stories from superior officers — was spoiled by the pock marks and twin scars marring the man's face, gashes across each cheek that had healed the old fashioned way.

"Captain John Jacobs of the *Horizon Cusp*, I am Captain Leopold Wirth of the mercenary ship *Ragnarök*. I want to first assure you that we are not after you, your crew, or most of your passengers."

"How very reassuring." Jacobs poked the gryphon illusion in the ship's mage's workshop and twisted his finger to open a channel, then pushed that finger all the way through to mute the incoming signal. "However, Starchaser Spacelines has a clear policy against piracy and hijacking."

Out of the corner of his eye, Jacobs could see Machado's head appear over the gryphon display, a separate channel from his main comm pad and a design detail that Jacobs had insisted on when he commissioned the *Horizon Cusp*. At the time, he only anticipated a need to have two conversations at once.

But Jacobs believed in adaptation.

"We aren't pirates because we aren't after any goods. And we aren't hijackers because we aren't after your ship. We're mercenaries, and in this case our target is very specific: Donatello Mancuso."

"Who is that?" Jacobs tried to sound blasé, but knew it came out forced. Such tones did not come naturally to him.

"Come, Captain Jacobs." Wirth shouldn't have tried for a patronizing look. Jacobs only found it irritating. "Perhaps company policies bar you from answering questions about passengers, but we both know that he is your business partner and we both know that he is aboard your ship. We want him."

"That's too bad. I'm not in the habit of turning over my passengers to the first punk kid who asks."

Jacobs turned on his command glare. The full weight of threat his experience could bring filled his face.

"Back off."

Wirth didn't even flinch. This mercenary captain must have stared down more than his share of commanding glares over the years.

"We're outside of Earth controlled space," said Wirth. "What I'm asking isn't illegal."

"Earth claims the space between Earth and Venus, whatever Venus and Mars may say about it. And this is getting us nowhere."

Jacobs waved one hand through the man's face, cutting the link. He turned to the head of his ship's mage, Machado's eyes narrowed in thought as he continued staring at where Captain Wirth's head had been.

Jacobs undid the mute, then said, "Did you get enough for a spell?"

"I ... think ... so."

"Take him down, Mash. Sow some confusion into their ranks."

"It won't be easy, but I'll get it done, Captain."

"Good man. Bridge out." Jacobs cut the link, then turned back to the bridge crew. "Ride that speed as hard as you can, Mr. Burke."

"Captain," said Grabowski, "The gargoyle ship is accelerating and moving to intercept. And they've launched a shuttle!"

13

Machado turned to Cromartie and said, "I want you reinforcing the wards. Something's coming."

Cromartie leapt to his feet, pulled out a pocket censer that looked like a thick silver cigarette case and lit the charcoal. He sprinkled onto it some of the incense he had been blending, a mixture of juniper, hyssop, and liquid amber.

Machado watched as Cromartie strode toward the far circle, the one with the strongest links to the wards, but the Initiate must have noticed that Machado had not moved, because he said, "Are you going to start the defenses with illusion?"

"No," said Machado, aware that his voice sounded distant, but not doing anything about it. "I've been ordered to take out their captain."

Cromartie stopped one step shy of the circle. He had the look of someone about to speak, but Machado already knew what he would say. He would know that Machado had always spoken against death magic, both as perverting the art form and as dangerous to the caster. But Machado did not give him a chance to ask the question.

"The captain likely expects me to murder this man, and you and I both know I'm not going to do that. But I have to shut him down hard and fast."

Cromartie still had not taken another step.

"Get to your spells, Initiate. Make me do both our jobs and I'll dock your pay."

Cromartie stepped into the circle and began his work. His deep, resonant voice chanted words not English, but not Gaelic either. Probably Creole. Machado had noticed that Cromartie cast in Creole whenever he got nervous.

Machado stood, called forth *Saravá* and walked into the largest circle, the one he had designed exclusively for himself as a general purpose circle, easily customized.

No. Machado stopped himself. *Not yet. I need more for the connection.*

Machado left the circle for his alchemy lab, where he closed his eyes and called to mind everything he had been able to put together through two communication links: the enemy captain's look, his voice, his expressions, and something of the man's feel. Machado held these qualities in his head, and let his hands work with his eyes still closed.

His hands found herbs, powders, philters, and oils, knowing which they found because Machado had used the same organization system since his first day aboard the *Horizon Cusp*. But Machado did not think about which selections his hands made. He trusted himself to his art, holding and analyzing his sense of the man while his hands brought together the right ingredients and blended a connection oil, which would strengthen the thaumaturgic link Machado would need to affect this Captain Leopold Wirth, especially over such distance, and across two sets of wards.

Then Machado's hands stopped moving, and he knew the oil was ready. He picked up the mortar, turned, and began to anoint that large circle at the cardinal points, while chanting the words of connection.

No, he would not *kill* this man…

Tunold paced as he could in the main Security Office, while all around him men and women of the ship's watch lounged like soldiers getting every last moment of rest they could eke out before the call to action came.

But the fire of need already burned through Tunold, and sitting still would not suit him.

He rounded on Chief Goldberg, reclining in his desk chair. "Why are we sitting here? We know there's a boarding party coming in and we know where they're going to hit."

"No. We don't."

"The Main Deck. It's the only place that makes sense."

Goldberg regarded him, listening but not impelled to action.

"Look," said Tunold, "the public sections of the *Horizon Cusp* are common knowledge. Hell, Zoltan used them in the advertising. So anyone after Mancuso knows he'd want one of the top suites, and that means he's on P1 or P2. But they have no way of knowing which, and speed is of the essence. If they cut in through at the Main Deck, they have the same distance to go either way."

"Except that they know we know they're after Mancuso. So they may assume we moved him."

Tunold leaned on the chief's desk with both hands. Not that he wanted to intimidate Saul, but if he didn't do something, he'd start pacing again.

"Why haven't we moved him?"

"I was just wondering the same thing," said a female voice behind Tunold. He craned his neck and saw Tai Shi in a form-fitting black bodysuit with low boots and her long hair bound. A hood lay behind her head and goggles dangled from her belt. Her version of a safety skinsuit?

"I suppose we could throw him in the brig for his own protection," said Goldberg. "Easiest to protect. But really, if we do, the other execs should get adjoining cells, in case the kidnappers have an unannounced secondary target."

"And why haven't we done this?" said Tunold, turning sideways to keep both the chief and the interloper in sight.

"I could say that moving them to the Security Deck risks giving the boarding party access to the crew portions of the ship, but it'd be just as true that I was trying to avoid this."

Goldberg pointed at Tai Shi.

"You can't keep me out of this fight." Firm, direct, confident words.

"He can," began Tunold, but the chief cleared his throat and Tunold decided to let him answer for himself.

"Keep you out of it? No. Try to avoid drawing you into it? I sure as hell can do that much." Goldberg gave Tunold a wry glance. "But it looks like I failed on that score. So, Kris, do me a favor and take a bunch of men to round up the top execs and any staff they want to have along, and bring them down here to the brig."

Goldberg turned his attention to Tai Shi. "I believe Ms. Tai Shi and I need to have a little talk about the chain of command during this upcoming soiree."

"We don't," said Tai Shi, and Tunold felt his neck twist around fast enough to bring his shoulders and hips with it. But Tai Shi continued, "This is your ship and these are your people, Chief. Strategically you have to answer to me, but tactically I'd be a fool to interfere."

She shook her head. "I'm here to help, not hinder."

Goldberg rose to his feet, a big smile on his face. "Then maybe you and I will get along just fine after all."

Goldberg turned to his resting men and women of the watch. "Wake up time, boys and girls, and I mean double-time. We have some executives to wrangle before company arrives."

"Gargoyle ninety seconds and closing, Captain," said Grabowski.

"What about that shuttle?"

"Thirty seconds tops, Sir. And they've launched a second."

Jacobs swore quietly. Burke was maneuvering to keep the shuttle at bay as long as possible, but with two the task would grow unmanageable even before they reached the pinch point.

And every juke and jink brought the speeding *Ragnarök* that much closer.

Worse, either or both of those shuttles might be decoys, but more likely both carried boarding parties. A ship the size of the *Ragnarök* might carry as many as three shuttlecraft and as many as ... two hundred ... armed...

"Mr. Grabowski, judging by size, how many men can those shuttles hold?"

"I estimate ten, plus pilot and copilot."

"Oh, hell! Mr. Burke, ignore the shuttlecraft, the *Ragnarök* intends to board us the old fashioned way."

Jacobs jammed his finger into the security section of the gryphon illusion, twisted, and started speaking before Goldberg's head appeared to acknowledge.

"Chief! The shuttles are decoys. These bastards intend to grapple and board us from the gargoyle itself."

But the woman who responded was a lieutenant. Not the chief. And though she would deliver the message, Jacobs knew the delay might cost the chief critical seconds of organization.

Jacobs could only hope the cost would not be dear.

— — —

MACHADO SWEPT HIS ARMS OUT TO THE SIDES IN A CIRCLE AND brought them together with all the force his not inconsiderable size could muster, releasing his spell at the apex of a resounding clap.

In that moment, that fleeting portion of a second so brief it might not have existed had not an magician as experienced as Machado known to look for it, Machado felt the spell strike its target.

But Machado could waste no time savoring the befuddlement he had cast upon Captain Wirth, not even to know that the captain would give orders the opposite of his intentions until the friction between desire and action generated enough tension for the secondary effect to render the good captain unconscious.

The spell was cast. Machado knew it would run its course.

In that moment, other matters needed his attention. He felt *Saravá* contact him from deep within the *Horizon Cusp's* tapestry, where the spirit panther kept tabs on the latest information from the scanners.

"Master," said *Saravá*, "focus has shifted from the twin shuttles to the primary opposing ship. It is believed that this ship will carry the attack to us."

"Why send the shuttles then? Just as a diversion?"

"What if they're rigged?" said Cromarite, who must have finished as much as he could do to reinforce the wards for the time being.

"Good point," said Machado. "Focus on shuttles. I'll see what I can do about this gargoyle."

"I ADVISE AGAINST THIS, MASTER," SAID THE *CÚ SIDHE* AS DONAL SAT cross-legged on the floor of his suite's social room and prepared to send his consciousness out into space.

"Noted," said Donal.

"I do not jest, Master. Ronaldo Machado barred this course from you specifically, and if you are elsewhere when the call comes, you may be unable to lend aid at a critical juncture."

Fionn leaned well forward on its forepaws, a gesture which, from a normal dog, might indicate a desire to play. But from Fionn, Donal knew that it was merely intended to draw his attention.

"I implore you. Choose another course of action."

The choice of words made Donal hesitate, clacking his teeth together lightly in his closed mouth as he thought. Fionn did many things: advise, recommend, suggest, point out, call attention to, and other similar turns of speech all of which made quite clear the fae deerhound's opinion while acknowledging that its master would do exactly as he wished.

But Fionn had never before implored Donal, and that made Donal think twice about his goal.

"I just want to see what's out there. If I do get called to help, I want a feel for the space around us so I don't waste time getting up to speed."

"Captain John Jacobs directs us to a narrow channel between asteroids and the feeding ground of the lacunae."

"Lacunae? There are lacunas out there?"

"I have not checked, but I should be surprised if there are not."

A smile spread slowly across Donal's face. A lacuna feeding ground. Only the violet clouds were known to draw lacunas the way a hunting ground drew predators. Donal did not know for certain that lacunas did eat, as humans understood it, but that mattered less than the idea that a great many lacunas might dwell near at hand.

Donal had once called a zuglodon down on this ship by accident, because he had sent his consciousness out into space without proper safety precautions. But conjuration spells required significantly less risk, and did not require Donal to bring the conjured spirits to *this* ship...

Donal cast a circle about himself and slipped into the proper frame of mind for a conjuration, one of his two magical specialties.

In fact, Donal began to see how he could incorporate his other specialty, the magic of deception, into his plan.

***

However much pacing might have helped Jacobs, he knew the right place to be was at his station. Seconds made all the difference in combat, and he could afford no delays no matter how badly his legs longed to stretch and...

But Jacobs knew that was a lie. He did not need to pace. He merely needed to act, and short of grabbing the pilot's station from Burke, there was nothing he could do. And Burke had done a solid job of recovering their course while keeping their distance from the gargoyle as great as he could manage.

Unfortunately, this time the *Horizon Cusp* was the slower ship.

"Mr. Grabowski..."

"Ten seconds before they're in range of grapples, Captain. Good news is the shuttles are flying drunk. One may even get in the gargoyles way."

"Good job, Mash," muttered Jacobs. "Now do something about that ship!"

Not for the first time, Jacobs wished he had armed the *Horizon Cusp*, even though it would have violated the laws of every recognized authority. Might not have been practical, but right then it would have been damned convenient.

MACHADO SWORE COLORFULLY IN PORTUGUESE, BUT FINISHED HIS QUICK rant in English, "And damn me if they don't have a Magister. Because someone is knocking down my defenses as fast as I can set them up."

"I've got the shuttles out of the way. What do you need?"

"Something to distract the opposition so I can get a solid defense in place."

Machado would have to leave the details of Cromartie's assistance to the Initiate. Machado had time only to raise his hands and keep casting.

TUNOLD STOOD BESIDE GOLDBERG AND TAI SHI ON THE MAIN DECK, the entire force of the ship's watch arrayed about them, some sixty men and women. All of them watched the great gray form of the approaching ship through the transparent portion of the hull commonly referred to as the Observation Wall, a lesser version of the Observation Deck at the bottom of the ship, which was almost entirely transparent.

Tunold knew the incoming ship was shaped like a gargoyle, but it was close enough now that he could not see the whole shape clearly. In seconds they would fire their grappling cables, magically augmented to link the ships together.

Boarding would follow shortly.

Tunold knew that they should be waiting on the Security Deck, along with almost all the passengers. But Tai Shi had picked this as the likely location for a breach on the basis of first its central location, and second its transparency, which would ease magical access when the time came.

Tunold wanted to argue because he neither liked nor trusted the woman, but Goldberg had agreed, and it was Goldberg's call. So the entire force waited here.

Any second now…

"Captain," yelled Grabowski, "bogeys! Dozens!"

"Details, Mr. Grabowski!"

"Lacunas, Sir." Disbelief twisted the poor man's words almost beyond the point of comprehensibility. "Big ones, small ones. Gotta be fifty of them all homing in on the *Ragnarök*."

"Mr. Burke, push us into the asteroid field. Once inside you can kill the speed all you like for safety, but not until there are at least two rocks between us and them."

Jacobs noted to give his ship's mage a bonus and started poring over what the charts could tell him about this asteroid field.

"Yes!" cried Machado as the illusion took hold. A simple spell, it would enhance the wards to make them extra-slippery to incoming grapples. Now he needed to do something about the gargoyle's firing mechanism if he could penetrate its wards.

Then he felt it, dozens of angry, simple minds with vast power. All outside the ship.

"Aaron, get ready to augment the wards. We've got—"

"Master," said *Saravá*, "lacunae from the hunting ground have been conjured to attack the other ship. Based on the information from the scanners, I estimate fifty-three, including six great lacunae."

Cromartie could never have conjured that many. Probably not Tai Shi either. Her magic tended toward the direct and personal. Conjuration was not her style...

But it was a specialty of Cuthbert's.

"Aaron, forget the wards. Go get the doctor and find Cuthbert. Damn fool's outdone himself this time."

Machado allowed a moment to perceive for himself what *Saravá* had seen through the scanners. He smiled, despite his concern.

"That brilliant, damned fool."

Machado could now ignore the *Ragnarök*. Once those lacunas started hitting the other ship, their wards would not last long.

But Machado had to ensure that these lacunas did not turn their attention to the *Horizon Cusp*.

DONAL REELED AS HE SAT CROSS-LEGGED ON THE CARPET, SWAYING SIDE to side despite how much he wanted to stop. Swaying made the nausea worse. Perhaps Magister Machado could stomach rich food before a major working, like the sausage and eggs he had sent to Donal, but Donal should have stuck to fruit and toast.

Then perhaps the room would not be spinning so fast.

Donal focused on his breathing, resorting to one of the basic school-taught patterns to try to control his body, to bring his physical form and mental form back into the alignment that the major conjuration, combined with an illusion no less, had knocked out of whack.

Fionn sat before Donal, then leaned forward and ever-so-gently nipped at Donal's shoulders, then his wrists, then his knees, mumbling Gaelic all the while that Donal felt as though he should have been able to understand, yet could not.

Still, by the time Fionn finished the ritual, Donal began to feel his stomach settle. He almost felt coordinated in his body again, but not quite.

Then the knock came on the door.

Donal tried to untangle his crossed legs, but they refused to cooperate. A moment later, the door opened and Doctor Ramirez hustled into the room, followed by Initiate Cromartie.

"Donal," said the doctor. "I apologize for using my access key, but the ship's mage felt you might have been lying here unconscious."

"He nearly was," said Fionn before Donal could reply.

"I'm fine," said Donal. "Really. A little nap and I'll be right as the morning fog."

"He nearly disconnected," said Fionn to Cromartie, and Donal felt just a little betrayed. "He held together, but he—"

"Needs blended salts in suspension, which I have," said the doctor, fishing a small sealed glass container full of greenish liquid from his medical bag. "And I suspect an alchemical mixture which I don't have."

"I know which one you mean," said Cromartie. "Saw it on the battlefield all the time. I'll go get some from Fredrickson."

"I'm telling you," began Donal, but the doctor shoved the drink in his face, leaving him no option but to open it and drink. It tasted all right at first, almost like lime, but by the end of the jar it didn't quite sit right in his stomach and the salty taste irritated his taste buds.

"I take it by that sour expression that it no longer tastes good?"

The humor in the doctor's voice made Donal suspect that the man had deep-seated sadism.

"Terrible."

"Good. That means you've had enough. When Mr. Cromartie returns with the potion, see that you drink all of it." Then the doctor turned to Fionn. "Please. See that he drinks all of it."

"I shall," said Fionn.

"I'm right here," said Donal.

"That's probably all you need," said the doctor, owlish eyes regarding Donal without blinking. "But if you feel off later, come see me for more blended salts. You magicians really need to keep better track of what your magics do to your bodies."

"Such as I have been saying no less for thousands of years," said Fionn.

"Seriously." Donal waved his hand back and forth. "Sitting right here."

The doctor turned and left without another word.

14

Seated once more in his office with Tunold and Goldberg in his guest chairs, Jacobs listened while Machado, reclining on the couch, explained how more than fifty lacunas happened to come rushing out of the violet cloud and descend on the *Ragnarök*.

"Cuthbert *again?*" said Tunold.

"The boy does have a happy talent for conjuration," said Machado. "Good thing, too. If he had managed a lesser familiar he'd have gotten himself into all sorts of trouble by now."

"Maybe we should have hired him for assistant ship's mage," said Goldberg.

"You mean so he could have gotten into more trouble than he does now?" asked Jacobs, drawing the eyes of the three officers and three short but different laughs. Tunold snorted, but it was a snort that rocked his head back and forth, even pulling his shoulders with it the least bit. Goldberg snickered, mostly with his nose, a sound that moved so little of his face that it would have gone unnoticed during a larger meeting. Machado chuckled, a rich sound that pleased the never-ending stream of women he always seemed to draw in port.

In Machado's case, the brief laugh ended with him saying, "I'm quite pleased with how Aaron has worked out. He's adaptable, for an Initiate, and his focus and dedication are admirable."

"What happened to the *Ragnarök*?" asked Tunold.

"They tore it apart," said Jacobs. "Freed its lacunas."

"Did the crew make it to lifeboats?" asked Goldberg.

"Some must have, but the total is unknown." Jacobs heard at least one of his officers draw breath to speak, but Jacobs only spoke louder. "No, we will not be rendering humanitarian aid. We have already sent word to the nearest military base, and beyond that we will leave them to their fates.

"It's bad enough I have Burke steering us through an asteroid field, but after that little display, there's no way I'm going to risk this ship flying anywhere near that so-called feeding ground."

"It *is* a feeding ground," said Machado. "They just don't eat the way we think of eating."

"Not the point," said Jacobs, thinking about how the other ship came apart. "They tore it apart at the seams, Mash. How does a spirit do that?"

"Well, it can happen with a ship that's carterite heavy because carterite requires more alchemy to mold into shape and more enchantments to maintain. When the lacunas ripped through the bindings, they literally tore through the ship."

Machado shrugged. "Honestly, though, by the time the hull came apart any crew still on the ship were probably already dead. The life support would have gone down well before the hull gave way."

All four men descended into a moment of silence. For Jacobs that moment was filled with thoughts of those he had lost at sea, in the skies, and at space, which made him think of that most recent loss.

Jacobs dug into his desk drawer past the bottle of Brigid's Own Irish Whiskey for a mostly full bottle of Butcher's Block Kentucky Bourbon and four tumblers. He poured two fingers worth in each.

Each man stood and took up his glass, faces solemn for the dead. "The *Beamrunner*," said Jacobs, "and all those we have lost."

They drank down the whiskey, Jacobs savoring the bitter burn all the way down. It tasted like mourning. Each man set his glass on the desk and returned to his seat.

"How did our guests handle the temporary change of accommodations?" asked Jacobs.

"Does it have to be temporary?" said Goldberg. "Because I think we could cut down on—"

"Saul."

"All right, all right. They're all out on their own recognizance anyway. Odd, though. The top people seemed to treat the whole thing as a matter of course. It was their second-tier folk who got put out about it."

"Probably expressing what the bigwigs thought for them," said Tunold.

"More likely," said Jacobs, "they just aren't as used to death threats." He shook his head. "Any signs of trouble among the passengers? Apart from Cuthbert, I mean. Tai Shi, for example."

Goldberg sighed. "I want to bitch about Tai Shi. God knows she's given me enough reason over the last week. But I have to hand it to her, she handled the crisis well."

Jacobs felt his eyebrows rise, and Goldberg snickered that almost silent laugh of his again. "No joke. She even showed up in a safety skinsuit of her own—"

"Fashionably black of course," said Tunold.

"—whatever color it was, she took orders and stood ready to fight. Didn't even offer suggestions unless asked. Said her role was strategy, but would leave the tactics to me."

"Did you tell her that, strategically speaking, we need more safety skinsuits and some upgraded Pacifiers?"

"Captain!" Goldberg affected a wounded look. "I know my job." He winked. "I also suggested a few slingers would be—"

"A terrible idea," said Machado. "I swear, all you physical combat types crave your lost firearms so much that you don't think through the consequences."

"Hands up all who grew up without firearms," said Goldberg, raising his hand. Tunold also raised his, as did Machado.

"They were never my favorite example of technology," said Jacobs.

"My point is," said Machado, "military research keeps trying to bring back firearms and ranged weapons. Slingers! The pathetic things are fragile, and probably as great a risk to the shooter as to the target. And I have no intention of wasting my time cleaning up after misfired shots that mess with *my* spells."

Machado stood, and Jacobs had to admit that he cut a formidable figure, despite his modest height.

"If we start using slingers, you can find a new ship's mage."

"Sit down, Mash," said Jacobs. "No need for threats."

"It was just a thought," said Goldberg, hands raised in surrender.

Machado turned his attention to Tunold, and Jacobs realized that the ship's mage wanted reassurance from the *Horizon Cusp's* next captain as well as its current.

Fortunately, Tunold realized this as well.

"I'd be fine with barring slingers from the ship." Tunold's eyes turned to Jacobs. "Even among the weapons we store for our passengers."

So Kris is still angry about a bunch of swords and trinkets in the safe?

"All right, gentlemen," said Jacobs. "If we can waste time arguing about what we will and won't carry for our passengers, then I'd say we're done with our after-action meeting."

Jacobs stood. "We have a ship to run. Let's get to it."

By mid-afternoon, Donal felt like himself again. The elixir the doctor had given him had helped his body. The doses of potion Initiate Cromartie had brought back from the alchemist had gotten Donal's mind and magic back in alignment.

But for Donal's money — not that he had to pay for it — the massage helped most of all. He stood now outside The Relaxation Station on the Main Deck and stared at the cloudless bright blue "sky" above him.

Donal stretched his arms and said to Fionn, "Think I could get any research money to study the thaumaturgic benefits of deep tissue massage for magicians? I could argue that nothing anchors the mind and spirit in the body better than a deep, muscle-by-muscle rubdown."

"I think that if you complete your doctorate, you will be able to persuade potential investors with words they do not understand. Monied people always like feeling that they invest in those smarter than they are themselves."

"True," said Donal, beginning to saunter down the path between faux-Greek designs of dance studios (classes daily!) and hydrotherapy offices (they claimed restorative powers, but Donal suspected that they counted on the soothing feel of hot, bubbling water).

"Wait, what do you mean 'if' I complete my—"

"There you are," came Li Hua's voice from behind Donal. He turned and saw her approaching from near The Relaxation Station, dressed casually in a low-cut but long-sleeved sweater, and slacks that hung tight to the waist and thighs, but flared out around her calves and soft leather boots.

"I checked the Observation Deck first, but I should have known you'd come for a massage."

"I had a busy morning," said Donal, trying to sound humble but unable to keep a pleased smile off of his face.

"I know. Here I was ready for a good fight and you stole all the fun." She stepped close. "I had to go work out. Too much energy."

Something about the way her lips formed those words made Donal want to kick himself for not being near at hand when she had needed ... exercise.

"Wish I could have helped, but I was kind of indisposed."

"Overreached again and almost disconnected?"

Fionn made a small canine sound that would have been innocent from an actual deerhound, but from the familiar had to have been a statement akin to "I told you that was overreaching."

When Fionn actually took Li Hua's side about something, Donal felt ganged up on. Fortunately for Donal, it did not happen often.

"I had to do something. I couldn't just—"

"Shhh," said Li Hua, two fingers over Donal's lips, her own lips coming closer, excitement brimming her soft brown eyes with their hint of caramel. She breathed her next words, a bare whisper.

"Admit it. Responsibility was not your sole motivation. You craved the risk, the razor's edge at the limits of your talent and ability."

Li Hua moved her fingers and her lips came closer.

"You love the adrenaline as much as I do."

And then she kissed Donal with only her lips, not touching with her hands, nor pressing her body against him. A soft and almost secret kiss that ended all too soon for Donal, though it did keep her lips near his.

"I don't know if anyone loves adrenaline as much as you do." He brought his hand to her cheek and kissed her then, his other hand on the small of her back pulling her to him. Her arms entwined about his neck as the kiss deepened.

As the kiss ended, Donal stroked her cheek again. He could see in her eyes that she wanted him to say more, to confess to sharing her passion for danger. Donal could not say for certain that he did, but he could not deny that such risks had done more for his confidence and his magic than anything else he had done since graduating U. C. Santa Cruz.

And he could not let the silence stretch any tighter between them or he would ruin the moment.

So he stretched the truth, just a little, as those who specialize in the magic of deception did best.

"But I do love what the adrenaline does for me."

"I knew it." Li Hua's words sounded definitive, and something changed in her smile, her eyes. Some certainty, perhaps about Donal or perhaps about the two of them as a couple. Donal wanted to ask, but she spoke again, excitement smoldering under her words.

"I have a few hours before my next meeting." Her fingers traced the line of his jaw. "What say we go back to my room and celebrate our mutual love of excitement? And afterwards, we can talk about what it could mean for our future."

Part of Donal recognized from her tone that she did not mean their future as a couple, but after the morning he had, his thoughts focused more on what awaited him in her room *before* they had this conversation.

After all, Donal told himself, *my professors always said that if the present is handled correctly, the future will attend to itself.*

When Machado stepped out of the bubble onto the Engineering Deck, he smelled Jang's work immediately. *Verbena,* he thought. *She always uses too much verbena.* So far as Machado was concerned, the scent of that herb should not be detectable ten meters from the Deception Drive's engine room. Yes, it sealed many of the key spells, but that did not mean that it needed to be slathered about like gouts of cheap aftershave used to cover a lack of personal hygiene.

He should certainly not be able to smell it here by the bubble.

She probably does it to annoy me.

Machado sauntered past the side rooms that held redundant systems, spirits kept dormant and constrained by spells one step shy of completion: an elaborate network of magic that formed a system of travel almost one hundred percent reliable. More out of habit than out of concern, he gestured for *Saravá* to check the rooms on the right while he examined the rooms on his left, in passing.

Everything looked in order. Machado mused that he might have occasion to question Jang's precision, but never her accuracy.

Continuing on, Machado took a side passage past the supply closet to Jang's office, where he paused to check the paper wheel affixed to the door for her location. In big black letters was written, "The Chief is," followed by eight options: in, asleep, pissed off, eating, Deception Drive, around, in a meeting, out. The small arrow in the center pointed to her current location: the Deception Drive.

Machado sighed as he moved sideways down a cramped hall, past rooms dedicated to communications, navigation, detection, and other systems.

No wonder Jitters never puts on weight. You have to be half-clothesline to work down here.

At the end of the hall, eventually, he reached the Deception Drive. Its door stood open, showing the three-meter square room with walls covered in layers of spells, runes, symbols and bindings that contained a single lacuna in a web of illusions that kept it content and happy, tied into certain key systems that motivated it to carry the ship where its captain wanted through positive reinforcement.

Sales material implied that the Deception Drive was so named because it was deceptively fast for an engine needing only a single space elemental. The truth was that the lacuna was the one deceived into doing its job, rather than forced and compelled as other engines had done before it.

Jang moved about the main circle in her potion-stained coveralls. Within that circle resided the lacuna itself, invisible but all too audible in the multi-tonal sounds it made: three just then, not quite harmonizing. Jang wafted incense toward the circle from her portable brass censer, the size and shape of a deck of cards. She spoke to it as well, in low soft tones. Machado could not make out her words, but he knew that she was not casting. No thread of power moved through her.

Still, he clasped his hands behind his back and tried to wait politely, even though he knew she wasn't casting. Which meant that what she did now could not be critical. Which meant that waiting was wasting his time, time that could be invested in another task for the ship.

Time during which Machado could not keep himself from remembering the pain that innocent-sounding spirit had seared through his system, when Machado's will alone stood between the lacuna and a slip in its bindings.

Finally, to break the silence and ensure that she knew he was there, he said, "More verbena, Jang?"

"Verbena seems to soothe it, and it dominates the grassroot portion of the incense." She paused and gave Machado an evil grin. "Plus, I know you hate it."

She wanted to get a rise out of him. Machado refused to succumb.

"How's it holding up?" he asked, his gaze dancing across the various spells inscribed along the walls, floor and ceiling, but saw nothing immediately amiss.

She clapped the censer closed and tucked it in her breast pocket. "Got a bit agitated when we had that unannounced high-speed chase."

"It wasn't unannounced. I warned you it might happen before I turned in last night."

"'Jang. Probable incoming pirates. Be ready.' Some warning."

Machado stared at her. Her complaint sounded almost right. Almost normal. But not quite.

"That's not what's bugging you."

"No! It's Burke up there playing fucking dodge ball with my ship!"

Machado shook his head and folded his arms. He felt *Saravá* take up a supporting position behind him.

"Out with it, Jang."

Jang started tapping her knuckles together.

"Look. I know Cuthbert's the hero of the day and all, but that spell of his almost sank us."

"The other lacunas ignored us. He augmented the conjuration with a clever bit of deception. Besides, I—"

"No. I mean he almost conjured *our* lacunas too. Damn near called them right out of their bindings. This one," — she jerked her head at the singing spirit in the circle to her left — "and the one in the scanners too. Never seen anything like it."

"Both at the same time? How did you hold them together?"

"Spit and bailing wire." She tried to laugh at their old joke about maintaining the *Horizon Cusp* while at space, but couldn't manage more than a half-hearted attempt. "No, the bindings held, but it was a near thing."

"That's why it's so verbena-heavy in here today."

"Really does help soothe them, though damn if I can figure out why."

"I'll add it to my list. Maybe I can figure out a way to use that detail to improve the deceptions."

"Not with whatever they call facilities on Venus," Jang said with a derisive snort. "Won't matter much anyway. We cut the lacunas off from the outside space any more than we do and they won't be able to do their jobs for us."

Machado thought about that as the two of them looked up at where they knew the spirit to be. Machado shifted more of his consciousness until he could see it, like the empty outline of a stream of water, shifting and twisting and curling about itself.

He sighed.

"All right. I'll ward the deck against conjuration magic. That should keep our lacunas where they belong — at least for the time being — and all our other elementals while I'm at it."

So much for Machado's plans for the rest of the afternoon.

"Excellent work, Mr. Burke," said Jacobs from the forward portion of the perimeter walkway that surrounded the bridge. Through the transparent ceramics of the hull surrounding the bridge, he watched the last of the asteroids pass to port, leaving clear space ahead for the rest of the day.

Beautiful, when he took the time to notice.

Jacobs turned to face his bridge crew. "Excellent work, all of you. I've served with many crews over the years, and I can't think of any I'd rather have around me during a crisis."

Jacobs savored their stunned expressions at the highest compliment he had ever paid them, but only for a moment. He turned and made his way to the stairs and continued on back to his station, hiding his pleasure at the elation they must be feeling behind his impassive mask of command.

But inside, Jacobs felt warm affection for them all, every member of his crew. But especially his chosen bridge crew, because he had meant every word of that compliment. They had earned it. Jacobs even allowed himself a sigh of pleasure as he eased into his captain's chair.

But then, to work.

"Mr. Grabowski, how is my space?"

"Clear as morning, Captain." Jacobs did not even have to see the man to hear the smile in his voice. "No threats emerging from the feeding ground, not even any sign of wild lacunas in the last hour."

That was good. That was as it was supposed to be, according to the charts that Jacobs even now reviewed to reassure himself that this quiet moment might last for a time.

At least until his next command performance at dinner that night.

But even then, Jacobs expected no more trouble until tomorrow, that final day of approach to Venus. That day would be fraught with possible dangers, from the nearness of the zuglodon hunting ground to the mysterious no-fly zone that Jacobs had chosen — perhaps in a fit of irritation — to skirt as closely as he could.

No. Tomorrow would present the sort of challenge Jacobs preferred to face as a captain, the sort that did not leave hundreds of men and women floating in space, men and women who would not likely survive the night.

At moments like this one, Jacobs felt glad to no longer serve in the Navy, pleased that such incidents were rare for him now, and never initiated by him. He also felt glad, if wistful, that Rhonda and Carl were not alive to explain this to.

Of course, if they *were* still alive, they would understand. They would have lived through too much, seen too much to blame him for what had happened.

But in Jacobs' mind, Carl was eternally a little boy, full of ideas and promise, and Rhonda was idealistic girl he married, a pacifist who struggled with her love for her Navy man.

To them Jacobs would apologize at length before he slept.

But right then, on the bridge, all Jacobs could do was dry his eyes and see about getting their flight back on schedule. Not that anyone would care but him.

"Mr. Burke, our little dance with the *Ragnarök* has put us exactly four-and-one-quarter hours behind schedule. I expect you to increase speed to compensate. Ms. Jefferson, I would like you to run that calculation as well."

Jacobs allowed himself a small smile at the surprised confirmations he got. He wanted to see how well they handled this task, but he knew they would get it right.

They really were a good crew.

Donal stretched like a contented cat, warm pleasure suffusing his being. Some of that, he had to admit, came from the well-enchanted bed and sheets around him, but more of it came from the fact that he was still half-entangled with Li Hua.

She reached the dozen or so centimeters between them and kissed his throat at the pulse point, then pulled back smiling as though at something more than their recent activities.

Then Donal remembered that Li Hua had said something about discussing their future. But just then the only future he wanted to discuss was how much time they still had before either of them — meaning Li Hua — had to be anywhere, and how that time might be passed.

A subject on which Donal had a few ideas, none of which necessitated leaving the bed.

But Li Hua spoke first. "How did you feel? After pulling off that spell?" She danced her fingers along the hairs of his chest. "Not easy, was it? Combining that big a conjuration with that intense an illusion."

"I admit it was quite a rush." Donal wanted to mirror her movement, but confined his fingers to her shoulder, at least until she signaled that she was ready to move beyond words. "Did you see it?"

"Oh, I had a front row seat down on the Observation Deck when your lacunas tore into that ship, battering apart its wards and freeing its lacunas." She kissed his shoulder, but the softness of her lips did a little less to stir him than it should have. "It was quite a sight."

"They tore the ship apart?"

"Split the carterite at the joins." She tilted her head in thought. "Heck of a salvage."

"What about the crew?"

"Not much left to salvage there."

Donal sat up. "That's not funny."

"Donal..." Li Hua urged him back down with her fingers on his shoulder. "They were trying to kill us."

Donal sat, staring at the peaceful depiction of a nebula on the opposite wall. *The whole crew, dead? Because of me?*

"Donal..." There was laughter in her voice, and she began to kiss her way up his bicep, speaking between kisses. "It was just like," — kiss — "Mars," — kiss — "them," — kiss — "or," — kiss "us." She paused to kiss the top of his shoulder, biting down just a little.

"You did what you had to."

Donal slowly shook his head.

"They were going to *kill us all*." She sat up now, grabbed his chin with one hand and turned Donal to meet her eyes. "You, me, Captain Jacobs, the steward who brought you wine at dinner last night, the tall guard who keeps escorting you places. All. Of. Us."

She moved her hand to stoke Donal's cheek now, and Donal let himself lean into it.

"If you hadn't done what you did, they would have broken through the wards, breeched the hull, and come after us with some two hundred mercenaries. They wanted Mr. Mancuso, and these are not people who leave witnesses."

Li Hua leaned in and kissed Donal again, and this time Donal could enjoy the sweetness of her lips, the subtle jasmine of her scent.

When the kiss broke, she said, "You did the right thing."

"I did the necessary thing." Donal searched her eyes to see if he could find even of a hint of the struggle he felt over what he had done, though he knew Li Hua had answered her own questions about such matters long ago. "I'm not sure they're the same thing."

"When survival is at stake, the necessary thing is always the right thing." She quirked a smile that arched one her eyebrows. "No playing martyr on me now."

Donal shook his head, then kissed her to reassure her that he was quite happy they were both alive.

"So you said something about discussing the future?"

"Later," Li Hua said, swinging Donal back down on the bed. "I only have an hour till my meeting, and I have to show the hero of the day my gratitude."

15

Jacobs sat at his desk, trying to fortify himself with fiction for the night's dinner with the passengers. He had found a series of thrillers by an up and coming author who set his works during World War II. Jacobs found them soothing: lots of action, clear good guys and bad guys, and reminders of what life had been like before the fall of technology.

Of course, the writer had been born some thirty years after the rise of magic, so he got all sorts of little details wrong, but Jacobs enjoyed the novels anyway. Though he did sometimes feel tempted to write letters of correction to the author.

Jacobs had just reached a scene where the hero, Arnie Steele, had crept into a Nazi compound to save the brilliant Jewish scientist (who, Jacobs expected from the pattern of previous novels, had a beautiful daughter). Steele had made no sound passing the guards, but he had not counted on the acute noses of their German shepherds...

Someone had the gall to knock on Jacobs' door.

Jacobs looked down at his novel, where the dogs had just begun to pull their guards in Steele's direction, then back up at the door. The knock returned, a confident two-tap pulse that Jacobs did not recognize.

Which meant it wasn't anyone on Jacobs' crew.

My own fault for sending Kelly to dinner early.

Jacobs stabbed the spot where he stopped reading, a frustrated poke with his index finger. That would trigger the refillable to open to that spot when Jacobs returned. He tossed the novel into a desk drawer and said, "Come."

The door opened. Mr. Mancuso, dressed for dinner in a black evening suit that was not quite a tuxedo, stepped in and closed the door behind him.

"Captain Jacobs. Or can I call you John, now that we're partners? Seems to me that our shared business interests ought to be sufficient grounds for using each other's Christian names. Mine's Donatello."

"I prefer Captain Jacobs."

"Course you do." Mancuso smiled, and Jacobs would have sworn the stretch of lips somehow managed to look predatory and sincere all at the same time. Mancuso continued speaking as he crossed the room in swift strides. "You're a military man, and I'm just the sort of successful businessman your type hates. Just as used to giving orders, but you don't feel I've earned the right because I've never fought anyone to the death."

Jacobs decided that those words were a trap and chose to sit, waiting for the man to get to his point, rather than rise to the bait.

"Nevertheless, you risked yourself and your crew to protect me from those pirates." Mancuso smiled, and this time Jacobs had no doubts about the predatory thoughts behind Mancuso's eyes. "Yes, I know they were after me. I even have a pretty good idea about who sent them. Not that I can do anything about it from here."

Mancuso gestured to the books and images on the walls. "I see you've redecorated. Does that mean you're interested in staying on with Starchaser Spacelines after this trip?"

"What can I do for you, Mr...." Jacobs felt his eyes widen at the implication in the man's words. "Wait. You saw this office recently? *Before* I moved back into it?"

"Couldn't buy a business sight unseen," said Mancuso in a chiding tone. "Your boy Zoltan gave me a tour of the facilities to prove that the ship had recovered after the damage from those zuglodons."

Jacobs hated the thought of that man, that *landlubber*, violating the sanctity of the crew sections of the ship. But this was not the time to let that show. Jacobs forced his lips to part, aware that the effect was more snarl than smile.

"What can I do for you, Mr. Mancuso?"

"I want Donal to join us at the big table tonight. Hero of the hour and all. But it's your table and I didn't want to invite him without talking to you first." Mancuso raised a sardonic eyebrow. "I can pay for his seat, if you'd prefer."

Jacobs felt a real smile intrude on his expression, but it was the smile he got when an opponent dropped his right in the boxing ring. Mancuso had been thorough in his research. Half the seats at the captain's table were only available through invitation from the captain, while the other half could be purchased for a set price. The contract for this flight had included seats for each of the top executives, but technically one purchasable seat remained unused.

Jacobs wanted to take Mancuso's money, both on principle and to avoid agreeing with the man. But damn it, in this case he was right. Jacobs would have already invited Cuthbert to the table, except for one detail.

"I'm not sure we'd be doing the boy a favor. If last night was any example, the conversation will run heavy on the business side."

Mancuso shook his head. "You're a brilliant captain, Jacobs. I don't mind saying it because I'm smart enough to recognize talent when I see it. Part of the reason I'm where I am today. But you sailors lose your sense of anything but sailing. Cuthbert gets his doctorate and he's going to need funding for his research."

Mancuso shrugged with a what-can-you-do gesture.

"I'd be happy to fund the boy for his entire life, but he might think I'm trying to buy him if he never receives any other offers of grant money. So let him start seeing what his options are. That way he can pick me because he knows I'm the best choice."

"Modest. Aren't you."

"I told you I recognize talent, and that means my own talents too. Far as I'm concerned, modesty is as big a sin as pride. Lose control of either and you're just as badly off."

"I want the *Daedalus Dream* as part of my retirement package."

"That's what I mean!" Mancuso rubbed his hands together, excitement brimming his eyes. "Have to have the confidence to go after what you want. The *Daedalus Dream's* profit margins are too sweet for me to just throw it in, but I'll do some thinking about this and get back to you."

Mancuso stood.

"The *Daedalus Dream*," said Jacobs.

"We'll see." Mancuso straightened his jacket, even though not a wrinkle or crease had intruded on its smoothness during the time that Mancuso had been sitting. "If that's a deal-breaker for you, realize that your buy-out offer will exclude the costs and profits of that ship. You'll either get a lesser ship for free or one way or another you'll pay for the one you want."

"I'm not asking for anything I haven't earned."

Mancuso met Jacobs' eyes, and Jacobs saw the merciless look he associated with commandos about to go into battle.

"You're entering my field of combat now, Jacobs. Stick to your guns and you'll find out how I earned *my* command."

DONAL STOOD IN THE BEDROOM OF HIS OWN SUITE, TRYING TO GET HIS suit to behave the way it had in the tailor's shop, to hang just right. But he could not stop fidgeting, and neither mirror on the back of the closet doors seemed to offer much guidance.

"I should attend the dinner," said Fionn, who lay on the floor, head on crossed paws as though completely uninterested in Donal's clothing problems.

"I'm not sure that's a good idea." Donal twisted and checked another angle. Donal liked the suit. In theory. Tailored navy blue silk with a scarlet tie, a light blue silk shirt. Combined with a black belt and shoes, even Donal had to admit that the suit looked good on him.

At least, it had looked good while he and Li Hua had been in that tailor's shop in San Francisco.

"Someone has already made one effort on Mr. Mancuso's life. The responsible party will likely be sitting at that table tonight. You need me to help you sort through the possibilities."

"That," said Donal brushing his hands down his sleeves one more time, "does not address the issue of Mr. Mancuso himself." From the look of his reflection, he almost had it right, except that now his shoulders looked off again. "I'm not sure we can afford to split our focus."

"Oh, for Rhiannon's sake," said Fionn, rising to stand. "Stop fidgeting. Close your eyes. Now take a deep breath. Let it out slowly. Now another. That's it. You're just getting dressed, not attending your own funeral. One more slow, deep breath."

Donal could hear the *cú sidhe* walk a circle around him, feel its presence as it passed, its not-quite-body-heat. Finally, Fionn spoke again.

"Now, open your eyes."

Donal allowed his lids to part as slowly as the breaths he continued to draw. The Donal looking back from the mirror looked just as good as Donal had remembered from that tailor shop.

"Much better," said Fionn. "And for what you paid for that suit..."

"I'll need it for certain school functions anyway." Donal turned to meet Fionn's fiery emerald eyes. "It doesn't matter how much good you could do me at dinner. Magister Machado would probably throw a fit if I brought you."

"Ronaldo Machado has no right to intrude on your safety."

"Unless I want to challenge his right to this ship as his demesne, he does."

"Foolish system," said Fionn.

"Maybe, but it's all I've got."

"Give me your word that you will summon me at the first hint of trouble. You can apologize to Ronaldo Machado later."

"I'll call you at the first sign of a problem."

"No, Master. Give me your word."

Fionn's seated posture was erect and still, its ears up and pointed, its eyes locked on Donal's.

Donal crouched to put his eyes on Fionn's level and said, "An we are linked, I swear by my power, my skill, and my blood that I shall summon you to my aid at the first sign of trouble while I dine in the restaurant Ambrosia this night, or if I suspect any possible danger as I approach or leave that place."

Fionn nodded once, then shifted into bright green light and moved into the silver faun pendant on the chain around Donal's neck.

JACOBS TOOK HIS SEAT AT THE HEAD OF THE CAPTAIN'S TABLE IN THE center of Ambrosia's main dining room. Above him the illusory sky shone with the stars of a clear Greek spring, leaving the room at a comfortable level of dimness: bright enough that all diners at a table could see each other and their meals clearly, but dark enough to give privacy to the neighboring tables. In the background he could just hear the strains of a Greek folk song, loud enough to add a touch of spice to ambiance, but too quiet to interfere with even whispered conversation.

Mancuso sat on Jacobs' right, and for the second night in a row Jacobs wondered why. The seat at the foot of the table was available. Mancuso might have claimed it by right of partnership, and considering that everyone at the table except Jacobs was Mancuso's guest, it could even have represented a shift in the location of the table's head.

And yet Mancuso chose to let Jacobs keep the head of the table, but sat in the position of most-important-guest: first among equals, but below the captain. Jacobs guessed that this was some sort of maneuver related to whatever business deal Mancuso was cooking up on this voyage.

Much like inviting Cuthbert had to have been. Oh, Jacobs did not doubt that Mancuso felt gratitude toward the boy for his role in the day's excitement, but Jacobs doubted that Mancuso was the sort to accomplish only one thing with a gesture.

Even now Cuthbert sat at Jacobs' left hand, dressed for the occasion, but lacking the self-possession to wear the suit the way it should have been worn. The poor lad looked every bit as uncomfortable as Jacobs had expected. He wondered for a moment whether Carl would have handled the situation better. Jacobs liked to think Carl would have. Jacobs liked to think he would have trained his son to understand that when you focus on mastering yourself, no one else can make you feel like less than a master.

But for all his study and introspection, Cuthbert seemed to have missed that lesson.

On Mancuso's right was the only man not dressed for a formal dinner, Farbod Kianoush. Kianoush opted for a dark cashmere sweater with slacks that could have looked formal with the right shirt and jacket. With the sweater, though, the effect could not have been called "dressy."

Kianoush was also the only one who had refused his share of Pinot Noir when the steward brought the bottle around. The opposite reaction from Saito Akio, who sat to Kianoush's right and had already finished that first glass of wine and gestured for more. Saito wore a finely tailored charcoal gray suit with a slim black tie, and Jacobs approved of the choice. It created a look that managed to be almost understated, while still conveying elegant quality.

Saito shared that quality with Natalia Romanova, who sat across from him. She wore a gown of deep forest green, high-necked and long-sleeved, yet cut so that a hint of iridescence — apparently a feature of the fabric — emphasized her movements as though she wore understated jewels all over her body. But the only actual jewelry she wore was a cameo that hung about her collarbone.

Ricardo Montenegro, seated to Romanova's right and Cuthbert's left, also wore a necklace that hung about his collarbone, but in his case a face had been carved in gold. Jacobs did not recognize the style, but believed it looked Mesoamerican. The gold matched

Montenegro's cufflinks, the only other adornment of his classic-design tuxedo.

But Jacobs was more curious about Montenegro's choice of seats than his decision to wear the only actual tuxedo at the table. Montenegro had looked as though he intended to sit beside Mancuso before he spotted Cuthbert, at which point he had moved quickly to claim the seat to the boy's left.

But what could Montenegro want with Cuthbert?

Jacobs hoped that the day's excitement had not put any of them on edge. But he knew that if any of them stepped out of line, Goldberg and his team would be all too happy to leave their table behind Jacobs and escort all disturbers of the peace to the brig.

And if any of them gave Cuthbert a bad time, Jacobs felt as though he might be tempted to let the chief do just that.

Donal held his wineglass by the stem and swirled his Pinot Noir, enjoying the brilliance of its red color. He brought it to his nose and smelled bright cherries with a hint of fresh earth in its scent. He sipped, and its complex flavors sorted themselves on his tongue: fruit, currant, Portobello, and a hint of smoke.

He felt the urge to gulp it down, to finish his as fast as Mr. Saito had. Not that the wine was that tasty, though it was, nor as a gesture of support for someone who clearly had been raised with a different attitude toward wine than Donal had.

No, Donal wanted to gulp down his wine and ask for more because he felt overwhelmed by the business discussions that had already begun. Either the other diners continued from previous topics with odd, pre-agreed-to jargon, or they conversed about business the way professional magicians discussed thaumaturgy: deeply and intently, with no regard for anyone who does not have the education to keep up.

Donal declined to gulp down his wine because it would waste a delightful wine, which he considered criminal, and because he had probably made others just as uncomfortable with his own shop talk as these tycoons now made him.

Donal could practically hear his father telling him to pay attention to the experience and learn from it.

A wine steward dressed as a satyr refilled Mr. Saito's wine, and Mr. Mancuso raised his glass.

"What is this now, Donal? The third time you've saved my life?"

Donal felt a flush creep up his cheeks as the other businesspeople turned calculating eyes on him. But before Donal could find words, Mr. Mancuso continued, taking in the whole of the table with a sweep of his finger.

"And today he saved all of you as well. And your assistants, and our dear captain, and everyone else aboard this ship. And so let us drink to Donal: may he prove as good in the lab as he is under pressure."

"To Donal," said the others, and all raised their glasses to drink.

Am I supposed to drink too? Or is that a faux pas?

Donal didn't know. Joke toasts had been made to him at college parties, but never anything serious or formal, and the rules were a mystery. By the time they had finished drinking the toast and replaced their glasses, Donal had managed to do nothing but hold his glass by the stem and fight down a blush.

Donal finally did manage a second sip, and as he replaced his glass, Ms. Romanova said, "I must say, Mr. Cuthbert, that I find this development quite irritating."

She arched an eyebrow, clearly waiting until all eyes were on her before she said, "I did so hope to find an excuse to challenge you to a duel after that business on Luna. But I can't very well continue to hold that against you after the events of the day."

She raised her glass to Donal again.

"In light of your actions today, the Romanov family rescinds its vendetta."

Now that was a toast Donal knew he could drink to.

"IN THE FUTURE, MS. ROMANOVA," SAID JACOBS, "PLEASE INFORM Security Chief Goldberg of any active vendettas against other passengers, including any you might still hold toward those on this flight."

The woman actually gave Jacobs a coy smile.

"I will, of course, keep that in mind, Captain. And I assure you that though the Romanov family has as many vendettas as any other comparable family on Luna, I am not aware of any current instances that would involve the crew or passengers presently aboard your ship."

Jacobs made a mental note to make sure Zoltan had not arranged for them to pick up any new passengers on Venus.

"But Natalia," said Montenegro, "there are no other families on Luna that compare in status to the Romanovs."

"No, there aren't." Her smile broadened a bit and took in the other diners. "Not anymore."

Kianoush shifted in his seat as though her statement had been for his ears alone.

Mancuso pointed at Montenegro and said, "Weren't you telling me just yesterday that you once fought off space pirates?"

That drew Jacobs' attention.

"Do not make too much of it," said Montenegro. "I was young and running a lifter on a cargo vessel. My first."

He smiled despite his humble tone, and Jacobs saw something like nostalgia in the man's eye, even though Jacobs considered him far too young to know what real nostalgia felt like.

"The ship had been forced to cut its speed. Something about an unexpected hazard in the route."

"That should have tipped your captain," said Jacobs.

"It did. He sounded the alarm. We didn't have much more than axe handles though. It was a low-budget operation." Montenegro shook his head. "When my buddies saw that ... *our employers* expected us to defend their cargo against armed pirates using nothing but axe handles, they opted to offer a few unpleasant words to their captain and hole up in the crew quarters."

"I keep telling people," said Mancuso, "cutting corners doesn't save money."

Jacobs agreed, but chose not to say so aloud.

Montenegro continued, growing more animated in his story. He leaned forward and held an imaginary axe handle in one hand.

"I wanted no part of their cowardice. I grabbed my axe handle and ran for the cargo bay. I pulled open the hatch...

"And ran straight into a pirate's Pacifier."

Jacobs laughed, and it seemed to break the spell. Montenegro followed and soon the whole table was laughing at his seated pantomime of taking a Pacifier blow to the head.

"I woke up two hours later with the worst headache of my life. These were the old Pacifiers, too, when they were made of wood instead of hard rubber."

"I read about those," said Cuthbert. "Magicians tried to tell them that the material didn't matter, as long as it had once been alive, but the marketing people insisted on making them from wood. Like old police clubs."

Jacobs had a story about old police clubs, the military police, a crew on shore leave, and a bar fire, but decided that this was neither the time, the place, nor the company to share it.

"Wish they had listened. I still can't watch baseball." Montenegro chuckled again. "Every time the ball gets hit, I take it personally."

The waiters and waitresses arrived and began taking dinner orders, and Jacobs noticed that Montenegro took advantage of the distraction for a private word with Cuthbert.

MONTENEGRO LEANED CLOSE TO DONAL, TAPPING A SPOT ON HIS OWN forehead as though showing Donal where the wooden Pacifier had struck him. But instead of talking about the blow, he said, "Something is amiss. I cannot explain now. Keep your wits about you."

Montenegro chuckled then, and Donal forced himself to smile as though at a joke. He wished Montenegro had told a joke. Donal had had his fill of cryptic warnings.

Nevertheless, Donal smiled ruefully at the half-glass of Pinot Noir he had remaining and swirled it just to savor its scent one more time. He had a feeling he should switch to water when the glass was empty. A decision he knew Fionn would approve of, which somehow made it worse.

All the money that went into the food on these voyages and Donal barely got to enjoy it.

He took a sip of the Pinot Noir and let the robust flavor trickle past his tongue and down his throat, then replaced the glass on the table. Only drinking the one glass meant that he could take his time with it, at least.

Donal tuned back into the conversation as Ms. Romanova pointed a comment at Mr. Kianoush: "Oh, you didn't keep us out of Mars, however much you like to tell yourself you did. No, your little pro-Mars movement only convinced us that Mars is cutting off its own nose on the trade front."

She smiled with a condescending tilt of the head. "Really, focusing on building local and buying local is all well and good, but until you develop your exports your cities will continue to hemorrhage money. If Mars runs out of carterite, the whole planet will turn into a ghost town in six weeks."

"You're hardly one to talk." Kianoush managed a good sneer despite being only a year or two older than Donal, which put Donal uncomfortably in mind of his brother. Not the sneer itself, but the level of success at a young age. "Luna is so tightly woven into Earth's economy that you might as well use their currency."

Even Donal recognized that trap. Luna *did* use Earth's currency. So had Mars until the start of 2026 when it began formally issuing its own and declaring an exchange rate. Donal never had gotten around to finding out how Earth had responded.

"Come now, you two," said Mr. Mancuso, though Donal thought he saw a glimpse of pleasure in the 4M magnate's eye. "The main course has yet to arrive. What say you lay aside your grievances before you ruin the meal?" He circled his finger to call for another round of wine. Donal reached to cover his glass and indicate that he had had enough, but Mr. Mancuso caught the movement.

"Don't spoil the party, Donal. Tai Shi has told me how you enjoy good wine, and I know that IIX can't be expecting any pressing work from you. Don't let their sniping stiffen you up."

Donal felt his hesitation leak out all over his face, but he started to pull back his hand as the wine steward moved to refill his glass.

"Skip Cuthbert," said Captain Jacobs to the steward. "Move on to the next."

MANCUSO LOOKED READY TO ARGUE, SO JACOBS CLARIFIED.

"No one will have a drink forced on them at the captain's table. Not Cuthbert, not you, Mancuso, no one." He turned to Cuthbert. "Want to call for something else? I usually let the chef pick the wine, but we have a pretty good selection."

"It's not that. The Pinot is excellent," said Cuthbert. "It's just that when I finish this I think I'll switch to water."

"I'm the same way," said Jacobs, who could not blame the boy for not wanting to drink too much around this group of sharks. Jacobs would have sworn that every word out of their mouths was intended to bite one of the others. Even Mancuso's "attempt" to make Kianoush and Romanova play nice was little more than a reassertion of his control, a reminder that he was the one in charge of their little group.

The wait staff began taking orders, starting with the captain, as tradition demanded. Jacobs ordered the buffalo steak with garlic cheese mashed potatoes and wondered if Dr. Ramirez would give him a pass on the potatoes for choosing the leaner buffalo over the fattier angus beef.

Cuthbert ordered grilled chicken with vegetables, which Jacobs considered a waste of the Ambrosia's chef. But the chef had plenty to deal with among the rest of the orders, as the businesspeople ranged all over the menu for their orders.

Except Mancuso, who had to order off the menu. Jacobs wondered if that had been a calculated part of ordering last, a way of one-upping his contemporaries. He decided that he didn't really want to know.

Instead, Jacobs tried distraction, using one of the ice-breaker questions Zoltan had given him back when Jacobs had complained that having to eat with the passengers every night meant trying to find something to say to a bunch of people who could not possibly understand the life Jacobs had lived.

Typical Zoltan. Ask him a serious question, get a pat, easy answer in list form. Jacobs had sometimes speculated that, as a little boy, Zoltan organized his toys daily depending on whether he expected to play by himself, with his brothers, or with various of his friends.

"One thing I do love about the *Horizon Cusp* is getting to dine at Ambrosia every night," said Jacobs. "I don't mind telling you that I've docked at many a strange port in my days as a sailor, and I've eaten many a strange dish. Some I couldn't recognize. Some I wished I couldn't."

Jacobs had their attention now, and that last line even got a couple of smiles, though the widest, of course, was Mancuso's. "But by far the strangest dish I've ever been served was a thousand year egg." Jacobs shook his head. "Yolk black as deepest space and consistency like jelly. Or maybe jellyfish. Either way, the taste wasn't so bad. Bit salty, almost like a cheese."

"How did you end up eating one?" asked Cuthbert.

"When you're a young man seeing new ports, you always want to try to local specials." Jacobs smiled. "Some even a Georgia boy like me couldn't stomach, but none stranger than that egg."

Jacobs looked around the table. "I know I can't be the only one here with a strange food story."

"When it comes to my stomach," said Mancuso, "I am risk-averse. I ate on the cheap until I could afford better, but once I could I never looked back."

"This information has not gone public yet," said Kianoush, "but we've discovered a species of animal native to Mars. Can't be the only one, because it acts like a prey animal: skittish, eating something like vegetation, though I confess I don't know what."

Kianoush glanced around the table and seemed to warm to his audience. "One of my guards shot one with his crossbow, thinking it was a stray dog with mange, maybe a small golden retriever."

Kianoush looked at his hands, fingers splayed on the table in front of him. Jacobs could not tell how the man felt about his guard shooting a "stray dog."

"But when he got to the body, he saw that the legs were all double-jointed, the body hairless, and the head too conical, and full of teeth made for grinding.

"The guard brought it back in, and our alchemists began dissecting it." Kianoush grimaced, as though at the memory. "We don't even have an official name for it yet. We've only caught the one, and the alchemists keep referring to it as the jackalope."

"Does it have antlers?" asked Jacobs.

"No. Is that important?"

"Only if they want the name to stick."

"What did it taste like?" asked Cuthbert.

"Please do not say chicken," said Saito.

"Not like chicken at all," said Kianoush. "And I made them consult an imam before I was willing to try it when they grilled a section." Kianoush studied the backs of his hands again, closing and re-fanning his fingers. "I would say it had the consistency of guinea pig and a taste similar to veal, but gamey."

"Could prove popular," said Montenegro.

"I guess the strangest thing I've eaten is haggis," said Cuthbert. "But it's better than you'd think. At least the way my grandma prepared it."

Everyone stared expectantly at Donal, but he wasn't sure what to say.

"She used to say that the secret was not skimping on the heart, liver, and lungs, and that the difference between savory and disgusting haggis came down to loving the dish."

Donal shrugged, a little embarrassed. "She said you need to put your own heart into the dish, not just the sheep's."

Donal half expected everyone to laugh, but during the moment's pause after his last word, Mr. Saito drew breath and said, "There must be some psychological switch that takes place when the third generation arrives that lends importance to tradition. My mother was a poor cook until I had children. Then, suddenly, she made the best *Nikujaga* I have ever tasted." He turned to Captain Jacobs. "Have you noticed a similar trend in your own family?"

"I lost my family during the fall of technology."

Captain Jacobs said the words without noticeable heat or inflection, but they fell heavy on the conversation, creating a lull that grew until Mr. Mancuso said, "Well I've got about a dozen nieces and nephews and my mother still can't cook."

Mr. Mancuso launched into an amusing anecdote about his mother's cooking, but Donal watched the captain. For a man with no discernable talent at thaumaturgy, he managed to seal himself tight enough to be as spaceworthy as his ship. Even shifting levels of consciousness, Donal could not spot any signs or traces of emotion in the man's bearing. He merely sat and watched the conversation with sort of simple attention Donal could imagine him using to watch for sea storms from the deck of a sailing vessel.

Donal turned back to the conversation, still lead by Mr. Mancuso, who had managed to lighten the mood to the point that humor showed in the faces of his listeners.

Well, all except the captain and Donal.

Still, Donal marveled at the way this man seemed to steer these experienced businesspeople, directing them like a conductor. He did not seem to Donal like a man who had to murder to get what he wanted. In fact, Donal had begun to think that Mr. Mancuso would consider murdering to get ahead in business a type of cheating.

But Mr. bin Zuka had been on the brink of publicizing Red Sun's theories about Mr. Mancuso trying to establish a shadow government when he suddenly dropped dead. And Mr. Montenegro implied concerns about how 4M did business, and so did that man who threatened Donal outside his own apartment.

Everyone seemed convinced that 4M was killing people. Convinced enough to try to pay off Li Hua so they could take their shot at killing Mr. Mancuso.

But Donal just could not believe it.

16

AT LEAST AN HOUR HAD PASSED SINCE THE END OF DINNER, BUT DONAL did not concern himself with the time. He stood on the Observation Deck in the aft of the ship, staring through the transparent hull at the space they had passed. The entire bottom and sides of the ship had been rendered transparent from the inside, apart from the dull gray walkways and the dull gray re-orientation room — a safe zone for those disquieted by the sensation of standing unprotected among the stars.

Right now great mists of red and green stretched across the sky to Donal's right and though battling for supremacy. Ordinarily Donal enjoyed such sights as he stood as though he floated among the stars.

But this night the thought chilled him more than the air.

Donal stood beside Fionn, his thoughts and occasional words concerning the ship he had destroyed, the crew he had marooned without real hope of recovery, and the man some decks above him who seemed to be at the center of everything: Donatello Michelangelo Mancuso, CEO of 4M and de facto leader of several related companies.

"So you will not try to kill Donatello Mancuso?" said Fionn, in its thick brogue that managed to come across as neither Scottish nor Irish, but somehow both.

"I don't see how I could. I'm not sure he's guilty of anything except excellence in business. Well, I'm sure he can be a jerk, but that's not a killing offense."

"There have always been those who have been slain for their inability to work within the boundaries of polite society." Fionn flattened its ears and perked them again. "However, that is a decision for his societal equals, a category that does not yet include you."

"You think it will?"

"This society seems to hold in high esteem its masters of the craft of the wise, as is proper. When you receive your doctorate, you will be among them."

"Craft of the wise?" Donal felt a lopsided smile creep up the left side of his face.

The *cú sidhe* tilted its head in a canine shrug. "Not the fashionable phrase, but it has not lost its accuracy."

"I'm not feeling very wise right now."

"I did not say you had mastered the craft already."

Donal turned a furrowed brow on his familiar, ready to say something about support, but Fionn chuffed a laugh and said, "And even the greatest wizards doubt from time to time."

"Do they also kill people they don't mean to?" Donal tried to keep the tremor out of his voice.

"I do not favor agreeing with Tai Shi Li Hua," said Fionn, "but in this case I have no choice. She is right. You took the steps you needed to take to save your own life and the lives of others."

"*You* agree with me?" said Li Hua's amused voice behind them. "At last I can die a happy woman."

Donal turned and saw Li Hua in a casual, lightweight dress of deep yellow that blended well with her reddish Martian-Chinese complexion. She wore matching low heels for a relaxed look that Donal had no doubt left her ready for a fight. She stepped in close and kissed Donal on the cheek.

"I had a feeling I would find you here. But I didn't expect to find you morose."

"Am I?" Donal tried to smile, but didn't quite make it. "How long have you been watching me mope?"

"Fortunately only a moment. Though if you ever do want to take a crack at field work, you'll have to learn to do your deeper contemplations alone in your room. If I'd wanted to kill you, I could have done so before you would have known I was there."

"You could not have approached my master with such intentions and escaped my notice and warning."

"True, but that's not enough for a field agent." Li Hua sighed. "I'd try to seduce you out of your bad mood, but clearly that didn't work earlier. So let's forget the past for a little while."

She turned partway, extending one hand to Donal. "Come on. Here among the stars is a place for a romantic talk, not the kind I have in mind."

Donal took her hand, curious, but aware that asking would not do any good until they stood someplace she felt was secure for their conversation.

But why did their conversation need security?

Jacobs returned to his quarters, fully intending to call it an early night. He was due to work out after dinner, but these dinners themselves felt like work outs, with all the back-and-forth among the "guests" at his table.

Missing his routine one night would not kill him. He could get back to his book, calm his mind, and maybe get a good night's sleep. Just as well. Jacobs would need all his wits about him tomorrow. They were due to pass near the zuglodon hunting ground in the morning and the military no-fly zone in the afternoon. Best to approach that day as rested and ready as possible.

Still, Jacobs couldn't shake the feeling that his day was not yet over.

He stepped up to the comm pad on the table beside his reading chair, that marvelously comfortable recliner that had stayed with Jacobs through dozens of ships and scores of moves. He slapped the comm pad, but stayed standing lest the lure of the chair change his mind about the link.

A moment later Jefferson's head appeared above the comm pad.

"What are you still doing on shift?" said Jacobs.

Jefferson had the grace to look embarrassed. "The whole bridge crew is, Sir. We know that, well, dinners on this ship get dangerous during charter flights, and we asked the ex oh's permission to stay on duty until we were sure everything was going to stay calm."

Jacobs snorted. He knew that not all of his crew had served in the military, but he tended to forget which had and which hadn't until they called his attention to it. Like now. If Jefferson had served, she would have known better than to waste an opportunity for rest.

But then, Tunold should have known better than to grant the request.

Furthermore, Jacobs should have known better than to contact the bridge for a status report during the rare hours of the day he was not on duty. But in Jacobs' case, he could excuse it. Jacobs had the experience to know when to trust his gut.

Then again, Tunold might have that much experience himself…

"All right, what has no one told me?"

"Linking you through to Mr. Tunold, Captain. One moment."

Jefferson's pleasant head morphed into Tunold's narrow head.

"Captain, what can I—"

"Belay that, Mister. What have I not been told?"

"It's nothing, John. I promise you."

"Ex Oh, you are on the brink of insubordination. I suggest you take a step back from it and tell me what the hell is going on."

"Sir, I assure you that I am not insubordinate. To the best of my knowledge, nothing threatens the ship, its crew, or its mission, which are the proper concerns of a ship's captain."

"Are you quoting regs to me, Mister?"

"No, Sir. I am reminding you of our agreement. I am not saying that there might not be an issue among the passengers that is mine to deal with as executive officer, but I am saying that if there is such an issue, I can promise you it will be in my overnight report and ready for your eyes when you come on shift at oh-six-hundred."

"Very carefully said, Kris."

"I do my best, John. Get some sleep."

"If whatever you aren't telling me gets me out of bed with no prior knowledge of what's happening, you won't like the end result."

"Acknowledged, Captain."

"Very well. Jacobs out." Jacobs passed his hand through the image of Tunold's head, severing the connection. Jacobs shook his head. He would go to bed, all right. But after a conversation like that, Jacobs was not sure how well he would sleep.

DONAL AND LI HUA STOOD WITHIN THE SOLID, GRAY CUBE OF THE Observation Deck's relief zone. Donal estimated each side to measure about five meters, and the walls bore large landscape murals of Earth, Mars, and Luna. Little reminders of land for those disturbed by space, that also served to refresh the air in the otherwise confined space. Plush couches and chairs in browns and greens completed the scene, would reassure a troubled mind of the colors of home. And if they were not enough, each corner had a small restroom unit.

Li Hua had already paced the room and cast wards against scrying, and Donal, at her request, had returned Fionn to the silver faun pendant.

Fionn had not wanted to go, but Donal assured his familiar that he would share the whole conversation later, and that Donal would not commit to any long-term courses of action without consulting the fae deerhound.

Donal was now alone with Li Hua, staring at her across the rows of seating and low, dark wood tables. Donal could see excitement lighting her eyes, but that excitement did not bleed through to make her smile. Even her posture held something back, stayed formal instead of the relaxed sexiness Donal had grown accustomed to. Her reticence made him hesitate to approach, and reminded him of something else.

"Are you sure those wards won't draw the ship's mage into our conversation?"

"Perk of the new title," she said. "I have license to ward whatever I want without question, anywhere 4M has business." She waved her hand to designate the assembled couches. "Where shall we sit?"

Donal picked a deep, forest green couch in the center, and Li Hua settled in next to him, close enough to be friendly, but not so close as to start something that would distract them from their conversation.

She turned to face him, one arm along the back of the couch and one knee pulling up onto the cushion beside her, her yellow dress long enough to keep the movement modest.

"Reminds me of the first real conversation we had, over that lovely Morgan Syrah."

Donal smiled. "I thought you were flirting, but you just wanted to talk about the people trying to kill us."

"I was doing both." She smiled, and Donal wondered if the evening might yet become something other than deep, serious conversation. The couch was quite comfortable...

"But before we get to that," she continued, "there are some things we need to figure out, you and I."

"About what's going to happen when I go off to CalThaum San Luis Obispo?"

"Oh, that's part of it." She leaned forward. "But before we get to the Hierophant you will become, let's talk about the Journeyman you are. You're an odd combination, Donal."

Li Hua shook her head with a slight smile. "You'd make a terrible field magician. I'm sorry, but it's true. Field magicians need to maintain a constant sense of their surroundings, but you get distracted by every interesting new spell you find."

"How can you not be? Opportunities to learn are all around us—"

"Let me finish." She held up her hand in a placating gesture, and the slight raise of her eyebrows told Donal she meant no insult. "But you've got a gift that can't be taught. Throw you into a pressure situation and you improvise spells on the fly better than anyone I've ever met. You proved it against the zuglodon, you proved it in your duel with bin Zuka, and you proved it again today."

Donal felt heat rise in his neck, but fought the blush down by glancing away from the admiration in Li Hua's eyes to the pastoral scene of rolling red Martian hills behind her, and drawing a single deep breath.

"But can you do that in the lab when the pressure isn't on?"

"I ... well..." Donal tried to think back over his impressive accomplishments in school, but had to admit that none of them compared to the spells he had pulled off when lives were on the line.

"I don't know. I don't see why what I'm learning out here wouldn't translate to the lab."

"What if I could offer you the opportunity to find out? Out here in the real world, not in the lab? What if I could offer you a chance to build your power the way the magicians of antiquity did it."

Donal thought about that. His brother Bran had parlayed his experiences on the edge of space to successfully challenge for the title of Magister without spending a day in graduate school. What if Donal could be the first person even to successfully challenge for the title of Hierophant?

"What would I have to do?"

Tunold turned from his comm pad back to his station. He knew he had gambled, not bringing Jacobs in on this, but Jacobs had to see that Tunold was ready to command a big ship. No matter who the passengers were and what problems they were having.

He glanced at the miniature phantasmal gryphon that floated above his workstation. The true keys to the ship. Tunold loved that little source of reports and direct connection to every system and department on the ship. Right now he only got access to it when the captain was off-duty, but soon enough Tunold would get the big chair and have access to the mini-gryphon as a regular part of his work day.

But he found difficulty taking joy in it just then, even when he touched the location of the main deck's security office and gave his finger a little twist to open a communication link. Goldberg should have answered within seconds, but as those seconds stretched into a minute, Tunold felt his shoulders hunch and jaw clamp in irritation.

Finally the chief's head appeared over the gryphon display. "Sorry, Ex Oh, my guests had to finish making a point before I could answer."

Diplomatic words and a neutral expression. That meant that Kianoush and Romanova were right there, probably close to arm's reach.

"Shall I presume that means they are insisting on their current course of action?"

"Aye, Sir, I'd say they sound quite eager for it." The image of Goldberg's jaw moved out to one side, tilting his head, and through the link Tunold could hear Goldberg's neck crack.

The chief was preparing for a fight.

"All right, Chief. Tell them I'll be right down to discuss this with them." Tunold cut the link, then turned to the bridge crew. "All right, folks, this is why I agreed to let you stay on duty late, but when I get back you'll all be relieved, so let your reliefs know now." Tunold stood. "I have to go deal with a potential situation. Mr. Burke, mind the shop until I get back, and if there's a problem, link me down in Goldberg's Main Deck office, not his Security Deck office."

Tunold did not wait for the acknowledgments he knew were coming. He trotted off through the door and down the sloping passage to try to stop a duel.

LI HUA SLID A LITTLE CLOSER ON THE COUCH, HER KNEE NOW SCANT centimeters from Donal's thigh. Plenty of privacy there in the safe room of the Observation Deck, especially behind her wards.

Donal wondered where this conversation was going. Did she want him to skip school and come to work for 4M?

"All you'd have to do is focus on your strengths." She patted Donal's hand. "Not just conjuration, but deception. I've pulled off a few stunts with deception magic that you'll be interested to investigate, when I point them out to you, but my specialties lie in the magic of movement and scrying."

The look Li Hua gave Donal then was half-lust, half-power. Donal wasn't sure if he should be turned on, or worried, and had to admit he was a little of both.

"I can't wait to see how you improve on my work," she said.

Li Hua slid closer, her one arm moving from on the back of the couch to around Donal's shoulders.

"Together you and I will be unstoppable."

Donal leaned in and kissed her and she met him with passion. When the kiss broke he said, "So when will I get to see these spells? Are they on Mars? Earth?"

"Oh, no, Donal," she said with a flirty flip of her hair, moving the long sheet of straight black locks out of the way so she could lean in and kiss Donal's neck. She whispered in his ear, "I'm talking about enchantments right here on the ship with us."

TUNOLD STEPPED INTO THE SECURITY OFFICE ON THE MAIN DECK AND noticed four things right away: Goldberg, seated, face neutral but hands gripping his desk like he wanted to break it in half; Kianoush, standing beside the desk, hands on his elbows and fingers drumming, dressed in slacks and a shirt that allowed a lot of freedom of movement; Romanova, standing across from Kianoush, hands folded over her stomach and thumbs circling each other in a patient pattern, also dressed in slacks and a shirt that allowed free movement; and no other members of the ship's watch present.

That last part told Tunold that Goldberg had been trying very hard not to throw the weight of his rank around. Jacobs would appreciate that, but Tunold was not sure that he did. If Goldberg could have dismissed the matter by acting like a security chief instead of like a diplomat — work for which Tunold doubted Goldberg had been trained — Tunold might be having a quiet end-of-shift on the bridge.

"All right," said Tunold. "What's so important about this grievance that it couldn't wait until morning?"

"The midnight hour approaches." Romanova looked over at Tunold, infinite patience in her deep brown eyes. "A traditional hour for duels and assignations. Space has no dawn nor dusk. During the noon hour tomorrow we shall both be too busy to fight a duel."

"It is in both of our interests," said Kianoush, "to conclude the matter to both of our satisfactions before business resumes in the morning."

"Whatever it is has waited this long," said Tunold. "I say you let it wait until you reach Venus. Then you can kill each other in peace and I won't have to deal with it."

"Kill each other?" Kianoush bubbled a laugh that rose and fell, bringing with it, then taking with it, a smile on his face. "Certainly not."

"Risk leaving my idiot brother in charge of the family name and business?" Romanova scoffed. "Never."

"Chief," said Tunold, "you want to grab these two some boxing gloves so we can settle this and get back to business?"

"Cretin!" said Romanova. "I refuse to brawl like some common thug."

"I must agree," said Kiaonoush, hands now at his sides. "We require our dueling swords from your ship's safe so we may fight a proper duel to first blood."

"You know what that means, Ex Oh," said Goldberg.

And Tunold did know. Retrieving anything from the ship's safe while at space could not be done without the captain.

Donal felt little alarms go off in his head at the thought of Li Hua having deception spells somewhere on this ship for him to examine. But the silk of her yellow dress felt so soft, and the plush couch beneath them so very private.

He cleared his throat and said, "I'm having difficulty concentrating while you're kissing my neck."

Li Hua purred a soft, pleased sound that included hot breath tingling along Donal's skin. But she pulled back, her eyes smiling into Donal's.

Donal furrowed his brow, and brought his hands back to rest on his own knees. He decided it was in the best interests of his focus to keep his hands by his sides.

"Thank you" did not feel appropriate, but he needed to say something. "What deception spells do you have running? Are you hiding wards or something?"

"Nothing so prosaic." She traced a finger along Donal's jaw. "No, this is bigger than that. Bigger than anything we've ever talked about."

Li Hua lay back against the couch, gesturing up with her hands as though taking in the entire universe.

"I'm talking about finishing the work that Lloyd Bird started."

Lloyd Bird returned magic to the world. What would...

And then Donal thought he understood, and immediately hoped he was wrong. Lloyd Bird brought the magic back. What if Li Hua meant to put the magicians in charge?

Tunold felt a fleeting wish that the dozen or so empty seats in the Main Deck's security office each held an officer of the watch. He might need them to keep these Kianoush and Romanova apart without getting hands-on.

He looked back at the two would-be duelists.

"Forget it," said Tunold. "I'm not getting the captain out of bed so the two of you can try to kill each other while pretending you're just trying to draw blood. We started this trip with twenty-one living passengers, and I intend to have twenty-one living passengers when we arrive on Venus."

"I assure you, Mr. Tunold," said Romanova with a sigh that clearly indicated that she thought she was dealing with a moron. "Neither Farbod nor I have any intention of trying to kill each other. It would be bad for business."

"Just, please," picked up Kianoush as though the two had rehearsed this, "get us our swords and let us settle this. We will not need more than five minutes to do so. You have my promise."

"I know you won't," said Tunold, trying to restrain the growl he heard starting in his voice. "I know a few things about fights myself, and unless a crowd gets involved, they don't need more than a few minutes to resolve themselves."

Tunold shook his head, a heavy gesture that involved a lot of shoulder movement. "I also know that fighters can get carried away, and that even a duel to first blood can lead to a dead body on the deck."

Tunold folded his arms, daring them to challenge him on this point. "I'm in charge while the captain is off-duty, and I say you want to duel? Fine. Mr. Goldberg, get them each a Pacifier."

DONAL FELT A CHILL SLIDE DOWN HIS SPINE, A DROP OF SWEAT TRICKLE down from his temple. He had to clear his throat to speak, which seemed to amuse Li Hua. His voice sounded rough when he finally managed to form words.

"That's why you're telling me this behind wards. Why you asked me to put Fionn away."

"Well, to be fair, I *am* planning to jump your bones once I'm sure we're both reciting from the same ritual script." She leaned closer as though to share a secret. "And I don't think Fionn approves of me."

"He thinks you're bad for me." Donal worked to keep the and-he's-right tone out of his voice. "He thinks that when I spend time with you I'm more likely to find myself in dangerous situations I'm not ready to handle."

"How does he expect you to learn to defend yourself unless you struggle under real duress." Li Hua waved a hand absently. "But you've already proved my point several times over. You shine brightest after a little tumbling."

Li Hua smirked at her choice of words, but Donal's thoughts were elsewhere.

"What's more," she said, "you love the action as much as I do, even if you have trouble facing up to that little fact."

"So." Donal tried to keep his voice steady, but her raised eyebrow told him he had failed. "What do you see as the ultimate culmination of Lloyd Bird's work? Because I don't think you mean teaching."

"I think you know exactly what I mean." Li Hua tilted her head and regarded Donal past lowered lids. "You know as well as I do that before magic fell the first time, magicians stayed out of politics." Her mouth formed a line, as though she found the thought distasteful. "And look what happened. Science rose, and without the ethics of magic to guide it, it led to strip mining, pollution, wholesale destruction.

"Mass gassings, the atomic bomb..." Li Hua leaned toward Donal, but this time the light in her eye was not sexual. "Science and technology damn near destroyed the whole human race. And what did it ever really do for us? We've come farther in sixty years with magic than we did in hundreds of years with technology."

"Well, we didn't exactly have the science equivalent of Lloyd Bird and his acolytes standing by to show us the way."

"But don't you see? That wouldn't matter. Science was impersonal. It worked equally for everyone regardless of personal talent or philosophical development. Magic requires both."

"True," said Donal, shifting uncomfortably in his seat. "But magicians can go bad too, regardless of their training. We haven't had a modern powerful magician go bad yet, but it's just a matter of time."

"We're getting away from the important point here, Donal" Li Hua's face and posture were serious now. "Under the rule of technology we had leaders who could kill thousands, even millions without any direct personal involvement. Other people had to get their hands dirty, giving the leaders more mental room to excuse and justify their actions.

"And now we have magic, but we've continued down the same path, allowing men and women rise to positions of power and importance without the ability to handle either, without the training that magic provides."

"You want magicians to hold public office?" Donal had to chuckle. Maybe he had read Li Hua wrong. "The idea has potential, but I don't think that most people are ready to let one person wield both political power and thaumaturgic power."

"Of course not."

A small smile touched her lips, a smile Donal remembered from Mars, from a moment when she had been proud of the elegant way she had killed the men who had hunted them.

"And that is where the deception magic comes in."

17

Tunold folded his arms and loomed over the seated Romanova and Kianoush as he waited for their response. Perhaps the silence of the late hour and lack of witnesses would work in his favor. Rich executives or not, with the Main Deck deserted and the security office devoid of anyone else except the chief, they *had* to feel a little intimidated by Tunold's ursine presence.

They were only landlubbers, after all.

"Pacifiers?" said Romanova, her contempt making the word sound obscene. "Ridiculous."

"I am willing," said Kianoush, bringing a glare from Romanova, but a smile from Tunold. "In truth, the weapon itself matters little to me. I would prefer a proper duel with swords, but it seems the executive officer will not budge on the issue."

Tunold only shook his head.

Romanova turned to appeal to Goldberg, but before she could speak, the chief said, "It's his call, Ma'am."

Tunold thought the woman looked even more irritated at the chief's choice of titles.

"He's right," said Tunold, as much to draw her attention from the chief as to back his point. "I'm the ranking officer on deck and it's my watch. You can try appealing to the captain in the morning, but a) he's likely to agree with me, and b) he'll tell you that crew and passenger matters are my jurisdiction unless he chooses to get involved. Which he won't. Not over something like this."

Goldberg nodded his head in support. Kianoush said, "If you must have swords, I know only one more person to whom we could appeal. But I do not relish asking him to intervene."

Romanova looked as though she swallowed a particularly large and ugly bug. Tunold expected her to turn green any moment.

"Very well," she said. "Fetch the Pacifiers."

SUDDENLY THE OBSERVATION DECK'S SAFE ROOM FELT UNCOMFORTABLY warm and close. The sight of the Martian landscape painting behind Li Hua now made her look more alien to Donal's eyes.

"You've enchanted Mr. Mancuso," said Donal. Saying the words aloud made him feel as though his stomach had ruptured and begun to leak its contents down through his abdomen and into his legs. "That's the deception magic, isn't it? Hiding a series of compulsions."

"Slowly, and over a course of years," Li Hua said, pride swimming through her voice. "Finest work of its kind I've ever done."

She reached out to stroke Donal's chin, and if she noticed that Donal had frozen in place, Donal couldn't tell.

"Though I can't wait to see how you improve them."

Donal could not speak. Had trouble even thinking. He might not have been sure he was in love with Li Hua, had not even been certain of their future once he went off to grad school. But he never dreamed...

But Li Hua was still talking. "...from the first day I met you. Remember? When I was getting you away from the Aetheric Dynamics hit men? I thought that maybe you had lost the package in all the confusion, but you just smiled and patted your bag, and suddenly I could see it. Like it just appeared out of nowhere. Instant distressed leather. I knew right then that you were already better at deception magic than I could ever be." She shook her head in admiration. "I just needed to know if you could handle the life. Deal with all the action."

Donal still could not find his tongue. His breaths had gotten shallow, and the room seemed to develop a slight twist, as though it wanted to spin around Donal, but wasn't quite ready to start. Li Hua finally noticed, but misinterpreted the lost look on Donal's face. She smiled, the humorous, infectious smile Donal remembered from that first day on Mars.

"Oh, it wasn't as calculated as all that," said Li Hua. "I really did — and do — want your body. Finding a partner who loves the action as much as I do and brings your skill with illusions and deceptions to the mix was a bonus."

"It's all you." Donal finally got the words out in a half-strangled rasp. "All the murders. The seizing power."

"Oh, *Donal*." The excitement ran out of Li Hua's face, leaving her crestfallen. Even her shoulders slumped. "Didn't we already go over all this? I do not murder. I defend myself."

Pride came back into her bearing, her features. She looked sure of herself again. Dangerous.

"I've killed to defend you too, remember. And I've killed to protect all the magicians everywhere."

"You've been killing to support your ideology."

"No, Donal." She shook her head, her cascading tresses like a curtain, opening and closing as she did. "Don't do this. Don't deliberately misunderstand." She grabbed Donal's hand in both of hers, and implored him. "Don't make me choose between you and the good of the whole human race."

"Funny," said Donal, without a trace of humor in his voice. "I was about to say the same thing."

Tunold smiled down at the would-be duelists, each in tailored, fashionable work-out clothes that would not doubt leave them unencumbered in a duel.

A duel, but not a fight. Her hair should be tied back the way Tai Shi's was, not in a simple ponytail that anyone could grab.

Tunold took a Pacifier from Chief Goldberg while the chief leaned on his desk. Goldberg looked as ready to laugh as Tunold felt.

"Who wants to go first?"

"I think you misunderstand..." said Kianoush.

"We want to duel *each other*, you dolt," said Romanova.

"I know what you want." Tunold spun the Pacifier around in his hand, forcing the two rich, self-important idiots to follow the movement. "But you aren't on Luna or Mars where you make the rules."

"I do not 'make the rules' on Mars," said Kianoush. Romanova drew breathe to add something, but Tunold did not give her time to get a word out.

"Neither is this San Francisco with its clear dueling code, or Venus with — as I understand it — its complete lack of laws. You are aboard the *Horizon Cusp*, a helioship at high space."

Tunold stopped twirling the Pacifier and pointed it at himself, which made the chief wince.

"And I have already told you, I am the ranking officer on deck."

"I—" started Romanova.

"Now in case you don't understand what that means, 'high' space is another way to say interplanetary space. In other words, we are outside the jurisdiction of any given planet. Even Earth."

Tunold saw understanding lighting in their eyes, so he finished his point. "That's right. And the *Horizon Cusp* only allows duels if the ranking officer on deck agrees. So I'm giving you two a choice: if you can both beat me, one at a time, I'll let you have your little duel. Either of you loses to me and you get no follow-up against each other."

"In that case," chimed in Goldberg, "I'd say the first one to lose to the ex oh is the loser in your dispute."

"That's hardly fair," said Kianoush. "You've chosen a weapon at which you have a clear advantage in terms of experience and training."

"I did." Tunold tried for one of the captain's evil grins, even though he knew that on his face it would come out more of a snarl. "That is what is known as R.H.I.P."

Neither of the executives spoke for a moment, then Romanova said, "Rank hath its privileges?"

"I learned it as 'has,'" said Tunold. "But close enough." He held the Pacifier in both hands in from of him, as a knight might have held a broadsword. "So are you ready to decide who goes first? Or will you go back to your rooms?"

Kianoush and Romanova glanced at each other, then away.

"You understand, Mr. Tunold," said Romanova, "that you are removing the only honorable and legal way we can resolve this matter between us aboard your ship."

"You both run corporations that move billions of dollars every year. You'll deal with it."

"You realize," said Kianoush, "that we will protest your actions here with both the captain and Mancuso."

"Yes," added Romanova with a dangerous look in her eye. "You are abusing your power."

"I don't know what your Mancuso will say about this, but I'll bet you two hundred that Captain Jacobs backs me."

Tunold folded his arms, letting the Pacifier dangle by his side.

Without another word, the two business leaders turned and left.

Once they were out of sight, Goldberg said, "I'll take a piece of that action. My money says that John will tell you that all you've done is force those two to find a way they can fight their duel without our supervision."

Tunold turned and saw the chief slowly shake his head.

Donal saw realization wash over Li Hua's face as she heard the resolved tone in Donal's voice, saw his posture straighten.

"Donal," said Li Hua, her eyebrows high and her lip not quite trembling, "swear to me that you will take a day and think about this, and speak next about it to no one but me."

"I'm not sure I can—"

"By this time tomorrow we'll be on Venus. I'll get Mr. Mancuso situated and then you and I can go someplace private and sort through all your questions and concerns. You'll understand. What I'm doing is what's best for everyone."

"What about Mr. Mancuso?" Donal felt sadness pulling him down from the inside, but pushed on. "Is it best for him that you're making his key decisions? Using him as a stalking horse so that if someone does get killed over your work, it isn't you?"

"I'd never let that happen," she said with a firm shake of the head. "You know how good I am."

"Was it best for Mr. bin Zuka that you murdered him for being almost right?"

"The man was obsessed." Li Hua let go of Donal's hand and sat back. She no longer looked at Donal, stared off at the mural of Earth on one wall. "If he had only been more flexible, he might have worked with us."

Donal squeezed his eyes closed. "There is no us here." The words felt cold leaving Donal's mouth. "This is about you and your own insane plan."

"You're not even going to consider what I have to say?" A tremor in Li Hua's voice opened Donal's eyes. Her own were shiny with unshed tears. "Donal..."

"You're murdering and ensorcelling people to amass power. What is there to consider?"

"I'm trying to prevent the mistakes of the past, to keep power out of the wrong hands."

"You say that magicians are trustworthy with power because our art demands ethics. But how does what you do *not* violate the Foundation Principle?"

"The Foundation Principle?" Li Hua laughed, an honest and sincere sound, when Donal thought it should have sounded desperate, unhinged. "Donal, we violate the Foundation Principle all the time."

Li Hua waved her arms to indicate the ship around them.

"How do we fly through space, Donal? Do we ally ourselves with the native powers of space and seek their permission to travel through their lands? No. We conjure those native powers and bind them to our will. Half of magic's great advances come from bindings, from our own ability to say 'yes you will' louder and with more force than a bunch of elementals can say 'no we won't.'"

She pointed an accusing finger at Donal. "You're no different. All your Enochian ideas, they're just more ways of making spirits do what we want." She leaned forward now, beautiful in her certainty. "And I have done nothing different. I have commanded Mancuso's spirit like an elemental. And those I have been unable to command, like bin Zuka, I have punished like any other recalcitrant spirit."

"It's different." Donal's voice had grown quiet. Heartsick. He saw now how this was going to end, and he hated that ending even more than he feared that he could not handle it. "And you know it's different."

"It's no different. Just because these spirits are incarnate—"

"You know it's different because you hid what you did behind spells of deception. And you want me to hide it even better."

That stopped her.

Li Hua blinked away her tears and stared at Donal. Donal knew his own tears would come later, when the dull shock of the night's revelations finally passed.

"There's no point in giving you time to consider, is there?" She sounded as tired as Donal felt. "You have no intention of listening to what I have to say. Your mind is already made up."

"I wish you could see that this is wrong, Li Hua. You've become exactly what you're trying to stop."

"Donal Cuthbert." Li Hua stood, hands absently straightening her yellow silk dress. "I hereby charge you to speak no word of what we have discussed with anyone else, ever. I charge you further to take no action to hinder or stop me in any way, now or in the future."

She pointed at Donal, and the divide between them made Donal almost feel as though he had been stabbed by that pointing finger.

"Swear these things to me upon your power, or I will challenge you to the *Comórtas Draíocht*."

"Tai Shi Li Hua," said Donal, standing and closing his eyes. "I charge you to release all those humans whom you have bent to your will, and to swear upon your power that you will cease and desist your efforts to amass power in such a way."

Donal opened his eyes and saw the amused look on Li Hua's face. "Or *I* will challenge *you* to the *Comórtas Draíocht*."

Li Hua laughed. Donal shook his head. It made little difference who challenged whom. He knew they would not leave that room without fighting the duel of magic.

That locked room, warded against scrying. Donal could expect no help, no support. He stood alone and overmatched, but he saw no alternative. She had been too careful, built up her power too slowly. Donal had only discovered the truth because she wanted to bring him in.

Only Donal stood between her and total victory. All he had to do was out-duel a woman who lived and breathed combat.

18

Donal's gut tightened as panic worked its way through his system. He needed some escape from the safe room, from the Observation Deck.

From Li Hua.

He knew he would have to face her, duel her, but if he did it now he would lose. He needed to buy time to think, to plan, to seek help.

But he could see no plans among the cushions and couches of the safe room, no allies among the murals, no escape route in the restrooms.

Li Hua shook her head, a slow, sad movement. She said, "*Comórt—*"

Donal threw a seat cushion at her and ran for the door. Nervous sweat stung his eyes. He banged his shin on an end table as he rounded the couch. Pain slowed him to a stumble.

Li Hua vaulted over the back of the couch into a diving roll that left her standing between Donal and the door. She smiled like a cheetah that has run down its prey.

Donal screeched to a halt that left him clinging to a chair to stay standing. He panted for breath, though more from stress than from his exertion.

Li Hua looked shower-fresh in her light dress.

Does she enchant all her clothes for fighting?

It was a silly question. Donal already knew the answer. He could see it in her ready stance, feet apart and balanced, weight low. In the smile that flared out from her eyes. Even if now that hint of smile faded and angry sadness began to resurface.

"Interesting stratagem," she said. "But as much as I might enjoy chasing you..."

Her brown eyes flashed, their touch of caramel fading to black. "Damn it, Donal! This should have been a fun chase that ended in a very pleasurable tackle. We should be naked and celebrating right now. Why can't you trust me? Why can't you work with me to build a better future?"

"Because you're trying to make magicians a ruling class. You want to give more power to those who already have power."

"Magicians are the only ones equipped and trained to handle power."

Donal tried glancing toward the other couches, toward the murals. No other exits. Just rest rooms. No escape there. Next to the door was a comm pad. Useless. If Donal could reach it, he would be better served to skip it and bolt through the doorway and make for the nearest bubble or access panel.

"And that's how you prove you can handle power?" He said, trying to brace himself for a mad dash despite the pain in his shin. "Use magic to manipulate your boss and kill your rivals? You sound more like a gangster than a queen."

"Fine then," she said, and Donal worried about the note of finality in her voice, forced himself to stand straighter as she continued. "Call me a gangster. But I am doing what needs to be done. And I can't let you stop me. *Comórtas Draíocht.*"

Her words rang out with an almost metallic echo, and the room felt smaller to Donal. She had issued her challenge to the duel of magic, and Donal had no choice but to respond.

Machado awoke among the heavenly sheets of his king-sized bed, all pleasures of sleep torn from him by an alarm in his mind. An alarm that had never rung before, and so he needed a moment to recognize it.

Not proximity. Not impact...

Then the cold fact all but slapped his round cheeks: someone had called for *Comórtas Draíocht*.

Before he even dragged himself out of his mess of enchanted, high-thread count sheets, Machado called forth *Saravá* and sent the ghostly panther soaring toward the duel along the deepest lines of the ship.

Machado thought fleetingly of wardrobe and appearances, but knew that he had no time. He pulled on the bathrobe he bought on Luna: some local material the blue-gray of moon dust, but softer even than satin, and ran for the door.

En route he shifted and sent some of his consciousness to ride along with his familiar while the rest of him ran for the bubble with as much dignity as he could manage.

After only three steps Machado had begun to sweat. The part of him that remained with his body tried not to think how sweat-covered and smelly he would be by the time he arrived wherever the alarm was leading him...

"Li Hua, don't do this." Donal's heartbeat thundered in his ears. Sadness overwhelmed him. He did not know that he had been in love with Li Hua, was not sure he had ever *really* been in love. He had imagined that when he went to grad school they would slowly drift apart. She busy with her work and he caught up in his studies.

He knew what was between them had to end.

But not like this. Not with her standing before him ready to fight in the belly of a helioship. Donal could see at least as much anger in her eyes as sorrow. But even a little sorrow meant that he had a chance to reason with her, to get her to see how wrong a course she was on.

He had to try.

"We could—"

"*Comórtas Draíocht.*" Li Hua's lips narrowed. Without so much as a word she called Pinyin Lung out of her brooch, a stream of dark gray smoke that condensed to form her sinuous spirit dragon familiar.

Twice now she had issued the challenge, and Donal had not yet responded. He could feel stillness seep in around him, a weight in the air as though he had seen a flash of lightning and now waited for the crack of thunder.

The call of the challenger demanded answer. If she issued it one more time, Donal would have no choice but to fight or concede. His mind reeled as he sought options, cast about for any way he could get her to see reason.

"Concede, Donal." Her words were quiet, almost mourning. "Concede and we can stay together. I would rather have you helping me, but if you will at least not oppose me I may yet find a way to bring you into this that works with your moral code."

Donal considered that, but the pressure of the challenge began to press on him. He felt almost as though he were being squeezed from the shoulders up. He looked at Li Hua, beautiful even in her anger, but she had been lying to him the entire time she had known him, hidden her personal agenda. She had shown Donal an adventurous face, a woman who lived for the thrill of action, but she concealed the manipulator, the woman who murdered Mr. bin Zuka to keep him quiet. The woman who ensorcelled Mr. Mancuso to direct his entire network of resources.

Donal could not have the thrill seeker without the manipulator. He drew a deep breath, used it to still his mind, and opened his mouth to accept her challenge.

Saravá phased down through the ceiling between the former lovers.

"I a...what?" said Donal.

"How?" said a slack-jawed Li Hua.

"My master adjures you both from participating in the *Comórtas Draíocht* and demands that you lay aside your differences for the remainder of this flight. This is the word of Magister Ronaldo Machado, master of this demesne. Let any who would dispute his word first challenge him for supremacy in this place."

"How? How did you get past my wards?" The fury in Li Hua's voice made Donal glance at her from the corner of his eye. She all but shook with rage.

Frustration at not getting to defeat Donal? Perhaps kill him?

"My master has added subtle connections throughout the spells of the *Horizon Cusp*. Never again will another's wards bar him from part of his own demesne."

"When you say we must lay aside our differences..." said Donal.

"My master declares your argument set aside. You shall not act upon it. You shall not discuss it. You shall seek no allies against each other. You shall not work against each other through intermediaries. You each shall seek no enemies of the other, nor plan actions against each other, save in your own heads or with your own familiars.

"Until you set foot on Venus, my master declares you in armistice."

Donal and Li Hua looked at each other, and though they stood no more than two meters distant, Donal felt that the space between them should properly have been measured in decans.

The door to the relief room opened, and framed in the doorway stood Magister Machado. The portly ship's mage should have cut a comic figure: drenched in sweat, panting for breath, and wearing only a thin robe that clung to his skin but did not quite close. Still, Donal could feel power crackling in the air around the Magister.

In that moment Donal realized that Magister Machado could have stood against himself and Li Hua combined and won. Here was the ally Donal needed. Magister Machado could take care of Li Hua and free Mr. Mancuso from her spells while raising less sweat than he had generated rushing down here.

"Magister," said Donal. "I—"

"Save it," said Machado, puffing for breath and hands going to his knees. "I did not ... leap out of bed ... and rush down here ... to listen to whatever little domestic problem you two are having." He stood straight, and despite the exertion and the speech, he already seemed to have his breathing under control. "Put it from your minds, or fuck your way through it, or do whatever you have to. But you will not fight about it on this ship."

Li Hua took breath to speak, but the Magister did not let her.

"I said save it. I don't want to hear about your title or what rights you think it gives you. One of you called for the *Comórtas Draíocht*. That makes this a matter of magic, and on this ship that means I make the call. If you don't like it..." Magister Machado slowly rubbed his hands together. "By all means, step on up and get put in your place."

Donal immediately raised his hands in surrender. He hadn't even had time to think first, to try to find a way to get the Magister to listen to him. He just knew he had no prayer of matching spells with this man, at least not now. And his arms acted before the brain could catch up.

Li Hua did not raise her hands. She merely looked down, then away, then nodded.

"I thought not," said Machado. "So let's make it formal, just in case either of you intends to try something sneaky."

The Magister began speaking Gaelic, his words almost slurring under the weight of his Brazilian accent, but still infused with a touch of power.

"Let this matter lie dormant between you. Speak no word of it to any save your bound familiars. Take no actions upon it. I say this matter is dead until you set foot on Venus."

Donal felt the words settle into his aura. A minor geas, hardly enough to call a spell, but so long as he remained where magic fell under Magister Machado's jurisdiction, Donal knew he would not be able to go against the command. Donal knew that from experience.

He had been under similar strictures when he took his Journeyman license examination.

"Cuthbert, go on ahead," said Machado. "There's something I need to discuss with Ms. Tai Shi here."

Donal left the relief room, and closed the door behind him.

CUTHBERT WALKED OUT OF THE RELIEF ROOM LOOKING LIKE HE'D LOST his best friend. *Poor kid,* thought Machado. *Must have been a bad breakup.*

Machado turned to Tai Shi. "I can't help but notice which of you had a familiar out and ready."

"I issued the challenge," she said, posture defiant, as though Machado had cheated her of her justice. "Would you believe he—"

"Didn't ask," he said, "and don't want to know. I have more than enough on my plate without getting into your personal life."

"Should have let us handle it then." She arched an eyebrow as though this Journeyman intended to teach a Magister a lesson. "The matter would be resolved by now, and you wouldn't have lost a second's sleep."

"You spend too much time with businessmen. Careful it doesn't give you an inflated sense of your skills."

"I know you could take me. Doesn't mean I have to agree with all your decisions."

"Look," said Machado, fighting a yawn. "I care less about your opinion of my decisions than I do about your personal life. I just kept you here, nice and secluded, to make something completely clear to you."

Tai Shi had both eyebrows raised now, and blinked a few times as though a vague curiosity lurked behind a façade of apathy.

"When you two get around to having your little duel you're going to stomp on him. We both know it. Cuthbert's talented, but you probably have more combat experience than a naïve kid like him can imagine. So I want you to remember *this.*"

Machado lowered his brow and brought his hands together in a gesture that a non-magician might mistake for prayer, but he knew that Tai Shi would recognize as the preparation of power.

"I like the kid. He has talent and he has heart, even if he's sometimes short on sense."

"You can say that again."

"I wasn't finished. If anything happens to him — and I *will* find out if it does — I'll come looking for you. And I don't just mean in the duel. If Cuthbert drops dead all of a sudden, whether from a 'mugger's' knife or just a collapse, say, in a spaceport."

Machado let those words ring for a moment, let Tai Shi realize what he implied. He waited until her eyes narrowed before he continued.

"That's right. I know no one can prove you killed bin Zuka, but his death sure was convenient for you and your boss. Now maybe that guy had it coming. He'd been responsible for one murder and attempted another. But Cuthbert? There's no way he's guilty of anything except occasional bouts of abject stupidity for the common good."

"Are you finished? Magister?"

"I believe so, *Journeyman*. So why don't you run along to your suite. I'll clean up these wards for you."

Tai Shi's eyes widened as though someone had given her an unexpected prostate exam. Machado spread his lips in an evil smile. *That's right. I get to take my time and analyze your wards as I pick them apart thread by thread. Handy information if you ever make me come after you.*

Machado gestured toward the door.

Tai Shi closed her eyes through a deep breath, then left the room, her familiar following in her wake. Like Cuthbert, she closed the door behind her.

Machado turned to *Saravá*. "Wish you'd gotten here in time to find out what was up. Officially I can't care because of their relationship. I have to assume it's a domestic issue."

Machado shook his head. "But I don't buy it. Cuthbert and his fumbling idea of investigation must have turned something up." He sighed. "But being Cuthbert, he probably doesn't have any proof he could point to."

"You could speak to Donal Cuthbert privately," said the spirit panther, its voice a deep, purring rumble. "I believe you would call it 'off the record?'"

"And get reamed out by Jacobs for violating protocol? No thank you." Machado looked toward the door. "Follow her until she returns to her suite, then report back. I'll want your thoughts about these wards before I dismantle them."

The ghostly *onça* drifted through the closed door.

Machado smacked the voice-only comm pad beside the door. "Bridge, this is Machado. I just broke up a domestic disturbance on the Observation Deck. Magical in nature, almost a duel. Details in my next report. Machado out."

Machado knew he should have waited for confirmation before cutting the line, but he didn't feel like wasting the time. He'd followed procedure, whether they understood what he said or not. It would all be in his report either way. It wasn't as though this were an emergency situation. And Machado now had a lot of work between himself and his oh-so-comfortable mattress.

Machado picked a spot at random and began an in-depth examination of Tai Shi's wards.

***

Donal closed the main door of his suite behind him, then pulled his tuning fork out and double checked that his wards remained intact and unmolested. But if anyone had touched them, they had left no trace.

Donal shook his head violently. This was not the time for paranoia. He had no reason to think anyone would have tampered with his wards. And based on Magister Machado's edict, Donal was likely as safe as he had ever been in his life, at least until he reached Venus.

He wandered deeper into the suite, on into the bedroom, and

collapsed face-first on the bed. He let out a sigh that must have started down in his toes and rolled through him like a wave. When it finished, he called his familiar out of his pendant. Fionn's emerald light coalesced into the more familiar deerhound shape on the floor next to Donal.

The *cú sidhe* perked its ears as it regarded its master, then flattened them, then rested its head on the mattress beside Donal.

"You have ended things with Tai Shi Li Hua."

Not even a hint of question to the fae hound's tone. Donal felt there should have at least been a question. He lay there and pondered that.

"The end did not go well," said Fionn. "But more troubles you than the simple loss of your relationship."

"Mr. Mancuso's not the problem. It's her. It's been her all along. She's in his head. Slow, subtle stuff, built up over time."

"And she knows you know?"

Donal managed to nod by shoving his face deeper into the sheets and pulling it back up far enough that he could breathe again.

"That she did not act immediately means nothing. She will come for you. We must—"

"We can't." Donal caught Fionn up on the almost-duel, Magister Machado's arrival, and finally his edict.

"Then we have time to prepare. Tai Shi Li Hua will be difficult, but she is not indefatigable. She has weak points. I have noted several."

"You have?" Donal rolled over and looked at Fionn. The deerhound had raised its forepaws onto the bed.

"I knew you would end up dueling her, so I have taken every opportunity to study her magic and her blind spots. By the time we arrive on Venus tomorrow night, you will stand ready to defeat her."

Donal sat up and offered a prayer to Lugh that his familiar was right. The fate of four worlds and billions of people were relying on him.

"Let's get to work," he said.

"Not now. Your heart grieves and your head needs rest. We will begin in the morning, when you are ready."

"All right, but I'm not going to be able to sleep just yet. Come on." Donal rose to a standing position, and stretched his arms and back as he did. "There's a spell I want to cast and I need your help."

19

At his station on the bridge, Jacobs took one look at the overnight reports and decided he had not had enough breakfast. Or enough sleep. Two near duels in one night? *Good thing the voyage is only three days. A week with these people and they'd kill each other.*

At least the status reports all came up clean. Some small issue in the Deception Drive, but it seemed that Jang had handled it without having to call Machado. All she had needed was some extra verbena from Fredrickson.

Verbena. Are they binding spirits or making tea?

At least the old mechanical engines looked and sounded like they were working as hard as the crews that maintained them. These sorcerous engines all seemed to rely on oils, scents and herbal remedies. They put Jacobs more in mind of the sorts of presents he used to buy for Rhonda than the types of materials that should keep a ship afloat, much less carry it through space.

Back to business, Old Man. You might not understand their methods, but you cannot question their results.

Jacobs stabbed the miniature gryphon image in the mid-section and twisted his finger to open a link to security. A moment later Goldberg's head appeared above the gryphon.

"Chief, what the hell are you doing on shift? You filed a report around midnight last night. What is my rule?"

"Even officers need eight hours as often as manageable." Goldberg breezed through the words to push on to what he wanted to say next. "But after last night there's no way I'm going to be off-shift today. Don't want to risk these idiots trying something before we land. Speaking of, we still on schedule for fifteen hundred hours E.S.T.?"

"Until you hear otherwise. And I'll let it go this time because I have something to tell you: Tai Shi and Cuthbert damn near had a magic fist fight down on the Observation Deck."

"Crap. I better have a couple of folks keep an eye on our courier."

"My thoughts exactly. Bridge out." Jacobs cut the connection and turned back to his bridge crew. "Mr. Burke, we are still on schedule?"

"Aye, Sir, steady as she goes right now. But I can't say I like the look of this space."

"Mr. Grabowski, what is Mr. Burke referring to?"

"The zuglodon hunting ground, Sir. It's bigger than the charts indicated."

Jacobs called up his charts and looked at the route as planned. Then he looked again at the scanners report and all the stars and landmarks looked to be in the right places. They were exactly where Jacobs course said they should be. Everything appeared to be in order.

"How do you know there's a problem?"

"It's the scanners, Sir. Ever since the Mars run when we got hit by zuglodons, the lacuna in the scanners gets shaky when it sees any sign of a zuglodon's passing."

"You didn't mention any zuglodons in your report."

"Haven't seen any, Sir. But the lacuna's acting like there are some out there."

Jacobs thought about that, then opened a link to Engineering. He started talking before Jang's head appeared. "Chief, how's the Deception Drive's lacuna?"

"Anxious, I'd say, Sir. Or maybe unhappy," said Jang, irritation all through her face. "Hard to say for sure, but it definitely doesn't like something."

"Understood. We may need speed and maneuverability today, Chief, so have her ready. Bridge out."

Jacobs cut the connection. They were still two hours from where he expected to start seeing signs of zuglodon activity. That meant that Burke and Grabowski were right: the zuglodons were near. And Jacobs had no intention of fighting more zuglodons if he could help it.

He might have considered re-plotting his course, adding a day for safety, but he had two problems with that. First, he needed to arrive on time or near to it. Otherwise official accounts could not confirm his route and his flight would get re-categorized from commercial to private. That would fail Starchase Spacelines, and ruin the whole point of the damned voyage. And second, the passengers had already started fighting among themselves. Adding thirty-three percent to their travel time would either exacerbate that tension, or focus it on the crew instead.

Neither of these were acceptable in Jacobs' mind. He saw only one reasonable course of action. He would have to guide the *Horizon Cusp* into the military no-fly zone.

MACHADO AWOKE WITH A HEADACHE. HE SHOULD NOT HAVE WASTED SO much time digging deep into Tai Shi's wards. What were the chances that he would actually need that information? Surely the Journeyman was not stupid enough to challenge him.

But why was he awake? His personal alarm was not due to awaken him for a few hours yet. *Probably just an odd bit of dream.* Machado began to settle back into his pillows, but then the comm pad went off again, bright scarlet light flooding out of the pad itself and carrying with it a slight mental jounce to attract attention, a feature Machado had long considered disabling.

Sheer desire for sleep encouraged him to ignore the device

anyway, to return to sleep where he would no doubt dream of smiting the damnable inventors of such an irritation...

The head of Captain Jacobs appeared above the comm pad. Machado had waited too long to answer. The link had formed a connection without his approval.

A priority feature that Machado felt the captain abused.

"Mr. Machado," said the captain, "have I called you at a bad time?"

Jacobs had at least three different patient tones that Machado had picked up on: the first said "I'm dealing with an idiot;" the second said, "You have thirty seconds before you've worn through my patience;" and the third said, "You are five seconds away from more trouble than you can possibly imagine." Machado heard that last tone in the captain's voice now.

Which meant this was not the time to point out that Machado's proper title was Magister, not mister.

"Sorry, Captain. I was up late working." Machado emphasized the statement by rubbing his eyes and face, trying to banish the last of his sleep.

"That was not reflected in your final report of the day. Do you need to amend it?"

"No, Sir. Personal matter."

"Then get your ass out of bed. Today we get to choose between zuglodons and pissed off Navy ships. Personally I don't want to deal with either. So you better get us ready for both. And Jang may need help with the engines."

Machado felt a momentary hope that the captain was joking, but knew better. Jacobs never joked about threats to the ship. Still...

"Need me to feed your cat while I'm at it?"

"If you do, stick to fish. None of that fatty pork or sausage of yours. Benny's not getting any younger." Jacobs raised one eyebrow. "Any real questions?"

"Time and priorities?"

"Sooner is better. Wards and defenses come first, but if Jang has urgent need, draft Cuthbert and Tai Shi and assign resources where you have to."

"Aye, Sir. Any chance I can draft them right now?"

"Not until there's pressing need you can point to. Keep it by the book. If we piss off Earth, I don't want them to start seeing conspiracies in our logs."

Jacobs' head turned as though he were listening to someone else report, but the sound did not carry through the link. When the captain turned back, he said, "Anything else?"

Machado shook his heavy cheeks.

"Then bridge out." Jacobs cut the connection.

Machado called *Saravá* out of the tiny onyx stud earring he concealed behind this left ear. The ghostly *onça* swirled out of a plume of soft gray smoke. Machado said, "Tell Aaron to grab us breakfast and get down to the lab as fast as possible. Then get down there yourself and start pulling together the threads of my special tricks."

Machado allowed himself a small, tight smile. "Time to see if they will work."

JACOBS LOOKED UP FROM HIS CLOSER COMPARISON OF THE OFFICIAL charts and the reports from his ship's scanners. No doubt about it. Despite what he read in the charts, the *Horizon Cusp* was no more than five minutes away from an unknown number of zuglodons of all sizes.

Two of those dangerous space elementals had once come close to tearing this ship apart, and only one of those two had been fully grown.

If a pack of those things got past the illusions and deceptions that should be concealing the ship from their senses, the *Horizon Cusp* would have no chance. They would shred it fast enough that even Mash could not stop them.

Jacobs stood at his station and addressed the whole bridge crew.

"Ladies and gentlemen, today we are going to be violating Earth General Space Travel Regulation number six cee: 'No civilian craft will violate space designated by the Earth Navy as a no-fly zone.'"

Jacobs gave them a moment for that to sink in and get any of their little sounds of shock or surprise out of the way.

"We're an Earth-registered ship on an officially logged commercial flight, so they can't legally charge us with spying. Not just for going where we're not supposed to be. But they might try to push for Theft of Military Secrets or even Treason, depending on why they designated the no-fly zone.

"The point is, I am about to break the law and take this ship with me. I have good reason for doing so, but that's no guarantee that I and my crew will not face repercussions. If any of you are unwilling to participate in this, step down from your station now. I will think no less of you and Starchaser Spacelines will still pay you for the full voyage."

The crew members looked at one another.

"Sir," said Jefferson. "Isn't there something else we could do? Another option?"

"A fair question," said Jacobs. "But in this case moot. I have examined our alternatives and concluded that this is the best and safest course of action." Jacobs glanced at the position of the *Horizon Cusp* as indicated on his charts. "And we are out of time for debates. Any who wish to step down, do so now."

None did.

Jacobs smiled, and for the first time since he discovered their situation, began to feel deep in his gut that they might yet come through this day intact.

"All right. Ms. Jefferson, broadcast a mayday into the no-fly zone. Mr. Grabowski, keep a weather eye on those scanners. The question isn't whether trouble is going to come, but when it will get here. Mr. Burke, ahead three-quarters.

"Take us into the no-fly zone."

Twenty minutes ago, Donal awoke and showered with ritual slowness. This turned the simple act of bathing into a deeper, contemplative technique that cleansed the mind as well as the body. It purged from him the stress of the last night's discovery and realization that before he left Venus — if he ever left Venus at all — he would have to duel his girlfriend. Donal was not sure that he had ever been in love with her, exactly, but he had expected a more amicable break-up than this.

Of course, he had never realized that he had been dating a megalomaniac.

But at least Donal had the better part of a day to prepare for the duel, and he came out of his shower refreshed and renewed in both body and spirit.

Ten minutes ago, Donal had breakfasted on fruit — fresh berries and melon — and a plain bagel, with water his only beverage. Magister Machado might have recommended a heavy breakfast to Donal before a full working day, but back in college Donal had established the routine of a simple meal on the days of magical exertion.

Since then the meal itself had become a sort of ritual for Donal, and he knew that the approach he took to his most important exams would serve him in good stead here. So he ate every bite completely in the moment. The explosions of raspberry and blackberry juice between his teeth, the tang of sweet fresh pineapple on his tongue, the palate cleansing bites of buttered bagel between each flavor. Even the swallows of water had their place in the rhythm of his meal.

And now Donal sat cross-legged in the center of the main room of his suite, his thoughts deep within himself anchoring his sense of balance, centering himself as completely as possible while Fionn walked a circle around him, supporting and checking.

Deeper into his own mind Donal went, past fears and responsibilities, past joys and sadness, to the core of Donal's truest self, the kernel of personality that held him together through all the experiences of his life, that made him who he was beyond anything he said or did or thought.

Donal sank deeply into himself, and prepared. Because when he came back to his own body, he would have to learn how to stand in battle against a woman who could smile when she killed.

At the long desk in his workshop office, Machado pushed aside his half-eaten plate of eggs and pastries and sat back in his huge roller chair. He looked at his tall, dark assistant — who had finished his own plate of food and was waiting for the go sign to begin casting — and said, "Repeat it so I know you understand."

"I'm going to reinforce the innocuous deceptions that are already in place to make us less noticeable to space elementals in general, and zuglodons in particular. But you *don't* want me to add any of my own."

"That's right. Your deception magic sucks." One of the benefits of working with Initiates — they know they suck at spells outside their relatively narrows areas of focus. If they were competent generalists, they would be Journeymen. "So signal me when you're ready and I'll layer a few more deceptions out there."

"And while you're doing that...."

Machado snapped his fingers. "Don't be shy, Cromartie. There's no time."

"While you're doing that I am to dig through the wards for the military keys and loop them to the tertiary circle...."

Another uncertain furrowing of Cromartie's brow, and Machado had to resist the urge to grab the tall man and shake him.

"What?"

"But surely only you can—"

"I arranged the sequence to respond to both our thaumaturgic signatures. You should have no problem looping them to the circle and getting ready to kill those keys on my command. I know it's illegal, but the captain doesn't want to leave us bare-assed to anything their little magicians can pull together and I say he's right."

"It's not that." Cromartie shook his head, his expression something like awe. "You can actually *key a spell for someone else's signature?*"

Machado grinned. "If you think that's impressive, wait 'til you see what I do when the diversions are in place."

"HELM," SAID JACOBS, MANEUVERING CHARTS IN THE AIR ABOVE HIS station as fast as he could read them, "how far inside the no-fly zone are we?"

"Two thousand klicks, Sir," said Burke.

"Good." Jacobs stretched three sections of the three-dimensional map. "I'll have a route update for you in about ninety seconds. For now, ahead full and when we reach five klicks bring us about. Hard to starboard and up ... fifteen degrees."

Jacobs rubbed his eyes and looked over the route he had in mind. It looked good: didn't go too far inside the no-fly zone, and would take them away from the zuglodon hunting ground at the same time.

Assuming anything about the charts proved to be reliable where the zuglodons were concerned. If all went well, Jacobs might have his ship out of harm's way within another hour.

For the best. The longer the *Horizon Cusp* was in the no-fly zone, the greater the temptation Jacobs felt to grab hold of the scanners and find out just what was so damned important that it merited cutting off civilian access to such a huge swath of space. Space Earth barely had any right to claim dominion over, except that the Navy had the might to enforce it.

No, better to get away from all of this before the ship got noticed. Jacobs had a crew to get to safety and passengers to drop off on Venus. Once they landed, so far as Jacobs was concerned, the passengers' safety was their own business.

"Captain," said Jefferson, "we're getting hailed."

"I haven't picked up anything on the scanners yet," said Grabowski.

"Have you been scanning into the no-fly zone?"

"No, Sir." Grabowski looked away.

Poor kid. Probably would have left his post rather than break the law, but didn't have the courage to be the only one to do it. Thought having the log show his scanning activities might help him by indicating what he clearly did not *do.*

"You'll catch the same hell wherever you look, Mr. Grabowski. Now kindly try to find out what's hailing us. Helm, take us down to half-speed just in case it's who I think it is."

Jacobs' nostrils flared in a quick, deep breath. "All right, Ms. Jefferson. Link them through to my station."

The square jaw and short gray hair of an Earth Navy captain formed above the comm pad at Jacobs' station.

"Attention unidentified vessel. This is Captain Etor Liatos of the Earth Cruiser *Orpheus*. You have entered restricted space. Under Earth authority I order you to reverse course one hundred eighty degrees and withdraw."

"This is Captain John Jacobs of the registered passenger liner *Horizon Cusp*. Listen, Captain Liatos, neither I nor anyone on my ship could give a lesser damn what secrets Earth is trying to safeguard. Fact is that the zuglodon hunting ground is nearly twice as big as you boys marked it on the charts. I've got nothing but civilians on this ship and I need you to help keep them safe so we can get them to Venus in one piece."

"Sorry, Captain, my orders are clear here. The security of this zone takes precedence even above the lives of civilians. You need to withdraw or I'll have no choice but to burn you down."

20

At his perch above the round layout of bridge stations, the cold stars of space all about him, Jacobs tried to reason with the Earth cruiser's captain over the link. He had a back-up plan, but he hoped to never use it.

"Captain, please, I need you to listen here." Jacobs rubbed that spot between his eyes. "We're not looking for a fight. This is just a commercial flight to Venus. You can board us if you like—"

"Look, Jacobs. I know your reputation as a damned good captain. My instructor back at the academy used to tell stories about you. But I've got no leeway. You have ten minutes to withdraw. Then…"

Captain Liatos looked away for a moment, but when he looked back Jacobs saw only steel in the man's eyes. "You have ten minutes. *Orpheus* out."

Captain Liatos cut the link.

"Helm! Bring us about. Ninety degrees to starboard, pitch us up ten and give me everything she has. Communications, tell Jang to push her beloved Deception Drive for all it's worth and maybe a little more. Scanners, what am I dealing with?"

"Cruiser and two gunboats, Sir. They mean business."

"So do I. Keep an eye on our new best friends, Mr. Grabowski. If they keep pace, fine. If they close or move onto an attack vector let me know immediately."

"Sir," said Jefferson, "Captain Liatos is back on the link for you."

"Make him hold a minute." Jacobs opened a link to Machado's workroom and said, "Mash! Kill those keys!"

THE SOUND OF A KNOCK FOUND ITS WAY TO DONAL'S AWARENESS. A seven rap beat, steady, urgent. Didn't match any knock Donal was familiar with. He began easing himself back out of his center and into his body, comfortable and ready for him on the floor of his suite.

The knock repeated as Donal stretched his legs, and Fionn said, "Tai Shi Li Hua stands at the door, but I do not know what she seeks."

"The Magister has put a moratorium on our duel." Donal shrugged and stood. "Maybe she's realized that, with extra time at my disposal, I'm likely to set up a way to expose what she's doing even if she takes me down."

Donal strolled over to the door, but stopped shy of reaching for the knob. He twisted his words so that only Fionn could understand them. "Is she alone?"

Fionn nodded.

Donal opened the door. There stood Li Hua in a formidable gray skirt suit. Donal felt underdressed in his tee shirt and jeans.

"I leave you alone for one night and you forget how to dress."

"I wasn't expecting a visitor." Donal leaned against the frame to ensure he did not imply an invitation inside. "What can I do for you, Ms. Tai Shi?"

Donal's words hit home. Li Hua blinked twice, and her lips started to pull to the side before she stopped them. Her eyes narrowed and she said, "A small matter, Mr. Cuthbert. I doubt it will take much of your time."

She held up a small, trifolded piece of paper. "I hope you'll indulge my use of actual paper. It seemed more appropriate."

Donal shifted enough consciousness to scan the paper and ensure that she had cast no spells on it before he took it.

"Not bad," she said, her voice almost a whisper.

Donal felt a momentary urge to smile at her acknowledgment of how far his skills had come. But then he realized that she had still spotted his shift in consciousness.

He had improved, but not enough.

Donal unfolded the paper. The business language of it took him a moment to parse, but when he understood what he thought it meant, his eyes grew wide and he felt a wave of cold sweep up his torso and settle in around his neck.

"But this means…"

"That's right." No hint of sorrow about Li Hua now, only a smile that stretched from her lips to her eyes. "In my capacity as Director of Security for Inter-Business Relations for 4M and its business partners, the *Horizon Cusp* now officially falls under my authority, as confirmed by Mr. Mancuso himself."

Li Hua tucked the piece of paper back into the inner pocket of her suit jacket. "In other words, Donal, this is now *my* demesne."

Donal closed his eyes. He was supposed to have hours to prepare for this. He was supposed to be ready to take her down, to hit the weak spots Fionn had noticed. But now he had no time at all, because Li Hua said those two little words he had been dreading: "*Comórtas Draíocht.*"

All Donal's careful plans made no difference to the abject fear he felt take hold of him. He would have to fight. And he knew he would lose.

"Master," said *Saravá*, "the Navy has arrived."

Machado wiped sweat out of his eyes. He stood in the second largest, second most complete magic circle in his workshop, surrounded by burning candles and two forms of incense to support and ease his casting.

Still, two dozen major diversions could take a lot out of even him, but they should keep any threat of zuglodons off the ship for a while, at least.

If there weren't too many.

If moving in a pack didn't extend their senses the way some theories said it might.

No time now.

"Mash!" came the voice of Jacobs from the comm link. "Kill those keys!"

"Cromartie," said Machado, "yank the loop!"

Cromartie used an actual yanking movement to free the *Horizon Cusp's* wards from the thaumaturgic links Earth mandated that every commercial and private ship include. Machado felt those weak spots leave the wards like buoys pulled out of water, with the wards — as designed — filling in their own gaps.

In that precise moment, Machado felt the pull of his *Comórtas Draíocht* alert. Tai Shi and Cuthbert had to be at it again, despite his decree.

But that shouldn't be possible ... unless....

But Machado did not have time to investigate. He felt certain that Tai Shi had issued the challenge. No way Cuthbert could cross him, much less any chance that he would try. No, Tai Shi had to have found some claim on his demesne. Unless she was stupid enough to believe she could go toe-to-toe with a Magister.

But Tai Shi was not stupid. And even if she were, Cuthbert was still stuck fighting her at a time and place of her choosing. She would crush him. And Machado might never get a straight answer about what had brought them to blows.

But that was all a worry for later. Right now, Machado had a ship to save.

JACOBS TRIED TO WAIT PATIENTLY WHILE THE HEAD OF *ORPHEUS* CAPTAIN Liatos screamed at him over the link. After all, Liatos had the authority of Earth's military backing him up.

But Jacobs had never been good at obeying authority.

"Enough!" barked Jacobs, a tone so sharp that Liatos stopped mid-threat. "You gave us ten minutes before you open fire and I'm not going to let you waste the other nine."

"Stop running from us or I'll kill your engines for you."

Jacobs cut the link. Nothing he could say right now would make a difference anyway. Liatos would not vary from his orders, and any moment he would discover that the *Horizon Cusp* no longer had those ward keys he could exploit. Then they would be in the heart of the storm.

Jacobs wanted as much distance as he could get before that happened.

"Scanners, how are they keeping pace?"

"Gunboats are falling behind, but the *Orpheus* is staying with us."

"Firing status?"

"They're out of line to shoot, and their chutes look cold."

"Helm, how's she handling?"

"Five by five so far."

"Captain," said Jefferson. "The *Orpheus* is back on the link and they sound pissed."

"Cut that link. There's no point in it. I'm not steering us into certain death."

"Done, Sir, but..."

"Out with it."

"Captain Liatos said he has summoned reinforcements. We are to surrender immediately or be destroyed."

"SO THIS IS WHAT IT COMES DOWN TO," SAID DONAL, STILL BLOCKING the doorway. "I don't suppose you'd care to talk about this."

"There's nothing to discuss." All playfulness had fled Li Hua's tone. Her words were crisp, sharp, the way Mr. Mancuso sounded when discussing business. "Before I leave here, I will put you under a *geas* to keep you from ever telling anyone what you know or think you know about me, Mr. Mancuso, 4M, and all related businesses."

She tried to smile then, but even the smile had grown cold as though, inside, she had already cut herself off from Donal.

"You can still go to grad school, get your Hierophant credentials, and do all the research you want. I don't want to ruin your plans, Donal. I just don't want to let you ruin mine."

But Donal barely heard her words over the pounding of his heart, the sense of loss dripping down his spine, the heat in his face and the tears that tried to escape, gave everything he saw a glossy sheen.

Was it really only a few days ago that Mr. Mohatar had told Donal how good a couple they made?

"*Comórtas Draíocht*," Li Hua said again. "That's two times, Donal. Accept the challenge or accept the *geas*." She shrugged. "Or try to do neither and weaken the power of your word. Erode your oaths. Sure, you'll lose your *cú sidhe*, but you always wanted to try for an Enochian familiar anyway—"

Give up Fionn?

That was the most insulting thing she had said yet. More than her condescension. More than her confidence of victory. That she would even *suggest* that Donal would sever his ties to Fionn...

True, Donal had not summoned a familiar in college like most of his classmates. True, Donal had once had plans of becoming the first modern magician to bind an elemental familiar using an Enochian approach of his own devising.

But Fionn had become more than a best friend, more than a partner. The familiar ritual had used the words as part of the alchemy to seal the bonds between them: "my tears, my blood, my sweat, your life." Donal had felt the truth of those words ever since. Fionn was no mere spirit. Fionn was a part of Donal.

And to imply that Donal would give up his familiar to avoid getting beat up?

"I accept your challenge." Donal turned and walked into his

room, certain that now he could safely turn his back. The challenge had been issued and accepted, binding her by its rules as much as him.

Perhaps Li Hua had been taunting him about the familiar, but even the implication that Donal would give up Fionn had been enough to make him angry. And Donal knew he needed his anger right now.

For all its art and precision, thaumaturgy relied on a magician's confidence and sense of authority as much as on his skill. Donal's confidence going into this duel was weak and he knew it, but perhaps he could make up the difference in anger....

MACHADO WIPED HIS FACE WITH BOTH HANDS. AS HE DID, HE EASED A slow, deep breath in through his nose, imagining it spiraling all the way down into the very soles of his feet, then let it out just as slowly through his mouth, reversing the spiral.

By the time he stepped up to the largest magic circle in his workshop his mind was clear and ready to cast.

Machado spared a glance for Cromartie, but the Initiate was doing his job. After pulling the keys, he had moved over to the third circle and begun augmenting the wards where and how he could.

Machado stopped just shy of entering the circle. He turned to Cromartie and said, "Enough of that for now. I want you to prepare a half-dozen distractions for the ships that pursue us. You don't have to stop them, just slow them down until I'm ready to deal with them."

Machado pulled from his pocket a small red cloth bag tied off with matching cord. Without looking, he tossed it over his left shoulder and into the burning brazier behind him. Machado had labored for weeks to determine the exact components necessary for that incense. He had driven Fredrickson half crazy trying to gather the ingredients, especially since Machado refused to say why he needed them.

But Machado had no intention of making her party to his crime.

And the moment he threw that incense into a fire he committed a crime against all laws governing civilian ships and the limits of their wards.

Machado had always pushed his wards as hard as the law allowed to protect the *Horizon Cusp* from the various hazards they faced. But this time, Machado crossed that line, and only Captain Jacobs knew that he had prepared to do so.

Machado stepped into the circle and began threading together the subtle groundwork he had built up over the course of months, interweaving the threads of scores of half-cast spells.

By the time he finished, the *Horizon Cusp* would have active wards at least as potent as those of their pursuers.

And if Machado had anything to say about it, the wards of the *Horizon Cusp* would be even better.

"CAPTAIN!" SAID GRABOWSKI. "TWO MORE GUNSHIPS AT TWELVE o'clock high!"

"Dive!" Jacobs' fists clenched and unclenched with the need to punch something, if only he could find a target. But the captain's station lacked a punching bag. He settled for finally smacking the gryphon image on the beak, sounding general quarters.

Jacobs reassured himself that Burke had proven himself a good pilot, would be able to handle all of Jacobs' orders. He did not need to seize the helm and handle this escape himself.

He *did not* need to do it.

The klaxon rang out, followed by the sound of his own voice calling the crew to their stations. The passengers would already be confined to quarters. Still...

"Communications, get me Goldberg. Scanners, what's our status?"

"The new gunboats are shifting course to intercept. The ones that accompanied the *Orpheus* have fallen off the chase, but the *Orpheus* herself is hanging with us. And, Captain, she's heating up her chutes."

Jacobs stood in his chair and twisted to regard the *Orpheus* behind them. It was about the size of the *Horizon Cusp*, but bore the outer shape of an old steel cruiser that would have sailed the seas before technology fell. The kind Jacobs first served on.

"All right, you bastards. You'll cut us off fore and aft and trap us against the zuglodon hunting ground? I don't think so." Jacobs pointed at Burke. "Helm! Hard to port. Take us deeper into the no-fly zone."

"Captain," said Jefferson, "I have the chief for you."

"Link him through." Jacobs turned to the forming head of Chief Goldberg. "Passengers squared away?"

"Everyone but Tai Shi." Goldberg's lips puckered like he wanted to spit. "Claimed I didn't have the authority and browbeat my men into letting her go. Want me to chase her down?"

"Damn her and damn her title, but we can't spare the time. I need your men ready in case the Navy boards us."

"You want us to fight armed and ready Navy spacers?" The head tilted and swayed as though Goldberg cracked his neck. "Do we have cause?"

"I'm logging their charts and response as recklessly endangering civilian lives at high space. At least three crimes in that."

"Good enough for me, Captain. My people and I will give them hell, but you know as well as I do that if they board us we're as good as sunk."

"You just get ready to fight and leave the rest to me. Bridge out." Jacobs slashed his hand through the image to cut the connection.

Under his breath Jacobs said, "Mash, your little trick better work."

***

Donal moved the coffee table and couch next to the round table and recliners under the porthole, then slid the two matching chairs back, making room for their duel. But not just any duel. The

Comórtas Draíocht had its own formal rules beyond what the law required; it was every bit as much a ritual spell as a fight.

While Donal cleared the space, Li Hua summoned Pinyin Lung. Then the two magicians moved to stand two meters apart, distant enough to give them space, but close enough to give their familiars room to create the circle around them. They faced each other, each with a familiar on the right.

Donal looked down for a moment of prayer, as the rules permitted.

Great Lugh, Skillful One, He Who Sits in the Seat of the Sage, guide me to victory today as you guided the Tuatha de Dannan to victory over the Fomorians at the Second Battle of Maige Tuired. I ask this not for myself, but on behalf of those my foe would make suffer under the yoke of oppression, those she would reduce to a servant class for the magicians among us. Great Lugh, you mastered all skills, and so you know that all people and all skills have value. Help me defend those whose crafts are not my own. I pray you, help me thwart her goals.

Donal went on to offer short prayers to the Dagda, Brigid, and Fionn MacCumhaill, seeking more divine assistance. By the time Donal finished, he felt clear once more and as ready to fight Li Hua as he would ever get. He looked up to see her, arms folded, her toe not quite tapping as she waited.

Donal met her eye and matched her timing, nodded, then together they recited the formal commencement, infusing their words with a touch of power: "I declare that this matter binds us. No escape, no interference, until I yield or prove my mastery by spell alone."

They turned to their familiars and said, three times, "Guard. Guide. Witness."

Cú sidhe and dragon began to circle in a slow pace around the duelists. Donal offered and received the formal salute, given with the first two fingers of the right hand: point down to acknowledge those who have gone before, touch the core of the self, the solar plexus, touch the link to the universe, the forehead, point up to acknowledge those who will follow, and sweep a final gesture of respect to Those Who Watch.

With these simple rituals, Donal committed himself to the task. The magic was in place. Until the duel had a winner, neither of them could affect anything outside the circle of their familiars. But inside that circle, each had a direct link to the other, not only facilitating targeting, but also broadening the scope of their capabilities.

While dueling, Donal and Li Hua would be able to call on spells in mere moments that would otherwise take hours to construct, if they could even be done.

And now the circle had been set, the familiars posted, and the formal words spoken.

Thus, the duel began.

MACHADO'S BODY SAT ON THE FLOOR OF HIS WORKSHOP, IN THE CENTER of the largest and most intricate magic circle on the ship, inhaling the piquant mixture of herbs and roots that formed this unique incense.

But Machado's mind was deep in the tapestry of spells he had woven to protect the *Horizon Cusp*: the wards. In each of those wards, Machado had woven additional threads of power that played hell on his maintenance budget and required him to spend twice as much effort keeping those wards ready at a moment's notice, even though in the six months since he had begun working little extras into those spells, no one but he would have noticed the difference.

A thread of power here, a half-finished spell there, little bits and pieces throughout the ship that lay dormant, waiting, in case Machado ever needed them.

Today, for the first time, he did.

Machado's mind raced from system to system, working through the right order of completion to begin the change that would take the *Horizon Cusp's* wards from high quality commercial grade to high quality military grade.

At least, that was the plan.

But in the moment, all Machado could do was work at full speed to catch every loose end, tying off and completing hundreds of spells faster than an Initiate could complete one.

Everyone knew that a Magister was more powerful than a Journeyman, and that a Hierophant was more powerful than a Magister. But what the laymen never understood was that the difference in grades meant more than channeling power. It meant mastering technique to finer and finer granularity, holding more and more complex spell structures in one's head, making essential choices in the flash of an instant.

Machado needed all of these skills and more as he worked. And more than even that, he needed *Saravá*. His familiar gathered and distributed power, the raw work, allowing Machado to handle the finer work and keep moving.

But even Machado needed time. He had never attempted anything so involved and complex while under such duress. He could only hope that Jacobs could buy him enough to finish.

Well, he could also hope for one other thing.

He could hope the wards would work.

In. Out. Slow. Steady. One breath follows the previous, as one movement follows the previous, as one spell follows the previous. Donal focused on the movements of his hands, pulling aside Li Hua's rapid flow of fiery orange dragon's teeth, almost a steady stream as part of her attack. He focused on shifting only exactly enough of his power to shunt the assault by, where it would hit the circle created by the two familiars and dissipate, its power strengthening their isolation and temporarily boosting the power of the familiars.

But most of all, he steadied his attention on his breathing. Each breath was life. Each breath was hope. Donal needed those breaths to keep his attention not on how the duel would end, but on precisely what he needed most to do each moment. That was how Professor N'kembe had told him to deal with complex spell tests.

The same technique served him well here and now.

It was Li Hua who had taught Donal to abandon the systems of breathing taught by the schools. Explained to him how they tipped his hand about the spells he cast.

But slow, steady, deep breaths did not trigger trained-in mental cues. They served Donal the same way they would serve anyone under pressure, and they served him well enough. Those dragon's teeth were the sixth straight attack he had defeated without raising the slightest sweat.

Li Hua scarcely spared Donal a moment to counterattack, staying almost entirely on offense. But her strategy did not trouble Donal. He was content to remain on defense for the time being, studying her attacks and letting her waste as much effort as she desired.

Donal even attempted to allay suspicion by throwing token attacks here and there. Small bits of illusion that shattered against her counterattacks, not even requiring direct defenses.

But she already believed herself the superior magician. Let his trivial attacks confirm this in her mind. In the meantime, Donal had noticed her tendency to lean on kinetic attacks. Perhaps he could find a way to exploit that.

In the meantime, to each breath its place. In. Out. Slow. Steady....

"Captain, it's the *Orpheus* again."

Jacobs didn't bother to say anything, just nodded at Jefferson and slapped his comm pad the moment it glowed red. He didn't wait for Liatos to speak, either.

"Make it fast, Captain. I'm trying to save lives here."

"Heading deeper into restricted space is your idea of *saving* lives?"

"No, getting a military escort past the *zuglodon hunting ground* that *your people* misrepresented on the *official* charts was my idea of saving lives." Jacobs gave the man a strong enough glare to make him blink. "But that's not going to happen, so I have to improvise."

"Time's up, Captain. Surrender your ship or be destroyed."

"We still have two minutes."

Jacobs knew it sounded lame, but stalling was never his strong suit.

"You've abused that time and my mages tell me your ship wards lack the mandated military keys."

"They were there until you threatened to murder civilians over an innocent mistake, Liatos. Our log will confirm it."

"Earth law does not recognize the civilian right to make that call. Even making the keys removable is a fineable offense."

"So fine me! The office is in—"

"I've had enough, Mister." Even over the link, Jacobs could see fire blaze in Liatos' eyes. "If you don't surrender in the next five seconds, we shoot."

Jacobs knew the man only did his job. Had been told that somewhere in this restricted zone were secrets worth keeping. Even at the cost of civilian lives. But damn it, this was still the military's fault for at least sloppy charting, maybe even deliberate mis-charting.

Jacobs cut the link.

"Helm, escape maneuvers. Damage Control, I want reports as fast as I can get them. We're in it now, ladies and gentlemen."

"Sir! Destroyer! Dead ahead!" Grabowski practically leaped out of his chair and dove for cover, but he somehow managed to keep his hands on his station's controls.

"I'd say we've gone far enough. Helm, ninety degrees to starboard and pitch us up thirty. And stay evasive!"

One advantage of a good crew. While they were doing their jobs, Jacobs had done his. All that poring over charts had let him plot no fewer than three escape routes, depending on when Liatos made them necessary. Gamma would have been best, but Jacobs never expected to get fifty thousand klicks into the restricted zone. Still, once the immediate dodging was finished, Jacobs would know which route to use.

"Incoming!"

Grabowski did duck that time, but at least he didn't abandon his station. Jacobs glanced up reflexively as twin fireballs bore down on them.

Alchemy made military shot burn hot enough to melt even hardened ceramics. Thaumaturgy made those shots lighter and truer than ever before. But Jacobs still considered the fireballs little better than the ancients had with their Greek fire and catapults.

But archaic design or not, they would do enough damage if they struck true.

Jacobs could tell immediately that the shots from the *Orpheus* would miss wide to port. They weren't in good position to shoot, and his yaw to starboard had taken their shots off line.

Unfortunately, the move must have been anticipated by the destroyer. It had loosed three fireballs of its own, and two of them bore straight down on the *Horizon Cusp*, likely to hit near the bridge and under the port wing.

Jacobs gritted his teeth and watched the fireball bear down on the bridge, bright light half-blinding him through squinted eyes.

The fireball splashed impotently against the wards.

"Yes!" roared Jacobs, thrusting one fist in the air. "Machado, I'm going to have a statue built to you!"

He grabbed the rail of his station and leaned over the crew. "That, ladies and gentlemen, is the work of our patron saint buying us time. Helm, get us the hell out of here. Follow escape route beta."

Jacobs started to turn back to his charts for emergency modifications, but an evil idea occurred to him. Right now the *Horizon Cusp* had better wards than it had ever had before, possibly better than those of the pursuing ships...

"Belay that, Helm. Take us into the hunting ground. Let's see if our Navy friends have the stomach to follow."

<hr>

Sweat crept down Donal's face, burned his eyes, stuck his shirtsleeves to his arms. Even his breathing grew shallow, his defenses less elegant. Meanwhile, Li Hua's attacks grew more intricate without losing any of their power.

Like right now. Donal needed almost all of his mental agility to spot and defeat each of the two dozen rings of fire Li Hua had thrown at his head. He forced as many as he could to slam into each other, but resorted to direct opposition to stop five.

Too many.

If he continued at that rate, her attacks would drain Donal faster than he could afford. Each such effort cost him a little more of his power and concentration.

Worse, the rings had been a distraction for the real attack. A kinetic loop tried to trip him and make him fall out of the circle, losing the duel. Fortunately he had been able to jump just as the loop closed and evade the attack.

Donal had to admit that his strategy was not working. He had hoped to wear her down, let her spend her energy. But her attacks had gotten stronger and tighter, while Donal's defenses grew slowly weaker.

Three straight attacks that might have killed him. Lethal, without a doubt. Li Hua did not have enough skill at deception magic to fool Donal. Her fire attacks had been as real as the acidic-looking liquids she sometimes threw.

If Donal survived this, he would have to join a dueling society. Get some formal combat training beyond the introduction he had taken at U.C. Santa Cruz.

But that was for later.

What had he learned so far? She favored two kinds of attacks: kinetic and evocation. Despite her claim about scrying, those had to be her specialties the way Donal's were deception and conjuring.

Donal pulled on that second specialty now, using the ceramics of the deck to call forth a gnome, an earth elemental.

But Donal had the gnome only half-formed, its granite and slate body still taking shape, when Li Hua countered with a gout of fire spat straight from her mouth. The gnome melted before it and Donal half-ducked and half-shunted the fire above him to defeat the counterspell.

The gnome's molten core dissolved, absorbed by the magic of the *Comórtas Draíocht* before Donal could try to tap into it for another spell.

Meanwhile, Li Hua swept her arms wide and brought them back together, directing a gale force of wind at Donal. She caught him square in the chest, lifted him off his feet. The edge of the circle a scant meter behind him and closing.

Donal snatched the gale and called from it a massive sylph, the largest air elemental he could control. The sylph, a beautiful naked woman with butterfly wings, formed three meters tall between Donal and the edge of the circle. She caught him and lowered him to the carpet as gentle as a whisper.

But the attack she carried to Li Hua shrieked and cut like an arctic windstorm.

Li Hua drew two swords from the air itself, their curved blades composed of green fire a meter long. She whirled in a circle, swinging the swords in tight arcs, and cut the sylph to burning ribbons of floating ash.

"Thank you," Li Hua said. "I so rarely get to work this spell into a duel."

She threw the swords at Donal and with an incantation quickly in muttered Chinese, caught him from behind with a wave of motion that pulled him toward the spinning fiery blades.

Donal wanted to use the blades to cut the motive force propelling him forward. Or at least use that force to try to knock Li Hua out of the circle. But he felt certain that she expected the second and he didn't have time for the first.

He had to settle for his third option: redirecting the kinetic energy of her rear attack to carry Donal upwards and clear of the swords. He would have a trick landing safely, but at least he would be safe from those attacks.

Donal needed to find a way to use her specialties against her and exploit her clear unwillingness to resort to actual defense.

But for now, he had to survive as best he could.

MACHADO HATED SWEATING. HE HATED SHOWING VISIBLE SIGNS OF work at all, especially when he was casting. In his mind's eye, Magister Ronaldo Machado was a smooth, effortless magician who could produce effects that impressed his peers and astounded the masses, all while looking and smelling good. Much of the time the reality matched that image.

But this was not one of those times.

Sweat drenched him now, making him wipe excess from his eyes with a slick forearm, and taste salt while he chanted. Looking good was no longer part of the equation, and smelling good even less so. But keeping these wards at military grade strength took steady casting and a tremendous amount of will. He had lain the groundwork necessary for this stunt months ago, hoped he would never need to use it, but even he could only push his preparations so far.

Government inspectors came through the ports every couple of months to check over all civilian helioships. They never gave actual spellwork more than a cursory glance. They took only as much time as they required in order to certify the intentions and power level of one hundred spells, chosen at random. Though Machado noticed that "random" system inspections always seemed to include wards.

But while those inspectors might have given the spells themselves little attention, they watched the related alchemical work like predators at a watering hole. And Machado knew they were right to do it. Advanced spells could be hidden among the standard arrays, but the supporting alchemy they needed stood out quickly to those who knew what to look for.

So while those pursuing ships had properly supported military wards that their ships' mages could maintain with a reasonable amount of effort, the *Horizon Cusp* could only sustain its advanced wards as long as Machado could handle pressing his limits.

But he could hold. He had to.

Most ships could not maintain top speed while firing, so either the pursuers would keep shooting until they dropped out of range, or they would give the barrage a rest and Machado would be able to take a break.

That would happen any second now…

"Master," said the smooth voice of Machado's familiar, *Saravá*, "a number of zuglodons have begun moving our direction. I believe we have entered their hunting grounds."

"What?"

Machado did not expect a reply, because the ghostly panther would know its master understood, even if he could not believe what he heard. A number of creative ways to kill Captain Jacobs flitted through Machado's mind in a fraction of a second.

Just buy me a little time, you said. Just enough to escape pursuit, you said.

"Aaron, forget the ships! Pour everything you have left into keeping those zuglodons off us."

Cromartie looked even less steady than Machado felt. Just an Initiate. Not trained for this kind of extended work, much less fighting off a bunch of hungry space elementals with delusions of grandeur. But Machado had been training Cromartie to deal with zuglodons, just in case.

If only Cromartie's deceptions were stronger. If only Machado had a Journeyman backing his play right now. But no, the only two Journeymen on the ship were busy fighting among themselves.

Machado wiped more sweat from his eyes, took a deep breath, and kept casting.

***

Jacobs stood with his hands on the rail that surrounded his station on the bridge. His grip had squeezed much of the blood from his fingers, but his voice dripped with calm confidence.

"Steady as she goes, Mr. Burke. Ease us back toward our course along the alpha line I've set up for you."

Burke and Grabowski looked pale. Grabowski shook with fear, but so far Burke kept a steady hand on the controls. They had reason for their fear. A pack of four zuglodons had moved within two dozen klicks of the *Horizon Cusp's* current location.

Jacobs could not see them with his own eyes, but he knew well enough what they looked like: giant transparent gray snakes, bloated in the middle, as though they've already fed too well. At one end — the head, for all intents and purposes — they had a series of tentacles.

Grabowski had already told him their relative sizes. Two of the pack were about the size of the *Horizon Cusp*. The other two were much, much bigger.

"Damage control, report."

"Wards are holding, Captain, but I don't know how many more volleys they can handle."

"Mr. Grabowski, have our friends decided to join us or are they content to keep this relationship long-distance?"

"They appear to be holding distance, Sir, but they're staying inside shooting range."

"They're discussing the matter, Sir," said Jefferson.

Jacobs looked down to see his communications officer twisting both hands to pinch together three strands of the snarl of blue-light spaghetti floating in the air above her console; a snarl that represented the entire link network of the *Horizon Cusp*.

"You know that for sure?"

"I can't hear everything they're saying, but I can pick up enough. The destroyer wants to let us go. Figures we haven't seen anything and that they've persuaded us not to come looking. But the *Orpheus* wants us, wants to prosecute us for entering the restricted zone, attempting to escape legal interdiction, and for using illegal wards."

"Damned good work, Ms. Jefferson. Relay that information to the ship's mage. Maybe he can use it."

That settles it. Jefferson, my last act before retirement will be getting you trained for promotion.

"Captain," said Grabowski, "the biggest one is moving to intercept ... now the others are following. No doubt, Sir. They've noticed us."

Help me, Dagda. She's everywhere.

Donal could barely stay upright. Li Hua's attacks came in without pause. Across the circle from him she seemed to dance, weaving her arms and singing a tune that accented every beat with a new attack, some new hazard from the depths of her mind winging at Donal, battering at his dwindling ability to defend himself.

Fionn may have spotted flaws in her technique, holes in her defenses. But Donal could not see them. Could not see anything but wave after wave of spells coming at him. Storms of red Martian sand, freezing cold, viselike grips, ghostly pounding fists, sirens that rattled Donal's ears and teeth, blasts of sound that he only just prevented from shattering his ribs.

Spells without hesitation. Spells beyond counting. And all without so much as breaking a sweat.

Fionn might have been able to tell Donal secrets that could have made the difference. But Donal could not imagine what those secrets were.

Donal clung to the shreds of his confidence. Patched together enough to maintain at least some of his power. Though most of it felt spent and lost to the duel.

His single, tiny thread of confidence came from defeating the last seemingly indefatigable foe Donal had faced: Imenand bin Zuka. But bin Zuka had failed to counter Donal's dual-core spell, a spell that called on both his specialties: conjuration and deception. But Li Hua had two specialties as well, and wielded dual-core spells with the same casual efficiency as everything else she did.

Donal had bought himself time with redirection, even turning the occasional spell back on Li Hua. But she could maintain this pace longer than he could. She would outlast him. Donal would lose.

That thought loosened something in Donal's head. Cracked away more of his confidence. Donal could no longer afford to wait. He needed to make his move. Now.

Li Hua would be watching for deception magic. It was the specialty of Donal's that she best knew him for. So Donal focused on conjuration, and not what he knew of her magic, but what he knew of *her*.

Li Hua loved action above all else. So Donal called on the Morrigan to guide his casting and brought forth a spirit of battle in the form of a huge crow. Added a touch of illusion to disguise his favorite feature of this spirit: the more one opposed it directly, the more powerful it grew. Donal hid that aspect behind the razors of its talons and beak, underscored the common association that gave rise to the collective term for crows: a murder.

Li Hua exploded a series of stars around the crow, clearly intending to fry it to a cinder. But the crow did not burn. Instead its black feathers flared red-orange, then faded back to onyx as the crow grew half-again as large.

Donal gathered another spell, tried to press his meager advantage.

But Li Hua did something he had never before seen in a duel: she dove for the floor, sliding toward him into a roll.

Donal pulled together a disorientation effect that would make him appear to surround her. It would never have worked if she had kept her place across the circle. But up close it might buy him time. A chance to evade whatever she reached for in the air above her. Time to allow Donal's battle crow to end the fight.

Images of Donal popped up in a circle around the crouching, reaching Li Hua. The battle crow banked and dove at her. Donal began a spinning loop that might catch Li Hua in an incomplete moment, force her to repeat ineffective steps and buy Donal more time.

But Li Hua was faster.

She once more drew from mid-air her curved fiery sword and spun in a tight circle, carving through the rib cage of not one image of Donal, but all of them.

Including the true Donal Cuthbert.

Pain burnt through Donal's whole body. Radiated out from his ribs through every nerve he had all the way to the tips of his toes and the follicles of his hair.

Donal saw her smile of triumph. He saw his battle crow fade from existence scant millimeters from her throat.

And then he saw nothing else.

21

Machado kept up his chants and timed additional herbs for the incense with the rhythm of his gestures. Every word had its tone and beat, forming a rocking drone as he finished each line, but a haunting refrain as he completed the entire verse.

Each sound, each movement, each scent had its place in the role of maintaining the *Horizon Cusp's* wards at a level more powerful than any comparable ship had ever boasted.

Any Journeyman could have handled Machado's words, his movements. Some might even have had the instincts to feel the timing as the casting grew longer.

But it took a Magister to understand how to channel the soreness such effort had cost his arms and fingers, the tightness in his back, the stiffness in his knees and hips. Every demand the working placed on Machado's body, he found a way to fold back into his spellcasting to work *with* the wards instead of against himself.

And only the Magister who had cast those wards — who knew every thread and nuance of them as he knew the scenes of his favorite books — only he could shift and balance those wards to keep maximum strength at the areas most under threat, while allowing the other zones to ease just a hair.

Only Machado himself could have handled finding little ways to rest part of his mind even while the remainder of him exerted his talents to his limits.

From the corner of his eye, Machado saw Cromartie collapse. Hardly surprising. Machado felt past ready to collapse himself. At least Cromartie had mastered Machado's anti-zuglodon spells to the best of his limited abilities. Machado could only hope the Initiate had gotten those spells in place fast enough to do the ship any good.

"Attention, Magister Machado."

Jefferson's voice, over the comm link. A pity Machado could not spare a moment to look over at her pretty face, but the spells he maintained had no forgiveness for distraction.

"Our pursuers argue among themselves. The destroyer does not wish to pursue. The cruiser wants to bring us in. The captain wanted you to know."

She grew quiet, but Machado could tell the link remained open. Her silence over an open link irritated him like a grain of sand between his toes. He had no time for such irritation, and focused tighter on his work. So tight he almost missed her final words.

"Four zuglodons on attack vector. The captain says that if you have any tricks up your sleeve, this is the time. Bridge out."

Any tricks up my sleeve? What does he think I'm doing down here? Now I've got to maintain the wards to keep those ships off our backs and *fight off the ... zuglodons...*

"Master," said *Saravá*, "I have a detailed message from Donal Cuthbert."

"Hold it 'til we're done." Machado grinned. "I'm going to need you for this next part."

Machado swept his arms wide and blew out a breath so great no onlooker would have believed that even Machado's impressive frame could have contained it.

As he did, he dropped those military grade wards.

"Captain, our wards just dropped back to normal strength."

"Say again, Damage Control?" Jacobs kept his voice steady for the sake of his crew, but it was a near thing because he wanted those words to rage out in disbelief. Those military grade wards were all that kept their pursuers from destroying the *Horizon Cusp* outright. Not to mention the zuglodons, which were so close Jacobs could see their sparking tentacles when he looked up through the transparent bulkhead of the bridge.

"All enhancements have dropped from the wards. They still hold steady at main strength for now, but I can't guarantee how long they'll last if those ships start shooting again, or the zuglodons reach us."

Jacobs covered his eyes. He should never have brought the ship into the hunting ground. Machado had warned that even he could not maintain those enhanced wards for long. But Machado had seemed so able to handle anything Jacobs required of him.

Magic. This was all the fault of magic.

In the old days of technology, if one man went down another could pick up the slack. Ships were kept afloat by teamwork, not single specialists.

Now Jacobs had pushed his mage too far. Machado had finally collapsed, leaving the *Horizon Cusp* defenseless when Jacobs needed him the most.

"All right," said Jacobs. "Speed is now our only defense. Mr. Burke—"

"I beg your pardon, Captain John Jacobs," said an ethereal voice over Jacobs shoulder. He turned to see Machado's spirit panther familiar. It said, "Ronaldo Machado requests that you bring the *Horizon Cusp* to a halt and maintain that position until I signal you, at which time he requests that you proceed on your course at top speed."

Jacobs' relief at the realization that his ship's mage was still in the fight gave way to the insanity of that request.

"He expects me to make my ship an easy target?"

"My master anticipated that question and has instructed me to tell you that he has had to reach far up his sleeve to find this trick."

Jacobs stared at the panther, considered saying something else, but the familiar vanished in a swirl of smoke. One magician against a host of enemies. Nothing for the captain to do, no way that Jacobs could affect the outcome.

The frustration of it ground his teeth. Ripped tension from his neck down his spine. Clenched his fists tight enough that his nails would have drawn blood had Jacobs not kept them as short as his hair.

But then he remembered that in the days of steel ships, every once in a while, needs of the whole ship would rest on the actions of one crewman, braving a storm to weld a key join or risking drowning to get a turbine turning again while others bailed madly.

Perhaps this was no different.

"All engines halt, Mr. Burke." Jacobs forced out the breath he had been holding. Sucked in another and said, "But be ready to slam us to full speed on my mark."

"Captain," said Jefferson, "Mr. Mancuso is requesting your presence, along with Chief Goldberg and as many members of the ship's watch as he can bring."

"Tell him I'll take care of it as soon as I can. Then wake Tunold and tell him what you just told me. But first warn Chief Jang that I'm going to want all the speed she can give me, as much as that Deception Drive can muster.

"As soon as Mash gives us the word, I want us out of here like we're fleeing Hell one step ahead of the devil."

Which, as far as Jacobs was concerned, was not far off from the truth.

Tunold snapped awake the moment his comm pad buzzed. He sat bolt upright, the sheets of his long twin mattress falling around him, one hand slapping the comm pad just hard enough to activate it.

Another man might have felt self-conscious that he was naked to the waist, but Tunold would not have given it a thought even before he began the regimen of daily running and light lifting that had given him his toned, trim physique.

He took the message from Jefferson without wasting words on questions. Goldberg might know something by the time Tunold reached him. If not, Tunold had no doubt he would hear more from Mancuso than he could possibly want to know.

Kristoff Tunold's quarters had once seemed downright luxurious compared to the accommodations he had dealt with in the military. But after only two days in the actual captain's cabin, they felt small. The bedroom measured four meters on a side, and the sitting room three meters. Total size probably two-thirds of the space the ship's captain enjoyed.

And Tunold had never really moved back into the executive officer's cabin after Jacobs took over the ship once more. All his personal possessions remained packed in his crates and footlockers, making the "social" part of his cabin seem more like a warehouse than a place to entertain guests.

Even the walls remained denuded of the black-and-white landscapes Tunold favored. Only his clothes had found their way back into the places they had occupied for most of Tunold's time on the *Horizon Cusp*.

But Tunold wasted no thoughts on reflection or comfort that morning. He showered with his habitual speed, using the dampen-soap-rinse style he had learned in the Navy to conserve water, then threw on and organized his uniform to inspection perfection.

Then and only then did he jog out the door and trot at long-distance speed for the Security Deck and Goldberg's office.

At least the Old Man didn't demand to deal with this himself.

JACOBS DUG THROUGH HIS THREE-DIMENSIONAL CHARTS, ZOOMING AND twisting the depictions of space at high speed. He dragged a miniature image of his ship along prospective routes, canceling and re-routing as he scrutinized the final two decans of space between the *Horizon Cusp's* current position and Venus. Any moment now Machado would send up the flag and Jacobs needed the course ready and perfect.

He needed to get his ship away from the zuglodons without dragging it back into the no-fly zone. He wished he knew what Machado had in mind. He wished he knew the position of every zuglodon between where he was and where he needed to be. He wished he knew if those Navy boys had called for reinforcements.

There!

Jacobs found what he needed. If the *Horizon Cusp* dove thirty degrees as it gained speed, then leveled off seventeen and banked soft to port for thirty seconds, hard to starboard for ten, then came up three degrees and straightened course for Venus, they should be safe.

Assuming nothing went wrong.

Jacobs dragged the tiny map image of the gryphon-shaped ship one more time through his intended course, a scarlet planning trail following it as he did. He then set his palm on the updates pad.

"This is Captain John Jacobs," he said. "Update course."

The rubbery pad sounded a low gong that would also notify the helm and ex oh's stations. The scarlet trail turned bright blue, then faded and the tiny *Horizon Cusp* returned to its current position.

Jacobs had done everything he could.

The rest was up to Machado.

Seconds passed at the breakneck speed of ice ages. Jacobs tried not to drum his fingers, tried not to let any of his nervousness leak through to the crew. They were nervous enough. Jacobs could see the sweat on their brows and shirts, the strain in their faces and hands. He looked up through the dome at the slowly approaching zuglodons.

That they still moved slowly was a good sign, he knew. They moved fast when attacking. Jacobs remembered that all too well.

Then the zuglodons began to spin their snake bodies, flaring their tentacles out wide.

"Captain, we're being hailed," said Jefferson.

"Captain, the zuglodons are moving off," said Grabowski with almost a cheer. "They're spiraling on an attack vector at something that isn't showing up on my scans."

That's it, Mash. You can do it.

"Hold position, Helm," barked Jacobs. "Communications, do not respond."

"It's the destroyer, Sir. The *Morganstern*. They're begging us to get to the lifeboats and swearing they'll save as many as they can as soon as they—"

"Sir! The destroyer has opened fire on the zuglodons!"

Now Jacobs wanted to cheer, but held his tongue. Particularly because any misses might endanger his ship.

Machado's familiar swirled into shape in front of Jacobs. "Now," it said and shifted back into smoke.

"Helm! Punch it!"

"Now the cruiser has opened fire. And the zuglodons are moving to engage!"

"Calm down, Scanners. Helm, report."

"Five klicks from battle now, Sir, steady on the new course... ten."

"Scanners, report. And I don't mean that battle."

"The battle is all I have to report, Sir. The zugldons appear to have called for reinforcements. A half-dozen more are moving to join. But they're all ignoring us. And the cruiser and destroyer are too busy to pursue."

Steady, Old Man. Save your people.

"We're not in the clear yet. Hold that speed, Mr. Burke."

They have weapons. You have a magician on the brink of collapse.

Jacobs yanked off his captain's hat, but resisted the urge to slam it down on his console. Still, his fist clenched with the urge to swing it or throw it. Something. Anything. Anything to distract Jacobs from what he had just done: left good men to fight overwhelming odds for nothing more than doing their duty.

Certainly Liatos could have given them a pass, could have even escorted the *Horizon Cusp* safely most of the way to Venus, all while safeguarding Earth's precious restricted zone.

But damn it, the man had done his duty. And Jacobs understood duty all too well. Which was all that kept Jacobs from turning his ship around, flying his crew back on a suicide mission to save better armed and armored ships from possible destruction under the tentacles of those great space monsters.

Jacobs' Navy days were long behind him. His duty was to his ship and his own mission now.

But leaving men to die cut him to the core. And now he was doing it for the second time on this thrice-damned flight.

The Naval ships might yet outfly those great beasts. They might even have defenses specific to fighting zuglodons. That was a possibility. It would explain why they were willing to fly so near the hunting ground, even understate it on the charts.

Jacobs told himself that he believed that as he forced one more deep breath down his gut. Then he put his hat on and got back down to business.

<hr>

With a soft metallic click, Machado closed the lid on his censer and cut off the flow of incense. He forced his tired legs to carry him toward his workbench. The spells were cast. Piggybacking on what Cromartie had set up for him, Machado had drawn the zuglodons to attack where they believed the *Horizon Cusp* to be. As they moved in, he had deceived the scanners on the Navy ships to see the *Horizon Cusp* getting torn apart.

Both illusions took tremendous effort to pull off. Neither would last longer than perhaps a minute. But they also helped hide the smaller deception that made the *Horizon Cusp* look like another zuglodon.

The illusions also lasted long enough for the ships to open fire on the zuglodons, trying to save the civilians. The zuglodons would take care of the rest.

Their own fault for opening fire on a civilian vessel.

Machado stretched his arms, then grabbed a towel from his bench to mop away the sweat from his face and neck. He would need a shower before his hair could be saved.

"Master," said *Saravá*, "there is still the matter of the message from Donal Cuthbert."

"In a minute." Machado pulled a second towel out of the workbench, and a small throw pillow. These he took over to Cromartie, who lay passed out in the middle of his circle. Machado slipped the pillow under the Initiate's head and set the towel by his hand.

"Now, what does Cuthbert want badly enough to..."

Machado remembered the alarm that had triggered as he was busy defending the ship.

"*Saravá, conta.*"

His familiar knew what he wanted to hear. In Cuthbert's voice, the panther began to speak.

"Magister, if you receive this message that means that Tai Shi Li Hua has challenged me to the *Comórtas Draíocht* and defeated me. She wants to prevent me from telling anyone that she has been building long term mental controls into Mr. Mancuso. She worked slow and deep, so they'll be difficult to notice, and she's using deception magic to further conceal them. She's done this as part of a plot to make magicians into a ruling class.

"Because she has beaten me, I can no longer confirm or deny this. And I know that sending you this message violates your direct order not to tell anyone about the matter was between us. For that I offer a formal apology. I have further violated your order by sending this message to Mr. Mancuso himself, though I doubt her mental control will allow him to believe it."

"That is the end of the message," said the ghostly *onça*.

"He must have bound the spell into his familiar last night. Keyed it to release if he lost a duel, used some of the dissipating power to deliver it." Machado shook his head. "Kid's a genius. An absolute idiot in how he does things, but in thaumaturgy terms, a genius. If he's still alive."

Exhausted as he felt, Machado wanted to hunt down Tai Shi and deal with her himself. But that would have been something Cuthbert would have done.

No. Machado knew what he needed to do.

Tunold leaned on Chief Goldberg's desk, trying to keep sympathy in his voice. Of course, he knew full well that the effort accomplished nothing more than modulating his growl into a quieter growl that sometimes came out menacing. But the chief looked more exhausted than Tunold felt.

Well, more exhausted than Tunold had felt before fury took over at finding out he had been allowed to sleep through an attack on the ship. He would have choice words for the captain when he next saw him.

But for now, he needed the chief.

"I know you've had a short night and a rough morning. Mine's not a lot of fun either. But our A Number One pain in the ass passenger — and new part owner so quite possibly our boss — wants you along with me when I go see him. And you know that the captain says about keeping customers happy."

"I know that I don't want to drag my ass along on a royal visit just to find out someone stole his cufflink. Let me send a lieutenant."

"Enough!" Tunold stood straight and put his fists on his hips. "Are you coming? Or do I have to make it a direct order?"

"You wouldn't." Goldberg said the words, but the narrowing of his eyes told Tunold he wasn't sure he believed it.

"The captain himself said you're going. Now on your feet or I get the pleasure of assigning you a punishment for insubordination."

Goldberg cracked his neck, then, grumbling words he wisely kept too quiet for his executive officer to hear, grabbed the arms of his chair and hauled himself to his feet.

"Sir. Yes. Sir. Chief Security Officer Saul Goldberg reporting for duty. As ordered. Sir."

"Wiseass. Come on."

The two men proceeded to the door when Tunold was surprised to see the doorway fill with the heavy frame of the ship's mage. Mash looked so spent and sweaty Tunold wondered if he had run all the way here from his workshop.

"Christ, Mash," said Goldberg. "You look like you've been pulling double shifts on the Flying Dutchman."

"I feel like I have. Mancuso's in trouble."

"That's where we're going," said Tunold. "Come on."

"There's more. You need to have men find Cuthbert and take him into protective custody."

"Protective custody?" said Goldberg, suppressing a laugh.

"Now. The anti-caster cell. Have men wake Cromartie and key the cell for Tai Shi's signature. He'll know how to do it. You'll find him on the floor of my workshop."

"You're serious," said Tunold.

"Bring people with us," said Machado who looked as though he were lecturing about magical safety. "As many as you can spare. This may get bad."

"Chief," said Tunold.

"On it."

"Mash, you better catch me up."

22

MACHADO APPROACHED MR. MANCUSO'S SUITE ALONGSIDE TUNOLD. Goldberg and a dozen men and women of the ship's watch followed in formation.

"May I take lead?" said Machado. "This is a matter of thaumaturgy."

"Mancuso called us. Let me take lead. That'll give you room to make any discrete checks you want."

Machado almost stopped walking. He would never have expected that level of subtlety from Tunold. But they reached the door, and Tunold knocked while Goldberg organized his people. Machado twiddled his thumbs and waited, only half his mind on what they were doing. The other half waited for the report he knew was coming and what he hoped it would say.

The door opened. A blonde woman. Stevens, as Machado recalled. Business assistant.

"Come in, gentlemen. I believe you know Mr. Davis."

Davis, the other blonde in a suit. This one a man. Social assistant, if Machado remembered correctly. Past Stevens and Davis the suite looked in good shape, from the clean furniture in the main room to the assortment of hors d'oeuvres on the coffee table and array of alcohols on the table between the recliners under the porthole.

Machado had to ignore a rumble in his empty stomach at the savory smell of the meats and cheeses on that table.

The door to the bedroom was closed. Mancuso had to be in there. No sign of Tai Shi, which was a help.

Stevens invited them in, and as they passed her, she said, "We were expecting the captain."

"The captain is unavoidably detained on ship matters," said Tunold.

"It has been a busy morning," said Davis.

Goldberg brought half of his team into the suite, with the other half taking up positions in the hall.

"Where is Tai Shi?" asked Tunold.

"We haven't seen her this morning, but after Cuthbert's disturbing message..."

Stevens continued talking, but Machado's attention shifted entirely to his familiar, who had phased into the suite through the bulkhead.

Mind-to-mind, *Saravá* said, "Donal Cuthbert is unconscious but alive, and under a *geas*. He now rests in the anti-caster cell, which Aaron Cromartie has tuned according to your orders. Aaron Cromartie has now gone to rest. He apologizes and says he can do nothing more for now."

"I wasn't sure he could handle that much," said Machado, in the same mental fashion. "Has the doctor been called?"

"Yes, and a dozen members of the ship's watch stand guard."

Machado thanked and dismissed his familiar to go about tracking down Tai Shi. By the time he tuned back into the conversation, Tunold was saying. "...understand."

"Mr. Mancuso," said Stevens, "refused to believe that he could be acting under anyone else's control. Fortunately, a contingency in some of our business deals includes a stipulation that any credible accusation of magical influence immediately halts all business, and requires that the alleged influenced person be isolated until the truth can be determined."

"What determines a threat's credibility?" asked Goldberg.

"Well, the formal definitions go on for three pages, but when a man who saved Mr. Mancuso's life on multiple occasions alleged that his girlfriend has been mind-controlling Mr. Mancuso, I immediately declared it credible according to a codicil of emergency provisions."

"I seconded," said Davis. "That meant we needed a respected third party. Though we do have many options on the ship right now, Stevens and I both agreed that the captain was the best choice."

"But you say he is unavailable," said Stevens. "I guess we can slide you in under the 'designated party' clause, if you can verify that you are empowered to speak on his behalf."

"I can and I do," said Tunold, and unless Machado was mistaken, he heard more than a little pleasure in that gruff voice. "My ship's mage here received a similar message about Mr. Mancuso and agrees that the threat is credible."

Both the suits turned to Machado, so he nodded gravely. If all business decisions took so long it was a wonder that corporations ever accomplished anything at all.

"All right," said Stevens. "So we all agree. Now what?"

"Now," said Machado, "I go into his head and find out what's going on."

JACOBS SLUMPED BACK INTO HIS CAPTAIN'S SEAT. THE SHIP WAS SAFE. The zuglodon hunting ground was behind them. No signs of pursuit. Clear space between Jacobs and Venus.

"Take us down to cruising speed, Mr. Burke. No sense in terrifying the locals."

And given the proximity of a large collection of some of the greatest space hazards Jacobs knew of, he had no doubt how the locals would interpret a civilian ship coming in at high speed. Even though Venus had negligible laws and landing conditions that sounded downright primitive, such an unconventional arrival would likely result in a poor reception.

Of course, if either of those military ships had linked ahead, Jacobs might be in for an unpleasant reception anyway.

If it survived, the *Morgenstern* would let them go. Jacobs didn't doubt that. But the *Orpheus*, well, Jacobs half-expected to see that cruiser appear on the scanners any minute, half-dead and on fire but riding them down like death late for an appointment.

And even if the *Orpheus* failed to arrive in person, Jacobs had no doubt that if it survived that battle, it would link ahead to have them arrested on Venus. Captain Liatos struck Jacobs as the sort to push this conflict as far as his rank could take it.

But there was another factor involved. Jacobs' reception on Venus would depend not only on whether those ships survived that last battle but also on whether they realized that the *Horizon Cusp* had escaped them. Given the *Morgenstern's* last link, they might think that the *Horizon Cusp* had fallen to the zuglodons.

That had to have been Machado's work, the reason he needed Jacobs to bring the ship to a dead halt amid a sea of threats. He must have tricked their scanners into seeing the *Horizon Cusp* destroyed by the great beasts.

Tricky work, but a good call if he pulled it off. Surely not even Liatos would call ahead to interdict a sunken ship.

Another sign that it was time for Jacobs to retire. He had tried to deal with space as he thought it should be handled rather than how it would be handled. Jacobs had known well what a no-fly zone meant, that any ship meeting them inside it would be as likely to shoot them down as talk to them.

But no, Jacobs had persuaded himself that humanitarian aid would rank higher than planetary secrets. He had risked his ship, his crew and his passengers on that little bit of persuasion, rather than taking a safer, longer route.

Perhaps he should let Tunold take the conn for the flight back to Earth…

Jacobs shook his head. The time for self-critique would come later. Right now, he had a mission to finish.

"YOU ARE WORRIED ABOUT SOMETHING THAT ISN'T REAL!" MACHADO threw up his hands with an exasperated sound, but Stevens looked unmoved. So certain in her perfect suit and luxury suite, backed by her male twin Davis. Machado needed to make them understand. And Goldberg and Tunold while he was at it, or their reports would miss the whole point.

Machado bought a moment by placating his rumbling stomach with a slice of Jarlsberg cheese from the hors d'oeuvres tray, then tried again.

"No viable methods for probing through the thoughts of another sentient being have ever been proven! Sure, some claim that powerful air elementals can be used this way, but I've never seen it done. The closest anyone has come involves summoning very dangerous spirits from certain old grimoires—"

"I don't mean to accuse you of anything. But we do not know what your investigation will turn up. If Mr. Mancuso's mind has been opened to manipulation—"

"I will not be 'manipulating.' I will be looking for evidence of certain types of thaumaturgic structures—"

"Structures you will have to test, which may lead to his revealing trade secrets—"

"I don't give a damn about your trade secrets!"

"Machado," said Tunold, his tone just under a roar. Though, to his credit, the ex oh looked ready to throw Stevens through a bulkhead so Machado could do his job. But when Tunold turned to Stevens, his tone came out even.

"I understand your concerns, and agree that you have every right to be there." He turned back to Machado. "Is there any risk that he could become violent if you try to undo any blocks?"

Machado grimaced, but refused to lie.

"Some. But under the circumstances I consider the risk minimal compared to the potential invasion of his privacy."

"Understood." Tunold turned back to Stevens. "You and Mr. Davis may be in the room to protect any secrets Mr. Mancuso might reveal." He waited until Stevens nodded before continuing, "And Goldberg and I will be in the room to defend Machado physically, in case Mr. Mancuso becomes violent."

Stevens shook her head and started to say something, but Tunold cracked his voice like a whip. "Either we protect ourselves against all potential risks, or we ignore all potential risks and Machado goes in alone. That is my decision as executive officer of the *Horizon Cusp*."

Stevens and Davis looked at each other as though they shared some unspoken communication that even Machado could not sense.

"Very well, Mr. Tunold," said Stevens. "I acknowledge that you have the right to make that decision and will abide by it. All of us then."

Machado stood back from the door to the bedroom and Stevens opened it. She started to enter, but Machado put a hand on her shoulder.

"Normally I believe in ladies first, but under the circumstances it would be safest if I lead."

"You make it sound as if I'm a serial killer," said the bored voice of Mr. Mancuso.

Machado entered the obscenely large and opulent bedroom — at least obscenely large and opulent compared to most of the *Horizon Cusp's* accommodations — where he saw Mancuso stretched out on top of the covers on his more-than-king-size bed, ankles crossed and a refillable novel in his hands.

Every stick of furniture in the room looked to have been hand-crafted from rich hardwoods and trimmed with silver and gold, from the frame of the sleigh bed to the armoire and chest of drawers, to the twin nightstands and even the doors to the walk-in closet and bathroom.

Mancuso himself wore his impeccable suit down to his fine shoes, with the only exception being his jacket, which lay draped across the mattress beside him.

Still not looking up from his novel, Mancuso continued, "I still say this is ludicrous. Tai Shi would never pull a stunt like this. Too much risk for too little reward. What has it gotten her apart from what she would have had anyway? The promotion?" Mancuso scoffed. "I'd first imagined a role like that in business school."

"If she did it at all," said Machado, "and I am not saying she did, she may not have had a plan in mind, but a contingency. Protecting herself against a future possibility rather than seeking immediate benefit."

Machado didn't believe any of that. Not for a moment. He thought Li Hua seemed arrogant enough that, if she had done it, she probably intended something like the sort of ruling class Cuthbert mentioned. But he knew the contingency idea might strike the right chord with a man like Mancuso.

Mancuso made a humming sound that Machado interpreted as polite disinterest.

"Not likely," the business magnate said. "But I'll grant that Cuthbert has my best interests in mind, so if he believes it, I'm willing to let you check it out. And at least this whole debacle proves that my executive business assistant is reading all the contracts the way she's supposed to. Good work there, Stevens."

"Then you don't mind if I get started?" said Machado.

"Do I have to stop reading? I'm almost done with this chapter."

"By all means, keep reading," said Machado with a placating wave of his hand. "It's good for your mind to be busy while I work."

Machado pointed at the door. Goldberg closed it. Tunold took up a position on the other side of the bed. Stevens and Davis stood on the near side, uncertain what they needed to do. Machado almost wished he could watch their faces while he worked, but that, alas, was not an option.

Machado stepped close to the bed until his knees touched the soft down mattress. He whirled his finger in a circle and enclosed the bed and himself in a magic circle. Mancuso shifted his shoulders, and

Machado raised an eyebrow. That might have indicated discomfort at being cut off from Tai Shi. Mancuso had no thaumaturgic training, nor any particular talent. With his focus on his novel, he likely did not even notice Machado's whirling finger.

But part of Mancuso responded to being enclosed within a magic circle. Interesting.

With that, Machado began.

Machado shifted consciousness into deep contemplation while calling his familiar back to him. The ghostly panther arrived and said to its master's mind, "Tai Shi Li Hua rests in her suite. A half-dozen members of the watch stand outside her door awaiting orders."

Machado said nothing. He pointed at Mancuso. *Saravá* moved into Mancuso's body and began looking from the inside for what Machado would seek from the outside.

As his familiar worked, Machado whistled a low tone, long and simple. He let the sound stretch until it filled his body. Then he let the tone vibrate, seeming to shake the world within his circle until it began to elicit echoes.

Outside the circle, Machado knew that the onlookers might hear his whistle, but they would not hear the responses, because they echoed not in sound but in magic.

First, Machado heard the answering call of his circle, his own magic harmonizing with his personal root note. The response came back pure and clear, shivering pleasure down Machado's face and arms. Little more than calibration, really, because Machado had only just cast that circle. The chances that someone could have already tampered with it lay somewhere between slim and none.

But they provided a secondary benefit: resonance. The circle amplified the root tone as it spread through the bed, where it came back muddled by the magical signatures of the magicians who had enchanted the bed for deeper comfort and relaxation.

Those signatures clashed against the pure, clear tones Machado produced, but he knew he heard them that way because their tones were not his own. Every magician's signature sounds clear and pure to that magician by its very nature.

But Machado did not dwell on his own signature. Instead he dwelled on the clashing sounds of the signatures he sensed from the bed, disconnecting and isolating each signature, each magical thumbprint, until he understood it. Then he ignored that signature and moved on, his senses now dismissing that signature's ability to interfere.

He found four signatures in the spells on that bed, none he knew personally. No doubt part of the original manufacture. That fit with the power levels he picked up from those signatures: all Initiates.

But they no longer mattered. Machado moved past them.

Mancuso's clothes showed no sign of enchantment. Machado double-checked that, surprised, but then when his second sweep came up clear decided that it was a status choice. Fine, expensive clothes made without the aid of thaumaturgy would no doubt cost even more. Or perhaps they were a trend, or exhibited a certain sense of taste.

The details did not matter, under the circumstances. The clothes were clean.

At least, *these* clothes were clean. Machado would have Cromartie sweep the rest of the man's possessions before Mancuso left the ship, to ensure that no contingencies had been established.

Check that.

Cromartie could handle the sweep if *Mancuso* came up clean. If Machado found that the man had been ensorcelled, he would have to check every possession himself, just to make certain.

But for now, Machado turned his attention to the man himself, Mr. Donatello Michelangelo Mancuso.

MACHADO CLOSED HIS EYES AND PAUSED FOR THREE BREATHS, DOUBLE-checking the signatures he had calibrated himself to ignore, then cleansing and purifying his own thoughts once more.

He wanted his mind as clear as possible for this last stage. No judgments. No preconceptions. No short cuts. By now *Saravá* would have prepared the way. Machado had completed the preliminaries. The time had come for the real work.

Machado opened his eyes.

He moved to stand by Mancuso's feet and began once more to whistle the low, root tone of his personal magical signature. Finding no echo, Machado slowly turned his head, forcing the tone to continue up Mancuso's calves and across his knees, then slowly past his hips, and up his torso and arms.

Nothing. Further then.

Still on that single breath, Machado sent his root tone the rest of the way up Mancuso's torso, then his neck, then up through his skull.

Nothing. That was to be expected, but not assumed. If any signs could have been discerned at that level, someone would have discovered any tampering before now. But the obvious possibilities had to be excluded before the subtle methods were checked.

With that in mind, Machado began again at the feet, but this time sweeping across Mancuso's aura, that region of self that extended beyond the body. Which was the only description of the aura that all magicians could agree on.

Many systems of thaumaturgy defined or interpreted the aura within their own context. Some used terms like "chakra" or "meridian" while others talked about the "spirit" or some form of "higher self." The trade magazines had some new theory or other every month, as yet more magicians tried to make their personal ideas apply to everyone.

Machado didn't care what any of them said. He had been raised with Catholicism and *Candomblé*, and he considered the presence of the aura proof of the soul. That the self extended beyond the confines of the body indicated to him that the self could well survive death and, *Oxalá* willing, find someplace better to spend eternity.

But Mancuso's aura showed no signs of tampering.

Again, not a surprise to Machado, but a possibility that had to be eliminated before he could move into the subtlest territory of all: the mind itself.

Auditory checks would not suffice for this. He would have to go deeper.

Machado spread his arms and gathered himself within the territory described by his hands. He turned so that Mancuso's head lay between those outstretched hands, if still a half-meter below where his hands would meet if Machado clapped.

But Machado did not clap. He closed his eyes and drew his hands together slowly, centimeter by centimeter, and as he did his attention moved down his arms at the same rate. His hands continued to ease toward each other as his thoughts flowed down over skin, muscle and bone. Machado's awareness left behind his own mind and body as it made its way down those arms, feeling where the air touched skin, where the shirt rubbed and where it hung.

Though Machado could not see Mancuso, he could feel him. The proximity of their auras tingled in the background of Machado's awareness as it slid past his wrists to his fingertips. When the hands stopped moving, if Machado had opened his eyes he would have seen Mancuso's face as though between his two hands.

But he did not open his eyes. He had no need to. By that point, Machado's awareness alighted the tips of his fingers and slipped across the tiny gap between the two men's auras and into the mind of Donatello Michelangelo Mancuso.

Machado had not lied when he said he would not be able to read Mancuso's thoughts. But he had not told the entire truth either. He had told as much as a layman could be expected to understand without panicking.

Because what Machado found in Mancuso's mind was close to his essential self, abstracted.

Another might have seen a spider web of goals and desires, fear and nightmares, or perhaps those same ideas played out in sculpture or landscape paintings. But for Machado, the mind appeared as a tapestry.

The general shape and form of Mancuso's tapestry depicted the man triumphant in the classical Italian renaissance style. He stood clad in bright plate armor atop a hill overlooking a harbor full of ships. One boot rested on the grass of the hill. The other was raised, and rested on a solid rock of granite. Each ship in the harbor had the name of some company or industry. In the distance were more lands and seas and sky, and the implication Machado picked up on was that Mancuso had conquered all of this territory. The coat of arms on his breastplate was a stack of gold coins against the background of a contract under crossed pens. He held a helmet under one arm, with a plume of solid gold. At his feet was an admiring hound that carried the sense that it represented politicians.

Machado could have sent his thoughts along through the image of that hound and learned of Mancuso's accomplishments and plans involving politicians. Not concrete details, but overviews, fragments of inspiration and dream. This is what Stevens, what any layman, could not comprehend. If Machado chose to, he could learn much that was hidden about Mancuso, but he would never come close to anything they would regard as business secrets.

But frankly, Machado had no wish to learn that much about this man.

The voice of *Saravá* came to Machado. "I have worked from the border in, covering much of the background, but found no sign of undue influence within the skies, the seas, the distant lands, nor in the harbor with its ships."

"Excellent. I have found no exterior signs. Continue as you have and I will begin now from the center and work outwards to meet you."

Machado considered whether the head or the heart constituted the true center of Mancuso, but decided that his head must rule. Machado was no businessman himself, but from what he knew of the type he believed they relied on numbers and logic over instinct and feeling.

He was wrong, as it turned out.

The moment he touched Mancuso's fashion sense — the part of his mind about the left ear where Machado began — he sensed the swirling connections of the threads emanating from Mancuso's solar plexus. It seemed this man trusted his instincts before his intellect after all.

The core of Mancuso's instincts swirled in silver and chrome, polished and refined...

But there was more.

Machado almost missed it. If he had started from the solar plexus he might have missed it, but having to move there from the mind had sparked Machado's curiosity. Instead of simply noting the structure, Machado had begun to wonder about the source.

The first thing Machado touched on was a teenager's love of gambling and the ability to pick up on nonverbal cues that indicated the motivations behind the plays of other players, beyond what any logic might have explained. It was that core of perception that taught Mancuso to rely on perceptions he could not readily explain.

But another thread led from this point to the armor, and that did not make sense. Machado could clearly pick up that the armor represented history and family, though more about the legacy he would leave behind than about what he could look back on. That was part of the reason the tapestry depicted him looking out over what he had conquered, not back on where he had come from.

And yet, that thread indicated protection, which did not fit with the rest. Machado dove into that thread, expecting to find an event in Mancuso's personal history that would explain the tie, explain how it all worked together.

Instead, he found a bit of satin amid the silk. A thread that someone else had woven in. Tiny. Artful. Easily missed even by a Magister.

But this Magister had found it. And he could read the signature of the weaver quite clearly: Tai Shi Li Hua.

DONAL AWOKE STIFF AND SORE. HIS HEAD POUNDED AS THOUGH HE HAD rented his skull out for an anvil. His ribs burned as though the blacksmith had stuck a dozen pokers in there to cool. His hands came to his temples, desperate to rub them. But when he craned to let his head meet his hands, his neck seized.

Too much pain. Too much frustration. Donal tried to scream.

The sound came out closer to a whimper.

Donal settled for shallow breaths until he could control himself enough to shift a bit of consciousness and distract his awareness from the pain.

Then and only then did Donal open his eyes.

"A cell?" His voice croaked. Donal hadn't actually intended to say the words aloud, but the shock of realization had done it. Instead of on his own bed, or even on the floor of his suite, Donal lay on a rough blanket, on a stiff bed attached to the wall. No doubt so it could fold against that wall easily.

A cage of bars surrounded Donal on three sides, with the dull gray walls, ceiling and floor making up the rest.

Reflexively Donal reached for a thread of power and found one. Not cut off from his magic then. So either he was being held during an investigation or...

Donal could not think of anything good to follow that "or" so he let it dangle.

He lay back, uncomfortable, and tried to work his fingers into the knots in his shoulders and neck. If he lay in a cell, then his gamble had failed. Not only had Li Hua beaten him in the duel, it appeared she had beaten him completely.

And now Donal lay in a cell. Whatever charge had been filed, he would be found guilty. Li Hua would see to that. Donal felt sure of it. So close to grad school. So close to his doctorate. Only to have it snatched away.

What would his parents think? What would Bran think?

Lying on his bunk in what he feared was his new home, Donal Cuthbert began to cry.

Donal's tears lasted only a moment before the need to act overcame him.

So Li Hua had beaten him in the *Comórtas Draíocht*, letting her put him under a *geas* against disclosing to anyone her plans and her control over Mr. Mancuso. So she had gotten him arrested on some kind of trumped up charges. So she had somehow defeated his twin spells to warn the Magister and Mr. Mancuso himself. And Donal's current residence implied to him that she had defeated those twin spells and sold the ship's watch on a story that made Donal look like the guilty party.

But who knew what she was doing didn't matter.

Even Donal going to prison didn't matter.

This woman wanted to establish magicians as a ruling class with herself in charge. She had to be stopped. And if Donal was the only one who knew, then he was the only one who could stop her.

Donal shifted more of his consciousness to allow him to ignore the pain in his head, neck and ribs. He would pay that when he finished his spell, but he would have plenty of time to convalesce later. He sat up and called Fionn forth from the silver faun pendant around his neck, not wasting time to wonder why the guards had been sloppy enough to leave it with him.

"The spells enacted as desired, Master," said Fionn. "Ronaldo Machado and Donatello Michelangelo Mancuso received their messages."

Donal puzzled over that while the *cú sidhe* tilted its head and it regarded Donal.

"You look dreadful. You need rest, food, and a massage, in that order."

"I'm in a cell, Fionn. So the messages might have been delivered, but Li Hua has to have undercut them. I don't know how, but she beat me there too." Donal shook his head and stood up. "As to your recommendations, I can get the first two later, but the third is probably out of the question."

The fae deerhound scrutinized the cell. "But this cell—"

"We'll worry about the cell later. Right now we have to stop Li

Hua."

"She defeated you once already. You must recuperate before attempting to face her again."

"I'm not going to challenge her. I'm going to beat her at her own game."

"You have no reagents. No incense, oils…"

"I know. But I've got you." Donal slipped his favorite tool from his shirt sleeve. "And I have my tuning fork. Come on."

Donal strode forward and began to cast a circle.

"Let's make Li Hua turn herself in."

The *cú sidhe* looked for a moment as though it wished to say something, then flicked its ears in a sort of canine shrug and took up the proper position to aid its master.

MACHADO THOUGHT THAT TYING THE INFLUENCE INTO MANCUSO'S instincts had been a clever touch. The man trusted his instincts, so he would trust what they told them. But that tiny thread of influence in the armor served as a mere tendril. Machado had yet to find the core of the control itself.

He called *Saravá* to him and together they began to trace the thread.

Saravá saw where the thread connected higher into the armor where it would extend through the breastplate and perhaps up into the image of the head, which would strengthen the sympathetic impact of any established control.

Machado continued the other direction, down the breastplate and into the greaves, and finally into the sabatons. It was there that he found the tiniest trickle fading from the silver of the armor to the grayish white of the rock under Mancuso's foot.

But it lead Machado into the rock, and it was there he found the core of the spell. It hid as a duplication of the original rock in the tapestry's design, but added a touch more gray to indicate that the rock came from deeper in the earth and represented more strength.

That was key to the spell. The control spells woven in established that this rock supported Mancuso, formed the core of his certainty and confidence, his ability to reliably make the best decisions. That rock formed the foundation of all he had ever accomplished and all he ever would accomplish.

And that rock's name was Tai Shi Li Hua.

Machado paused for a moment to admire the subtlety of the work, the skill and patience necessary to establish that degree and depth of control. Mancuso would weigh her advice above all others. If her familiar carried ideas into the core of the rock, Mancuso would treat them as his own. They might even manifest through dreams. The poor man would never have had any way to notice that what she implanted came from outside himself.

But Machado had found the core of the spell, and anything a Journeyman could assemble, Machado could disperse. He would need to take care, though, and work slowly to ensure that he returned everything to its original state. Fine, precise work, of the sort that specialists in magic of the mind excelled at.

Would that Machado had such a specialist here now. But he could not risk the time to get Mancuso to one. Tai Shi might have woven contingency commands into the spell to protect herself. It needed unweaving as soon as was practical, which meant—

Just then Pinyin Lung entered the tapestry. Machado turned, tried to raise a defense of the poor man under his care, but whatever the Tai Shi's spirit dragon familiar had come to do, it abandoned the plan as soon as it detected Machado's presence.

The dragon turned tail and fled.

Machado took advantage of his position deep in Mancuso's mind to command him to sleep, then withdrew to his own body as fast as possible.

The moment Machado shook his head, Tunold said, "What's the verdict?"

"He's under Tai Shi's control. I've made him sleep to protect him for now." Machado stood up. "And she just found out we know."

"Let's go," said Tunold.

23

Donal began with a basic circle, dividing all that existed into two categories: that which was within and that which was without.

Within knelt Donal and his magic.

Without lay the rest of the universe.

Such a circle would sever any basic spells on him, cut them off from their caster and their source of power. But it would not free Donal from his *geas*. The nature of a *geas* made the magic part of Donal. It would persist until either he died, Li Hua released him, or something greater broke it.

But Donal did not need to free himself from the *geas*. He just needed to stop Li Hua.

That thought sounded fatal in its finality as it flitted through Donal's head, but he had no intention of killing her. What he needed to stop was her plan, not her breathing. And stopping her plan required two steps.

The most important step would be the most difficult deception Donal had ever attempted, and he would need to thrust it deep into her mind. He would need to convince her that she had already succeeded so completely that she no longer needed to take any direct action at all. She would see every person and every decision around her as acting in harmony with her goals and plans, interpret every single action as though it worked to fulfill her goals.

Her direct influence would no longer be necessary. She would have gotten the process to the point that it could continue without her.

But Donal could not implant so deep and complex an illusion against an awake and aware foe, especially the trained mind of a magician. For this spell to work, he would first have to have her unconscious mind available to him, preferably when she did not have the protection of strong wards. Of course, she never slept outside strong wards, so to create the opportunity, Donal would have to first render her unconscious.

He had no direct link. No physical tie such as hair or blood, no imagistic tie such as a still illusion. But Donal did have his depth of personal experience with her to draw on. And so he began to build his link memory by memory.

He began with her smile, then added the amused confidence in her voice when she called someone else's work "clumsy." Next he added the flirty arch of her brow, the hint of caramel in her brown eyes, the promise in her tone when she needed to delay a date…

Memory by memory Donal built the image of Li Hua in his head, crafting his thaumaturgic link bit by bit. From the feel of her hair to the taste of her lips to the camaraderie of theoretical discussions and the passion of their lovemaking, Donal dredged up every detail he could. Each snippet would tighten the link, make his magic that much more effective.

If Fionn noticed the trickle of tears from its master's eyes as Donal worked, the fae deerhound gave no sign.

JACOBS LEANED FORWARD IN HIS CAPTAIN'S CHAIR, HIS HUNGRY EYES ON the bright yellow ball of Venus, growing ever larger before him. Still just a ball, but soon he would begin to make out details. Soon he would see the details of its surface. Not long after he would finally set foot on the morning star itself.

Almost there, thought Jacobs. All systems were reporting in clean, and any minute now Jefferson should be able to reach whatever passed for port authority at Gilgamesh, the first colony on Venus and the only one with anything like a spaceport.

He rubbed his hands together. Soon his ship would touch down again. Soon the voyage would be over and port authority could officially acknowledge his route, ship's manifest and passenger list, the three keys necessary to getting Jacobs — as well as the *Horizon Cusp* and Starchaser Spacelines — officially acknowledged as the first captain, ship and company to successfully complete a commercial voyage from Earth to Venus.

His last great accomplishment. And then, finally, he would be ready for the ending line of Masefield's "Sea Fever." Everyone remembered the line about the tall ship and the star to steer her by. But Jacobs sometimes thought only he remembered the rest, especially the ending, which he had found himself thinking about more and more as the years went by: "And quiet sleep and a sweet dream when the long trick's over."

Jacobs had sailed the seas, the skies and the stars for more than sixty years. He was ready, at last, for the long trick to be over.

But he was not done yet.

"How does she look, Mr. Burke?"

"Steady as she goes, Captain."

"Ms. Jefferson, any word from—"

"Security report, Sir," said Jefferson, cutting him off with an urgent tone. "The chief had men around Ms. Tai Shi's suite."

She looked up at Jacobs and he saw fear in her eyes. "A dozen of them, Sir. She took them out."

For what felt like the hundredth time on this little three day cruise, Jacobs slapped the control to sound general quarters.

Why would she bother? Where could she think she's...

"Damage Control," barked Jacobs. "Lock down that hangar bay. Use the emergency repair override."

As Jacobs received confirmation of the order, he regarded his miniature gryphon display. Tai Shi now had no escape from the ship, but she might find a place to hide...

ONCE DONAL HAD HIS LINK TO LI HUA AS STRONG AND CLEAR AS HE could get it, he held onto it with part of his mind and began the next section of his spell, the part that would separate her from consciousness.

Donal might have hesitated about this part of his plan, except that he knew he was still aboard the *Horizon Cusp*, which meant that the ship had yet to land. He knew from a previous voyage that the ship turned prisoners over to port authority before disembarking the rest of their passengers.

If they were still at space, then Li Hua could not be engaged in anything particularly dangerous.

True, her sudden collapse would draw attention to Donal, if it happened in the presence of Magister Machado or Initiate Cromartie. But if Donal cast the spell right, to most people she would appear to have collapsed from overwork.

Here, Donal's relationship with Li Hua gave him an advantage. He had seen her asleep, seen her falling asleep, seen her so exhausted she could barely keep her eyes open. He knew what every step of the process looked like, sounded like, even felt like, the growing weight in her limbs as she fell asleep.

At the time, he had paid attention because he had found those little details charming. Now, sad to say, he found them useful.

Donal focused on those details, first separating the stages and getting them clear in his head. Once he had them isolated and distinct in his mind, Donal crossed his wrists before his chest, tuning fork in his right hand and fingers near his eyes.

He began the first of a series of chants to raise the power he needed.

The initial chant was an internal call to arms, awakening the power Donal stored within himself, rubbing it to moving life, letting it swirl about him, building in the trickle of power that flowed through all living beings.

Words began to come out of his lips as he summoned the elements to support his cause:

"Air, flicker of the mind's whimsy, lend distraction to my power that my foe shall lose her focus."

Donal felt the chill of air power join the growing swirl about him.

"Fire, roar of the mind's will, lend your consuming power that my foe shall weaken."

Donal felt that chill blend with the heat of fire power entering the swirl.

"Water, slip of the mind's flexibility, lend fluidity to my power that my foe shall dream while waking."

Donal felt the tingle of mist that does not quite touch the skin mix into the swirl of growing power.

"Earth, foundation of the self, lend solidity to my power that my foe cannot resist."

Donal felt the swirl gain fathomless depth.

Now, where most magicians would have either moved on from the elements or called upon the element of spirit, Donal broke from tradition to go a direction he did not expect Li Hua to have prepared for.

"Space, limitlessness of the self, lend scope to my power that dwarfs my foe."

Where earth had given the swirl depth, Donal now felt space enter the building power and stretch it every direction at once.

The sudden expansion pressed at Donal's mind. How could he wrap his head around infinity? Every effort to expand his thoughts to encompass more only created more to encompass.

But Fionn was there, a counterbalance, a pole with which Donal could resonate, and Donal understood. He did not need to encompass infinity, only embrace it.

Donal did that, and his power flared brighter than he had ever experienced before.

Ready then, Donal began the first spell, chanting in Gaelic. His words were commanding, but the tone of his voice was soft, rising and falling like a gentle lullaby. Fionn overlaid a tune and Donal's spell became a song.

And together, they began to sing Li Hua to sleep.

Tunold wanted to run flat out through the carpeted passage past the most expensive accommodations to the bubble, heading full speed for the problem the way he would have if he were alone.

But he was not alone. He had Goldberg and a dozen ship's watch with him. But they were fine. Might have been able to keep up. The problem was that beached whale of a ship's mage. Machado ran about as well as Tunold cast spells.

Tunold itched to run on ahead. Just let Machado catch up when he could. Maybe even take care of the problem himself. But he knew better. Tai Shi had already taken down a dozen armed ship's watch, which meant that even he and Goldberg together might not be able to stop her. At least, not without Machado's help.

So Tunold had to settle for a slow jog, and tried to ignore the adrenaline boost he got from the call to battle stations echoing all around him.

At least he did not have any civilians tagging along, though that had been a near thing. Stevens and Davis wanted to witness for some kind of legal reason that Tunold had no time to figure out. Especially since his gut told him it was a business reason, not a true legal matter. They certainly lost their eagerness to debate the matter when Machado had pointed out that Tai Shi might have enchanted them with contingency plans.

Even Tunold had to admire Machado's speed and efficiency when he cast a fast set of wards on that stateroom. It might have cost them valuable seconds, but Tunold had learned the hard way not to ignore Machado when he insisted that something was important. The man might have been arrogant and out of shape, but Tunold had never met a better ship's mage.

They finally reached the bubble and Tunold almost died of shock on the spot: it sat waiting for them, steel cage open and everything. He dove in as though he expected it to get called away before he could board. Goldberg and his people filed in after him, Goldberg issuing quiet orders to organize how they would move when they found Tai Shi.

After what felt like half an hour, but probably only took another ten seconds, Machado huffed and puffed his way into the cage beside the others, sweat bringing out the musk in his cologne and giving his face a glossy look. Hands on his knees, he bent forward and tried to catch his breath.

"Gangplank," said Goldberg, using the crew's term for the formal arrival and departure deck, to tell their destination to the water sprites that carried the cage up and down the tube in its warded bubble of air.

But before the cage could begin to move, Machado said, "No ... Observation Deck."

"Ridiculous," said Goldberg. "She needs to escape, not take in the sights."

"Ship ... incoming..."

"Executive override," said Tunold to the water sprites. "Take us to the Observation Deck." He turned back to Goldberg and saw dawning realization. "That's right, Chief. She plans to meet her ship at the emergency hatch."

"Ship incoming," said Grabowski. "Looks small."

"Military?" asked Jacobs. *Could be a gunboat. Could be that the* Orpheus *reported in enough information to draw the curiosity of the local patrols...*

"Can't tell from here, Sir. No transponder code."

"Shall I hail them?" asked Jefferson.

"Hold off, Ms. Jefferson."

Jacobs called up his station's feed from the scanners. He normally avoided using it because it lacked the precision of the actual scanners station, and he would rather let his crew give him accurate information than estimate himself from an imprecise view. But a ship not sending its transponder...

Very unusual. Definitely not military or anything official. Not commercial either. Even pirates used fake transponders to lull ships into ignoring them. He looked closer at the image of the small ship, crafted to look like a flying squirrel. A runabout. Probably enough ship for a private Earth-Venus run, but not to make it as far as Mars.

But why no transponder? A ship that small could get lost in normal traffic, which would be dangerous...

"Mr. Grabowski, you said it's coming this way?"

"Aye, Sir. Definite intercept course."

"Sir," said Jefferson, "I've got Port Authority on the line. They're ready for us to land and feeding us the route they want us to use."

"Acknowledge, Ms. Jefferson, and send that route to my station too."

What could that runabout want?

The answer occurred to Jacobs almost as soon as he asked himself the question: Tai Shi. That boat had to be her escape hatch.

"Mr. Burke, evasive maneuvers. Looks like you'll have a fun landing."

***

DONAL DID NOT NEED TO HAVE FIONN SEEK OUT LI HUA TO KNOW HIS spell failed. He felt it in the sink of his heart as he knelt in the middle of his cell. He had done all the stages properly, built his power the way he needed to, focused on his objective, even worked through the link in his head to get it as precise as possible.

But his spell failed. Probably never even reached her. If she noticed it at all, Donal suspected that Li Hua shrugged it off with a twitch of her shoulders.

All the steps had been perfect, but thaumaturgy demanded more of the magician than the ability to follow the steps of a formula. Even alchemy required more of the alchemist than rote repetition, and thaumaturgy settled for nothing less than the complete dedication of the magician.

Donal had failed because on some level he had fought himself. Even though he had locked away the pain of his injuries and forced himself to dedicate as much will as he could muster to stopping Li Hua's heinous plan, on some level he had been unwilling to work against her.

Donal held his head in his hands, rubbed his temples with his thumbs, pressed his palms against his closed eyes. He heard the soft padding of his spirit deerhound approaching across the ceramic cell floor.

"Any magician may fail a spell. You only become a failure if you give up."

"How?" Donal heard his voice break on that word, but pushed more words out anyway, confident that his familiar would interpret the broken sounds. "This is all my fault. I should have seen it months ago. And I have to stop it. And I don't see how."

"Admit the truth."

"That I'm a blind idiot?"

"Some have said as much, though I have not. You know what truth you must admit."

"But I don't—"

"You must understand power to call it. And you must understand yourself to direct power. Your spell was fine, but it did not strike Tai Shi Li Hua. Tell me why."

"Well," started Donal as though answering a professor. His hands were on his knees now, and though he still knelt on the floor, the mere act of answering a theory question helped him recover some of himself. "My mental sketch of her seemed thorough in its detail—"

"Tell. Me. Why." The *cú sidhe* pressed its nose against Donal's. The courage blazing in its emerald eyes commanded Donal to tell the truth.

In that moment, Donal understood what he had hidden from himself for months, what he had been unable to face because he knew that, logically and logistically, it was wrong. But what he faced had nothing to do with logic and logistics. It had to do with her smile, the playful tone she used just for Donal, the fiery way she debated thaumaturgy with him, and the quiet way she welcomed him after a long day.

"I love her."

"Yes. You do. Now can you let her go?"

Donal's nostrils flared in a deep breath. "I don't want to."

"But can you?"

Donal thought about everything he had learned about Li Hua in the last twenty-four hours, about the details that showed truth about her that she had concealed from him. Donal centered himself with three words.

"Yes. I can."

"Excellent," said Fionn, and Donal thought he heard relief in his familiar's voice. "Let us begin again."

THE *HORIZON CUSP* ROLLED AND TWISTED, BUT JACOBS MANAGED A wolfish smile as his chart indicated that Burke stayed within two degrees of his designated approach pattern. *Great flying.*

That runabout stayed with them, though. Its pilot clearly had experience with its smaller size and knew how to take advantage of its maneuverability.

Jacobs leaned over the rail to look at Jefferson, who had her fingers in the snarl of links. "Any luck hailing our little pest?"

"Not yet, Sir, though Port Authority wants to know, and I quote, just what the hell you're doing?"

"Primitive setup probably can't see a ship the size of that flying squirrel." Jacobs shook his head. "Tell Port Authority that I'm testing my pilot to see if he's ready to handle the landing himself." He turned to the helm and said, "My apologies for that, Mr. Burke." He turned back to the communications station. "And if the runabout won't talk to us, just send it this message: we've got its description. We've got a good idea about its range and ports of call. And we will interpret any attempt to reach us as attempting to aid a fugitive from justice and endangering a ship attempting to dock."

Jacobs sat back in his seat, mumbling, "That should at least give the bastards some pause."

He tapped the security section of his miniature gryphon display, but the reports had not changed in the last five minutes.

That meant that Tai Shi was still at large.

***

Tunold ripped open the cage door the moment he saw the open space of the Observation Deck. The ride had seemed to take forever, long enough that even that fat ship's mage recovered his breath, though he wasted it now mumbling to the air.

But they had reached the Observation Deck. A whole deck wasted because some tourists might want to look through the transparent ceramic hull in several directions and pretend they stood among the stars themselves.

At least the deck would come in handy this time. Wide open spaces with no tourists about meant plenty of room to fight. Plenty of room to rush Tai Shi all at once with a dozen ship's watch. Plus Goldberg and himself leading the way while Machado hung back and did whatever it was that Machado did.

With any luck, Tunold himself would get to throw the knockout punch.

The moment his boots hit that ceramic bulkhead, Tunold's eyes spotted Tai Shi. Aft, port side, near the hatch. Waiting for what looked like a giant flying squirrel to catch the gryphon's belly and let her escape.

Tunold roared and charged. All around him a dozen voices echoed him while more than two dozen boots followed him, sounding like an avalanche.

Tai Shi spun to face them, dressed as though for a casual day at the office: slack and a scoop neck sweater with high heels. But her stance looked balanced and ready, as though she knew those clothes would not impede her. In her right hand she held the handle of a combat knife, its blade waiting along her forearm. In her left hand she held a small, silver bauble.

Let Machado worry about the bauble. Tunold worried about the knife.

"Tell me, Magister," she called in a taunting voice, "do you have the confidence to stand by while I dispatch your friends? Do you have the courage to give a mere *Journeyman* a fair fight?"

Rage burned through Tunold at her obvious disregard. As though only a magician could possibly stop her. He used his momentum to dive at her, trying to drive his shoulder through her midsection, confident that Goldberg, on Tunold's left, would adjust and deliver the knockout blow if Tunold failed to land it himself.

Tai Shi dropped to the floor as Tunold's dive took him over her and into the bulkhead. Pain jolted through his shoulder and back, but he broke his fall well enough to avoid serious injury.

He turned and saw Tai Shi, standing again, throw a kick that took Goldberg in the jaw.

The chief had the wherewithal to grab for that foot, but it was already gone, so he threw a left. She tried to block it with her knife, but Goldberg adjusted enough to avoid the blade.

Tunold was on his feet again and coming at her from behind. The chief moved to flank, ready to make her fight two directions at once while the rest of the ship's watch moved in...

But she just slumped to the floor, unconscious.

"Damn it, Machado," yelled Tunold. "We had her!"

"Don't look at me," said Machado, raising his hands. "Hadn't finished my spell." Then the portly mage blinked. "Cuthbert. *Saravá, vai!*"

Tunold shook his head. Those last two words had been addressed to mid-air for all he could see.

THE MOMENT DONAL COMPLETED HIS SPELL, HE KNEW IT HAD GONE better. Even standing in the center of his cell in the ship's brig with only Fionn for company, he knew. He could not explain how he knew. He could not feel it in the warm, little-moved air. He could not smell it in pine scent lingering from the cell's last cleaning. He had no real sensory cues at all that his spell had performed one way or the other.

And yet, he knew he had done it right this time.

Donal believed that the nature of a solid link allowed for just enough communication that a caster could intuit the effect he had on his target. But this was hotly debated in scholarly circles.

All Donal knew for certain was that he had fired off a much better spell than his previous effort. Which meant that the way likely now stood open for his second spell. Or at least it was as open a shot as he would ever get.

He drew a cleansing breath and turned to his waiting familiar.

"All right, Fionn. Now this one will be complex. I'll need you to hold parts of the illusion as I assemble it and check my work to see that the seams will fit together without any gaps her mind might catch." Donal rubbed his hands together. "First, we'll—"

Donal stopped speaking as the gray misty spirit panther *Saravá* melted through the cell's floor to hover before him. Machado's familiar. Donal began to hang his head. He had taken too long. The Magister had caught him.

"Donal Cuthbert, my master wishes you to cease your workings. Your first spell was sufficient to bring down Tai Shi Li Hua, and he bids you to rest now and leave her to the ship's watch. You will soon be able to safely leave this cell."

"What?" said Donal. "I'm not under arrest? Then why am I in the anti-caster cell?"

"I did try to tell you earlier," said Fionn. "The cell has been tuned against the magic of Tai Shi Li Hua, not to inhibit your spellcasting."

"I knew they hadn't tuned it for me, but... So, the Magister got my message?"

"That is correct," said the spirit panther. "As did Donatello Michelangelo Mancuso, whom Ronaldo Machado has now proven to be under the control you warned against. The day is won. You may rest."

Fionn turned and began to confer quickly with *Saravá* in that language that only familiars seem to understand. As they did, Donal allowed that information to seep in. He had done it. He had stopped Li Hua, and proven that she was the one behind the conspiracy bin Zuka had warned of.

Donal dropped back to sit on the rough cot, sighing out his tension and letting himself relax. Unfortunately, when he did, all his pains came screaming back, all the worse for Donal's movements and spellcasting that had not taken their warnings into account. Donal felt as though fire burned through his ribs, his neck, his shoulders and the back of his head.

Donal cried out and tried to squirm for comfort on the cot, unable to focus on anything but his excruciating pain.

Suddenly Fionn was in his thoughts, the image of the fae deerhound's face drawing Donal's attention, forcing Donal to regard him.

Donal saw Fionn standing beside him, face scant centimeters above his own as he lay on the cot.

"*Saravá* has gone to fetch Doctor Ramirez. You will have help soon."

"Sir," said Grabowski, "the runabout's breaking off."

"Let it go," said Jacobs with a weary shake of his head. "It never latched on, so Tai Shi can't be getting away. Though if you can get me any updates, Ms. Jefferson, I would greatly appreciate them."

"Trying, Sir, but all I've been able to get so far is that Cuthbert needs a doctor... Wait. Tunold is on the link for you."

"Finally. Link it through to my station, please." He turned to the helm. "Mr. Burke, think you can set her down without any more aerobatics?"

"I was thinking of throwing in a few for your entertainment, Sir," said Burke in a tight voice as he nudged the ship back onto the precise requested route to bring the ship into the atmosphere and down toward the planet. "But if you'd prefer..."

"I would." Jacobs turned to the floating head of his executive officer. "Status?"

"Tai Shi has been secured. Mash says Cuthbert brought her down." Tunold grimaced. "Timing was terrible, too. Saul and I had her on the ropes."

"You'll have to tell me all about it later, but if everything is under control I have a ship to land."

"Nothing pressing, Captain."

"Then bridge out."

Jacobs stood and hurried down the stairs from his station to the walkway surrounding the bridge. He got to the very front as fast as he could without actually running, out of a desire to maintain at least a modicum of decorum.

From that spot he could enjoy, for the first time, the growing sight of Venus before him: a great yellowish-white ball that seemed to glow of its own accord. Jacobs knew from the charts that much of its land was split into two great continents, but only one — Istar Terra — was settled. From where he stood, Jacobs could see mountains and canyons, craters and ... a bright yellow column of light. Canary yellow, almost like...

Of course. Gilgamesh had erected a barrier, just as the cities on Mars had done. Jacobs knew that within he would find an environment conducive to human life and comfort, while life outside the barrier, though possible, he understood, would prove ... less accommodating.

But Jacobs knew that on Mars, the spells adapting the planet for human life had begun adapting humans to Mars. Anyone could see it in the red pigmentation humans developed when they spent enough time on Mars, a permanent condition for the natives. He wondered how, over time, Venus would make its own marks on the humans who had chosen it for their home.

But no one would know that for years to come yet. Settlements on Venus were too recent.

Burke flew the *Horizon Cusp* in through the barrier, where the sky around them changed from a barely discernable yellow to the blue of home. He touched the ship down in a lit circle, one of perhaps thirty in the bare dirt field. Only two others were occupied.

The ship had landed on Venus. Now all Jacobs had to do was get rid of those troublesome passengers.

24

JACOBS SAT AT HIS OFFICE DESK AND WIPED THE EXHAUSTION FROM HIS eyes. Tunold, Goldberg and Machado had just left. Their reports had been thorough, and complete, and covered the sort of infighting and bullshit that Jacobs wished landlubbers would keep to themselves.

Why couldn't they try to kill and control each other on their own time? Why did they have to come aboard his ship to do it?

In any event, to all reports, Tai Shi was under control and would remain in her charmed cell until she could be dumped on the proper authorities back on Earth. Tunold had wanted her off the ship as soon as possible, but he should have known better. Venus had little law, much less proper authorities. Dumping her here would have been the same as letting her go.

Machado had, he said, freed Mancuso from Tai Shi's control. He offered details, but Jacobs had declined them, told him to save them for Earth.

Cuthbert appeared to have come through the encounter scathed but intact.

Poor kid probably has a broken heart, but that'll mend. It's not like they were married with a kid of their own...

Jacobs distracted himself before he got lost in thoughts of Rhonda and Carl.

The other passengers complained about the voyage's troubles, and the hardship of the times they had spent confined to their spacious, ridiculously comfortable suites. Jacobs felt no sadness for their plight.

Their impatience to disembark was another matter.

The *Horizon Cusp* had sat on the ground of Venus for six hours now with no one leaving, which had been enough to even get the port on the link again to see if Jacobs needed any help.

The answer, of course, was no. But Jacobs refused to let anyone disembark until Machado had cleared Mancuso and his assistants. Jacobs wanted to make sure no other little details popped up in the process, anything that might have pointed an accusing finger at another passenger.

But no, as far as Machado had been able to tell, Tai Shi acted alone. At least, on that level.

And now Mancuso had asked for a meeting before disembarking, and the man was taking his sweet time in showing—

Jacobs heard the precise knock of Kelly.

"Come," he called.

Kelly opened the door just enough to allow him to lean in at a thirty degree angle. "Mr. Mancuso is here to see you, Sir."

"Let's get this over with," Jacobs said with a sigh. "Send him in."

Mancuso entered the room with slow, precise steps. A far enough cry from the whirlwind Jacobs was used to that he felt an inquisitive eyebrow raise. Despite himself, he gestured with one hand to offer Mancuso a chair.

"Thank you," said Mancuso, with something like his normal tone, if his voice had been slowed down a hair. "Not feeling quite myself yet. Though your ship's mage tells me I'll need some counseling to sort out what's me and what isn't."

Then his voice grew faster and some of his normal presumption returned to his tone. "Though I can't see why I'd need someone else to tell me what's me and what isn't. Not like there'll be a better expert on the subject than I am."

Jacobs said nothing. He merely sat, thinking longingly of the bottle of Brigid's Own Irish Whisky in his desk drawer.

"But that's enough of that," said Mancuso, waving one hand as though dismissing a servant. "Need to talk to you. Partner to partner." The man actually had the gall to smile, though the smile would have worked as well on a shark. "Yes, I know that word rankles you. Especially coming from me. Last time I'll need to use it. I promise. Got an offer for you."

He pulled a tri-folded piece of paper from the inner pocket of his expensive dark blue suit. He slid the paper across the desk to Jacobs, waited while Jacobs read it. Jacobs would have sworn he had managed to keep his expression flat, but Mancuso smiled again.

"That's right. It's about four times what you're expecting, plus the retirement package we talked about, plus free premium passage on any Starchaser Spacelines flight for the rest of your life."

Mancuso fiddled with his cufflinks, then looked back at Jacobs and Jacobs saw in the man's eye the one thing he never expected: gratitude. "You and your people have saved my life time and again. And this time your mage cleared my head from a problem I would never have known was there. I never forget my friends, and I never forget those who help me." He stood. "Take time to think about it if you like, but I think you should take the deal. Retire. Live a little. And if you need anything else, let me know."

Mancuso left the room, closing the door after him, and Jacobs spent several minutes just staring at the door and the offer.

Donal stood beside Fionn near the comfortable seats lining the pale gold and sandstone-colored waiting area. At the far end sat the hippogriff shuttle in its nest-like dock. Soon they would board and Donal would set foot on Venus, ready to deliver the package that had almost gotten the ship attacked by mercenaries. Mercenaries Donal had killed defending the ship.

But Donal's thoughts were not on the mercenaries, nor on Venus, nor even on the package tucked safely inside his messenger bag and concealed through Donal's spells. No, his thoughts were on Mr. Mancuso and the strange conversation he had just had.

Donal half-wondered whether Mr. Mancuso would still fund Donal's education, or whether that had been Li Hua's influence. But Mr. Mancuso re-affirmed that 4M would pay for as much education and research as Donal wanted.

But Mr. Mancuso was not done.

He established a retirement fund for Donal's parents.

Donal's parents loved their woodworking, and when Donal was growing up they spoke as though they never expected to retire. But as Donal had grown older, he had come to realize they they did not think they could ever *afford* to retire.

Now Donal held in his zephyrpad evidence and written promises establishing a solid retirement plan for Robert and Colleen Cuthbert, along with a detailed explanation of why 4M was doing this and how Donal was to thank for it.

Donal's throat refused to allow words out when he read that. His throat had all it could manage to allow air to pass. Bran had all the accolades, all the moments that would live on in the history texts, but Donal had been the son to make sure his parents were looked after in their old age. Donal had tried to think of a way to thank Mr. Mancuso for that, but his throat remained choked up.

But Donal continued to think about that, even after the call to disembark had sounded.

Jacobs left Tunold to deal with the new port's paperwork. Kris would make a good captain, and he would have to learn to deal with the bureaucracy sooner or later. Besides, Jacobs wanted to be the first person off the ship to set foot on Venus.

He took the shuttle down before the passengers had been alerted to gather at the gangplank. Just Jacobs and a pilot, and the pilot would have to get the shuttle back in place before the passengers started gathering. Wouldn't do to let the privileged people know that a mere ship's captain had beaten them to the surface.

Jacobs disembarked the shuttle and stood on the morning star for the first time, his eyes closed in reverence for the moment. The air was hot, dry. Almost too dry, like Jacobs remembered from Arizona in August, decades ago. The air smelled fresh, though, as though cleaned recently by rain at a high elevation. Denver, maybe, not Arizona.

One more breath and he felt ready to perform his landing ritual for the first time on Venus. Perhaps for the only time.

Jacobs crouched with one knee on the Venusian ground as though he bowed before a king. He closed his eyes and picked up his customary handful of local dirt. He rubbed the thin soil through his fingers. He held it to his nose and smelled its tang, almost citrus. He opened his eyes at last and looked at the dirt. Pale. Yellow. Fine. Venus. He stood.

From where he stood, the main part of the spaceport looked little better than a shanty town: wood and luminescent stone structures built in cylinders and cones. Sealed, but with big windows.

With all the official work left in Tunold's hands, Jacobs clapped his hands clean and set off to have a look around the last new space-port he ever intended to see.

The hot air of Venus smelled of lemons and clover, and carried so little moisture Donal's shirt clung to itself. As he and Fionn moved through the dusty areas that passed for roads and streets in Gilgamesh, Donal found himself glad for their field work games. They gave him something to focus on so he would not get distracted by the strange, seemingly untamed magic of Venus. Donal could feel it in the air around him and in the ground beneath him: wild, yes, chaotic, yes, but power waiting for a magician to tap and channel it, to study it and learn its secrets.

Magic unlike anything he had touched on Earth or in the heavily organized sections that were all Donal had seen of Mars.

Venus did not feel like anything Donal knew, and the researcher in him badly wanted to stop and rubberneck like a child at an amusement park. Focusing on the field work game kept Donal present, paying attention to where he was and where he was going.

Of course, it would have helped if he had had more people to choose from for potential threats to watch. He barely saw a dozen people on his way through the empty, undecorated spaceport, and the "city" itself looked like little more than a temporary settlement. But the customs agent had recognized the delivery address as the Zanzibar. He had insisted that Donal would know it when he saw it, calling it the fanciest hotel in Gilgamesh. A superlative that meant increasingly less to Donal, the more he saw.

He recognized the conical buildings as alchemical products. The sort that were stored in meter-square cubes, and when the right reagents were added they grew into two or three story furnished buildings, some customized for housing, others for small businesses. They would last at least a decade, and the ones Donal saw widely spaced among the yellow-white grounds of the settlement looked to have more than half their lives left.

Donal did not recognize the cylinder shapes, but restraining himself to a glance left him speculating that they were of similar design, though for different purposes. Donal had seen at least two such buildings back in the port proper, but had not taken time to find out their purposes.

Despite these potential distractions, Donal kept himself oriented according to his directions and watched strangers on foot with mock suspicion. It might have become real suspicion, except that what few strangers he saw were on foot and all clearly going about their own business.

Even what passed for streets were quiet. So far Donal had spotted no more than a handful of horses — Arabians, which suited what

Donal understood of the settlement, that the colonists had come primarily from the Middle East and India — and only three runners.

Perhaps twenty minutes after Donal and Fionn had made their way out of the spaceport, Donal set eyes on what had to have been the Zanzibar.

The sight almost made him fall to his knees. So much gold and marble, wrought into a fine four-story palace of the sort Donal had imagined when he read the tales of Scheherazade. Surrounded by fountains and gardens, it could have served as a palace to any of the great sultans from those stories.

Donal felt Fionn's teeth lightly dent his hand, and recovered himself. He checked his surroundings but still saw no sign of threat. *Probably nothing to worry about. The package already did its work when it let that other ship home in on us.*

But then Donal noticed an eddy of power twist past like a fluke of the breeze, and double-checked the nearest strangers to keep from his mind on his business.

He covered the final few hundred meters to the Zanzibar, and noted that even the walkway leading up to it had been carved from marble and enchanted to keep the pervasive dust from soiling it. The trickles and splashes and gurgles of the fountains had a soothing quality. Not magic, just the reassuring presence of water in so dry a land. They also lent a cool feel to the air near them, and the nearby gardens smelled of rich blends of flowers with roses leading the way.

Donal half-expected giant eunuchs with scimitars guarding the front door, but instead found twin statues of dervishes, finely detailed, with swords still in their scabbards. Donal felt an itch between his eyebrows. He wanted to shift consciousness and really examine them, find out if they held any enchantments.

If he had designed this place, they would have.

But Donal steadied himself and stayed on his task. He reached for the fine bronze handle of what looked to be a double-door fashioned from teak, but before he could grasp it the doors opened inwards.

Cool air hit Donal's face, saffron and lilies a bare undertone of a scent. The interior of the Zanzibar exceeded Donal's expectations. A high domed ceiling, enchanted to trap echoes instead of sharing them. Creamy blends of rich colors everywhere his eye alit, from the ceiling to the fine stone tiles of the walls and flooring, from the polished woods of the reception desk and concierge to the broad, deep couches with their end tables and coffee tables. Art on the walls enhanced the beauty with its fine blend of history, legend and religion.

Once more Fionn's teeth dented Donal's wrist and brought him back to attention. Though he promised himself that he would take time to visit Venus properly. Between the mysteries of its magic and the puzzle of this amazing building among so many temporary structures, he had more questions than he had time to answer.

Donal approached the front desk, where a man about Donal's own age stood behind the counter, wearing a pale suit, and a nametag that read, "Ahmed."

Ahmed smiled and said, "Good day, Sir. Checking in?"

"I wish." Donal reached into his bag for the package. "I'm an IIX courier with a delivery for R. A. M. in room two-oh-one."

"Certainly, Sir. But I will need to confirm your employment."

Donal reached into his pocket and slipped out a piece of enchanted silver shaped like the three letters of the IIX logo. He held it up for inspection. Ahmed picked up a silver-chased letter opener with "Zanzibar" engraved down it in fine script. He tapped the tip of the letter opener against the logo, and the logo flared green and chimed a sweet b-sharp note.

"Thank you, Sir. One moment, please."

Ahmed reached under the counter and plucked a link. Donal recognized the type, common in hotels: voice only and tuned to allow for subvocalized communication. A few seconds later Ahmed smiled at Donal. "You may go up." He pointed to the far corner of the room. "That stair will take you there."

Donal began to turn away, but quickly turned back before Ahmed returned to his duties.

"I have to ask. Why such a fancy hotel among all these temporary buildings?"

Ahmed's smile broadened and he said, "Allah grants..." Ahmed glanced left and right, then leaned in a little closer. "You are a courier, not a visitor, so I will tell you the truth. Leave the spaceport in any direction and you will find our true homes, our fine restaurants and parks and museums. But only if you know where to go. We do not want you to find them. We do not want tourists. We have come here to leave Earth behind, not bring it to us."

"But everything about the Zanzibar—"

"Resembles Earth, yes. By design. A great glory to fill your eyes—"

"To keep us looking where you want, so we don't see what you don't want us to see. Like slight of hand."

Ahmed smiled, as though pleased to have finally told someone, but hesitation entered his eyes. "But I have said more than I should. I hope I may trust your discretion."

"Of course," said Donal. Not that he could see why it mattered. After all, if most tourists were told that Venus did not want tourists, they would probably not bother to come. But he would hold his silence on the matter. "Thank you."

Donal did turn away then, and as he crossed to the stairway he muttered to Fionn, "All this opulence and they make their patrons walk up flights of stairs?"

But the moment Donal's foot touched the second stair, the stairwell began to move. The stairs themselves moved beneath him, carrying him up, around the bend, and depositing him on the second floor. Fionn actually chuckled, a disturbingly human sound from so canine a throat.

"You saw that coming?"

"I wasn't staring at the art."

"Fine. Then you get to lead us to two-oh-one."

Donal began to look around the hallway, with its rich red carpeting and pale, almost delicate walls, but Fionn struck the mocking pose of a pointer, his nose clearly indicating a door a scant two meters away.

A door that had three digits engraved in its varnished oak surface: 201.

___

Donal knocked on the door, and it opened before he could finish. Standing in the doorway, wearing a high-necked chiffon dress the color of cream, stood Rowan MacPherson. There, amid such opulence, she stood like a waking dream. Perhaps his mother's dream. She would have killed to find Donal such a woman.

Donal felt as though he should have been surprised to see her there, but he was not. "What does the A. stand for?" he asked.

"Alanna."

"Of course." *Of course your middle name is "beautiful."* He held up the package. "I need your I.D. for the records, but since you're also the sender, you can wave that if you like."

Donal held up his signet with his other hand. "Just identify yourself by name and say to the seal that you're waving the recipient I.D. requirement."

"I'll get my I.D." She turned away to walk down a small hall into her room proper, but spoke over her shoulder. "Why don't you come in?"

"I'd just as soon wait here, if you don't mind."

That stopped her. She turned back.

"Donal, we need to talk."

"This package was used by a ship full of mercenaries to try to kill everyone aboard the *Horizon Cusp*. Including me. I don't think I have anything else to say, and I can't imagine that you have anything to say that I'll want to hear."

"And what if I told you that those mercenaries only carried weapons capable of stunning opponents? That no one aboard the *Horizon Cusp* would have suffered lasting harm?"

"Including Mr. Mancuso?"

"Well..."

"What if I told you that your mercenaries were after the wrong man?"

Rowan MacPherson tilted her head, draping her long red hair in a way that Donal guessed had to be deliberate.

"That's right. Tai Shi Li Hua had him in her thrall. Subtle work, built up over a long time." Donal watched Rowan MacPherson's finely sculpted eyebrows raise as her green eyes widened in surprise. "So whatever you had in mind for Mr. Mancuso, you would have been doing it to a victim of your target instead of your target."

"We would have discovered that before acting."

"Of course you would have." Donal didn't bother to hide the contempt in his voice. "Not that you've admitted what you had in mind for him. But you aren't the sort to admit to crimes. Hell, you didn't even admit to anything about those mercenaries, just asked a 'hypothetical' question. You didn't even acknowledge that they were your mercenaries, even though they homed in on *your* package."

"Two dozen other people know what that package contains, in case you're curious," she said, closing the distance between them again in a few long strides. "Donal, please come in and talk to me. I don't want you to walk away thinking that I represent trouble. We could help each other, you and I."

"I'm sick of corporate espionage. And I'm sick of beautiful women telling me half-truths."

Rowan MacPherson sucked in a breath through her nose while tightening her lips in an expression Donal read as realizing something obvious.

"I'm sorry about how things went with you and Li Hua—"

"You have no idea."

"No. I don't. I could guess, but I'm sure I wouldn't get close to the truth." She met Donal's eyes and he saw nothing but sincerity there, not that he had any intention of trusting what he saw.

She said, in a softer voice, "This is the wrong time to talk to you. I understand that much. When I had planned to meet you here I had no way of knowing you would suffer such a loss. Although you don't want my sympathy, you still have it."

She shook her head. "As the sender, I, Rowan Alanna MacPherson, waive the I.D. requirement for the package I have sent to Venus with IIX courier Donal Cuthbert."

"Thank you," said Donal. He held out the package and she took it. Donal turned and walked back to the stairs quickly enough to reach the third one down before they began to carry him to the first floor.

Donal's shoes clicked across the tiles of the Zanzibar's lobby. Fionn, beside him, said in words that only Donal could understand, "You will hear from her again."

"She does seem the type," said Donal in the same fashion.

"Better to hear what she has to say now."

"No. I've had enough corporate espionage to last me a lifetime."

EPILOGUE - DONAL

The *Horizon Cusp* may have landed at the San Francisco Spaceport around noon, but Donal did not get back to his Tudor-style apartment house until close to midnight. The Port Authority had thousands of questions about Li Hua and Mr. Mancuso, then about a ship full of mercenaries, and finally something about a no-fly zone. But Donal didn't know anything about that last one.

Then, after Port Authority finally let him go, he had to answer a thousand more questions at IIX. But Donal couldn't help it if his combat clause got activated yet again, and Magister Machado and Captain Jacobs had both been good enough to certify both what happened and Donal's role. Mr. Mancuso even threw in a letter of commendation and thanks.

Donal suspected that the letter drew more curiosity than anything else, but Donal was tired of answering questions by then and gotten monosyllabic.

Fionn had tried to prompt him to give them more details, but Donal felt so sick of the whole process that he had sent his familiar back into the silver faun pendant.

The entire time Donal sat in the IIX office, all he had wanted was his final paycheck. Now they were delaying even that a few days. At least Ms. Stevens had gotten Donal's stipend started, so he felt comfortable quitting on the spot, to Ms. Washington's face.

Donal thought about that as he trudged alone up the stairs. No more courier work. He had months to relax now before classes started. First he would go visit Mom and Dad, tell them the good news about their retirement plan and why they had it. Donal smiled, his eyes half-closed as he pictured looks of astonished gratitude on his parents' faces. He pulled out his apartment keys...

"I hear Mancuso is still alive." Donal recognized the cold voice even before he turned. The sword-carrying businessman, dressed in a black suit this time, though cut the way the last one had been. He leaned casually against the turn of the stairs, both gloved hands near the hilt of his sword. His belt buckle was still enchanted, and this time the sword at his belt had a spell on it as well.

"Mr. Mancuso's mind was being controlled. He was never the threat your people thought he was."

"Believe that do you?" The man raised his eyebrows in mocking disbelief, giving his head a slight shake. "So, naïve, Cuthbert."

"I know it for a fact." Donal turned his key in the lock, determined to get behind his wards before the man could draw his sword. "So leave me alone."

"Hand off that door if you please." The man held up a small throwing knife, which had been concealed in his left hand. "This is poisoned. You'd be dead before you took a step."

Donal raised his hands, letting the look on his face remind the assassin that though the gesture might have meant surrender for most people, for a magician it was a ready pose. The man quirked one corner of his lips without a hint of real amusement in his eyes.

"I understand you worship the old Celtic gods," said the man. "I'll give you a moment to make your peace."

"I believe he means it," said a male voice that Donal recognized but could not place, coming from down the stairs. He could hear two sets of shoes begin to ascend. "What do you think?"

"I'm sure of it," said a female voice that sounded familiar to Donal as well. "Drop the knife and sword belt, assassin."

The authority in that statement helped Donal place the woman's voice just as she came into view: Hierophant Jane MacDougall, her sandy hair freshly cut short and her dress fashionably long. And next to her stood Hierophant Nicholas Mason, a smile in his eyes and his rapier on his hip.

The assassin dropped the knife and quickly worked his belt buckle. It seemed the man's storehouse of information included prominent Hierophants.

"You are going to go to the twelfth precinct," said Hierophant Mason in a lecturing tone, "and turn yourself in to the police, naming everyone you know who was involved in the conspiracy that required your attempt on Donal."

"And we have some idea about who those might be," said Hierophant MacDougall.

"We will check on you by dawn. If you have not done as we asked..."

"There will be a period when you will wish we had killed you." She smiled and even Donal shuddered. "Then, oh, how you will long for those days, how they will seem like heaven compared to what follows..."

The assassin bent to pick up his weapons.

"Oh, no, Jeremy Smithson," said Hierophant Mason. "Leave the evidence there. Jane and I will bring it to the station with us at dawn."

"Oh," said Hierophant MacDougall, and she flicked her wrist. A bare gesture, but Donal felt a tremor of power flow from it. "You have now been marked with a tracer. Nicholas and I will know every move you make and every person you speak to until I remove it. So I suggest you go directly to the station."

"Bring your driver with you," said Hierophant Mason. "He should turn himself in as well."

"We will hold you responsible if he does not."

"See you at dawn."

The two Hierophants looked at the assassin, Smithson, and the man bowed his head and walked out.

"Um," said Donal, his exhausted brain still trying to catch up, "can I invite you both inside?"

"Please," said Heirophant MacDougall. "We have much to discuss."

Donal opened the door and the wards and gestured for them both to precede him. The moment the door and wards were closed behind them, Hierophant Mason said, "Current law enforcement is insufficient to the task of keeping magicians in line. You proved that with Tai Shi. Conventional means might never have caught up to her plan."

"And so some of us want to put together a special, interplanetary task force for just this purpose," said Hierophant MacDougall.

"Magister Ronaldo Machado recommended you."

"And you do seem to have a knack for trouble. Goodness knows you made an enemy or two in the business world after your actions en route to Venus."

Both Hierophants paused long enough to finally give Donal a moment to think. He liked the idea of working on such a task force, thought it was necessary. But still...

"Can I finish school first?"

The Hierophants smiled.

EPILOGUE - JACOBS

Six months into his retirement, John Jacobs lounged in the sun on the deck of his new personal vessel, the *Sweet Dream*, at the sea dock in Mazatlán. With a novel waiting on the deck beside his reclining chair, Benny Sugg sunning his belly next to it, and waves rocking them both like a soothing nanny, life could get little better.

Jacobs had spent so much time in space that he had all but forgotten the simple pleasures of the sun on his skin, the sea air in his lungs, the cries of hungry seagulls. They came back to him now like childhood friendships rekindled.

The boat itself had cost more than Zoltan's house, but Jacobs would not know what to do with a house anyway. He had commissioned his new vessel to look like an old U. S. Navy utility boat: nearly fifteen meters long, with a round bottom, plus three good-sized cabins, a galley, and a beautiful oak library. He even had leftover cargo space, for long runs. Like Australia. Or Mars. The *Sweet Dream* could handle any of them.

That thought made Jacobs smile while the sun baked his dark skin. The seas, the skies, and space were all open to him now, with no partners to answer to and no passengers to please. Maintenance could still give him headaches, but he could handle most of it through a few idiot-proof places to dump specific alchemical reagents in precise quantities. Machado himself had checked the work and assured Jacobs that the ship should run smoothly and reliably, so long as Jacobs had it serviced by a competent magician whenever he reached dock.

In two days he would land the *Sweet Dream* at the air base in Milbrae. He would don a casual shirt, and slacks, and have dinner with Zoltan and his wife. And unless Jacobs missed his guess, Zoltan's wife intended to play matchmaker. Jacobs' old partner had complained often that Jacobs spent too much of his time alone. Likely Zoltan and his wife intended to change that.

Jacobs could not imagine any woman measuring up to the golden memory of Rhonda. But maybe Zoltan had a point. Maybe Rhonda would forgive an old man for finding companionship in the twilight of his years.

Maybe Jacobs could meet a woman who could appreciate a fine novel, a fine ship, and a fine glass of Irish whisky.

But just at that moment, with the sun, the sea, and his cat, Jacobs needed nothing else in the world.

ACKNOWLEDGMENTS

Thanks again to my wonderful beta readers: Bill, Lori, Rob and Wendy.

SIGN UP FOR STEFON'S NEWSLETTER

Stefon loves to keep in touch with his readers, and loves to keep you reading. The best way for him to do both is for you to sign up for his newsletter.

Sign up at http://www.stefonmears.com/join

If you sign up for Stefon's newsletter, you get...

- Monthly updates about his publishing and travel schedules
- His latest news, in brief, and answers to reader questions
- A free short story for signing up
- List-only offers and occasional specials
- Plus a free short story every month!

ABOUT THE AUTHOR

Stefon Mears would love to tame the wild magic of Venus. Stefon has more than thirty books to his credit, and he never stops writing. He earned his M.F.A. in Creative Writing from N.I.L.A., and his B.A. in Religious Studies (double emphasis in Ritual and Mythology) from U.C. Berkeley. He's a lifelong gamer and fantasy fan. Stefon lives in Portland, Oregon, with his wife and three cats.

Look for Stefon online:
www.stefonmears.com
himself@stefonmears.com

www.ingramcontent.com/pod-product-compliance
Lightning Source LLC
Chambersburg PA
CBHW031617180726
48284CB00005B/1583